CATHERINE ISAAC was born in Liverpool and was a journalist before she became an author. She wrote her first novel, *Bridesmaids*, under the pseudonym Jane Costello and her eight subsequent books were all *Sunday Times* bestsellers.

You Me Everything was her first work writing as Catherine Isaac. Translation rights have been sold in twenty-four countries and a movie adaptation is in development by Lionsgate and Temple Hill. She lives in Liverpool with her husband Mark and three sons.

www.catherine-isaac.com
catherineisaacauthor
@CatherineIsaac_
CatherineIsaacAuthor

ALSO BY CATHERINE ISAAC

Messy, Wonderful Us
You Me Everything

Catherine Isaac

The World at my Feet

SIMON &
SCHUSTER

London · New York · Sydney · Toronto · New Delhi

First published in Great Britain by Simon & Schuster UK Ltd, 2021

1 3 5 7 9 10 8 6 4 2

Simon & Schuster UK Ltd
1st Floor
222 Gray's Inn Road
London WC1X 8HB

Simon & Schuster Australia, Sydney
Simon & Schuster India, New Delhi

www.simonandschuster.co.uk
www.simonandschuster.com.au
www.simonandschuster.co.in

A CIP catalogue record for this book
is available from the British Library

Paperback ISBN: 978-1-4711-7811-5
eBook ISBN: 978-1-4711-7810-8
Audio ISBN: 978-1-4711-9141-1

Typeset in Bembo by M Rules
Printed and bound by CPI Group (UK) Ltd, Croydon, CR0 4YY

MIX
Paper from
responsible sources
FSC
www.fsc.org   FSC® C020471

For Mum, with love and gratitude.

The World at my Feet

Prologue

Ellie

One of the most common dreams you can have involves flying. Imagine that. Feeling your heels rise and a lightness in your limbs, before registering a gap between the ground and your feet. Then you'd look down to see they are no longer touching and at first hover, drifting across your back garden in a gentle ascent. You'd reach the trees and rise high above the lawn and it's then that you would begin to soar, over rooftops, hills and forests, with the chill of night air on your arms. You wouldn't feel afraid, just elated.

I'd love to dream like that, just once. To be Supergirl, or Wendy clutching Peter Pan's hand, swooping in the dark as the faint light from a sleeping city twinkles below. But then, I'd happily take any of the themes that skip through other people's minds: being naked in public, having my teeth fall out, sitting an exam on a subject I know nothing about – standard Freudian fare that supposedly says something deep about our fears or shortcomings. But when the arms of sleep fold over me each night, my subconscious leads me somewhere else entirely.

My dreams begin with walls, though they're not like those in my bedroom at home, which are smooth and matt with designer paint. Next, I register the noise, or lack of, a deadening, black hum that hurts my ears, despite the feeling that I am not alone.

By now, I am already terrified, gripped by the overwhelming feeling of impending threat. It's not just the fear of violence that smothers me though, it's something else more abstract.

Here, I have nothing. No possessions. No family. No identity. In this dream, I am no longer sure if I'm even human.

Out of nowhere, the face of a girl appears by my bed. My heart clangs and I grip the edge of my mattress. I can feel her breath on my skin and see the outline of her hair in the dim light. I already know every detail of her sweet face. It is more familiar than my own, with almond-shaped eyes in a dark brown hue, high cheekbones and a defiant smile that reveals two new, uneven incisors.

I push myself up in bed, briefly relieved that it's her, but she raises a finger to her lips, silencing whatever she thinks I am about to say. She shakes her head. Blinks away the oily glint on her eyes. Before I can ask what's going on, she reaches out and wraps her arms around me, hugging me tighter than seems possible for someone so small.

A noise startles her and she looks up quickly, scrambling away from the bed. I can see the rapid rise and fall of her chest before she looks at me again, then turns and begins to tiptoe away. By the time she's at the window, I already know what she is about to do, but I can only watch as she pushes it open. I want to scream now, so loud that it might tear my lungs. But I can't.

She climbs onto the sill and pauses, long enough for me to think she might change her mind. But she never does, no matter how many times I have this dream. Instead, she simply looks down and jumps into the abyss.

Chapter 1

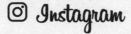 **Instagram**

EnglishCountryGardenista

650
posts

56.6k
followers

938
following

ELLIE HEATHCOTE

Ramblings and photographs from my English country garden. If you're a lover of plants, vintage gardenalia and gardening inspiration, you're in the right place.

The sight of tulips on a spring day always makes me feel nostalgic. They were the first flowers I ever bought to give to someone else. I was nine and had counted up my meagre savings in one and two pence pieces, before I went to the florist with my dad to pick out a bouquet for Mother's Day (it was amazing what you could get for 23p when he was around). Mum was brought to tears, though that might have been hay fever, and I insisted she keep them in a vase on our kitchen table until THE BITTER END, refusing to let her dump them, even after their stems started to ferment.

The varieties in the picture — goblet-shaped 'Ballerina' and 'Burgundy' — will grace my garden with colour for a few more weeks yet. I planted the bulbs in November, keeping them close together in trenches before adding a mixture of compost and soil, plus a layer of sand, which helps with drainage. The ones at the front are 'Montreux', which begin as a light cream with a delicate blush of pink that deepens as the flower matures, like a

My fingertips hover over the keyboard as I try and think of something poetic but, after a full day of digging, I'm running out of steam. What else would make a blush deepen? A medieval maiden beholding a handsome nobleman? Too long on a sunbed? I sigh, defeated, and delete the last sentence before adding some hashtags — #gardenersofinstagram #Englishcountrygarden #tulips #femalegardener #thisgirldigs #Englishgardenstyle — and scheduling the post.

You can't be poetic every day, though I do go to great efforts to ensure the quality and consistency of everything I put on here. I am also a social butterfly, engaging with as many people as possible; basically, I talk to anyone.

Despite this, no Instagram influencer could tell you a guaranteed formula for success. If there was one, everyone would be at it. Certainly, when I started on here two years ago, I never in my wildest dreams thought that I'd end up with nearly 57,000 followers and earn actual hard cash from it. This has left me with raging imposter syndrome, which I'm trying to overcome on the basis that we all accept when we visit social media that what we're seeing can't possibly be as good in real life. We scroll through a polished version of reality, life through a filter, a world in which blemishes are Photoshopped and less than perfect images are dumped straight in the Trash.

Visitors to my account wouldn't want to see the stacks of rubbish that languish behind my shed, or photos of poorly drained patches of lawn. They don't want to know about the stink under my arms after a day of hard toil, or the dirt that clings to my cuticles. They don't want ugly or messy, and why should they?

'We live in a nasty enough world as it is, don't we, Gertie?'

My dog tilts her head, a gesture that gives the appearance that she finds everything I say riveting. It's a nice quality in any pet, especially when they are the only other living thing her owner has to talk to on some days. 'I think we need to book you into the beauty parlour,' I add. I've been fighting a losing battle with her tufts of black and white fur ever since she first ran into this garden, dived in a puddle and bathed in it like it was Cleopatra's milk. I'd intended to get a big dog. I didn't mind what breed, as long as it was either a large, lolloping creature straight off the cover of *Country Life*, or the kind of marauding beast that would deter burglars and carpet salesmen.

'But we never get burglars or carpet salesmen around here,' my dad had argued.

'A Labrador then. Or a German shepherd,' I'd suggested.

So he brought home a shih-tzu. Or, rather, a half-shih-tzu — the other half, according to the woman in the dog's home, being 'God knows what'. Gertie had apparently been found pregnant as a stray, aged approximately two years old. Nobody knew where she'd come from, only that she was un-chipped, malnourished and had been keeping the wrong kind of company. While the four puppies she had a few weeks later were snapped up by eager buyers, Gertie was a less attractive prospect. She'd been there for nearly seven months, until Dad arrived and rescued her. It wouldn't have been the first time he's felt the urge to do this sort of thing. He is an unlikely-looking hero, between his thinning hair and a wardrobe dominated by corduroy and old concert T-shirts, which give him the air of a school librarian who got lost on his way home from a gig in the late 1970s. But he refuses to sit by and watch anything in trouble without stepping in: Pigeons with broken wings. Caravanners on the A40. Small, stray dogs.

Of course, at two and a half years old, Gertie was com-pletely untrainable, hence the fact that I still regularly have to defuse her homicidal tendencies towards the postman and have never succeeded in persuading her to stay off the sofa when her paws are muddy. Also, despite being surrounded by countryside, she is not allowed off the lead after previous, unfortunate examples of antisocial behaviour. None of this information is shared on Instagram of course. I prefer her to remain a star in her own right and Gertie is still responsible for my most successful posts to date. One picture – of her head poking out from behind a stack of plant pots – unleashed a deluge of likes and new followers. So in that sense, I consider Gertie and me to be like some of those old silver screen double acts. She is the Marilyn Monroe to my Jane Russell. The public didn't need to know about the grubby reality of *their* lives either. No matter what might have happened behind the scenes, those ladies would paint on their smiles and step on set. The show must go on.

My life as a social media gardener has been rich and fulfilling – that bit *is* authentic. I get a buzz out of doing what I do. Plus, there's the bonus of not having to work in an office, exposing myself to #MeToo incidents with a boss called Brendon and listening to Julia in Compliance drone on about her daughter's achievements on the French oboe. Instead, I spend every day creating something beautiful right outside my doorstep. I get to nurture life, feel the soil between my fingers and the crunch of grass underfoot.

If I was still seeing her, my therapist Colette would definitely agree that being outside contributes positively to my mental health. It's also more cost effective for the NHS than all the Citalopram, Prozac or Seroxat I've been on and off over the years.

I try not to think about Colette too much though. I hate being a disappointment to anyone and I'm fairly certain she hasn't filed away my notes in a folder marked 'Success Stories'. I don't think it would keep her awake at night, but at the very least she must walk into her office on some days and think: *How in God's name did that one get away?*

It was a nice office. The kind a psychiatrist would have in a mid-1980s Harrison Ford movie, with tan leather chairs, ethnic rugs and shelves full of books with snappy names like *Desensitisation and Therapy for Advanced Practitioners* and *Attachment Disturbances in Adults*. The room added to the general feeling when I first met her – more than fifteen years ago – that our relationship would be a success. She had that rare quality that inspires admiration without making someone unapproachable; she was well read, wore a lot of cashmere and had warm brown eyes that, alongside a mildly husky voice, made me hope for her sake she was not treating any men for sex addiction.

The thing I liked most about her though was her optimism. She had an unshakeable conviction that *everything was going to be all right*. I like that in a person. And things absolutely are all right, even if her definition of the term almost certainly diverges from the situation in which I find myself today.

I'm sure she thought I'd be easy to treat. I *should* have been. I couldn't have asked for a more stable upbringing than the one my parents gave me – a nice, normal childhood, full of birthday parties and sleepovers, lifts to Brownies and weekends away to Center Parcs. I have no right to any hang-ups really, though I comfort myself with the thought that, compared with all the other juicy problems and weird quirks Colette must have had trailing in from that waiting room all I had, really, was one issue.

Everyone's got at least *one*, haven't they?

I close down my laptop and head to the kitchen units directly opposite the living room. I love open-plan living, though the size of my annexe means I couldn't really have it any other way. My Grandma Hazel lived here when she was still alive and there's only enough space to separate off a single bedroom and small bathroom.

But even if I lived in a huge town house with a husband, lots of children and friends who'd pop over for prosecco-fuelled book club sessions, I'd still like the idea of blending living areas. *Perfect for entertaining.* That's what the articles on Pinterest say. I've had to wean myself off Pinterest though; it's lethal. The intention was to decorate this place on a budget – with reclaimed this and repurposed that – but after a couple of evenings browsing, only Farrow and Ball would do. Still, I had oak beams, stone windowsills and an arts and crafts front door to complement, so it would've been a travesty to slap on any old magnolia. So I got six tins of paint and some tile grout for the birthday after I moved in here, both of which I put to excellent use. You can learn to do anything from the internet these days. I laid bathroom tiles, plumbed in the toilet, wallpapered the bedroom. I'm sure I could perform open heart surgery with the right YouTube video.

I peek out of the front window to check the coast is clear, then stand on my tiptoes and reach on top of the kitchen cabinet (Card Room Green, F&B #79) to take down my stash of cigarettes.

Smoking is an unbelievably expensive pastime these days. I could never afford it if I didn't have a special arrangement that allows me to purchase them in boxes of two hundred at a knockdown price. I get them from Ged, who works at the local branch of Green Fingers garden centre, as a warehouse assistant, horticultural delivery man and supplier of boot-legged fags – though the latter is an unofficial role, of which his managers have no knowledge. I consider him a godsend, in the same way that busy new mums and self-employed freelancers rely on Ocado. I sent him a text three days ago, requesting my usual, and he told me it would be here today when he delivers my legitimate order.

He doesn't just deal in cigarettes – the main focus of his business activities is marijuana, for which there is a surprising amount of demand around here. But personally, I stick to the Marlboro Lights, which he gets from his sister, an air hostess based out of Heathrow, and smoke them out of my bedroom window, when the wind is blowing in the right direction – away from the main house.

It's not that my parents are especially puritanical but they definitely wouldn't approve of this and I couldn't bear giving them one more thing to try to understand or, worse, help me overcome. They are health-conscious in the way the middle classes are when they reach their sixties these days: pilates-practising, Evening Primrose oil-taking, pelvic floor-exercising, red meat-limiting moderates. Furthermore, I might recognise this as a filthy habit, but it happens to be one I don't *want* to overcome. I need to keep some things private from my parents, even if I do live next door to them.

There are precisely eleven steps between Chalk View, where they live, and my annexe. These eleven steps are significant as they mean that I don't *quite* still live with my mum and dad at an age when most people are thinking about having children of their own. A lot of self-respect is riding on those eleven steps.

Besides, who *wouldn't* want to live here? I've long considered this spot, high on the grassy hills of the Chilterns, as my own piece of heaven. I can't think of anywhere on earth that could make me feel happier. Which is why I haven't set foot beyond my garden gate for more than two years.

Chapter 2

My mother doesn't merely park her ancient pea green Volvo on the driveway, she reverses it in at high speed, screeching to such an abrupt halt that if there were passengers they'd be nursing whiplash injuries.

'Where have you been?' I ask, expecting her to be setting the table for Sunday dinner.

She slams the car door and clicks the lock. 'I popped into the village for some double cream for your dad. He's having trouble with the dessert so thought dousing it in this might help.'

'What is it he's made?'

'Citrus and stem ginger pudding or something. I'm sure it'll taste wonderful, but it looks like it's been vomited up by a bilious cat.'

I follow her into the house and we find Dad in the kitchen, swearing as he frantically tries to plaster a large, glutinous mass together with the back of a spoon. 'Well, of all the rotten bloody things,' he mutters.

Mum peers in, frowns and gives a brisk shrug. 'Oh, it looks all right to me, Col,' she says, patting him on the back. 'Deconstructed desserts are all the rage at the moment.'

I head to the fridge and take out a bottle of Sauvignon Blanc, pouring a large glass.

'Here, have this,' I say, handing it to him. 'It'll make it all better.'

'No, it won't,' he sighs despondently. He does a double take, picks up the glass and knocks back a mouthful. 'Actually, that is a bit better, now you mention it . . .'

Despite living next door, I don't eat with my parents every night – only on Sundays, when they take it in turns to cook. It's the one time of the week we're guaranteed to get together, not because of my own packed diary, obviously – but theirs. Both my parents have busy lives, especially my mum. She's semi-retired but never puts her feet up, instead filling every day with something new and interesting. She still loves work too, though it's been many years since she was employed full time in a newsroom and even longer since her decade-long stint as a foreign correspondent, covering some of the biggest news events of the late 1980s and early 1990s, from the first Gulf War to the siege of Sarajevo.

Though the days of her flying off to a war zone are behind her, her byline remains a regular fixture in newspapers: she writes freelance analysis and feature pieces and every so often appears on *Newsnight* or BBC *Breakfast* as an 'expert'. She comes across as knowledgeable and serious on television, rather different from the woman friends and family know as being the first to agree to a game of Twister at a party.

Over dinner, the conversation is the usual mix of village gossip and politics – they consider a good debate to be a family sport. After we've covered the GMB, MPs' expenses and the situation in Syria, the talk moves closer to home: my mum's friend Lizzie has been having an affair.

'I'm appalled,' Mum says.

'Well, she's been miserable for years,' Dad replies.

'I don't mean about the affair, I mean that I hadn't worked it out. I should've realised nobody can lose that much weight just from playing badminton.'

Theirs is a large kitchen and dining room, with soapstone countertops and copperware that jostles for space on the shelves. It is cosy and unselfconscious, a touch chintzy, though there are a few mod cons and stainless-steel gadgets. It's mainly filled with mismatched furniture dappled with the imperfections of time and picked up from anywhere and everywhere. Kilims from the Balkans. Batiks from Indonesia. Walls full of books and art and a 'good' oak table that might have been worth something if it wasn't dented by roller-skates and patchy from decades of buttered crumpets devoured by my sister Lucy and me.

'Can't be long before your concert, Dad,' I say, finishing the pudding.

'End of May. I can't wait. It was worth turning sixty-five for that.'

The two tickets to see the Rolling Stones at the London stadium were from Lucy and me. They went on sale more than a year ago and it took both of us, plus Mum, simultaneously hammering websites on five devices before we eventually hit the jackpot.

'I still haven't decided who I'll take with me,' he says, as Mum stands to start clearing the dishes.

I look up, surprised. 'Why aren't you going, Mum?'

'I've got an after-dinner speaking job, sadly,' she says. 'He won't be short of takers to accompany him though.'

'Hey, what was that concert I took you to as a teenager?' Dad asks. 'It was at the Forum in Kentish Town.'

'Macy Gray,' I tell him. 'She was brilliant.'

He holds my gaze long enough for me to realise that he is considering an alternative reality, in which the person he gives the other Rolling Stones ticket to is *me*. In which we leap up and down to the music, buy the T-shirts, drink the beers, feel the thrum of sixty thousand voices singing along to one song. The thought sends a prickle along the back of my neck. 'Your friend Alistair would be a good choice for the Stones, I think,' I say decisively. 'Don't you?'

He smiles in a way that doesn't reach his eyes. 'Yes, I'm sure Alistair would love it.'

Afterwards, Mum goes to watch the news in the living room and, after finishing the washing up, I find her curled on the sofa, bare feet tucked underneath her legs. Her hair was a vivid ginger when she was younger, but has faded to a peachy blonde. She has a fine bone structure and thick lips that once prompted someone from her tennis club to ask if she'd had collagen implants.

'Certainly not,' she replied, though judging by the number of times she's since repeated this anecdote, she was secretly pleased at the suggestion.

I sit next to her and wait for the closing credits while my eyes drift over the photos on the wall, an identity parade of badly cut fringes, braces and teenage spots, clutching graduation scrolls or running trophies.

I last won one when I was fourteen, when I competed at county level. I think it had been a surprise to everyone that I could run as fast as I could, me included – and it certainly kept the pounds off more easily than I can manage now. If Mum wasn't away, she'd be the one to drive me to the fixtures. She'd been a good runner herself as a girl and loved watching me compete, judging by the volume of her cheers if I won, at least.

Of course, when I first started those races, aged nine, she was still working abroad all the time. I used to seek her out on the sidelines and, if I saw her with her mobile phone at her ear, anxiety would bolt through me, because back then only one person ever phoned on that – her news editor. It was a sure sign that, later that day, she'd be packing her little brown bag, ready to fly off to God knows where. I never got used to it.

'Our new cleaner starts next week, did I tell you?' she asks, as the programme's credits roll.

'Oh, Mum, I've already said I'm happy to clean for you,' I protest. 'It's such a waste of money when I'm only next door.'

'No,' she replies firmly. 'I don't want you doing that.'

'But you walk Gertie for me. It's only fair that I do something in return.'

'Walking Gertie isn't a chore. I enjoy it. Besides, I've got Mandy starting next week now.'

'But—'

'Ellie,' she says, interrupting, as she pats my hand gently. 'It's out of the question.'

There's no point in arguing. Dad doesn't always agree with her, but he'd back her up on this. The thought of me being stuck at home, scrubbing a floor, instead of putting my university education to decent use is unbearable for them. Because however they imagined I'd turn out, it was a long way from that.

Chapter 3

I wake the following day to the soft thud of Gertie's paws as she jumps on the end of the bed and scampers to me to say hello. It's been a long time since anyone has tried to nibble my earlobes, but it's so gross that I prise her off immediately.

'You silly thing,' I murmur, ruffling her fur as she wags her tail, apparently ecstatic at the mere fact of my existence. I pick up the phone and check the response to the tulip post. It has attracted a solid 948 likes and lots of comments, though I discover as I scroll that this was largely prompted by a question from one of my followers.

@DaisyFallowes
Could you settle a difference of opinion between me and my boyfriend? He recently grew a man bun, started drinking craft ale and, as well as showing an interest in bee-keeping, is obsessed with making our garden organic. I'm all for this, but he claims that 'human urine is the most effective fertiliser known to man'. I'm now worried about him 'fertilising' the botanicals in broad daylight. The neighbours are a nice bunch but I'm pretty sure they have limits. Is he pulling my leg? 😄

@EnglishCountryGardenista

@DaisyFallowes I prefer Growmore, but your boyfriend is not wrong: human urine is a rich source of nitrogen, phosphorus and potassium. However, I wouldn't recommend applying it directly (and not merely for the sake of your neighbours). It works best when diluted ten to fifteen parts water. Happy fertilising!

I make sure I reply to everybody – @patti.74, who tells me that tulips are *her* favourite too. @Urban.gardener.NYC who wishes he had the space I have on the terrace of his loft apartment. @Dorinda.Smythe from Winnipeg, Canada, who says she's waiting patiently for her own tulips to poke through a blanket of deep snow . . . and dozens of others.

It's time-consuming but I was brought up to believe that if somebody takes the trouble to start a conversation, it's only polite to respond. I like to think of social media as a cocktail party. You get to chat to all kinds of people; some you hit it off with, others you don't.

This connection with the outside world is one of the reasons why I don't *really* think of myself as agoraphobic, whatever my medical records might say. I don't closet myself in a room with the windows nailed shut, unable to go to the bathroom without fearing what might jump out of the loo and get me. Also, it's not as though I don't go outside. I am *constantly* outside, where I feel not only relaxed but positively content, as long as it's within the perimeter of the garden, which is looped by a high stone wall and dense hedges that provide an atmosphere of seclusion and privacy. Compare this to some poor bastards on the panic forums. Some of them never even leave their *bed*.

I could leave if I had to, but the life I have constructed here is one I happen to like – and is all the better for the fact that it allows me to do a job I'm passionate about. I don't get paid a fortune as an influencer, but the sponsored content that I create, curate and publish online amounts to more than when I first started out, when I'd have done anything for a free watering can. Now, my paid-for posts are planned in advance with the marketing manager of one of the firms who employ me – everyone from online plant stores to clothing companies and publishers.

I like to think that one of my key attributes is flexibility, so when I was approached this morning by a firm I've partnered with before – The Creative Planter – to ask if I could squeeze in a sponsored post before Wednesday, I immediately said yes, despite the weather forecast. With rain promised later today, I need to get cracking. After wanding my hair into long waves, I apply liquid eyeliner and pull a pair of Hunter wellies over my jeans. I step outside with my tripod and camera, as milky morning light shimmers through the buds on the fruit trees.

Our garden wraps around my parents' house on a perfectly sized plot of around three quarters of an acre. The main house has the nicest aspect: from the top floor, where my mum's home office is, the view is an idyllic slice of English countryside, a carpet of green hills, church spires and woodland. Inside the walls, my aim was to create the perfect cottage garden, an exuberant and informal display of peonies and foxgloves, snapdragons and pansies. There are berry and fruit trees, as well as rambling plants that grow right up to the main house, weaving into each other and cascading onto the pathways. Right at the end is a huge weeping willow, with graceful, whispery leaves.

I start on the first few shots on my list – pictures in which I prune a fig tree and or tie back the rambling roses. But by 11am, the sky looks ominous, so I prioritise a now-or-never shot to illustrate a post about lily bulbs that the marketing manager of The Creative Planter was desperate for. It involves a side-on view as I kneel with a trowel, a splash of colour from the bluebells in the background. I set the timer and get into position, when a burst of sunlight shines through the clouds. It's a winning shot.

'Er . . . hello?'

With a second before the shutter clicks, I ignore the arrival of Ged with my Marlboro Lights – and fix my smile.

'Is everything all right?'

But I realise that the voice isn't actually Ged's. As footsteps approach, my breath catches and I look up without actively making the decision to do so. I register as my stomach plummets that a total stranger is standing in my garden.

Chapter 4

'Don't leave the gate open, I've got a dog!' I yell, though Dad took Gertie for a walk an hour ago.

He freezes and looks round, alarmed. 'Oh, sorry.'

I glance at the logo on his polo shirt and realise that, while he isn't Ged, he *is* from the garden centre. I remember my camera and check the last photo it took, discovering that as a result of the confusion all I've achieved is an unusable shot of my elbow. I groan as he heads up my garden path, carrying a tray of alpines.

He is a bear of a man, with the kind of height and bulk that you can't ever imagine fitting into an economy airline seat, or emerging from a gift shop without having broken a couple of knick-knacks. He wears grubby workman's gloves and an unironed shirt, and has a spongy midriff that, harsh as it sounds, does not compare favourably with the Nordic male supermodels I'm used to seeing on Instagram. His muscular forearms are milk white and his hair light brown, the colour of dust in the summer. He looks vaguely familiar though I realise that this is because, beyond thick, solid eyebrows and long lashes, his face isn't one you'd pick out from a crowd.

'Are you okay?' he asks. 'I let myself in when I saw you from the gate. I thought you might have fainted.'

I frown at this bizarre assumption. 'I was *planting bulbs*.'

'Ah,' he laughs, looking sheepish. 'Good job I didn't call the air ambulance then.'

The sky is leaden and oppressive and I need to get that picture urgently. 'Just leave the plants on the patio. Thanks.' I smile politely, hoping he doesn't take it as an invitation to stop and chat, then reset the camera.

'There are another couple of things in the van,' he says, heading away as something occurs to me with a crunch of alarm.

'Where's Ged?' I ask.

'Oh, the last guy? He got a job at Cuthbert & Sons.'

I blink. 'What – doing deliveries?' I decide there and then that, *wherever* he works, I'll be taking my business there immediately.

'Kind of – they're undertakers. Don't worry though. I'm only on a temporary contract but I've been told you're a big customer. If you've got any special requests, just ask.'

I pause, trying to work out if I imagined the inflection in his voice. 'What *kind* of "special requests"?' I ask tentatively, wondering if Ged has let this guy in on his sideline, perhaps in some kind of franchise arrangement.

'Well, carrying any heavy stuff. Supplying the goods at short notice.' He shrugs. 'Doesn't sound all that special really, does it?'

'But when you say "the goods" . . . exactly *which* goods are we talking about?'

He pulls a piece of paper out of his back pocket. 'Half a dozen alpines, a bag of fertiliser and some all-purpose linking supports. Is something missing?'

'No. Forget it.'

As he returns to the van, I take out my phone to text Ged.

There's a different delivery guy here and he
says you've left. I've completely RUN OUT.
Can you get here tonight?

I look up to find Ged's replacement stacking fertiliser against
the house wall. 'Sorry if I ruined your picture,' he says.

I'd forgotten about that, though by now the otherworldly
gloom that's descended has entirely put paid to capturing that
shot. 'They mentioned at the garden centre that you're a social
media star. Is it on Twitter?'

'Instagram.'

'Oh, right. I'll have to look you up. Not that I'm on
Instagram – or any of that stuff.'

I glance up. *'Nothing?'*

'I tried setting up a Facebook account once. All kinds of
people kept coming out of the woodwork.'

'That's the idea.'

'Yeah, but then I found out that the lovely little old man
next door was actually a Britain First supporter and my
Aunt Sarah kept posting mad, anti-vaccine rants and saying
garlic could cure cancer. I basically discovered that I was
surrounded by lunatics.'

Then, as if someone has switched on the setting on a shower,
great thick gobbets of rain begin to fall. I gather up my equipment and race across the patio, until I push open the door and
scramble inside. I tip them out onto the kitchen table, then
become aware that the delivery guy is hovering at the threshold, his hair plastered to his forehead in a kind of weird, knotty
fringe. 'You left this outside.' He holds up my make-up bag.

I walk to the door and he hands me a soupy cauldron of
foundation and Charlotte Tilbury eyeshadow.

26

'Oh, great,' I sigh.

'It's ... Ellie, isn't it?' he asks, inching further under my small porch roof.

I look up, surprised. 'Yes.'

'I *knew* it was you.' He crosses his arms and smiles.

'Sorry?'

'We went to primary school together. We were only in the same class for a year. I remember the day you started.'

'Oh, right,' I say awkwardly, feeling heat radiate to my neck. 'Do you need me to sign for this?'

'Oh. Yeah.' He takes the signing device from his back pocket and starts clicking on it. Thirty seconds later, he is still clicking, mumbling about technology and repeating the fact that it's his first day.

I'm not going to offer the information, but now he's mentioned it I do remember him from school. I recall seeing him emerge from the office behind his mum one day, as the head teacher was telling her that they 'took bullying very seriously'. I only had to glance at this hulk of a boy, his head hanging between the shoulders of his blazer, to know he was the victim, not the perpetrator. I felt sorry for him, but my overwhelming feeling was: thank God I'm not him.

'Got anything planned this weekend?' he asks, as he finally hands over the machine. 'It's meant to be nice and sunny tomorrow.'

'I'll probably do some gardening,' I say, scrawling my name.

'Great!' He smiles pleasantly. 'Nice to see you again anyway.'

Then he turns and heads back towards his van, closing the gate and leaving me to breathe a little easier.

Chapter 5

That night, I have one of my dreams. I knew it was coming. I can feel these things, in the same way that some people with migraines say they are preceded by certain distinct, peculiar feelings. In my case it was the overwhelming sense of dread that accompanied me as I curled up with Gertie in front of *Gardener's World* and made me fight to stay awake for as long as possible. I eventually became so tired that I'd hoped I could sleep through anything. I did drift off, but the valleys of my mind were soon infiltrated by the same thoughts and images that have haunted me for years.

Now when I wake, I am irradiated by fear and flooded with cortisol, my heart thrashing so hard it feels as though it might give way.

But I know the drill. I know to breathe, to turn on the light. To pull myself together.

It is only Instagram and Gertie that get me through the next few, sleepless hours. The dog doesn't mind that I cling to her like my life depends on it, occasionally getting out of bed to smoke a cigarette or top up my water. There is no point

28

in trying to do anything other than scroll through gardening accounts to occupy myself until daybreak.

It's around the time when the sun is filtering through my curtains that a photo appears on my feed with a hashtag that I follow: #Chilterns. It was taken from Coombe Hill, a chalk downland site that's one of the highest points in the region, with sweeping views of the Vale of Aylesbury. Mum used to take Lucy and me for walks up there. My sister wasn't even a teenager by then, but she'd still grumble endlessly about it, as if no more pointless endeavour had ever been invented than *walking*. But I used to love it, at least when I was in the right frame of mind. Mum would roll up a picnic blanket and stuff a rucksack full of egg and cress sandwiches, peaches and macaroons. Once we were at the top, I'd eat until there was an exquisite ache in my belly, licking the sweet zing of lemonade from my lips, savouring it as if it were my last.

The picture that has caught my attention features a striking male silhouette against a sky smeared with thunder and charcoal. He's holding a yoga pose in which the weight of his body is upheld by his hands, his legs raised in front at a 45-degree angle. It looks like an unfeasible, impossible position, yet he is as strong and steady as an oak tree. The caption reads:

Do not let your past define you. Being happy and fulfilled is a choice, as long as you're willing to open your heart to the magic all around you.

#yogaman #positivity #positivityquotes #passion #inspiration #crossfit #goodvibes #fitness #Chilterns #wellbeing

I re-read the caption and like the sentiment so much that I click on the account. Its owner is called @Firefly_Guy. He has just over nine hundred followers and a biography that reads: 'Yoga man, traveller, positive thinker'.

His pictures have been predominantly uploaded in the last few weeks, though some were taken a while ago. Most are in locations within a twenty-mile radius of here, but a few feature shimmering snow in Austria or rocks glittering with dust in Picos de Europa, Spain. His six-pack could have an Instagram account of its own judging by the level of interest it has attracted. Though undeniably impressive, it is his face that I'm mesmerised by. Everything about it is twinkly and alluring – artistic-looking hair that's tied back but falls onto a tanned forehead, a soft, dark beard that obscures his chin and eyes as blue as a swimming pool. My fingertips hover over the keypad for a moment, before I begin to type.

@EnglishCountryGardenista
That caption was a welcome thought today. Thank you for posting it. (Also, I love that spot – I made lots of childhood memories there!)

I press return, shut down my iPad and don't give it a moment's thought for the rest of the day. It's only after the light has faded, I've finished in the garden and showered, that I slump on the sofa with my phone – and discover that @Firefly_Guy has responded.

@EnglishCountryGardenista It's a beautiful view from there, I agree. One of my favourites.

I am contemplating whether to say anything back, when a private message icon appears in the corner of my screen. I open it up. It's from @Firefly_Guy.

> I ought to have said: thank you for your kind words
> about my post 🙏. It's nice to hear these things
> mean something to someone out there. Feels like
> I'm shouting into the abyss at times ☺.

This is significantly more exciting than my usual standard of direct messages, the last one of which asked if I could recommend a wormery starter kit. I compose my response eagerly.

> I know that feeling. I might have a few followers
> these days but it wasn't always like that.

In the lull afterwards, I click on one of his pictures, tilting my head to examine the beaded bracelet that kisses the veins on his wrist. I run my fingers over the screen, idly tracing its outline, when another message arrives.

> Okay, I've just seen how many followers you have.
> I am ridiculously impressed. How long did it take
> you to grow to that? And how? I have a million
> questions!

I can't deny I'm pleased he noticed. I reply coolly.

> I've been here for just over two years.
>
> Wow. Quite unbelievable . . .

Thanks, but lots of others on here have built
their followers far faster. It's actually slowed
down for me a little recently.

**You can't fool me with your modesty. Come on,
what's your secret? I realise this is starting to
sound like I'm asking for a consultation but I'm
genuinely curious ...**

Oh, just the usual. The photography has to
be top notch (but you already seem to be on
top of that judging by your most recent post!).
I always plan well in advance to make sure
I get lots of pics – sometimes 100 or 200 –
before I whittle them down to one. That's the
case whether it's for a post that a sponsor is
paying me for – or one of the others. The main
thing is letting your personality shine through.
Instagram Stories are good for that.

I hardly have to wait between messages; his replies arrive
faster than I can keep up with, making my heart flutter every
time a new one pings onto my phone.

You realise you should be charging me for this!

I snort.

These top tips are probably worth a
fortune ... about the price of a packet of
Smoky Bacon crisps I'd say.

Well . . . I wouldn't know. I'm vegan ☺

I wince. Of course he's vegan. You don't get a body like that from a diet rich in sausage rolls. I decide to steer the messages back to more comfortable territory.

Re. shouting into the abyss. I felt like nobody was interested too at first. You just need a couple of lucky breaks.

Hey, you're an inspiration.

My eyes narrow.

Hmm. Now you're taking the piss . . . I think?

Of course not. Why would you assume that?

Oh, I don't know. Maybe sarcasm is just hard to detect online. But if you're sure then I'll just soak up the glory.

Take it where you can, I say. Besides, it's obvious your breaks haven't been lucky. I'm not surprised people want to follow you. I've been clicking through your pictures. Your garden is lovely and your passion shines through. It also helps that you're incredibly pretty, of course.

My insides flip. I turn to the dog. 'Blimey, Gertie. What do I say to that?'

That's not offensive, is it?

'God no,' I say out loud, though restrain myself from actually writing it.

Not at all. It's nice of you to say.

Ha! Okay, good. What would have been the point in pretending I hadn't noticed, after all?! 😊.

It's been such a while since I've engaged in anything you could call flirtation that it's hard to know how to respond to this kind of thing. I've had approaches from men online of course, but they're rare in the gardening community, and I don't count 'hey sexy' when they land with sledge-hammer subtlety in my inbox. Though the internet is awash with people to message, meet up with, have sex with, all of that would mean taking a step I wouldn't contemplate.

Nevertheless, this feels different. This feels *wonderful*.

It continues for most of the evening, until I eventually retire to bed, my head full to the brim with thoughts about him, as one final message arrives.

Sleep tight lovely gardener. And dream well x

I allow myself one last look at his photograph before I turn off the light, gazing sleepily at the silver rings on his tanned fingers. I imagine what it must be like to be touched by those hands, to feel his skin against my own. It's a surprisingly easy thought to conjure up, one that prompts me to release a long, slow breath. Because, above anything else, it serves as a reminder of just how long it's been since I've been touched by anyone at all.

Chapter 6

Harriet, 1989

Harriet would have to admit that, several years after she'd won her first job in Fleet Street, there was still the odd moment when she felt out of her depth. The key, she'd worked out, was simply not to show it. Most of the men never did. This was particularly the case on foreign assignments, when she was among a press pack that was still predominantly male, with a few notable exceptions. Even though she considered most of her colleagues to be generous, unpatronising and fun to be around, it didn't do to broadcast bouts of self-doubt. Not when she still encountered the odd one who seemed positively troubled by her presence in a war zone.

'Do you think you'll ever get married?' asked Frank, as they sat in the back of a bullet-riddled Volvo having just left the airport in Beirut. While they were preparing for landing, the pilot had warned passengers to exercise caution when they exited the aircraft – and advised them to run as fast as possible to the terminal building to avoid being caught in any crossfire.

'Absolutely no idea. You?' Harriet said.

From the quirk of his eyebrow, he hadn't considered the question to be relevant to him. It wasn't as if he was an old duffer either – Frank was younger than her, in his early twenties and fresh from Cambridge.

'All I mean is . . . don't you think that if you did marry your husband would *mind* you being in places like this?'

'I'm absolutely certain that my imaginary future husband would be very supportive.' She grabbed the handrail of the door as the car swung around a corner.

They'd been sent by the foreign desk to Lebanon in the immediate aftermath of General Michel Aoun's declaration of a 'war of liberation' against Syrian occupation. The next 48 hours had been devastating, with Aoun's forces shelling West Beirut and Syrian forces targeting East Beirut, resulting in 40 dead and 165 wounded. As their car hurtled through the wreckage in the streets, the ring of distant gunfire peppered their conversation. In other words, you'd think there was quite enough going on to occupy Frank's mind outside of Harriet's personal life.

'Don't you ever think about staying in the UK to do something a little . . . *safer?*'

'Such as?'

'Oh, I don't know. Health reporter. Education, perhaps,' he suggested.

'I applied for the job of Knitting Correspondent but didn't get it,' she replied.

His head snapped towards her. '*Really?*'

'No, Frank.' She smiled. 'Not really.'

She'd never been able to work out who decided why certain specialisms constituted 'soft' news and were therefore especially suited to a woman. She counted her blessings that the succession of news editors she'd had were rather more enlightened – if by that was meant that nobody had batted an eyelid before sending her somewhere she could potentially get her head blown off.

The only issue had ever been whether she could get the job done and Harriet had worked very hard to prove that she could. She was fast and accurate, but also reported compassionately. She'd developed a pin-sharp ability to appraise risk, knowing when to keep away from danger and when it was worth trying to blag her way through a barricade. Despite a near miss by a rocket-launched grenade – which occurred while she was sharing a bottle of Scotch with an NBC cameraman in Afghanistan – and a brush with kidnappers in Angola, she was known for a refreshing absence of fuss.

'My aunt was an art critic for *The Lady*,' Frank continued, clearly considering this to be a helpful suggestion.

'But I do this, Frank,' Harriet said firmly. '*This* is what I do.'

If someone had told Harriet when she was a little girl that this was what she'd end up doing for a living, she'd never have believed them. She'd wanted to be a gymnast and was obsessed with the sport until she turned fourteen, when her body had grown in all the wrong places and scuppered her ambitions, apparently overnight.

She'd grown up with her teacher father and housewife mother in a neat semi-detached house in a small town in the West Midlands. At school, she liked English and History but rarely came top of the class. She was bookish and shy, with no particular interest in, or knowledge of, current affairs.

There really was no single moment that led her to this point. It was more a series of opportunities, curves in the road. Her father had a job at a good private school which she then got to attend as a pupil. Her first work experience was as a messenger on the *Coventry Evening Telegraph* – and she only chose that because it sounded more interesting than the alternative: photocopying clerk in a building society. A year in Rome as part of her History degree at Birmingham University sparked a period of joyous self-discovery, in which she learnt to shed off her introversion, chat to strangers on the tram and develop a life-long love of travel. After that, she would simply never have been happy working in any building society.

She quickly graduated from local newspaper hack to doing weekend shifts in the London newsroom of a broadsheet. She was chosen for her first trip to cover a conflict while she was working as a general reporter, for the typically illogical sort of reason that newsrooms specialise in: she'd had a long-term boyfriend from Ballymena while at university, which meant she was one of the few journalists they had capable of consistently spelling Northern Irish names correctly.

Since first seeing a tank roll into an urban street during the Troubles, her job had taken her to conflicts further afield – everywhere from Sri Lanka to Angola and Iraq. She was often terrified, occasionally moved to tears, but never anything less than fascinated. She also liked the idea that she was doing something that might make a difference, in small and occasionally very big ways.

Now, as their driver hurtled down a narrow alleyway, she clutched the small leather holdall that accompanied her on every trip. She'd picked it up in Lisbon airport on her first stint abroad as a reporter, to cover a more sedate royal visit. Within were the bare essentials: torch, toothbrush, notebook, official documents and a novel, in this instance the new Anne Tyler.

Suddenly, a blast resounded from somewhere, and their car wobbled. Frank grabbed her by the arm, his complexion chalk white.

'Do you think we need to try and buy some guns?' His voice was trembling. 'The driver said he knows somewhere he can get us a couple of pistols. Apparently the local press are all fully armed.'

'Don't be silly.' She tutted. He removed his hand and looked at her, exasperated.

'But why? Are you worried about trying to claim it on expenses?'

'If you and I go around toting those, we'd be far more likely to end up in a gun fight with some local militia and frankly I don't fancy our chances. Besides, it would mean breaking my number one rule as a journalist.'

She crossed one hand over the other and looked out of the window. A crack of gunfire echoed through the street.

'And what's that?' he asked.

She turned back and fixed her eyes on him. 'To keep *myself* out of the story.'

Chapter 7

Ellie

As someone who has shown a remarkable talent for losing friends over the years, I've reflected a lot on the first person I was ever really close to.

My childhood best friend wasn't a sister in the biological sense, but what she was to me transcended anything you could compare with a straightforward playmate or chum. Even though it was years ago, a whole lifetime away, I can still recall how much stronger, taller, better I felt for being around her. It sounds coy to say we were inseparable, but it's true. I assumed she'd be in my life for ever, the way children do. When you're young, you don't think much about the future, only the next hour, or day. Funny how it's only when someone is gone that you can reflect on the weight of their absence in any meaningful way.

Now I'm an adult there is really only one person who fulfils a role you could compare to that of a best friend and that's my sister Lucy.

She turns up on Saturday, while Mum and Dad are out. It's

been a couple of weeks since we've seen her, so I pre-empt what Mum will say by asking it myself. 'Why didn't you let us know you were coming over?'

'Last-minute decision,' she replies, as if she ever makes decisions that aren't. She sinks into my sofa and takes a bite of a sandwich that's clearly the result of a raid on my parents' fridge – half a baguette stuffed haphazardly with brie and grapes.

'I needed to get out of the city,' she says, between mouthfuls. 'Breathe in a bit of fresh air.'

'You're hungover then?'

'I think my brain might be bleeding. I'm giving up drinking as of today though.'

'I thought it was your favourite hobby?'

'Don't joke. Please,' she says, finishing off the sandwich and closing her eyes as she slumps further down the sofa. Gertie jumps up next to her and curls against her leg, as I bring over a glass of cold cordial from the kitchen. I place it on the table with two Paracetamol.

'Oh, you're good,' she murmurs.

'Anything else I can do for you?'

'Donate a liver?'

'You hide the fact that you're a human cesspit pretty well, I'll give you that,' I say, sitting down on the chair opposite her as she knocks back the tablets. Her chestnut hair is piled in a messy topknot and she's wearing white trainers and a floral print dress that goes down to her ankles, but shows off at least four inches of sumptuous cleavage.

Despite growing up in the same household, with the same parents and rules, Lucy and I couldn't be more different. Perhaps it's the ten-year age gap.

I, as the eldest, was obedient and anxious to please. I was an enthusiastic Brownie Sixer and deputy head girl, and my hand was always the first to shoot up when a teacher asked for a helper. Lucy on the other hand was averse to conformity. She lasted five minutes in ballet classes and chess clubs and was the kid who, when asked 'What's the magic word?', would not reply with 'Please' but 'Abracadabra'. As a teenager she hung around with the goths, the punks and the weirdos; she had pink hair with shaved sides for eighteen months and gave the impression that her Doc Marten boots were surgically attached.

She was clever enough to get into UCL to study Ancient History, graduate with a 2:1 and, after teacher training, begin work at a highly regarded sixth-form college, where her repertoire of amusing trivia about Roman orgies goes down a storm. You could never accuse Lucy of being boring. She is big-brained, big-hearted, funny and loyal.

'Do you want some tea?' I ask, taking two cups from the kitchen cupboard.

'Yeah, that'd be nice.' She lifts Gertie onto the floor and eyeballs the dog momentarily, before issuing the command: 'Sit!'

Gertie doesn't move, other than to blink.

'She only does it for me,' I say, flicking on the kettle.

Lucy is undeterred. 'Sit, Gertie!'

The dog yawns. I leave the tea and walk back to the living room. 'Sit!' I say.

Gertie looks from one of us to the other, then back again. 'Sit,' I repeat. 'Sit. Come on now. *Sit*. Please, Gertie. *Sit*.'

'I thought you were training her?' Lucy snorts. 'She's hopeless.'

'She's clearly just not in the mood to sit,' I say defensively.

'I think what you mean is: the dog is in charge,' she replies. I decide to go back to making the tea.

'So tell me: why are you hungover? What happened last night?'

'Oh, it's quite uninteresting,' she replies dismissively, which is what she'd say if she'd spent the evening entertaining Russian diamond traders at the Folies-Bergère. The scene of her downfall was a gin tasting at the Donovan Bar in Mayfair, which she attended with her friend Trudi.

'I'd been planning a quiet night, but you've got to get your money's worth. Anyway, there was this *awful* guy there. An advertising exec, originally from New York. He was arrogant, obnoxious. Also, you know the way some men are good-looking in a certain light but if you focus on them for a second you realise they're like a Picasso painting, with features that are in the wrong places and—'

'I get the picture. He was your worst nightmare. What happened?' I bring over the mugs and place one in front of her.

'I slept with him.'

'Oh Lucy.' Her shoulders slump. 'Well, at least you'll never have to see him again.'

'Apparently so. He hasn't returned my calls.'

'You . . . what?'

'Also, he's married,' she sniffs.

My jaw lowers.

'I only found out when I looked on Facebook this morning. His wife looks like Reese Witherspoon and she knits novelty bobble hats for charity. What kind of tosser would you have to be to sleep with someone else when your wife makes woollens in the shape of baby owls to raise money for sick children?' She shakes her head as a message lands on my phone. My heart compresses; I already know it's going to be from @Firefly_Guy – or, as I now know him, just *Guy*.

We've been texting each other non-stop for nearly two weeks now, though it feels as though it's been longer. Somehow, we are never short of something to talk about. Because, though I can't entirely match his knowledge of sub-titled movies, Japanese poetry and Puerto Rican night clubs, we have also found plenty of common ground – in social media and favourite local beauty spots. I'm interested in his job too – teaching yoga at a trendy studio, which he's clearly good at given the five-star reviews on their Facebook page.

His messages are wonderful in the most destabilising way. He is completely unselfconscious about telling me that he's been looking at my pictures, or that he likes the shape of my lips. My whole body prickles with warmth at this statement, made so matter-of-factly that you'd think we were discussing the weather.

So tell me @EnglishCountryGardenista ... do you think we might get to meet IRL one day? x

My small intake of breath piques Lucy's interest. 'Oh, who's sending you messages?'

'A company selling wellies. They're a potential sponsor.'

'Oh right,' she says, clearly underwhelmed. 'So ... anything else new with you?'

'Oh, you know. Thought I'd jet off to Paris to catch the opera tonight.'

She looks at me from under a pair of heavy lids. 'Ellie, your situation is far too tragic to joke about.'

'You don't need to worry about me, Lucy. I'm getting along just fine. I know you find it impossible to believe, but I'm actually happy.'

She responds with a muffled grunt, which could be derision or brie-induced indigestion. I suppress the temptation to point out that I enjoyed a thoroughly pleasant, sober evening last night and awoke feeling optimistic and energetic, rather than in bed with a married man who I then spent the morning stalking on Facebook.

Lucy won't accept the way I live my life. None of them will really, but she least of all. I think she hates the idea that I am fallible; it's against the natural order of things and every assumption she made about me when we were growing up: that I'd be the one to hold her hand and steady her through life. The rock solid one. There is little chance of that these days.

Chapter 8

 **Instagram**

EnglishCountryGardenista

620
posts

56.9k
followers

944
following

ELLIE HEATHCOTE

My British followers will know that there are only three things May bank holidays usually bring: rain, more rain and people grumbling about the rain, as they trudge round IKEA having abandoned plans to be outdoors. But, for the first time since the Magna Carta, we've got a long weekend in Britain and the sky is clear. I have a few chores to catch up on, but it feels wrong using that word about the garden somehow. It's hardly like cleaning the loo, is it? My first job is to take some softwood cuttings then get back into the lawn-mowing regime. My grass is growing strongly already so it'll be once a week from now on. How are you spending this May

Day? Whatever you're doing, have a gorgeous weekend!
#gardening #gardentherapy #girlsthatgarden #girlgardener
#wildandrustic #Maydaygardening #englishcountrygarden

My room this morning is not filled with the glorious sunlight
the forecast promised, but there are just enough glimmers to
post what I'd planned. Afterwards, I head outside to find the
air cold and bright, as dew drops hang from the frills of my
David Austin roses like little tears. I spot a weed in a container
and bend down to pluck it out but as soon as I've done so I
notice another. There's something magnetic about being in a
garden: one tiny thing catches your attention then, as soon as
you've addressed it, you're drawn to something else. Before
you know it you're brandishing a hedge cutter and going at
the evergreens without having even brushed your hair.

I never feel frustrated by weeds though. To be a gardener is
to accept that flawlessness is neither achievable nor desirable.
As Gertrude Jekyll said: 'It is not the attainment of but the
pursuit of perfection from which I gain the most enjoyment.'

Jekyll was a horticultural trailblazer and one of two
women to whom I attribute my love of gardening. The other
is my Grandma Hazel, Dad's mum and the previous occu-
pant of my annexe. She'd learnt basic gardening skills from
her father and as a young woman during World War Two
maintained a flourishing vegetable patch in her childhood
home in Lancaster. She moved to Chalk View three years
into her unhappy marriage with my dad's father before, six
months later, he died in a boating accident somewhere near
Wallingford. She never remarried, nor gave the impression
that she wished otherwise.

I recall slipping downstairs one morning when I was

about nine and I'd had one of what my parents would call my 'difficult nights'. I left Mum and Dad asleep in bed and found Grandma outside in the cold sunshine, pinching out the side shoots of her tomato plants. She had a thick frame with a sturdy bosom and proudly declared herself to be 'built like an ox'. Yet her features were soft: a wide nose, plump lips, eyes the colour of bluebells. She looked up and smiled. 'Hello, petal. I'm glad to see someone's up early. Where's everyone else?'

'They're still tired, I think.'

She straightened up. 'Did you have them up in the night again?'

I lifted my shoulders and nodded guiltily.

'Oh dear,' she sighed. 'Come over here. I think you need a hug.' She pulled off her gloves and enveloped me into her cardigan. I pressed my cheek into its thick weave and closed my eyes. She smelled of soil and Coty talc. A lovely smell. When she pulled away, she examined the bruises beneath my eyes. 'Gosh you look exhausted. Are you *sure* you don't want to go back to bed?'

I shook my head.

'Well, as it happens I was looking for a helper. Grab a trowel.'

We planted out some of her greenhouse veg that day – French beans and brussels sprouts – before she showed me how to thin out the beetroot and lettuce rows. I got muck on the hem of my nightie and my knees were pockmarked with stones as I knelt to help her. And though I was dirty and tired, it was the happiest of mornings.

I often helped her after that and still maintain that little vegetable patch to this day. I'd give anything to spend another morning with her, filling trenches with compost and planting onion sets as Radio 2 crackled out of the window.

The cancer swept through her like a bush fire, though perhaps I just wasn't told about it until there was no hope. She died when I was twelve and the garden faded fast. It had never been a passion for either of my parents; they were both too busy. So it became just a patch of grass they could never keep in check, whose only purpose was to accommodate a climbing frame and a patio on which they could enjoy a G&T with friends.

It never occurred to me that I could do anything about it myself until I discovered Jekyll. I was in my mid-teens and had volunteered to man the book stall at the school fete and found myself on duty with Neil, one of the students Dad tutored. He was in the year above me and, judging by the ferocious knit of his eyebrows, was there under duress.

The more popular books had already been snapped up: *Lace* by Shirley Conran and a complete set of *Carrier's Kitchen* part works. I was the only one who opened the crumbling edition of *Gardens of Gertrude Jekyll* – even then only because, when I'd asked Neil if he felt 10p was appropriate for *Microwave Cooking for One*, he'd replied: 'Who gives a shit?'

That book, I now know, was a 1900 edition and, though it was a little tatty, had originally been finely bound by the Chelsea Bindery, with wine-coloured endpapers and gilt edges. Its black and white pictures had been taken by Jekyll herself and, though grainy and monochrome by today's standards, hinted at the lavish displays at her home in Munstead Wood. One picture drew my attention: of an area tucked into a triangle of ground between a flower border and a kitchen garden. There were ribbons of tulips, amorphous patches of

Arabis and wisps of wallflowers. A thought occurred to me.
Could *our* garden look like this?

I bought the book for £1.50, about a decade before I spotted a similar first edition – in pristine condition – fetching
£1,250 on eBay.

I'd been flicking through it for weeks by the time I had
the row with Mum. Our dreary little domestic came at a
time when war was raging in Afghanistan and she'd had
the call telling her to fly to Kabul the following day. By this
point in her career, her role as foreign correspondent was
largely behind her. After Lucy was born, we'd had several
years of her being based in the newsroom in London and
all assumed that she'd never head to the front line again.
But now she was needed. A one-off, apparently, something
to do with their existing man being shot, though that little
nugget of information was something I only knew because
I'd overheard it.

Panic screamed through me like an alarm and I said things
that would later make me burn with shame. I accused her of
being selfish, stupid, putting her job before us, her family.
I told her she was going to leave us motherless – because I
knew with absolute certainty that if she carried on like she
was, she'd end up with a knife in her throat or a bullet in her
back. One of the super-powers possessed by every teenager
of course is the ability to predict the future with unstinting
accuracy. She'd tried at first to reason with me as I vented my
rage. But eventually she held my gaze silently, unbreathing,
with a glimmer behind her eyes caught directly between
deep-seated defiance and aching regret.

'Ellie, you mustn't say those things to your mum,' Dad told
me after she'd left.

'I can't help it. All my friends think what she does is cool, but they have no idea what it's like. I'm scared for her.'

'I understand,' he said gently. 'You're not the only one who worries about her, but I've seen her at work. She doesn't make silly mistakes. She's careful, smart and tough, which is why we love her, isn't it?'

'No,' I said bluntly. 'That isn't why I love her at all.'

As I headed outside, I was so wound up that I kicked over a terracotta container that had languished on the patio for years, being gradually smothered with moss and weeds. I gasped, unsure of whether I'd *meant* to do it or not.

'I think you should clean that up,' Dad said, crossing his arms at the patio door. I felt my blood chill at this new and unfamiliar tone.

I cleaned up the mess of course, simmering with anger and hormones. After I'd done it, I carried on. I had to. I don't know where the compulsion came from but perhaps it was the only thing I could think of to say sorry, even if I didn't mean it. So I weeded the flower beds, trimmed the fruit trees, strimmed the edges of the lawn that had become the bane of their precious weekends. On the way home from school the following day, I diverted to the garden centre, where I bought my first pack of seeds, a blue meadow mix, and a tray of marigolds. Then I got home and started digging.

Chapter 9

Ged has been in touch, but it's not good news. As well as his job switch, the arm of his corporate enterprise that deals in knock-off cigarettes has suffered an indelible blow: his sister has decided to retrain as a midwife. It's an admirable move of course, but will personally cost me a fortune now I've got to order my tobacco with the supermarket shop. I'd been certain that I had an unopened pack tucked somewhere on the top shelf of my wardrobe, but when I stand on my dressing-table chair to look for it, I can't find anything other than the plastic crate I keep up there containing old school certificates and photos.

I've a vague recollection of having had a 'sort out' of the shelf at some point in the past, even though my efficiency drives usually result in me losing a load of stuff, rather than achieving any great streamlining. I pull the crate down and start taking items out, when I come across a photograph that causes my stomach to lurch, like I've missed a step in the dark.

There are two little girls in the picture. We aren't smiling for the camera, just holding hands, a team of two. I realise that it's been a while since I looked at this. There was a time when it sat next to my bedside and I'd obsess over it. I was a different person back then.

I tuck it away and return the box, before heading into the kitchen to check my phone. I'm drawn again to the question Guy asked while I was with Lucy last week: *Do you think we might get to meet IRL one day?*

He probably thinks it's a reasonable suggestion. It probably is. But it's also one to which I can't give a straight answer, at least not without sounding like a lunatic. He has laughably interpreted my squirming rebuttals and attempts to change the subject as playing hard to get. Yet, as impossible as it is to say yes, I am also tingling with the sheer, blissful idea of it. Seeing him, touching him, looking into those eyes directly, without the vacant filter of a phone screen.

I step outside into the garden with my camera and tripod as the first notification of the day lands on my phone. I feel a delicious pulse in the pit of my belly.

> **What are you up to this morning? I had to get up at 5.30 for a power yoga session with a private client. Think I'm going to have to schedule an afternoon nap in at some point! x**

> 5.30? That's virtually the middle of the night.

> **Worth it to see the sun come up though. Hey, I've realised who it is you remind me of. It's been bugging me since the moment I first saw your picture.**

I frown.

Oh dear. Go on . . .

**There's a Spanish actress in a movie I used to love
when I was a teenager. I don't mind admitting that I
had quite the crush on her** 😎

Er, okay. But if you tell me it's Penelope Cruz,
I won't believe you . . .

As I attempt to conduct today's photo shoot, Gertie circles the
garden at high speed, for the sheer hell of it. With Mum and
Dad out until this afternoon, she hasn't yet had a walk and
the result is a bundle of looping, yapping energy that jumps
up to lick my ears every time I bend to straighten a foxglove.

'I love you, dog – but *please* stay out of my way,' I plead,
ruffling her fur as I set up the tripod in front of my summer
hanging baskets. I've planted a strawberry and mint display
that will stay in the greenhouse until they're established, or
until Christmas if Gertie gets her way. She deposits a tennis
ball at my feet and barks. I pick up the ball and throw it to the
other end of the garden, watching as she scampers off after it.

No, you're far better than Penelope Cruz!

Yeah sure. Anyway stop. I'm blushing.

**Ha ha! All right. I would still love to see that in
person though . . .**

Over the course of the next hour, I achieve very little in
terms of the photo shoot. This is partly my fault for pausing

every time my phone pings, but what am I supposed to do in the face of such a rare and lovely distraction? However, in between trying to think of something luminous and clever to write, Gertie's desire to play is completely unquenchable, leading me to the conclusion that I'm not quite as good at multi-tasking as I thought. Even when there's a lull between messages, each shot has to be taken in a narrow window of opportunity – basically while the ball is airborne and the dog is sprinting after it. I throw it further and further away, in the hope of buying myself more time – but even then it's hopeless and eventually my frustration gets the better of me.

'Oh, for goodness sake Gertie!' I say, grabbing the ball and flinging it as hard as I can, before darting to my camera to set the timer.

'Hey, wait!'

My head snaps up and I see the delivery guy from the other day. He's at the gate, with a box of plants at his feet, shouting at the field beyond. 'Hey, come back!'

'What's going on?' I ask, as he turns to me.

'Your dog ran out.'

I gasp. *You let Gertie out?*

I race to the gate, pushing him out of the way before coming to an abrupt halt. 'Gertie? Hey, Gertie!' I call out.

'She zipped past my legs when I opened the latch. She was chasing after a ball then spotted a bird and hurtled after it.'

Saliva sticks in the back of my throat as realisation seeps through me. I knew I'd thrown that ball hard, but had no idea there was enough force to propel it over the gate. 'Where the hell is she?' I ask frantically, gripping the gatepost.

The countryside unfolds beyond it like a familiar painting that I haven't looked at for a very long time. The grassland and hills that swarm with daisies and buttercups. The pastel grey sky and clumps of beech and ash woodland in the distance. To the south is Missenthorpe, the prettiest of villages. This is an England of cricket greens and church spires, of flint-built houses and duck ponds. An England I haven't seen up close in two years.

'GERTIE! COME ON!'

'Hey, it's okay,' he says, which really gets my back up. 'She can't have gone far. We can just go and look for her. I'll take one direction and you take the other. We'll find her soon enough.'

Jamie Dawson. That's his name – I remember now. Why this fact springs into my mind as I'm standing at my gate, infused with panic, I have no idea. The path outside follows two directions. Upwards leads to open farmland and the peak of the hill upon which our house nestles, overlooking the ribbon of countryside below. Downwards takes you into the village, a cluster of once-familiar shops and pubs, churches and people. I don't know which choice is worse, but in the event he makes the decision for me. 'I'll head down the hill and if I find her I'll phone you.'

'But you haven't got my number!'

'It's on your order form.' He turns to leave but, after a double take, pauses. 'Hey, don't worry. We'll get her back.'

His voice is spongy in my ears. My head pounds. The flesh on the lower half of my face begins to tingle and sweat has gathered at the base of my spine. He disappears down the hill, calling Gertie's name, and all I can do is stand, immobile, choking on my own fear.

My body is experiencing a fight or flight response, an acute stress reaction that occurs when threat is perceived. My central nervous system is in a state of hyperarousal, prompting a hormonal cascade from the adrenal gland. As you might be able to tell, I've read a lot on this subject. This physiological response is a good thing usually: the ability to detect and react to threats to survival is what enables zebra to escape from rampaging lions and human beings to dive out of the way of oncoming traffic. But mine, for whatever reason, is faulty. It's prone to misfiring. I do know this. But telling someone who suffers from panic attacks that their terror is irrational will do little to still their threatened mind.

These thoughts tiptoe through my head as I stand trembling at the gate, every breath like a crushing weight in my lungs. My limbs buzz. A thick, sticky sound throbs in my ears. I close my eyes, ball my hands into fists and turn to face the hill. I don't need to force myself to think of Gertie; she already looms in my thoughts as I turn and I run.

The dry thud of my feet as they scuff the ground leaves me with an intense feeling of detachment, as if someone else's legs are carrying me, that this is happening to another person. I look up and the sky, now grey, appears to be scowling at me.

'GERTIE! *Come on!*'

The thought that she isn't wearing her collar hits me. I didn't put it on this morning after she'd woken up. Why would I when she wasn't going for a walk until later today? She's chipped of course, but that would only be any use if someone approached her, put her in their car, drove her to a vet and asked them to scan her.

I remind myself I'm catastrophising, yet my negative thoughts begin to tumble over themselves, into a tight ball of despair. What if she gets as far as Kingwood Farm, where there are sheep grazing? Mum never takes her that way because she barks at them – she's had a number of near-misses when Gertie has become over-excited and, as amiable as Ed Sawdon is, no farmer would let a dog threaten his sheep.

A vision of Gertie crashes into my brain: of her lying prostrate with a bullet in her side and blood seeping into her fur. I physically shake my head to get rid of it and start to run faster, stumbling over the gravel on the path, as I frantically search the fields. 'Gertie!'

When I reach the section that is surrounded by hedgerows, the light dims. My limbs begin to shake, though it's not really that cold. Even the smells beyond my garden gate are different from those inside. Out here, the smothering scent of wormwood and sage radiates from the hedgerows. I reach a stile and pause, then scramble over, catching myself on the rotten wood. It splinters into my shin and when I look down, the skin is torn, a trail of blood sliding down my leg.

'GERTIE!'

I see the peak of the hill and begin to run again, staggering upwards with a feeling that the sky is engulfing me, swallowing me whole. When I finally stop, I am gripped by a certainty that I am going to die. I don't know how or why but I am.

I hear a bark. It's distant and I can't tell the direction from which it's coming, but it's her.

'GERTIE!'

The sight of my dog bounding over the hill, yapping as she hurdles over rocks and branches, makes me fall to my knees. I bury my head in her fur but the relief doesn't last beyond the initial moments. When I snap back to reality, it leaves a violent ache in my belly.

I pick her up and begin to head back, tripping over my

own feet as I cradle her in my arms. By the time I reach the house again, Mum is standing outside the gate, talking to Jamie. She looks up.

'Here they are!' Jamie has the relaxed and unaffected smile of someone for whom my own particular brand of madness would be totally incomprehensible. 'Oh, well done. Told you she wouldn't have gone far.'

'Where was she, Ellie?' Mum asks, looking at me anxiously.

Jamie begins ruffling Gertie's head and the dog springs into his arms, her tail in overdrive. 'Just went on an adventure, did you, little one?' he laughs.

'Looks that way. All okay?' Mum asks, in a tone that suggests she knows I'm not. I nod noiselessly and push open the gate to enter my sanctuary. My safety net. My home.

Chapter 10

I spend the evening in the company of *Garden Rescue* and half a pack of extortionately expensive Marlboro Lights. I can't face anything to eat and my thoughts about this afternoon's events jerk around my head like a twitching muscle that refuses to stay still.

When I gave up therapy a few months after I moved to the annexe of Chalk View two years ago, at least one of the reasons was that I'd learnt all the *theory* about agoraphobia that I possibly could. This was my second course of treatment with Colette. The first had happened after I left university more than a decade earlier and had been very successful.

This time, I'd been feeling better after a few weeks, at least I'd thought so. Then she suggested a 'new approach'. She wanted to get to the root of the problem. I knew what she wanted me to do wouldn't work. I told her it would have been counterproductive, could set me back years, no matter how well intentioned her motives.

Part of me also hoped that one day my problem might get better on its own, simply lift like a storm blowing over. Because, although I have lived with an irrational, agitated mind in one form or another for most of my adult life, that doesn't mean I've never been happy, or felt relaxed and normal. On the contrary.

I might limit my sphere of movement now, but I did spend more than ten years living in London. A whole decade when I was functioning in – and a lot of the time enjoying – a city inhabited by 8.1 million people, in which it's impossible to get from A to B without using an underground transport system. In other words, plenty to feel anxious about even for the non-agoraphobic. I also had friends back then, or at least colleagues I spent time with outside work, whiling away boozy summer evenings in Shoreditch bars or kicking off my Saturday mornings with a step class.

The pattern of my agoraphobia over the course of a life-time has ebbed and flowed. Until this afternoon, I think I'd assumed – without ever articulating the thought – that I would one day be okay again. But I feel shaken by what happened, I must admit. By the intensity of it and its stubborn insistence, even after all this time. As much as I'd convinced myself that I am happy living this life, the thought that I might be here for ever suddenly sits uneasily with me.

I gently push Gertie off my lap and head to my book-shelf, taking out a copy of *The English Gardener* by William Cobbett. I bought it from an antiquarian bookshop on the corner of Charing Cross Road, a shop that smelled divine, that sweet, musty scent of decades-old dust. It had a small but well-stocked gardening section and soon my Gertrude Jekyll book was joined by Derek Jarman's *Garden*, *The New Book of Apples* by Joan Morgan and Alison Richards and many more. My collection is a source of comfort to me, a literary blanket that soothes in a way that gardening advice on the internet could never hope to match. I do try though. The feeling those books give me is one I've attempted to emulate on Instagram, though I'm nowhere near as talented a horticulturalist as any of those authors. Still, the idea that my words might have an effect comparable to when I rub my fingers over the pages of a beautifully illustrated botanical guide is a nice ambition to have.

Tonight though, as I pick up *Classic Roses* by Peter Beales, none of this – not Gertie, the cigarettes, not the voices of Suzanne Vega, Etta James or Stevie Nicks, all of whom I've played all evening – changes anything. Nor does my incessant flicking through Guy's Instagram Stories. I feel agitated and upset and I've only got myself to blame.

The following morning, I am in the garden when Mum steps out, with a coffee in her hand.

'How are you doing?' she asks.

'Fine, thanks,' I reply.

'Do you want to talk about what happened yesterday?' she asks.

I shrug. 'Nothing to talk about, apart from what a naughty dog I've got. That's a nice top. Very trendy.'

She ignores my attempts to divert this conversation. 'Listen, sweetheart. I was thinking and . . . I wondered whether you should give Colette a ring again?'

I blanch at the suggestion. 'No, I'll be fine. Don't worry, Mum, honestly. I'm just going to be careful about the direction I throw Gertie's ball from now on.' I smile.

'This isn't about the dog, Ellie,' she says, gently. 'You got on well with Colette. You seemed to be making progress. I've never really understood why it was that you left so abruptly.'

'I didn't *really* make progress, Mum. And it was such a lot of money.'

'Oh Ellie, that doesn't matter,' she sighs. But it does. I've already cost them so much and, while they might live in a lovely – inherited – house they're not swimming in cash. 'How about someone else then?' she persists. 'Don't you think you need to do *something*, sweetheart?'

'Mum, it's fine. Really. I know you just want me to be happy, but I am.'

She looks unconvinced. 'Please just think about it.'

A beat passes. 'All right,' I say, which basically means, 'I already have and the answer is no'.

She decides to drop the subject. 'By the way, I got a text from Mandy, the new cleaner. She's struggling with childcare for her five-year-old son on Tuesday. Her mother has a hospital appointment and . . . well, there was some convoluted story but, rather than put her off, I suggested that she should bring him with her. I said he could play in the garden.'

'What?'

'I'm sure he won't be any trouble.'

'But that's not going to work,' I insist. 'I've got loads to do and there will be tools out there . . . it could be dangerous. It's really not a good time.'

'It's only for a couple of hours and I'm going in to the *Observer* office on Tuesday about a possible feature,' she replies. 'I'm sure you can keep him out of trouble for that long.'

Chapter 11

The little boy arrives with his mother just before 11am. He's cute, if you like that sort of thing, with dimples in his cheeks and a gummy gap in his bottom teeth. Gertie instantly recognises him as a new and exciting creature to leap on, sniff and make friends with, until he 'pats' her on the back like he's trying to get a racehorse to gallop and she decides to disappear instead into the annexe.

Mandy has very tanned, slender legs, breasts encased in the scaffolding of a push-up bra and long, groomed hair the colour of butter. Despite the fact that she'll shortly be scrubbing a toilet, her make-up is applied with the precision of an Italian old master and set off with a pair of false eyelashes. I feel a bit grubby and unkempt in her presence.

'Isn't your mum amazing?' she says, as she pulls a pink overall over her head. 'I couldn't believe it when she told me about her old job. You just can't imagine her in all those bloody awful places, can you?'

'Well, I tried my best not to,' I say.

'I like my luxuries too much to go off doing something like that, don't you? If I don't get my bath and Crunchy Nut

Cornflakes every night, there's no way I'll sleep. What do you do, work-wise?'

'I'm . . . well, I'm an influencer. And I run a kind of online garden business.'

She widens her eyes. 'Oh brill. You never thought of following in your mum's footsteps then? Flying off to all those mad places and putting the world to rights?'

'No. That wasn't for me.' I force a smile. 'So, are you taking the little boy inside?'

'Your mum was quite insistent that I should keep Oscar outdoors while I clean. I think she was worried he might break something.'

'Oh, I'm sure that wasn't it. If you'd prefer him to go inside where you can keep an eye on him, that'd be absolutely fine by me.'

She shrugs. 'To be honest, I think he probably *would* break something. Some kids only have to look at a vase to destroy it, don't they? And at least he can't do much damage out here. Right, I'll leave you to it. Oscar!' she beckons him over. 'Are you going to be a good boy?'

She rummages in her bra for a tissue that she proceeds to wipe over his cheeks. 'If you need the toilet, come inside. Don't do it in the flower beds like at Mrs Weaver's house.' She glances up at me. 'This isn't a problem, is it?'

'Erm. No, it's fine.'

Now she looks suspicious. 'You're *sure*?'

'Yes. I love kids.' I have literally no idea why I say this, beyond my pathetic need for approval.

'Ah, that's lovely. Have you got any of your own?'

'Me? No.'

'I'm not sure if I'll have any more, if I'm honest,' she

says, lowering her voice. 'One's enough for anyone, isn't it? Though my mum was one of nine.'

'Gosh.'

'I *know*. That was in the days when motherhood was respected as a job, mind you,' she says earnestly. 'My gran was a full-time home maker and mother, and loved every minute of it. Apart from when she had the nervous breakdown.' She appears not to be joking.

As she disappears into the house, I turn to the boy, wondering how Mum would handle this. 'Would you like some juice?'

'No. I just want to play with the dog.'

'The dog kind of does whatever she wants, but let's see if we can persuade her, shall we? *Gertie!*' She trots outside and looks at the boy.

'Does he like having a ball thrown for him?' he asks.

'It's a *she*. She's called Gertie. She'd probably like that as long as you don't throw it over the gate.' I pick up the hoe and slip on my headphones, clicking onto Florence and the Machine. As I prod the tool into the soil, I feel a tug on my sleeve.

'Yes?' I ask, looking down.

'I need a ball so I can throw it for him.'

'For *her*.' I put down the hoe. 'Yes, sorry. My mistake – I'll go and look for one.'

Inside, I rummage for a tennis ball in Gertie's toy basket. I pick one up and turn to leave, only to find the child standing less than a foot away, causing me to inhale sharply.

'I'm going to be an inventor when I grow up,' he announces, apropos of nothing.

'Great.' I hand him the ball and usher him out.

'Have you ever invented anything?'

'Nothing at all,' I say.

'I'm going to invent trousers that don't go inside out when you take them off. Then I'll put them on YouTube so everyone buys them.'

'Super. Off you go.'

He starts to wander off, then hesitates. 'Would you like me to teach you how to moonwalk?'

'No, you're all right. Thanks.'

For an hour and a half, he's one minute hovering over me – silently examining what I'm doing – then bombing around the garden as if he has a firework in his shorts the next. Gertie circles after him, yapping hysterically as they plough through a heap of weeds and jump over bedding plants.

'Look, I know you're only trying to enjoy yourself, but do you think you'd just be able to be a bit . . . a bit less . . . Arrgh! *Would you just stop!*'

'Hi there.' I look up to see the delivery man. Jamie. 'Am I okay to open the gate?'

I wince over the racket as I walk towards him. 'Yes, come in.'

'Just a little order today,' he says cheerfully, closing the gate behind him. 'Where do you want it?'

'The bench will be fine.'

'Looks like you've got company,' he says, nodding at Oscar as he puts down the box.

'Yes, I'd have thought you could've heard them from halfway down the hill.'

'Is he yours?' he asks.

'God, no.'

'Hello mate, what's your name?' Jamie asks. The child stops

and looks up. His face is blotchy and red like the inside of a pomegranate and steam is rising from his hair.

'Oscar.'

'Pleased to meet you.'

'Can you moonwalk?'

'Well, it's been a while . . .'

'I'm going to be an inventor,' Oscar announces.

Jamie widens his eyes. 'That *is* cool. What are you going to invent?'

'Trousers that don't go inside out when you take them off.'

'Awesome,' Jamie replies, as if he'd said *a cure for cancer*. 'Then, maybe you could invent . . . a trampoline that gives out popcorn every time you bounce?'

Oscar's mouth drops. '*Yes!*'

'Or, a jumper with a secret pouch that you can hide your dinner in when it tastes disgusting.'

'Or a time machine!' Oscar finishes.

Jamie looks as if he's in the presence of genius. 'A classic.'

'Well, I'm sure you're very busy,' I say, gesturing to the gate.

'Actually, I'm ahead of schedule. I whizzed round to try and finish early because I'm going to see Florence and the Machine tonight.'

'Oh, that's strange. I've been listening to their new album.'

'Isn't it great? You didn't fancy the concert then?'

'No. I mean, I would have liked to but . . . the thing is . . . I tried to log on when they went on sale. But then . . . *no*.'

But I quickly realise that there is no need to flounder for an explanation. As Oscar giggles with delight, Jamie is already moonwalking in the direction of his van.

Chapter 12

I can't deny feeling a shiver of satisfaction at Lucy's approving reaction when she clicks through Guy's Instagram feed. 'He's hot, I'll give him that. I don't believe he's got a body like that from only doing yoga though. It hasn't had that effect on all the ladies in pink leotards at our gym.'

'He does cross fit as well,' I tell her. 'But yoga is his thing.'

'He's very ... *positive*, isn't he?' She says the word as if it has a slightly odd taste in her mouth. 'Has he sent any nudes?'

I tut. 'No.'

'Only asking. I'm not slagging off the positivity guru stuff, either, by the way. I do love an optimist, even if some of it is a bit cheesy.'

'No, it's not,' I object.

'Oh look, I approve wholeheartedly of him. The very fact that you've found someone who gets your blood pumping is fantastic. I'll even push the boat out and let him off for making the statement: "If you can face your fear and dance in the rain then today has been a good day".' She snorts. 'He's no Plato, is he?'

'Oh, don't slag him off.'

She straightens her face. 'I'm not! Honestly, he's a complete catch.'

I decide to go and make some tea. I head to the kitchen while she idly picks up a copy of *English Garden*, discarding it after glancing through two or three pages.

'What happened about the New York advertising executive?' I ask.

'I've got bigger fish to fry these days.'

She reveals a tale of woe about how she went to see *Hamilton* for the second time with Pooja from work and bumped into her ex-boyfriend Mark, with his new wife Suki. Who is pretty, friendly and smart — a combination, it seems, that has made Lucy rather miserable.

'But *you're* pretty, friendly and smart,' I protest. 'Plus, *you* dumped him, remember.'

'I know,' she sighs. 'I was so depressed I re-joined Match.com.'

'You said it was full of losers.'

'Yes, including me.' I bring the tea and come and sit down next to her. 'So has he asked you out yet, this Guy?'

'A few times.'

'How are you going to get around that one?'

'That's the million-dollar question.'

She takes a sip of her tea. 'Are you not tempted to just get him over here? I mean, it's a thought, isn't it? As long as you're reasonably confident he's not an axe murderer, there's not a great deal you've got to lose. I know it's not the usual venue for a first date, but needs must.'

This has already occurred to me. Of course it has. But I have been prevented from acting by the sheer pointlessness of it: the issue of what happens *after* the first date. Part of me thinks I should take a leaf out of Lucy's book and not worry about the consequences. But she and I are hard-wired differently. We always have been.

She reaches over and rubs my back. 'Must be shit being an agoraphobic sometimes.'

I sigh. 'It's certainly starting to feel a little inconvenient.'

The first panic attack I recall in vivid detail was in Disneyland Paris. The happiest place on earth. I was twelve and at the time felt as though it had come out of the blue, though of course these things never do. Something had been festering inside my brain for years, like a cluster of benign cells waiting to grow into something solid and malignant.

I'd dreamed about going to Disneyland for ages. Most children do, of course, but I'd harboured an obsession with a variety of princesses – The Little Mermaid primarily – long after the age when children are supposed to have moved on to something more grown up. The journey there passed without incident. A seven-hour drive. Obligatory roadworks on the motorway. 'It's A Small World' on a loop on the CD player as Lucy yelled, 'Again! Again!'

'I think this is what insanity feels like,' Dad sighed as Mum chuckled and we approached passport control at the Channel Tunnel. He wound down the window and handed the family's documents to the official in the booth, a man with a bowl haircut and eyes as grey as the cold sea. There was a malevolence in those eyes, I could see it instantly. I shifted in my seat and tried to ignore his gaze, feeling the hairs on the back of my neck prickle as he said: 'Look up, please.'

He asked questions in a tone that felt accusatory and suspicious. A tone I was sure had irritated Mum, even though afterwards she pasted on a smile and cheerfully slotted the passports into her bag. She reached back and rubbed my leg reassuringly. 'Nothing to worry about, Ellie. So, who's ready to go and see Ariel?'

The moment I stepped into the Magic Kingdom, my travel sickness, which was what we all decided was making me feel queasy, disappeared. The sun was shining on Main Street and the laughter of children was carried by the breeze, mingling with the scent of candyfloss and sun cream.

We started with Aladdin's flying carpets then went on Peter Pan's ride. I was a little old for them probably, but Lucy was only two and I didn't mind. We met Mickey and Goofy and Dad and I went on Splash Mountain. But it was as we stood in a queue waiting to meet the princesses that I felt the first bristles of something sinister. There were three kids behind us – two girls, one boy, all much younger than me. The boy didn't want to be there and was pulling and complaining, flicking at his sister's ear, annoying everyone around him.

'Will you just *stop* with the whingeing?' his mother pleaded. 'Have you any idea how much it cost us to come here?' She grabbed his hand and yanked him towards her. He started crying. I felt my blood chill. She was going to hurt him. I knew it. Tears pricked in my eyes.

'Nearly there,' Mum smiled, squeezing my hand. 'All okay, darling?'

I nodded. Concern appeared in the wrinkles of her brow. 'Are you sure? Ellie, you're covered in goosebumps. Are you cold? Do you want to borrow my jumper?'

It must have been 27 degrees, but I shook my head. 'I'm all right. How long will we be in the queue?'

As we moved along, the boy continued to play up, until

eventually his mother threw in the towel. She abandoned their place in the line and herded all three wailing, shrieking children in the direction of the toilets. I couldn't shake off the thought of what was going to happen to the boy.

When we reached the front, Lucy toddled to Sleeping Beauty and threw her arms around her. I skulked next to them. I tried to act *normal*, but felt the opposite, overwhelmed by a force I couldn't explain, hypersensitive to everything around me. The noise and sunlight were amplified. My breathing felt hard, as if I was labouring to draw air into my lungs, and could never fully expel it. I had a sudden and intense feeling of threat. I gazed at Sleeping Beauty's lipstick which, up close, was as thick as tallow, fatty and gleaming.

What's your name? Are you having a magical time? Smile for the picture!

Mum lowered her camera.

'Er . . . thank you,' she said to Sleeping Beauty, taking my hand as I scurried away.

'It's all right, Ellie,' Mum said softly, not entirely knowing what she was reassuring me about.

'I just feel sick,' I explained, though that didn't begin to describe the pounding of my heart and the nausea in my throat.

'Perhaps it was Splash Mountain that made your tummy go funny?' she suggested.

'Yes. That was it,' I replied, though I already knew it was nothing to do with a ride.

Chapter 13

My mum's study is in the attic, in an oak-beamed room packed with orderly clutter: tightly stacked bookshelves, piles of sun-faded foolscap folders and biros that stand in brass pots on squares of ethnic-looking tapestry.

'Are you busy?' I ask, as I reach the top of the stairs and find her tapping away at her computer.

'Oh, hi,' she says, saving her work. 'I'm sure I can spare a minute.'

I sit on the rocking chair next to her desk and wonder how to broach this. 'Has Lucy been in touch?'

Her brow crinkles. 'No. Why?'

'Oh, it's nothing bad. Quite the opposite, actually. I've ... look, this might sound strange but ...'

'Go on,' she says.

'I've met someone.'

There is a moment before she answers when she tries to reconcile this information with my current personal circumstances. 'What do you mean?'

'Online,' I say.

'Oh. I see,' she replies, obviously trying to work out what she thinks of this.

'He lives locally. His name's Guy and he's a yoga teacher. We got chatting a lot and kind of became friends.' Heat begins to blotch on the skin under my ears. 'Maybe more than friends.'

She sits back and clasps her hands together, clearly startled by this news, but pleased too – at least, I think so. 'So I wondered if you'd mind if I asked him to come over one night?'

'Of *course* not, Ellie,' she says, her face lighting up. 'You don't need our permission for that. Your father might want to hang around to check him out, of course – but I'll make sure he makes himself scarce.'

'Thank you, Mum.' Though I'm happy about her reaction, I want to end this embarrassing conversation as soon as possible.

I look up at the wall behind her, where there's a framed map and a couple of Victorian botanical paintings. 'I'm surprised you've never put up any photos from your days abroad,' I say, nodding at it.

'Perhaps I should,' she says idly. 'I always thought it a bit odd to have pictures of myself up, but there are absolutely tons of them somewhere in those drawers.'

'Really? I thought people in the eighties and nineties hardly took any pictures, at least not compared with my social media-obsessed generation. You didn't have smart phones back then ...'

'No, but in my case, I almost always travelled with a news photographer. They're not exactly holiday snaps though, I assure you.'

She's right, they're not.

There was one in particular that I recall seeing, and being upset by, when I was younger. It was taken during the Bosnian war, in Sarajevo – a place I knew nothing about, beyond the fact that I certainly didn't want my mum there. The image showed her standing in a hotel bedroom, surrounded by shrapnel and lumps of shattered breezeblock. I found out when I asked her about it, years later, that a heavy night of bombardment had led to a direct hit on the very room where she'd slept for the preceding five nights. She'd only escaped because she'd been reading in the bath, wrapped in a sleeping blanket as protection. The thought made me weak with anxiety.

'What are you working on at the moment?' I ask.

'I wanted to mention that to you, actually,' she says, tentatively. 'Do you remember I said I was meeting the *Observer*'s features editor? They've asked me if I'll do a piece about Romania, to see how things have changed since the revolution in 1989. It would mean me travelling to Iaşi for a few days.'

I am aware that most of the locations my mother visited three decades ago are different places today, including Romania. She doesn't need to reassure me that things have changed there, that she'll be safe – I know all that, technically. But my brain doesn't always work like this. There are times when it doesn't succumb to logic of any kind.

'Is that all right, Ellie?' she asks.

'Of course,' I mumble, as my tongue suddenly feels too dry to swallow.

Preparing for my first date in three years is a large-scale undertaking. My legs haven't been hair-free since

Christmas and even then it was only because Lucy bought me a wet and dry epilator, insisting unconvincingly that it wasn't a hint. Tonight, I emerge from the bath with pink, throbbing limbs and no area of my body that hasn't been plucked, waxed, exfoliated, or moisturised. Not that I am presuming I'll have sex, of course. I'm probably not ready to take that step, even if my libido has reawakened like a roaring dragon.

I've never felt quite like this before and can't decide whether the cause can solely be attributed to abstinence. Guy is so different from the men I've been with in the past. With the exception of a fling with a Mancunian called Dave who went on to forge a successful career in musical theatre, all my previous boyfriends were deeply strait-laced – the sons of opticians or conveyancing lawyers, now pursuing similar careers themselves. They pop up on Instagram occasionally, sharing baby scans and, once a year, pictures from Glastonbury, as if to prove how far they are from middle age, whatever the Laithwaite's subscription and enthusiasm for cycling gear suggests. More than anything, there is something magnetic about the sheer *newness* of Guy.

After a fitful night's sleep, I take delivery of a supermarket shop that is heavy on rustic-looking vegetarian pies and artisan fare; items I don't intend to claim outright I made myself, but I won't object if he leaps to that conclusion. I then spend the morning in the garden while Mum and Dad disappear clutching maps and rucksacks for a day of walking, followed by supper in one of their favourite pubs, an old, eccentric place with low beams, peat fires and a barmaid who calls customers 'my love'.

Guy arrives at 12.30pm, bang on time – and just as I am

instructing Alexa to 'Play 6 Music'. I'd thought that would be cool to have on in the background, but she replies with, 'Playing Sex Music from Spotify,' which sends me scrambling for the off switch before I let him in.

I'm left flustered, though I would have been anyway, without the shenanigans over the playlist. But then he's here, on my doorstep, and just the sight of him makes my heart feel as though it is about to spill over. He is a mosaic of tiny details that his online pictures were incapable of capturing. Pale flecks in the irises of his eyes. A forehead burnished from sunshine. He's not as tall as I'd imagined, but he's taller than me, with a torso so lean there can't be a single extraneous ounce of fat. He is, quite simply, beautiful.

'You must be EnglishCountryGardenista,' he says, as his face breaks into a smile that goes straight to my knees.

'I am!' I reply giddily. 'I'm so pleased to meet you.'

I offer him a hand to shake, but instead he leans in to kiss me on the cheek. The bristles of his beard brush my skin, and I breathe in a scent that's peppery and mossy and just divine. He brushes raindrops off his shoulders and steps inside. Gertie bounds over and I grab her to lift her up as her tail thrashes manically.

'Sorry . . . she gets excited and jumps up when people first arrive, but she'll calm down in a minute.' I take her into the kitchen as her backside wiggles. 'Would you like a drink? Tea or coffee maybe?'

I grab a doggy treat and lower Gertie to the floor, feeding it to her as a distraction before she trots away in the direction of my bedroom.

'I hate to be a bad influence, but I brought this.' He lifts up a bottle of Riesling.

'Now you're talking,' I say, as I take the bottle from him and look for a corkscrew.

'So this is where you live ...' He glances around before taking a seat on the sofa. 'It's lovely, Ellie. Is it some kind of outbuilding?'

'I ... well, yes. It's small but it suits what I do to be here. The garden is so pretty that it's ideal for my Instagram page. It works well for all of us.'

I pour the two glasses and join him on the sofa, leaving an intimate but unpresumptuous space between us. I hand him his drink and he clinks my wine glass. I have to hold it with two hands to stop my fingers from trembling as I bring it to my mouth.

'So, what – the garden's yours as opposed to the people who live in the main house?'

'No, it belongs to them ... I'm technically, well, kind of a lodger. I thought it'd be temporary when I moved in, but everyone's happy like this – including me as it means I can work on the garden.'

'Ah,' he says. 'Who lives in the main house then?'

A heartbeat passes in which I consider lying. But I just can't. 'My ... parents.'

'Oh. Right,' he says politely. He takes a moment to digest this information, before saying, 'Everyone seems to be trying to get on the housing ladder at the moment, don't they?'

I decide not to correct his assumption, as his gaze settles on me. 'You look different from in your photos,' he says.

'Do I?' I ask, feeling a shot of heat in my neck.

'Yeah.' He takes a sip of wine and I watch the movement of his hands as he lowers the glass. Then he smiles the sexiest smile I've seen in my life and adds: 'Better.'

We get through two glasses of white before lunch and it is clear even without the benefit of the alcohol that he is not fazed by any of this. *Well, of course he isn't,* I tell myself. He probably goes on dates all the time, the way people do. My own nerves, on the other hand, do not settle at any point.

I know this is only to be expected, but there is one moment when I actually begin to wish it was all over so that I can just bask in the memories. I worry about saying something stupid, without the benefit of those seconds I have when messaging, precious time in which to draft and redraft my typed responses until they are just right. Now, any old thing is liable to spill out of my mouth.

'It's a bit strange finally coming face to face, isn't it?' I say, lamely.

'Does it sound weird to say that I kind of feel like I know you already?' My heart constricts. He tilts his head to try to gauge my expression. 'Sorry. Is that too full on? I didn't mean to—'

'No,' I interrupt. 'Not at all. I feel exactly the same.'

'I mean, when did we send the first message? Three weeks ago? Can't have been much longer than that?'

'Sixteenth of April.' I look up and wince. 'About then anyway.'

But now he laughs and it's clear that I don't *need* to be nervous. He really does like me, of that I'm fairly certain.

Over lunch the conversation turns to travelling, and while I could watch him talk so animatedly all day, it also makes me acutely conscious of the dearth of stamps in my own passport. I shift the topic to his yoga, and we chat about how and where he learnt it, before we drift to the subject of meditation. He tells me not to knock it until I've tried it.

'I wouldn't dream of knocking it!' I insist. 'Though I'm not convinced I'd be very good at it.'

'Well, I thought that too once. But I guess it just ... enhances my appreciation of the world. Improves my self-awareness. Does that make sense?'

'Yes, I think so. Did you say you write poetry too?' I ask, recalling one of our messages.

'Oh ... did I tell you that?'

'You did,' I confirm.

He inhales. 'I must have had a couple of glasses of wine.' He grins. 'Well, yes I do – but I don't tend to show it to anyone.'

'Why not?'

'Oh, I don't know. I only write it for myself really. Though ... maybe I should share some. I've been writing every day since I met you. You seem to have inadvertently become my muse. How did that happen?'

'No idea, but happy to be of service.'

We drink some more. We talk some more. I never allow the conversation to drift to the dangerous territory of why exactly I'm here, living eleven steps away from my parents' house.

Eventually, when he says he's going to have to make a move, it feels like it's come to an end far too soon – though when I glance at the clock I realise he's been here for more than three hours. I try not to show my disappointment.

'I think you should give me a tour of your garden first though, now that the rain's passed,' he says.

Outside, sunshine is pushing through the clouds and rain-drops are glistening on the petals. The garden always looks good in early summer, with the irises and peonies in full, succulent bloom and fuchsias spilling out from the hanging baskets and pots that line up against the house. I babble about herbaceous borders and mood boards and some of the challenges I've had with drainage, until it occurs to me that this is a subject particularly ill-suited to seduction.

'You really are good at this, aren't you?' he murmurs. Then he turns and gently slips his arms around my waist. Exhilaration blows through me like a gale.

I have a heightened awareness of the iron rigidity of his arms. The hard breadth of his chest. And that scent, the top notes of which I now realise cannot be attributed to any essential oil, but the smell of a living, breathing man.

As he leans in and brushes his lips against mine, my heart surges. He kisses me as though it is an art, guiding and gliding. The rhythm of his mouth directly related to the tension in my shoulders, which falls away like a silk scarf drifting to the floor. I eventually become aware that he is pulling back, and my eyes flutter open to find, mortifyingly, that he is smiling at me.

'You are utterly gorgeous,' he says emphatically, as he backs away. 'I'll be in touch, okay?'

Chapter 14

Harriet, 1990

Harriet felt as though she'd hardly set foot in her Clapham flat lately. She'd only just unpacked after her trip to Sri Lanka, where civil war was raging, when her news editor phoned with the next foreign assignment. She didn't mind too much. Her love affair with London was already teetering at its pinnacle, like a diver about to plunge off a board. She'd become so irritated by the dirt and heat on the Tube lately, not to mention how much it was costing her to live in a glorified shoebox.

This time, she was to join a convoy of humanitarian volunteers who planned to travel to a crisis-hit corner of Eastern Europe in lorries and vans packed with supplies sent by members of the British public. Her spirits were lifted by the numbers involved, ordinary folk doing their bit in a corner of Europe nearly a thousand miles away from the United Kingdom. There were nurses and builders, doctors and electricians, all of whom, in this case, had been mobilised by a small group of teachers from the Bucks Catholic

Primary Partnership. Among their ranks was a maths teacher called Colin.

He didn't look to her like a teacher: her preconceptions came from her father, a sober and disinterested parent who'd had a 26-year career as a physics master, something he'd considered to be the direct cause of his later needing a triple heart bypass.

Colin, on the other hand, was optimistic and kind, the first to roll up his sleeves and get stuck in with anything that was required, from loading up to making tea. He had sleepy eyes and a smile that changed the shape of his face altogether, rendering him all teeth and laughter lines. He clearly didn't take himself too seriously and wasn't especially well read beyond an apparently limitless number of sports biographies, but he was interested in politics and cared about the state of the world. His old-fashioned sense of decency shone through and was one of the reasons she pegged him as a man prepared to stick out his neck, to get things done.

'Have you been involved in anything like this before?' she'd asked, scribbling on her notebook to make it clear this was an interview, not merely that she was interested ... though she definitely was.

'Nothing,' he confessed, with a look that suggested he was still surprised he was doing it. 'I don't think I'd ever considered myself the type. But then, nobody probably *is* the type until they just do it. After we'd seen the news reports, I got chatting in the pub with Martin the deputy head and Diana, who teaches the first-years. We'd had a few, admittedly, but it got us wondering whether we could do something practical, instead of just watching on the television.'

The three launched an appeal that ultimately involved local

churches, other schools and small businesses. There were three-legged races with the infants, bring and buy sales in the juniors and endless appeals for all the 'junk' – his words – contained in the lorries. That included gallons of paint, toothpaste, soap, shampoo, blankets, two brand new hi-fis, toys, bikes, boxes of chocolates, medical supplies, mattresses and vitamins. Colin had twisted the arm of someone in the PR department of P&O to give them free ferry travel, while Diana had negotiated a substantial discount on the petrol.

There had been reports of similar convoys being ambushed by bandits in the hills, yet after mobilising so many people and businesses, there was a strange and possibly inappropriate air of excitement as the volunteers made the slow trek across Europe. But nobody could help it. They were doing a Good Thing, possibly the most significant they'd ever done in their lives. It was as Colin was expressing this that Harriet realised she'd stopped scribbling and was instead focusing on the faint line that ran all the way from his hairline to the bridge of his nose.

'Scary, eh?' he said, touching the scar with his finger.

'Oh! Sorry, I didn't . . . I wasn't . . .' Oh, but she was.

'I got it sledging when I was a kid.'

She chuckled. 'You might want to keep that story to yourself if we run into those bandits. Tell them it was a shark attack.'

The four-day trip turned out to be blessedly bandit-free, though one of the lorries did get a flat tyre in Germany and Nigel, who was driving one of the vans, had an acute attack of lumbago that meant Colin had to take over. He was unbelievably slow. Ordinarily, this would have frustrated the hell out of Harriet, but the main thing she would remember later involved listening to 'Black Velvet' by Alannah Myles on the radio, while Colin asked her about her job. There were so many questions about *her* that more than once she said, 'Who's interviewing whom exactly?'

'In all these dangerous places, have you genuinely never thought to yourself: *This is it, I could really be in trouble here*?' he asked.

They were somewhere in the vicinity of Vienna at the time and the weather on the autobahn was torrential and cold. Harriet felt surprisingly warm.

'You mean have I ever thought I was going to die?'

'That would be the blunt way of putting it,' he said, amused.

'Generally not, though Uganda was a close thing,' she replied.

'What happened?' he asked, clearly anticipating a hair-raising tale of gunmen, hand grenades or power-hungry militia.

'Tummy troubles,' she shrugged. 'That's the polite term. I lost a stone, then lost consciousness and ended up spending eight days in casualty.'

'God.'

'My photographer just about managed to get me to the airport. I passed out as we landed on British soil, at which point I was dispatched into an ambulance and off to hospital.'

'Was it something you ate?'

'I suspect it was the water. It's fine if you boil it, but it's not always easy to find somewhere to plug in a kettle.'

They talked about friends and families, journalism and teaching. He was a good listener and she found herself discussing things she usually avoided, for the simple reason that they were difficult to articulate.

'It's sometimes hard trying to convey why I love this job so much,' she told him. 'I've seen some awful sights, I can't deny it. But I don't feel hardened to any of it. There would be something very wrong with you if you did. I've discovered that you see the best of humanity, as well as the worst. Enough to make me steadfastly optimistic about the future of the human race.'

They pulled to a stop at a traffic light and she decided to stop talking now, for fear that she was rambling. But he turned to look at her.

'What is it?' she asked, touching her neck self-consciously.

He merely shook his head and looked back to the windscreen, smiling. 'Nothing,' he replied. 'Though you might be the most fascinating person I've ever met.'

Chapter 15

Ellie

The story of my life and how I came to be living in my parents' outbuilding – because I'm aware that that's what it is, Farrow and Ball paint or not – is not one I plan to tell Guy any time soon.

The incident at Disneyland felt like the start of something. I never mentioned it to anyone in the year or so afterwards, when I oscillated between suppressed, low-level dread and occasional, fully realised panic. It felt as though my internal alarm system was faulty: I would be hit by bouts of irrational fear in situations the sane part of me knew posed no threat whatsoever.

I kept this mysterious eccentricity to myself. On the surface, my life as a young teenager was exactly like that of every other girl I knew. A time of raging insecurities, laughter on the bus that leaves you woozy and aching, behind-the-back whispers and sleepovers every weekend.

I attended a Church of England all-girls school, where I thrived. I got a kick out of achieving, being in the top set, seeing the pride on my parents' faces when I brought home an A-plus. My abilities by this stage felt like a gift: I didn't know who had bestowed them upon me and why, but I was not going to waste them. The centre of my world was not exams though, but my little circle of friends. Unlike my sister, I always loved the idea of fitting in, of belonging.

Colette once suggested that might be why I'm drawn to Instagram, not merely for the camaraderie, but the validation. Who knows? But in my early teens I was part of a close-knit group of four that made me feel a part of something, a piece in a jigsaw, a cog in a wheel. I loved that.

Of those, my closest friend was Jo. We were so perfectly attuned that we would finish each other's sentences like an old married couple. We shared obsessions about Buffy the Vampire Slayer, Lush bath bombs, the books of Judy Blume and cross-country running. Jo had the benefit of sporty parents and very long legs – and until I met her it had never occurred to me to put my own to competitive use. I loved making her happy. I hated it when she was sad. When her first big crush walked onto the bus with his arm round another girl, I spent my pocket money on a glittery notebook and took it to her house with cupcakes I'd baked and topped with luminous blue buttercream.

In those days, I could never imagine a time when I would be without her – though this assumption turned out to be completely wrong. I had no idea at the time how easily I'd go on to lose her. And for reasons that were all my fault.

Still, despite all the embarrassing secrets we shared back then, the idiosyncrasies of my brain were not among them. Eventually, the point came when I could hide them no longer.

One weekend in January, when we were about thirteen,

our foursome went to spend our Christmas money in Aylesbury. After several hours of applying make-up at Helen's house, we emerged linking arms and feeling invincible in the way only teenage girls can. I was standing in HMV as Jo picked up the new Spice Girls album, when fear swept in like a cloud of dry ice. I began to hyper focus on my breathing, engulfed by an almost supernatural feeling that if I didn't consciously draw in air and expel it, I would not be able to breathe at all.

'Are you okay?' Jo asked, lowering her CD.

'I feel a bit weird.'

She reached out and clasped my fingers. 'You're all clammy. Come and sit down.'

A crowd began to gather, peering faces that made the sides of my head pound. A woman knelt in front of me and, although her green eyes were kind, I felt an overwhelming urge to topple her over like a skittle and run for my life.

'I just feel sick,' I managed. 'I need air. Sorry.'

I scrambled to the door as a film of cold sweat gathered on the back of my neck. I heard Helen tell Isabel that she'd seen something on the news about Mad Cow disease and wondered if they needed to seek urgent medical attention. Once I got outside, I pressed my back against the glass and slid down to the ground. Jo appeared and I began to shiver. A couple of concerned onlookers followed us out and were talking about deep breaths and ambulances. I felt weak with fear and my hands began to shake, movements that were sur-really dramatic, as if I was doing a bad impression of someone having a fit.

Above all, I was certain I was going to die.

'You should go and see a doctor,' Jo said, her expression

filled with concern as she sat on the pavement and put her arm round me.

'I just need to go home.'

The conversation between my friends continued as if we were underwater. Helen couldn't leave yet as it was absolutely essential that she went to Boots to get an exfoliator. Isabel needed to stop at WHSmith for some new ring binders. Jo was raising her voice angrily at them and she never did that. Later, she and I sat on the bus and she held my hand, releasing it only to give a middle finger to two boys who called us *a pair of lezzers*. By the time I was back home and Jo was filling Mum in, I felt as if I'd dreamt the whole thing. I described it as best as I could after my friend had gone. The thudding in my ears. The rushing of blood around my body. My certainty that death was imminent.

Mum tried to swap her shift the following day to take me to the doctor, but she had a big court case to cover so I went with Dad instead.

The GP was a locum. She had black hair flecked with silver and worn in a bun at the nape of her neck. Her name suggested south Asian ancestry and she had an air of total serenity, in sharp contrast to the harassed receptionist battling with her computer keyboard on the way in.

'Are you worried about exams, Ellie?' she asked, checking my blood pressure.

'No,' I said truthfully.

She unstrapped my arm and turned to Dad. 'Would it be possible for me to speak to Ellie alone, please?'

Dad looked surprised, not offended or worried as such, but something like it. When he left the room, the doctor turned to me. 'Is anything else troubling you that is going on at home?'

There was no subtlety to her suggestion. Her implication was clear and made the heat of anger rush up around my temples.

'Absolutely not. I've got the best parents in the world. There is nothing going on at home.'

Sufficiently convinced – or more likely bombarded – by this defence, she invited Dad to return.

'Physically, I can't see anything to be concerned about,' she told us. 'But, Ellie, you're at an age when you're going through lots of changes and the symptoms you've experienced can be the body's response to the idea that you're in acute danger.'

'I was only in HMV,' I pointed out.

'The brain is a magical thing. Sometimes it can play tricks on us, make us believe we're in danger when we're not. I think you had an overload of anxiety.'

'But I've got absolutely nothing to be anxious about,' I protested.

'I wouldn't worry about the reasons for it. These things are common in teenagers. You just need to remind yourself that if you have these feelings again, there is no emergency. It will pass, exactly like it has before.'

Dad turned to me and forced a smile. We hoped that was that. It wasn't.

Chapter 16

My first date with Guy is followed by another. Again, it is at my place and involves lovely food that I'm too nervous to eat, a little too much wine and long conversations that stretch into the night. He talks about his childhood and his experience of boarding school from the age of nine. The fact that he even went surprised me at first. He doesn't seem the type, though I'll admit I am no expert on what the type is. Either way, he hated it and says he spent the first year bewildered about what made his loving, devoted family put him through it.

'Did you ever ask why?'

'Oh no, I always understood. They wanted the best for me and were convinced I'd settle in eventually, like my brothers. But I was never going to do well there. Apart from anything else, I'm no good at being told what to do.' He laughs.

After shunning a university place, he spent several years unable to find his vocation, trying one career, then another.

'Office work sucked the life out of me,' he says. 'It became a means to an end, to save money so I could travel. I'd stay in a job long enough to make a bit of cash, then hop on a plane to South America or Asia.'

He discovered yoga in Cambodia and ended up working on a retreat for nine months with his then girlfriend. The relationship ended, but his passion for the disciplines and practices he'd learnt didn't. When he returned to the UK, instead of looking for another short-term contract with an insurance company, he knocked on the door of a wellbeing studio. This led to a very different career path from that of his older siblings, one of whom is a Tory backbencher, the other a cardiac surgeon.

'In my father's eyes, this still makes me a virtual dropout. He's never actually *said* he considers me a waste of space, but he might as well have. Being fulfilled doesn't count for much unless you're on your way to having a second home in Tuscany and a strong investment portfolio.'

'What about your mum?'

'Oh, she's terrific. We're very close. The youngest child can do no wrong as far as a mother is concerned, don't you think?' He grins.

'Hmm, not in our household.' I shrug. 'I'm the eldest by a decade but Mum always treated Lucy and me the same.'

'Then you're lucky,' he says, and I couldn't agree more.

He gets to meet my parents as he's arriving for our third date. Dad is still buzzing from his Rolling Stones gig three days earlier and drops the subject into conversation before I've even completed the introductions. I'm fairly certain that Guy's musical tastes diverge wildly from my father's, but he is charm personified. Dad is won over instantly and I think Mum likes him too, though I get a sense that she is reserving full judgement until she knows more about him than can be gleaned in a ten-minute conversation. But I already know he has all the right ingredients. She likes people who've done a lot of living, and Guy certainly has.

He is open about every element of his past. He doesn't need to spell out the names of every woman he's known for me to work out that he has a fair amount of experience under his belt. But this merely feels like one part of the rich tapestry of his life and it's all spoken about in the past tense. The only name in the present is mine and the sound of it on his lips electrifies me.

There's just one topic that feels slightly tricky and that's his three-year-old son, Elijah. The little boy lives with his mother and was the result of a toxic on-off relationship that ended badly a couple of years ago. Guy is troubled by the situation, that all his efforts to remain amicable with Stella, his ex, have so far been fruitless.

Every conversation – whether in person or online – leaves me in a state of ongoing, heightened desire. This is possibly to be expected given how little contact I've had with a human male for so long, and isn't helped by him telling me about a random dream he had, in which we were lying in my garden on a hot day while he massaged sun cream into my arms and across my shoulders.

After this, the thought of him undressing me looms almost as large as the ongoing management of the setting for our dates. By the time the prospect of a fourth is discussed, he is insistent that we go out for a drink and, although I know this is going to reach a critical point soon, I get around the issue by mumbling something about house-sitting for my parents while they are away – which they are, as it happens: Dad is at a stag party for his friend Gary, who is getting married for the first time, aged seventy-one, while Mum flew off this morning for her trip for the *Observer*.

Guy is the most pleasant distraction from this. When he arrives for our date, he brings champagne and we eat outside, devouring ribbons of tagliatelle with one of Mum's sauces from the freezer, followed by a sorbet made from rhubarb from the garden. A hot, sultry night descends upon us and light from a swollen summer moon shines overhead. Clouds of melodramatic scent rise from the ruffles of the sweet peas as he recalls a trip he took to Koh Phangan a few years ago and tells me about Leela Beach, where the sand is so white that it glitters.

'Where do you think your love of travel originally came from?' I ask, topping up his glass.

He looks at me and considers the question. 'You know, I'm not sure. I went to Kenya as a child to visit my Uncle Richard and have fond memories of that. Generally, though, I was always one of those kids who needed to escape. I was always running away from school.' He laughs. 'I don't know about you but I've always found it hard to relate to someone who doesn't feel the need to see the world. People who haven't travelled have no perspective, don't you think? Total tunnel vision.' He shrugs. 'Perhaps I'm being unfair, but I could never be on the same wavelength as someone like that.'

I lower my eyes, but quickly realise that he's expecting me to add to this discussion. 'I know but . . . travelling the world is a uniquely modern phenomenon, isn't it?'

'What do you mean?'

'Well, a couple of centuries ago, the idea that someone had to experience new cultures or leap on a plane to lie on a beach in Dubai to better themselves never occurred to anyone.' The stupidity of this statement hits me like a ton of bricks, but once it's out there all I can do is continue with a theory that I am making up as I go along. 'For all humans have spread their wings, are we *actually* better off? Mental illness is on the rise. Societies are fragmented. How can we say our twenty-first-century obsession with personal enrichment and global travel – with ticking this and that off our bucket list – has improved our lives?'

His eyebrows pucker. 'So . . . we should all stay at home? Never go beyond the supermarket or the pub?' The bemusement in his tone makes me worried.

'Oh God no, of course not,' I say, backpedalling. 'I mean, I agree with you. I'm just saying that there's another perspective that . . . I don't know what I'm saying. Forget it.' I shake my head.

He laughs gently and reaches out to touch my hair, allowing a strand to drift between his fingers. I notice his eyes dipping lazily over the curve of my shoulder.

'You know, Ellie, I've told everything there is to know about me, but sometimes I feel as though I hardly know a thing about you.' I realise I should be flattered by this, warmed by the idea that he wants to know me. But panic jolts me.

'Um . . . surely that's not true,' I mumble.

'It's not a criticism,' he says quickly. 'I can't decide if it's because you're mysterious or I've just been talking way too much about myself again.'

I feel a shot of heat behind my ears. 'It's neither. Talk all you want – I'm interested.' I grin. 'But I'm not mysterious, I promise. That makes me sound far more exciting than I am.'

My mouth suddenly feels dry. It occurs to me that if I was going to discuss some of the more unpalatable realities of my life with anyone, then logically it *should* be him. But the thought of it so early in a potential relationship is abhorrent. Way too soon. Though any time probably would be.

'What is it you want to know?' I say these words without fully accepting responsibility for them and the questions that might come next.

'Well, let me think,' he begins, pausing for a beat. 'You've told me how you won all these followers, but why don't you tell me about going self-employed? It must have been such a great moment to leave a job knowing that you were never going to have to answer to a boss again. You're living the dream!'

The relief that sweeps through me at this innocuous question is tempered by the knowledge that I am going to have to be economical with the truth even when answering this. I wish I was a more accomplished liar, comfortable with the idea of . . . not exactly being dishonest, but certainly not correcting his assumptions. I try my best to give him an accurate version – of something at least.

'Leaving my job was definitely a big step. Though . . . I didn't hate what I did beforehand or anything.'

'You worked for a marketing agency didn't you?'

I nod. 'Not a big one, but it was expanding rapidly and everyone was really nice so I was by no means desperate to leave. And I can't claim that being self-employed is *all* a bed of roses.'

When I look up, I realise that he looks perplexed by this description, wondering where it's going. 'But, yes, overall, it's incredibly rewarding.'

What I can't tell him is that I didn't leave my job in a blaze of glory, with a successful Instagram career established and waiting for me. I left after being signed off with 'stress', after

I'd already spent weeks cowering at home in my childhood bedroom, drowning in self-loathing every time I thought about the colleagues who were picking up my slack.

'I'm stunned, Ellie,' my boss James had said on the phone at the time. 'I never expected this from someone like you.' I think he meant it as a compliment.

James Cavendish was ambitious, energetic and as alpha male as they come. He considered me to be his right-hand woman, someone he'd promoted young, who was always the first to arrive in the morning and last to leave at night. Clients said I had a quick, creative brain, I was prepared to roll up my sleeves and get stuck in to anything. Less than a year before that conversation, James had asked me to consider buying shares in the company. He wanted me to become a director.

I liked James. Other people found him pompous and fond of the sound of his own voice, which was probably true though they're hardly the worst traits in a boss. I admired his self-belief, his unshakeable certainty that, with the right team, it didn't matter what storm the company faced, we were all in it together.

So when my breakdown happened – though I hate that word – I didn't need to imagine what he must have been thinking about me slinking off work, communicating only via email to let him know intermittently what was going on. I eventually agreed to a phone call, which I took from my bed with the curtains shut.

'I never even realised you got *stress*,' he'd continued. His tone suggested I now belonged in the same category as he'd put malingerers with hormone problems or obscure food intolerances, the sort who announced they were pregnant three weeks after returning from maternity leave. This was a category that solid, hard-working people like him – and until now me – wouldn't ever find themselves in.

I look up at Guy now, as his gaze settles on my mouth and I feel my pulse quicken. I wonder if he's going to ask me any more questions, but he simply smiles and says, 'Well, I think it might be time for me to phone for a taxi.'

Disappointment needles me in the side at what feels like an abrupt end to the date. 'Are you sure you don't want to stay for another one?' I ask, hopeful that I don't sound as needy as I feel.

He reaches out and touches the knuckles on my left hand then slowly begins to slide his fingertips up my arm, inch by inch. I watch them at first, listening to the sound of my own breath, until he is at the nape of my neck, resting at the warm spot beneath my hair.

He leans in and kisses me, slow and assured. But it doesn't take long before we tumble into something altogether more urgent. My desire is like a hot wind rushing in, sweeping us from the garden into the house and then into bed, with barely an awareness of the changing environment. We undress amidst the feathers of my duvet and it's there that his hands stray from my neck to my belly, my waist to my hip, my shoulder to my breast.

When they reach the inside of my thigh he hooks his fingers around my knickers and slides them deftly down my thighs. He kisses my neck, then my lips, before climbing on top of me. Suddenly, every anxious thought I've ever had is engulfed by the exquisite novelty of another human being's skin pressing against mine.

Chapter 17

The next few days ought to be bliss, but my sweet, pornographic flashbacks are tempered by the realities of this situation. It does not take a genius to work out that Guy would never understand why I can't leave this place. Even if he did, it would be an instant turn-off. All of which means that, on what must be the most beautiful afternoon of the summer so far, I'm feeling agitated. It's not helped by the fact that I am desperate for a cigarette and, though I'm resisting, I'd forgotten how hard it was to give up smoking, even with patches.

The sun has cast a soft, peachy light on the garden and the nostalgic smell of freshly cut lawn fills the air. I close my eyes and drop my spade, before walking to the bench and sitting down. Gertie appears at my feet, then jumps up and climbs onto my knee. I let my eyes drift over the garden.

This isn't just the place where the wild thrashing of my heart ceases. It's a source of endless, ever-changing interest, where colours are blousy and flirtatious in the summer, muted and subtle in autumn. Nothing is static in this space. Not the texture of the soil, nor the patterns in the walls, from which daisies sprout in spring and frost gathers in winter. I love my slice of paradise, while also starting to recognise that my passion may not be wholly a force for good. Love and happiness are not the same things, I suppose. And it strikes me every bulb I've planted and climbing rose I've coaxed up the bricks will mean little if I manage to blow this glorious intense thing with Guy before it's even close to full realisation.

I press my lips onto Gertie's little head, before putting her on the ground and standing to walk to the gate. I click the lock. Push it open wide. I look out.

Blond fields stretch in front of me and my heart begins tripping over itself. I close my eyes and recall some of the techniques Colette introduced me to, casting my mind back to the first day I met her. I was nineteen. Still technically enrolled at university on the course at which I'd been desperate to win a place and now hadn't attended for months. We were in her office. She'd insisted that I had to go and see her, not the other way around, explaining that her policy is not to visit the client's home.

'Travelling to see me is part of the treatment,' she'd said. 'If we held our sessions in your home that would reinforce "safety behaviour". It stops patients from growing. Is that okay by you?'

It was far from okay by me. The single, short journey to see her had been difficult beyond words. But then I thought of my poor parents, now onto their second machine coffee in the waiting room, and I nodded.

I was on the chair adjacent to hers – she had a desk, but didn't sit behind it – while I filled out a basic questionnaire, with a fountain pen she'd taken out of her handbag to let me borrow. It was heavy and expensive-looking; and it felt oddly inappropriate to be writing with this, not merely an office biro. Afterwards she scanned the form in silence, before removing her glasses and folding one hand over the other. 'Okay, Ellie. Let's start with what has been happening lately. Tell me what brought you here.'

I described the panic attacks, palpitations, hyperventilation and occasional vertigo. I explained how it began with a general feeling that something bad was going to happen and intensified to the point that I thought I was having a heart attack. I told her that it was smothering, crippling, that no matter how many times I tried to reassure myself that it was illogical, it didn't seem to matter.

'Are you embarrassed when these things happen?' she asked.

I shrugged. 'Having a meltdown in front of everyone certainly sucks. I've never *actually* lost control of my bodily functions, but I'm sure I've come close a few times.'

'A lot of people with agoraphobia fear public scrutiny or embarrassment.'

'Except, this doesn't only occur in busy places, when I'm surrounded by people. It's happened when I've been out on a walk with Mum and nobody else is around.'

'That's because you've learnt from experience what a panic attack feels like and you're afraid of it.'

'So I'm afraid of being afraid?' I said tonelessly.

She said that the reasons why people have anxiety attacks and agoraphobia are many and varied. For some, there's a genetic link. For others, it's a life event, such as a bereavement or trauma. But many studies show that agoraphobia is learnt; if a person has a panic attack out of the blue when they are outside their home, they then associate that anxiety with every time they go out.

'Have you talked to anyone about this, Ellie?' she asked.

'My parents,' I said. What I didn't say was that I didn't think they could truly comprehend some of the things that went through my head. This applied to Mum in particular. That's not to say she didn't *want* to understand, because I'm sure she did. People think of my mother as ambitious – and she did love her work. But our family became her biggest priority; she made enough sacrifices for me to believe that being a good mother was at the top of her list of aspirations.

Nevertheless, I could never shake the feeling that her unwavering reassurances about my panic attacks – her insistence that they *aren't silly at all, I mustn't ever think that* – were as much to convince herself as me. How could the woman in those photos, the one with the bulletproof vest and super-human level-headedness, ever truly understand something like this?

We had a row once when I said as much. She was shocked, I think, because I'd been such an unrebellious teenager. There had been the odd minor conflagration involving the half-hearted slamming of a door, though I was never as good at it as Lucy. But, after she'd found out I'd written to the university telling them I wouldn't be coming back, we had a stonker of an argument.

'I realise I'm a disappointment to you,' I'd shrieked, with the breathless fury of a toddler on the verge of a tantrum.

'What? How could you ever think that, Ellie?' she asked, as if there were no greater insult I could hurl at her.

'Don't deny it,' I shot back. 'You've got balls of steel. You've spent your life dodging bullets. Evading kidnap. Yet somehow you've ended up with me, who can't even get on the Tube without wanting to piss my pants. You're ashamed of me.'

'Ellie, stop that immediately,' she'd snapped. 'There is not a word of truth to that. Not one.'

I rolled my eyes. Shook my head. Snorted.

'Why are you saying this?' she said, almost growling with exasperation. She put her hands in the sockets of her eyes and inhaled deeply.

'Ellie, I am *proud* of you. I'm proud of everything you've ever done. The same is just as true now that you are a grown woman as it was when you were a little girl.'

My thoughts were snapped back to the treatment room by another question from Colette. 'What about any friends?' she asked.

'Jo was kind of aware of it. My best friend from school.'

'Was she supportive?'

'Yes, at first. She did all she could. Jo was a lovely person, but ultimately it all proved too hard to explain – or too *big* to explain. She found my behaviour frustrating. I have no doubt it was – I had tried to be a good friend but turned out to be a crappy one. I couldn't ever really convey to her that the way I acted was not something I had control over.'

'Are you still in touch with Jo?'

'No.'

She wrote something down on her notepad. 'You said earlier that this doesn't happen when you're at home. That's why you haven't been out much lately.'

'Well, it happens in my room at uni, but never at my family home. I'm always fine there. I'm always better. I feel like myself.'

'You must have found it difficult to come here today then?'

'Very.'

'But you still got here. No panic attacks.'

'True, but I was afraid the whole time. I won't relax until I get back. No offence, but that really is the only place where I feel normal.'

She held my gaze momentarily. 'The problem is, that by retreating to your home and staying there, you're only *relieving* the anxiety, not confronting it. By staying inside, you're reinforcing the association between going out and panic attacks. That only makes it worse.'

I felt the sting of tears behind my eyes.

'But, Ellie, and this is important,' she said, leaning onto her elbows, 'this *is* something that you can overcome.'

The expression on her face was one of utter conviction. It said, I've seen this before a hundred times and you are going to be *just fine*.

'I think we should begin with a course of CBT. It will initially involve a little homework,' she continued, taking a document from her folder and handing it to me. 'Perhaps you could fill this in before our next session.'

There was another list of questions on a single A4 sheet. The first one was: 'What do you think caused your agoraphobia?'

Chapter 18

I reach out and grip the gate, but when I shut my eyes to try and compose myself, my mind closes in on itself. A fuzzy sound rises in my ears and I register the slam of a car door.

'Hi there!'

It's Jamie, cheerful and oblivious to my distress as he marches to the back of the van. I press the ball of my hand against my cheek and brush away a sticky mess of tears as he approaches. It does not go unnoticed. His steps slow, his expression shifts and he lowers a tray of bedding plants to the ground, at a speed that is proportionally slower the wider his eyes become.

'Sorry,' he half-coughs, though he clearly doesn't know what his apology is for.

''S fine.'

He turns away, mutters something about another part of the delivery and returns to the van. All I want to do is run, but the better option is to just see this through, hold myself together long enough for him to complete the delivery and go.

'Shall I . . . just put these on the patio?' he asks awkwardly, returning with another box. I gesture for him to go straight through as I hang back, my arms crossed. But the more I think about not crying, the more pressure begins to build in my face. He returns, looks at me and hovers.

'Are you okay?'

I inhale deeply. 'Yes, thanks.' It comes out not as fully formed words, but a sob. I turn and hurry to the annexe, my feet almost tripping over themselves until I'm inside. I close the door behind me, submitting to the relief of tears.

A few moments later, the rattle of an engine starts up outside as I kick off my shoes and sink into the sofa, pressing a cushion into my face. I stay there for a minute or two, perhaps longer; I decide that I need a cigarette. I get up and go to rummage for one in the kitchen, intending to lean out of my bedroom window and savour every toxic drag.

I have my hand on top of the cupboard, when there's a knock on the front door.

'Shit!' I freeze, juddering like I've been caught shoplifting in my own home. The thought racing through my head is that Mum has returned home from London early, where she was meeting a producer from *Newsnight* for lunch. I sniff myself straight but realise it's more likely that Jamie hasn't left yet after all.

I drift to the door and open it, to find him on the step, filling most of the frame. His forehead is pink from the sun and a smattering of freckles has appeared over the bridge of his nose, making him look more like the kid I remember from school than ever before. The homely, chemical scent of fabric conditioner rises from his T-shirt and his hair carries a glisten of fresh sweat.

'Forgot to get your signature I'm afraid,' he says.

I take the machine from him, and as I'm signing my name

feel an unstoppable urge to try to explain the unexplainable. 'Look, about before,' I begin. 'I just have some stuff going on at the moment, that's all.'

'Of course,' he says stiffly.

I hand it back to him and nod. 'Bye then,' I say.

'Yep. See you next time.'

He goes to walk away, but stops and turns around. 'This is none of my business but ... why don't you call a friend? Get someone to come over. It always helps.'

I swallow, feeling mortified. 'My sister is at a conference in Frankfurt,' I reply, as it occurs to me that he assumes I have a support network beyond immediate family. My eyes drift to the floor. 'But, yeah. I'll call someone.'

I wonder briefly if I'd ever be able to reach out to the people I know from Instagram. I call them friends without ever really delving into the meaning of the word. Until this moment I'd always told myself that a relationship is no poorer simply because it began online. But suddenly the idea of having a heart to heart with anyone I've met through my page feels ridiculous.

'Take care then.' He steps back and I click the door shut, hearing his footsteps fade down the path. I scramble with the lock to open up again.

'Jamie?'

He turns and a crease appears above his nose.

'Fancy a cup of tea?'

I lean on the door frame and replace my nicotine patch with a fresh one, as Jamie sits at the patio table, drinking from a mug.

'I gave up smoking recently,' I explain. 'I nearly caved in just then and had one.'

'Ah. Another thing I interrupted. Sorry.'

'No, I'm glad. I'd have regretted it.' I look up and sigh. 'I feel a bit embarrassed about the state I was in at the gate before.'

'Ah, don't worry about it. Girls are always bursting into tears around me.'

I snort. 'I'm sure.'

He lowers his cup, serious now. 'You know, if you can't talk about it with a friend, it goes without saying that you could talk now, if you want. I know we hardly know each other but, sometimes that's better. You know, the way people in movies always share their troubles with a barman.'

'But you're not a barman ...'

'I was once.'

'Really? Did lots of people confide in you?'

He thinks for a moment. 'Not one, now you mention it.'

I smile. 'Thanks for the offer but I really couldn't.'

'No, it's fine,' he says. 'I have to remind myself sometimes that not everyone was brought up in a household like ours.'

'What was that like?' I ask.

'Well, having a stiff upper lip was not allowed. If you had a problem, you had to get it out *right* there, on the table, so everyone could discuss it in detail and come up with a solution.'

'God, that sounds awful. Weren't you allowed the odd secret?'

He laughs. 'Are you kidding? I was outnumbered. There was my mum, my sister and me – the only male. MI5 couldn't have kept anything from them.'

'Do you get on well with your sister?'

'We do now, but not when we were younger. She was two years older so thought of me with the kind of affection you might reserve for a boil on the bum. Still, living in an otherwise female household was insightful in some ways.'

It occurs to me that talking to a virtual stranger about this stuff would certainly, paradoxically, be easier than talking to my family, with all their expectations and knowledge of everything that's happened to me.

'Okay then. You asked for it. Where do I begin?'

When I pause, unable to speak, he raises his eyebrows expectantly.

'I'm ... screwed up,' I say.

He takes a long, contemplative breath. 'Well, that does sound like a pretty terminal case.'

I roll my eyes. 'You need to stop joking around here. I'm absolutely serious.'

His features soften. 'I'm not dismissing whatever it is you're going through, just to make that clear. But "screwed up"? Are you sure you're not just finding life a bit hard at the moment? Lots of people do at times.'

'I don't know.'

'Well, what's the quote: "You're mad. Bonkers. Off your head. But I'll tell you a secret. All the best people are."'

'I wouldn't have had you down as an *Alice in Wonderland* fan,' I say.

'Oh, you know it? My niece's favourite book. I bought her an illustrated edition when she was about five and I've read it to her more times than I could tell you.'

'How old is she now?' I ask.

'Nearly thirteen, so she's grown out of picture books altogether, which is a bit sad. It was nice having someone who thought I was a superstar when she saw my name on a front cover.'

I move towards the patio table and sit down opposite him. 'What do you mean?'

It turns out that delivering garden supplies to Green Fingers customers in the Buckinghamshire area is not Jamie's only job. His career – his passion – is illustrating children's books.

'I'm freelance now and the work can be intermittent, hence the fact that I've had to take on the delivery job. I worked in the art department of a big publishing house for the best part of ten years, until . . . for one reason or another, I had to leave.'

'Very mysterious,' I say, noting his careful phrasing. '*Had* to leave? You were sacked, weren't you?'

'No.' He laughs. 'My mum was unwell.'

I straighten up. 'Gosh. Sorry.'

'No, it's fine,' he insists quickly. 'Gemma – that's my sister – was going through a divorce at the time. Very messy. Her ex was a dickhead. It felt as though the whole family was imploding. Anyway, there was a redundancy package on offer and the idea was that I'd take it and become self-employed so I could also look after Mum.'

'And has it been successful, the work you have had published?'

'Now you mention it, I've had a number one bestseller . . .'

'Are you serious?'

'In Sweden,' he adds.

'Sweden? Well, that's brilliant. Isn't it?'

'Yeah, it's nice,' he shrugs. 'Though Sweden is a pretty small market, to be fair. Hence the fact that I'm still delivering compost for a living.'

'Well, if I were to choose a place to be a number one bestseller, it would definitely be Sweden. This is the country that produced ABBA, after all. And Ingrid Bergman – and the Nobel prize.'

'Don't forget the IKEA Billy bookshelf,' he adds.

'Exactly. Culturally, Sweden is where it's at.'

He takes a sip of his tea and we fall silent. 'It's nice to see you smiling.'

I nod. 'It's nice to smile.'

'Though we have digressed ...'

I look up self-consciously. It's been such a long time since I've talked to anyone about this who wasn't family or a therapist that for a moment I think I'm not going to be able to do it. Yet, when I start talking, it feels surprisingly easy. 'You've heard of agoraphobia, right?'

'Fear of open spaces?'

'It can be, and also crowds or travelling. But for me it's simply fear that comes on when I leave home.'

'Is that why you looked so unhappy when you went to look for Gertie?'

'I hadn't left here in quite a long time before that day.'

'How long?' he asks.

I swallow. 'Two years.'

His shock is instantly visible. 'Shit.'

'I told you,' I say, tapping my temple with my forefinger. 'Screwed up.'

'No. Not at all,' he says emphatically, then he falls silent for a moment. 'So how does that work? I mean, don't you *have* to go out sometimes? What about to buy stuff, or if you're sick or ... I don't know, there must be other things.'

'Not really. You can do anything online these days. Order food, clothes, plants, see a doctor, run a business. There's never been a better time to be a nutcase.' I grin. 'You know what, I'd become reconciled to my life here. I've been happy, generally. Then I met someone through Instagram. We've been seeing each other . . . and I really like him. I mean, *a lot*.'

'He's a good guy then?'

'He's wonderful,' I say emphatically. 'Only, I haven't told him about this issue yet.'

'Ah. And I guess he wants to take you dancing?'

The phrase makes me smile. 'I'm not sure he's the *take me dancing* kind of guy. But he definitely wants to go out.'

'What's the possibility of you giving that a go?'

'It makes me want to regurgitate my lunch,' I say. 'Which I think you'll agree would not be a good start to any date.'

He runs his fingers through his hair. 'Wow. Yes, I can see why you're concerned about this. Relationships are complicated enough.'

'Do you have a girlfriend?'

'Not at the moment. I was living with someone who I'd been seeing for a few years. We were hoping to buy a place together but then events took over. We split up when I moved back here.'

There's something about his expression that suggests it was her choice, rather than his. 'That sucks.'

'Yeah. It happens. But, moving home for a while was the right thing to do.'

'And how is your mum these days?'

He looks at his hands briefly then says: 'She died at the start of March. So, I was glad I left London. I made the right decision, because it meant I got to spend a bit of time with her beforehand.'

I press my fingers of both hands to my mouth. 'I'm *so* sorry.'

'No, it's fine. We're all doing okay most of the time. Grief is a weird thing though, isn't it? Sometimes you think you've pulled yourself together then the smallest thing can set you off. The other day, it was walking past the toiletries aisle in Marks and Spencer and a woman her age was buying the same peach hand lotion she loved. It just undid me.'

'Oh, Jamie. You did a really good thing,' I tell him, but he pulls a face as if it was unworthy of this description, then looks at his watch.

'I think I'd better get going. Thanks for the tea.'

'Thanks for the chat,' I say.

He picks up the keys to his van. 'Sorry I didn't really come up with a solution to your problem.'

'Oh, don't worry – nobody has. I enjoyed the cuppa though.'

He smiles. 'Yeah, me too.'

Chapter 19

I haven't always been the way I am. There were long periods when the more intense panic attacks of my early teens almost disappeared, hidden out of sight. Attributing them to my hormones seemed reasonable, because by sixth form I was doing pretty well for myself.

It was around that time that I got my first boyfriend, Jo and I went on an exchange visit to Madrid, my cross-country running fizzled out while I concentrated on my A levels, but I still volunteered at an old people's home on Saturday mornings – which had begun as something to put on my CV, but that I thoroughly enjoyed in the event. I found it rewarding and I liked the residents there, who were an endless source of good humour and anecdotes.

By the time it came to leave school, Jo and I said goodbye to the two other members of our group – Helen went to Southampton and Isabel to LSE – while we both won places at Bristol University, me to study History, her Law. Until that point, I'd felt so completely on her wavelength that I could never have imagined what was to come.

When we arrived at Bristol, Jo wanted to suck up

Catherine Isaac

everything that was to be had from a university experience. Her brother Chris depicted his own time there as a long round of parties, friends and getting hammered. She wanted the same, ideally emerging with more than a third like him. In theory I shared her desire to embrace life as an undergraduate, to meet new people and make memories, but when I got there, I slowly began to feel myself retreating from it.

There was also something about the ferocity of Jo's approach to the first term – the way she'd manically sign up to obscure political societies and sports clubs and every gate-crashed party in Freshers' week – that left my nerves jangling. I tagged along with her at first, but when it didn't slow down, I'd make excuses, tell her I had to finish an assignment as she went off on another night out, meaning that I was left alone in digs that I despised, praying that my roommate Carolina would be out.

My issue at university was absolutely not with Jo though. Not at all. With hindsight, I don't think I was fully prepared to embrace the realities of communal living, not by that stage in my life. If this makes me sound like a snob, then you'll have to take my word that this is far from the case. All I can say about the hall of residence I ended up in was this: I could not *stand* it.

It was a purpose-built 1960s building composed of blocks of accommodation, basic kitchen facilities and a series of shared bathrooms. There were 748 students living in there, some in single rooms, others – like me – in a twin. Each was no better or worse than the average student habitat: a shoebox starved of light and packed with cheap furniture, in which musty carpet tiles failed to conceal a series of grim-looking spills. But it wasn't the standard of accommodation that bothered me, nor any of the obvious things – milk being stolen from the fridge, toenail clippings left in sinks or the stench of a stranger in every toilet you went in.

It was the noises at night. I would lie in bed, separated from 747 other souls only by a honeycomb of paper-thin walls. Spongy silences would be broken by the rowdy clatter of someone stumbling in from a party, or the distant sound of early-hours toast drunkenly being made in the kitchen. Stairwells carried the echoes of laughter or arguments; even hushed voices could be heard if they were outside our door.

I'd thought I'd enjoy being in a twin room, even though my roommate was allocated randomly and I wasn't allowed to specifically request Jo. I thought that having someone else there would stop me ever getting lonely. But it had the opposite effect. There was nothing wrong with Carolina, a medical student from Devon, but for reasons I could never put my finger on, while we could chat politely, be considerate of each other's space and schedule, we never really gelled. And on particularly difficult nights, it was the sound of her more than anything else that rattled me.

The squeak of her teeth as she ground one molar against another. The rhythm of her breath as she inhaled and exhaled. The occasional soft grunts as she turned on her side. Permanent reminders of another human being's proximity, underlining that I was away from the privacy, comfort and safety of a real home. Paradoxically, these noises left me with an intense feeling of aloneness, of desolation and, above all, fear.

I was plagued by nightmares. The most frequent was the one that began with the walls, before a small, familiar face appeared next to me – and ended with her jumping out of the window. But that wasn't the only one. My dreams covered a multitude of topics, though always in the same setting and ending with my awakening amidst a burst of adrenalin, like firecrackers under my skin.

I couldn't claim my nightmares stopped when I went home to Chalk View of course, but they were nothing like as bad as they were at university. And over the course of that first year, while Jo always stayed in Bristol at weekends to attend a party, I was magnetically pulled home.

Sometimes I'd fight it and stay so I could join her, not wanting to let her down. But too often we would end up being separated. She knew a lot of people and would drift from group to group, whereas I'd find a quiet corner with whatever ally I could pick up, usually someone from my course with whom I'd sit and smoke weed or drink cider to ease the course of the evening.

Returning home at the weekends, the relief felt like sinking into a great big feather pillow. I told myself that going back made sense. After Grandma had died, there was nobody but me who weeded or mowed the garden regularly and I couldn't stand it being neglected. Plus, I enjoyed the company of my parents. If they had friends over, I'd sit up chatting, drinking red wine and playing Trivial Pursuit. If not, Dad and I would dig out the Scrabble or I'd read a book in front of the log burner. By Sunday afternoon, as the time approached when I'd have to go back to uni, there would be an ache in my belly that only got worse.

It was on the train back to Bristol one Sunday in the final term when I had my worst panic attack in years. The train was packed and I'd given up my seat to a woman with a small baby. The bags under her eyes made it clear she needed it more than me, but as a result I had to stand for most of the journey, pressed against a fire hydrant next to the toilets. It began with nothing new, just the usual cocktail of sweating, racing heart and a total conviction that some bad, undefined *thing* was going to happen.

I tried to ride it out, but at no point did these feelings show any sign of passing and, as the train rattled on its tracks, I was overcome by their intensity. I made it back to the halls of residence but couldn't tell you how I got there, beyond a few jagged flashbacks: my hand trembling as I tried to get the key in the door. Carolina opening it as she was on the phone. Climbing into bed while still in my coat and pulling the duvet up to my chin. I struggled to function for a week afterwards, though I tried to force myself to do all the things I was supposed to be doing – writing essays, attending lectures. But I was hardly present, smothered by anxiety at every turn. I retreated to bed.

I was curled there one afternoon, staring absently at an A4 sheet of notes about 'The Origins of the British East India Company' that I'd written in calmer times. My bladder was full; the idea of having to leave the room, travel down the corridor and make it to the communal bathroom filled me with dread. Even in that little room with its feeble window, I could see that the sun was incandescent outside. People were picnicking on Doritos and boxed wine on the lawn below.

There was a knock on the door. 'Ellie, are you there?'

It was Jo. I thought about pretending that I was at a lecture, but she continued to knock. 'Ellie, I know you're in there. I bumped into your roommate. Come on. Please open up.'

I pushed off the quilt. 'Coming,' I said, wincing as I

realised that I'd brushed neither my hair nor my teeth today. As she stepped in, her eyes darted around the room, to my unmade bed and then to me. 'What's going on?'

'What do you mean?' I asked.

'You haven't responded to any of my texts,' she said.

I'd been aware of her messages pinging onto my phone for several days. I'd meant to text back. It was only then that I realised I never had.

'Sorry,' I mumbled, 'I'm just really behind on some of my revision.'

'It's okay,' she shrugged. 'So, are you coming?'

'Coming to what?'

She blinked at me. 'On my birthday night out, Ellie. We're all meeting in town, making the most of the weather. We talked about this. You told me you were coming. You promised. I've been looking forward to it for ages.'

I listened to her with growing alarm as shame flared inside me.

'Did you forget it was even my birthday?'

This was not my usual style. We'd always made a fuss over each other and I took pride in buying, if not the most expensive presents, then those that were most *her*. A Virago Modern Classics edition of *The Weather in the Streets* by Rosamond Lehmann. A necklace with a tiny, silver pendant in the shape of a lobster or – the one she'd loved most – a cushion embroidered with tiny cactuses in her favourite shade of turquoise. I'd long given up on baking cupcakes, but on birthdays both she and I bought each other a set of four from the bakery in our village, which would be swirled with chocolate buttercream and iced with our initials. I'd intended to look for a cake shop in Bristol so we could continue the tradition, but the thought had gone entirely out of my mind.

'I'm really sorry,' I said. 'I don't know how . . .'

'Hey,' she said gently, touching my arm, sensing my distress. 'It's really okay. I'm not bothered about presents or cards, as long as you're coming with us! Make sure you bring some sun cream. The weather's amazing. A proper heatwave.'

I registered an icy layer of sweat on my skin. 'What time are you meeting?'

'Now!' she laughed. 'We're all getting the bus in, so get your skates on!'

'I'm not ready,' I said.

She was about to protest but looked me up and down. 'Well, look, don't worry, we can wait for you downstairs. How long will you be?'

'Why don't I just meet you in town?' I suggested. 'I'll follow on. I won't be long.'

She frowned, unsure. 'Are you sure, Ellie?'

I nodded.

'Okay, but don't be long, will you, otherwise we'll be miles ahead of you and it'll be a complete shit show by the time you arrive. I'll save you a seat wherever we end up. Text me when you're on your way.' She hesitated. 'You promise you'll come? Ellie?'

There was something about her tone that irritated me.

'Why are you asking me like that?' I asked.

'It's just . . . there have been so many things lately that you've said you'll do then let me down. I'm starting to feel like a mug.'

She forced a laugh but I didn't find the accusation funny. 'Don't be ridiculous. That's untrue.'

'But it's *not*, Ellie,' she insisted. 'Look, I really don't want to fall out with you. I'm just saying—'

'But you're accusing me of doing stuff that I haven't done.'

She frowned, indignant. 'You *have*, Ellie. You were supposed to come for a run with me at the weekend and left me standing by myself like an idiot, without even bothering to text. Then there was the party last week. I thought we were going *together*, but you messaged me with, like, twenty minutes' notice. There have been countless other examples. I don't get it. But I do know that *it's not on*. Everyone I've told about this thinks it's a terrible way to be treated by a friend.'

I felt a surge of heat to my chest, stung by the accusations. 'Oh great. So you've been bitching about me behind my back?'

She winced and shook her head, apologetically. 'No. Not at all. I just . . . I don't really get it, Ellie. That's all.'

'I'll be there today, all right?'

She stood up. 'Yes. Good. And thank you. Text me when you're on your way and I'll order you a drink so you don't have to queue.'

Obviously, I never turned up. She had every right to be upset on the phone the next day, and get even more upset when I furiously told her I resented her accusations. It all culminated in her telling me I was a terrible friend and me telling her I never wanted to see her again in my life.

I don't remember anything about the next couple of days, beyond the moment Carolina touched me on the shoulder as I lay in bed. I rolled over to find her crouching next to me. She said I needed to phone my parents.

'You need help,' she told me, in an even voice. 'You need to go home.'

I didn't sit my end of year exams. Instead, I spent the

summer going to see Colette once a week and in quiet recovery in the garden. Mum had spoken to the university, who'd agreed that I could restart the first year, but the thought of returning settled in my stomach like a greasy knot. The idea of going back became so terrible that I simply made the decision not to. Instead, I enrolled on a course at the Open University and commenced what would become a three-year degree from home.

I lost touch completely with Jo, as well as all my other friends. She'd tried to phone me a few times after our argument. I couldn't face her – or any of them. I felt ashamed. I couldn't locate an explanation that would make sense of any of it to them. So I continued to ignore their calls until, eventually, they stopped altogether.

Chapter 20

Harriet, 1991

Harriet and Colin were married at Wandsworth registry office just over a year after they'd met, on a balmy autumn day that, except for the odd falling leaf, could have passed for high summer. Some people thought it was a rather precipitate union, but not entirely out of character. There goes Harriet again. Flying off to the scene of an earthquake one minute, marching down the aisle with a virtual stranger the next.

Was it too simple to say that it didn't feel like haste when the two people involved were in love? It probably was, on balance. Perhaps when you've worked in a job in which your main preoccupation is retaining life and limb, your definition of risk diverges from that of the average member of the public.

Harriet loved her wedding day. The fashion was for huge, full-skirted dresses with stiff corsetry and reams of taffeta and silk. But after several visits to a bridal shop on the King's Road, she felt like a little girl with a dressing up box and that really was not the look she'd been going for. So she found a simple, floor-length design with a cinched waist and a bolero that swept around her shoulders. Colin could not take his eyes off her.

'You two are *perfect*,' Harriet's friend Jeremy had said, linking her arm after Colin had kissed her on the registry office steps. 'You realise that this whole whirlwind love affair is ridiculously romantic. If it wasn't you I'd find it sickening.'

Jeremy and Donato lived in the flat above hers. She was going to miss them enormously when she moved out, though she suspected that would be the only thing she would miss. They'd taken turns to cook for each other every couple of weeks and what had started out as a relaxed affair featuring pasta and a cheap bottle of plonk had evolved into something distinctly flashier. Outdoing each other had become a standing joke that none of them could resist, though it would have been cheaper for Harriet to take everyone to a Michelin-starred restaurant than create the lavish menu of a few weeks earlier: Coquilles Saint-Jacques, lobster medallions and some fiddly dessert that took her most of the day.

'I do somehow seem to have landed on my feet,' she said.

'God, you have. He's gorgeous,' he grinned, gesturing at Colin.

'Not everyone has been as supportive. Some people think we're mad.'

'Well, some people just need to mind their own business, I'd say.'

The guest list was bigger than they had initially planned, but they hadn't liked to offend family and weren't about to exclude any friends. It was particularly heavy on journalists, whose company Harriet had always enjoyed for their gallows humour, eccentricities and intolerance of bullshit of any description. They were the biggest drinkers, of course, which astonished Colin, but Harriet was used to stints in the newsroom that would involve half of the staff adjourning to the pub over the road as soon as deadline passed.

Both she and Colin had a week off work ahead of them after the wedding and, although they couldn't afford a honeymoon, they intended to make the most of it. She loved being home, no matter how much she enjoyed work. When some people heard what she did for a living, they assumed that her natural habitat was in a muddy trench, surviving on a raw donkey leg, but nothing could be further from the truth. Harriet liked clean sheets and silk blouses; she liked moisturising her elbows and going to the theatre. All the things, in fact, that would fill the next week.

It would be a time to cherish, they'd both said that, because afterwards life was never going to be the same. They hadn't gone public with their other bit of news yet. The last thing they'd wanted was people concluding that this was the reason for the wedding. As far as Harriet was concerned, there was no haste involved in her decision to marry. All right, perhaps a touch – but they'd have done it sooner or later anyway, she was sure of it.

Chapter 21

Ellie

'Can I pick some flowers too?'

I place a sweet pea in my basket and turn to Oscar, who has a blob of snot glistening on his top lip like a strip of glue.

'I don't think that's a good idea. These secateurs are sharp,' I reply.

'My mum told me to be helpful,' he says.

'You can be, by sitting down nicely somewhere.'

'This isn't fun,' he sighs.

'Why don't you go and help your mum with the cleaning?' I suggest.

'That's boring.'

'So is this,' I shrug. 'Gardening is a complete drag.'

He frowns suspiciously as I examine my posy, the ruffles of zinnia, calendula and sweet peas picked from the best crop I've seen in years.

'How come you're here today anyway?' I ask him. 'Shouldn't you be at school?'

'I'm off because I've got a cold.' He inhales deeply, causing the snot trail to withdraw into his nostril before reappearing to slide further down than before. I rummage in my pocket and pull out a tissue. 'Here.'

He takes it from me, contemplates it briefly and begins to wipe his hands.

'It's for your *nose.*' He presses it against his face, then tucks it in his pocket. He now has a beard consisting entirely of mucus.

'Shouldn't you be in bed if you're not well?'

'Fresh air is good for me. Anyway, bed is boring.'

'Is *everything* boring?'

'No,' he says. Then he stands up and starts wiggling his hips from side to side, swinging his arms in the opposite direction. 'Can you floss?'

'No.'

'I can teach you if you like,' he says, going faster.

'I'm good, thanks. Happy doing this.'

'You said it was boring.' He has now stopped flossing and has a red face. I don't even want to contemplate where snot has gone.

'You've got an answer for everything, haven't you?'

He shrugs glumly. 'You won't tell Mum I was annoying you, will you?'

I pause, as guilt slaps me on the cheeks. 'Don't worry, you weren't. Not in the slightest.'

I pull out my phone and Google 'gardening ideas for kids'.

'All right, I know something we could do.'

Over the next half-hour, we plant out a series of tomato seedlings that I'd grown from seed.

'Will they be ready tomorrow if I come back then?'

'No – and please *don't* come back tomorrow. Not because you've been annoying,' I say hastily. 'Just ... don't, okay?'

'I'll probably be better tomorrow anyway,' he says. 'Unless I puke or get the trots.'

'So are you going to take your tomato pots or do you want me to look after them to make sure the plants grow? Then, next time you're here – because I feel sure there will be a next time – you could pick them. If they're ready, that is.'

'I'll leave them here,' he says. 'My mum's not very good at that kind of thing.'

'Not very good at what?' Mandy laughs as she steps out of the patio door of the main house, snapping off her marigolds. 'Oscar, I told you not to make a nuisance of yourself. Is he being a pest?'

'Not at all. Good as gold.'

She smiles. Her eyelashes flutter. They're so big they cause a breeze. 'Oh, you're so good with him. He didn't stop talking about you after last time he was here.'

I scrunch up my nose sceptically, finding this hard to believe.

'He *loved* your friend too.'

'My friend?'

'The one who can moonwalk.'

'Oh. He's not my ... he's just the delivery man. He's nobody. Well, not nobody but ...' Then an idea occurs to me. 'Hey, would you mind if I took a photo for Instagram? My account is mainly about gardening and I think people would like it.'

'You want to put Oscar on it too?'

I shrug. 'I mean, I wouldn't include any details, just his first name maybe.'

She turns to Oscar. 'What do you reckon, buddy? Will you be Ellie's helper for the internet?'

'YES!' he replies, as Mandy peers at him and says, 'I think we need to give that nose a wipe first though.'

◎ *Instagram*

EnglishCountryGardenista

665
posts

57.3k
followers

949
following

ELLIE HEATHCOTE

Today, I had a helper. He's called Oscar and he's five. I noticed he was bored, so I thought I'd see what we could come up with to occupy him and we ended up planting out these tomato seedlings. He's a lot younger than I was when I was first introduced to horticulture by my Grandma, in this very same garden.

I was about nine or ten when she taught me the basics. She started me off on easy, fast-growing varieties – sugar snap peas, marigolds and everyone's favourite, sunflowers. I think I'd assumed at that age that all plants would grow that quickly and easily. If only, hey? But I'll never forget the thrill of that moment when I measured myself against my first sunflower's oversized stem and discovered that it had grown taller than me. It felt as though there was magic in the soil. Have you introduced your kids to gardening? What kind of projects have fired their enthusiasm? #kidgardener #gardenersofinstagram #Englishcountrygarden #tomatoes #femalegardener

#thisgirldigs #Englishgardenstyle #gardener #gardening #garden #gardenlife #flowers #plants #gardens #nature #gardendesign #growyourown #gardeninspiration #instagarden #gardenlove #growyourownfood

I publish the post and click on a new photo of Guy. He's standing on his head in a brightly lit studio, his legs twisted above him like a corkscrew. I pick up my laptop and turn it upside down, confirming that he is still outstandingly hot even with gravity working against his jowls. His caption reads:

Wake up and decide that today is going to be as beautiful as life itself. Live with a heart full of hopes and a soul full of dreams. Happiness lives within you, waiting to burst forth like a bright sun.

I gently bite the fleshy inside of my mouth, hoping that Lucy doesn't stumble on this. I probably shouldn't read his captions anyway. In the hour since this has been published, his groupies have descended like the Brides of Dracula. Their responses range from the fawning – 'so inspiring!' to the completely bewildering: I still haven't entirely worked out what 'Vinyasa Flow' is, beyond a certainty that it isn't anything to do with what size tampon you should buy.

He's *liked* all of them, which he started doing religiously after I told him that to succeed on here he has to engage with as many people as possible. I'm starting to regret that piece of advice. Ironically, the only person Guy no longer chats to on here is me. This is based on an important, unwritten rule – that, once you start sleeping with someone, you do not continue to communicate with them on a public forum.

I'm above that now. The last thing I want is to have to vie for his attention online, like I'm no more important than the woman who casually commented that she'd *downward dog with him any time he likes.*

Our private messages are showing no signs of abating and, in addition to this, we have carved out two days of the week – Tuesday and Thursday – when Guy will come here to see me in person, come rain or shine.

As that's the only time when he's guaranteed to be free from other commitments involving the studio or Elijah, they have become 'our' days. The very best of days. He has made one or two attempts to suggest we meet elsewhere for these, but each time I've managed to casually steer him back to my place without too much fuss (though I'm a little concerned that he might think the reason for this is my enthusiasm for the physical side of our relationship).

Obviously, I wish it was more. I'd see him every day given the choice. But I am old-fashioned enough to never say this out loud; being needy is not a personality quirk I want him to add to any of my others. That said, I did casually mention that it was my birthday this Friday and that I had nothing special planned. He held my gaze for a moment, then brushed his lips against mine and murmured, '*Is that so?*'

I am trying not to let my expectations rise.

Looking for a distraction, I click onto my search bar and type in google.se – Swedish Google – before searching for the name Jamie Dawson. I'm rewarded with several pages of links offering the book he illustrated for sale. *Danny och isbjörnarna* – Danny and the Polar Bear – was written by an Ulrika Sjöblad and is clearly as big as it gets in the Swedish children's book market, five to seven age bracket.

It's got hundreds of five-star reviews and, when I click on the image on the front I'm slightly surprised by what I find. When he said he worked in watercolour, I expected something traditional, like those old-fashioned Ladybird books they used to stock in every primary school library. But this illustration is theatrical and mysterious, with layers of pencil and paint. The intricacy of the drawings suggests a vivid imagination, a fine attention to detail and something else – a warmth. None of the Swedish websites deliver to the UK, but I manage to find a copy of the book on eBay. 'Buy now' it urges. So I do.

When I click back to Instagram one last time, I note that the post featuring Oscar's greenhouse has over fifteen hundred likes, which already makes it my most successful in months and it's only been up for an hour and a half. I carry on scrolling to read the responses, most of them telling me how cute and adorable he is.

'He's a peach!' says @hopsandhouseplants. 'Absolutely the image of you!'

My mum and dad don't argue a lot. They occasionally bicker but only recreationally, and never snipe like some of my friends' parents did at school, venting opinions on dishwasher-stacking techniques or underpants dropped on the bathroom floor. But they're by no means always of the same opinion, something that becomes apparent as I let myself into the house and overhear sharp voices above the hiss of a stir fry.

'Don't you think it would open up a can of worms?' Dad asks.

'It might. Is that necessarily a bad thing?'

'She hasn't spoken about it for years, Harriet,' Dad says. 'She doesn't *want* to. She's been quite clear on that.'

'But that's part of the problem, don't you think? Not talking about these things *ever* ... I'm no expert but that can't possibly be good for anyone.'

'I disagree. Why would anyone want to rake over it?'

'If you don't mind me saying that's a pretty male attitude, Colin. And if—' She stops abruptly.

'Ellie? Is that you?' Dad asks. I hear urgent footsteps approaching the door, and start backing away when it flings open. 'It's okay!' I say brightly. 'I've just realised I need to do something. I'll leave you to it.'

'No! Come in and have some dinner,' Mum insists, removing the wok from the heat. 'It's only a Pad Thai but I've made tons of it.'

'Yes, come on,' Dad says gently, beckoning me in.

'I don't know what you overheard but it's nothing to be concerned about,' Mum says.

'Don't worry, it's fine. I'll catch you both later,' I add breezily, already on my way back to my annexe.

Chapter 22

'Happy Birthday!' Lucy toasts me with her cocktail, then narrows her eyes. 'Have you been having sex?'

I feel my complexion deepen, unclear about how she worked this out while she's six and a half thousand miles away in Malaysia and speaking to me through a video call on her phone.

'What makes you say that?' I'm also in a dressing gown, haven't yet brushed my hair and am wearing flip-flops jammed over socks. I'd like to think that if I was *recently* post-coital I'd have made a little more effort.

'There's only one thing that makes a woman's skin glow like that and it's not a spray tan,' she says.

'Don't,' I tut.

'Just let me say this: I'm happy you've even *got* a sex life. Even if it is with someone who says, "the moon exists in the soul of each and every one of us",' she chuckles. 'He is a card, isn't he?'

'Why are you pouring scorn on what could be the best thing that's happened to me in years?'

'Oh, you know I don't mean it. Look, I'm the last person

who wants you sitting at home polishing your chastity belt. I just want to know this: is he *nice*?'

'He's more than nice. He's amazing,' I say.

'Well, that's great. So what's he said about your agoraphobia?'

When I don't answer she leans in. 'You have told him that you have agoraphobia, haven't you?'

'Not yet, no.'

The liquid in her straw slips downwards. 'But you've been seeing him for, what, a month?'

'It just hasn't come up.'

'Oh come off it, Ellie! It's up to *you* to bring it up. Doesn't he want to go out?'

'Of course he does, but he hasn't mentioned it for a while, thankfully.'

'Believe me, he'll mention it again soon, so you need to get in there first. Either that or ...'

'Or what?'

'Why don't you go back to your therapist again? Try to knock this thing on the head.'

'You say it as if it's as simple as giving up chocolate for Lent,' I say.

'Sorry.' She slumps in her seat. 'I know it's not that easy. I do understand, Ellie. We *all* understand. It's not your fault, any of this. I think you forget that sometimes.'

'How's your holiday?'

She's there with her best friend Emma Wraithmell, with whom Lucy first started travelling during their gap year. These days, Emma is married and a mother of one, but in Lucy's eyes that hasn't changed anything; she's still somehow ended up on holiday with her, along with her husband Andrew and their son William.

'It's fantastic. It's a gorgeous place and we've met some great people. A couple of girls from Edinburgh who are a real laugh and a guy from Barcelona, who runs his own marketing company.' A coy, soft look appears on her face. 'He is *hilarious*. He had me in stitches the other night.'

'Have you slept with him?'

She pulls a mock sad face. 'No.'

Something catches my eye from outside the window. Guy is walking down my path. On a *Friday*!

'I need to go!' I slam shut the computer as I pull off the flip-flops, followed by the socks. I dive into the bathroom and brush my teeth for twenty seconds, before there's a knock on the front door.

'Just a minute!' I throw on yesterday's jeans and a T-shirt, then dart to the door and open it.

Guy has his hands in the pockets of a pair of linen trousers that sit low on his hips. A slow smile brushes his lips. 'Hello, birthday girl.'

I smooth down my hair self-consciously, as Gertie circles around his feet, yapping for attention.

'What a surprise! I wasn't expecting you.' I'm conscious that my parents haven't even come over yet. Much as I'm desperate to fall into his arms and take him to bed immediately, I can't do that when my dad is liable to turn up with an armful of presents at any moment.

'I wasn't going to miss your birthday,' he says, sliding his hands around my waist. He kisses me on the neck and I feel a burst of concentrated, mindless bliss. 'I have a surprise.'

'Oh?'

He reaches to his back pocket and takes something out. 'You and I are off to the Mind & Body Show at London Olympia.'

I blink at what appears to be two tickets. 'What's the Mind & Body Show?'

He turns one over and begins to read: '"Join us for an array of world-class workshop leaders, presenting new ideas on awakening, inspirational living, meditation, yoga, angels and NLP."'

I feel the blood drain from my cheeks. 'When?'

'Today.'

I realise I haven't released my breath for several seconds.

'Is that all right?' he asks.

I nod rapidly. 'It's great. Thank you. That's ... so kind of you.'

'No problem. I'm looking forward to it.' He kisses me on the lips briefly, then nods to the kitchen. 'Mind if I help myself to a coffee while you're in the shower?'

I look down at myself, noting that I really do need a shower. 'Sure, go for it,' I say, watching him head to the coffee machine as Gertie jumps up at his legs, refusing to give up.

I turn around and walk to the bathroom. I close and lock the door. Then I numbly take off my clothes, turn on the shower and step under it, rivulets of water soaking into my skin as I wonder how the hell I'm going to get out of this one.

Chapter 23

I hear voices in the living room while I'm dressing. I pull a cardigan over my summer dress and prise open the door to see Guy with his arm over the sofa, a mug in his hand. Mum is leaning on the kitchen work surface, nodding as he talks. Something about her demeanour seems strained, her smile forced. I realise why when I hear him telling her about the plan for today.

I push the door slightly open to try to hear more, when she looks up sharply in my direction. 'Oh, hi there!'

I straighten my spine and open the door wide. 'Morning,' I say. As I head into the living room, she approaches to envelop me in a hug.

'Happy birthday, you! I've brought some presents over,' she says, gesturing to several small, prettily wrapped parcels on the coffee table. 'Your dad's on his way though so maybe wait until he gets here to open them.'

'I was just explaining the plan for today,' Guy says.

Mum's worried gaze fixes on me. Neither of us move but I am pleading with her with my eyes, begging her to get me out of this, to do anything she can to make it go away.

She inhales deeply and turns to Guy. 'Sorry to be a pain, but we actually have a family get-together organised for today. I hope you understand. You'd be very welcome to join us for dinner though, later. Hopefully you'll be able to get a refund for your tickets?'

Disbelief spreads across Guy's face like spilt milk. 'I ... I doubt it,' he replies eventually, before turning to me. 'Ellie – I thought you'd said you weren't doing anything today?'

'I just meant I wasn't going out. I'm so sorry, Guy,' I say, looking mortified – which I am. 'Thing is, we always do this for my birthday. It's a family tradition. A big posh dinner. Mum goes to so much trouble.'

From the expression that flashes across his face, it is clear that he is pissed off. Trying not to show it, but definitely pissed off. It reminds me exactly of the look I saw on Jo's face more times than I could count all those years ago. I feel a crunch of despair.

'Oh, hang on!' he exclaims. 'If it's dinner rather than lunch, we can leave now, stay for a few hours and we'll get you back in time.'

My temples begin to throb. I turn to Mum, who catches my eye briefly but looks away. 'Look, why don't I leave you to discuss it? Let me know what you decide, Ellie.'

The logical part of my brain knows I should be capable of dealing with this, but I feel a stab of resentment as she clicks the door closed. It occurs to me that she could well see this as a positive thing. That this might finally be the incentive I need to step out of my comfort zone. As if it were that easy.

'There we go, all sorted,' he concludes.

'Okay ... I'll go and put some make-up on,' I mumble, with an acidic churn in my stomach.

I get ready in the bedroom, where I am gripped by violent stomach pains that feel like a staple gun is puncturing the lining of my gut. On top of all my other thoughts, I become fixated on the terrible, unpredictable consequences of the human digestive system in this state of high anxiety. On the idea of being out with Guy, in London, and for my body to simply fail me – in front of him and everyone else.

'All set?' he asks.

'I'll get my keys,' I hear myself saying.

Before I am even conscious of releasing my breath, we are outdoors, then at the end of the path, through my gate and I'm in the passenger seat of his car. My heart is pounding in my ears and all I want is to be in bed, cocooned in my duvet, safe, secure.

He is about to drive away, when he reaches over to kiss me. His hand touches the inside of my knee and he slides his fingertips gently upwards, tracing my bare skin. I try to respond as though I'm enjoying it, but an erotic rush is entirely absent. He withdraws. 'Must keep my hands off you,' he smiles. I force a laugh to lighten the mood, before he puts the car into gear and pulls out onto the road.

It is a beautiful day. The meadow outside our house is replete with wildflowers, harebells and foxgloves that peep out from the long grass like a swathe of tie-dyed chiffon. The air smells of high summer, hot and over-sweet.

I open the window to force a blast of cold air on my forehead as we approach the village, then the duck pond and the pub. We pass young mothers with pushchairs, couples strolling in the sunshine, a postman unloading letters from a pillar box, a builder working on the roof of the village store. We pass the church and its war memorial, then the community library, as an

elderly couple emerge, struggling with a bag of books. It occurs to me that these vignettes of village life have continued for two years and will continue to continue, with or without me.

We turn left at the parsonage and approach my old primary school. It looks almost the same as it was when I was ten: boxy, beige, functional and welcoming. The only difference is a brightly coloured banner pasted on the wall next to the entrance, which reads: HOW DO YOU FEEL TODAY? It is surrounded by cartoons of small animals each offering a suggestion: *Excited? Confused? Relaxed? Happy? Worried?*

We turn onto Nightingales Lane and Guy puts his foot down as we head into open countryside. I got used to being the passenger in a fast car when I was young. With Mum at the wheel even a trip to the supermarket involved going at full throttle, as if she was ready to perform a handbrake turn should the occasion require it. Perhaps I'm just unused to it these days, but the speed with which Guy drives – comfortably over the limit – only adds to my anxiety.

I become aware that he is talking and I am responding, but the moment words are out of my mouth I have forgotten what they are. I look straight ahead, feeling my eyes blur as I press my hands into the seat, sweat leaking into the upholstery. If Guy is aware that something is wrong he does not show it. The words *You Can Do This* are on repeat in my brain, but like the man who says *Mind the Gap* on the Tube they lose all impact as soon as they're spoken. No part of my body any longer feels within my control.

'I feel sick,' I blurt out. I don't know how long we've been in the car. Two minutes. Five minutes. Whatever it is, it feels like more.

Guy glances over. 'What, travel sick?'

'Yes.' I nod. It's the easiest explanation.

'Okay, don't worry – we're nearly there.'

My head snaps in his direction. 'What do you mean?'

'The station is at the end of the road.'

'But I thought we were driving?' Even as I say it I realise I haven't been thinking straight. He was never going to drive all the way into central London and we're almost at Chalfont and Latimer, which is on the Metropolitan line with a direct route into the city.

'Only to the station,' he says. 'You'll be fine once you're out of the car.'

A metallic taste rises into my mouth. 'I can't go on a Tube.'

'What do you mean?' he asks.

'I mean . . . could you just take me home?'

He glances at me again. 'You do look a bit rough, now you mention it. Do you need me to find something to be sick in? There are some bags for life back there.'

I shake my head.

'It'll pass once you're out of the car,' he continues. 'If we turn around now, you'll have another ten minutes before you get home. You'll be better just getting there. Look, here we are.'

We pull into the car park, only to discover that there are no spaces. Guy performs a slow tour of the tarmac, becoming increasingly frustrated, as the heat in the vehicle makes my jaw loll. As it becomes clear that there is literally nowhere to leave the car, my hopes begin to rise that he might give up on this whole idea.

'Aha!'

A guy with a baby in a papoose approaches a minivan and clicks the lock.

We hover next to his space as Guy's indicator blinks

insistently, while the new father wrestles the child out of its fabric binding and into its car seat. He eventually pulls out and Guy goes to turn in, when a small, dusty Citroën approaches from the other direction and slips into the space. A middle-aged woman is at the wheel, with hair that resembles an apricot shower puff. Though it's clear that she's made a genuine error, Guy slams his hand on the horn, forehead flushing.

'Silly cow,' he mutters, winding down the window. '*Hey! What do you think you're doing?*'

She slams on the brake, her eyes wide. 'Awfully sorry! I'll move!'

Guy retreats as she evacuates the space, before taking her place. 'Thank God for that, eh?' he says, opening the door to climb out.

But I am unable to move. My hands grip the sides of the seat, as the pulse in both palms throbs against the fabric.

'Are you coming?' he asks, leaning in. 'There's a train in four minutes. We'll make it if we're quick.'

I glance at him, then back at the dashboard. 'I feel terrible, Guy.'

'Well, you will in there. It's red hot. If you get out, you'll be fine.' I don't move. 'Ellie?'

I take several deliberate breaths, before a sentence bursts out of my mouth. 'I just want to go home, okay?'

He jolts back, as if he's been slapped on the cheek. 'Are you . . . *joking*?'

'No,' I plead, shaking my head. 'I'm *really* sorry.' I'm engulfed by a wave of self-loathing.

'Well, *okay*,' he says gently. But I get the impression that the tone in his voice does not match what he's really feeling. 'Seriously, Ellie, why don't we just get on the train?'

'I . . . can't.'

He straightens up. 'So . . . what am I meant to do with these tickets?' He's angry with me now, of that there is no question. He also has every right to be.

'*You* can still go,' I offer weakly.

'Well, yes,' he replies, making me wish I hadn't said that. 'But how are you going to get home from here?'

'I . . . I'll have to phone my parents.'

He lets out a long sigh. 'No, don't do that.' Then he gets back in the car. He glances at me. 'Well, this has turned into quite the shambles, hasn't it?'

'I'm sorry,' I say.

'No, don't keep apologising. If you're sick, you're sick.' He turns to look at me. 'You *are* sick, aren't you?'

All I can do is nod.

I try to make small talk on the way home, but the words blood and stone spring to mind. Even when I manage to think of something to say, he answers in monosyllables. He's polite enough, just quiet, so much so that by the time we are nearly home I am awash with paranoia. He pulls on the handbrake outside Chalk View.

'This probably seems a little . . . weird,' I offer.

He shrugs. 'It does a bit.'

'I should explain. Though . . . now really isn't the time.'

He turns to me and exhales. 'Don't worry about it,' he says softly. The fact that he looks genuine makes no material difference to how crushed I feel.

'Thanks again. And sorry,' I add quickly, before I open the door and scramble to my annexe, feeling like a fish gasping for water.

Chapter 24

'Happy birthday to you . . .'

Dad's voice trails off as he registers my expression and he places the cake on the table. The candles continue to flicker, dripping wax on buttercream, determined that the party – if that's what you could call the three of us – will carry on. I lean in and blow them out, as ribbons of smoke fill the pocket of air above us.

'Shall I do the honours?' Dad asks. He cuts three large slices and hands us one each on a plate.

'I believe you had a rough day, Ellie?' he asks.

'Yes, you could say that.' I pick up a crumb between my finger and thumb and place it on my tongue. There's nothing wrong with the cake, but it feels like swallowing sand. 'I think I might have messed things up with Guy. I think I've messed things up *full stop* really, haven't I?'

Mum picks up a fork and digs in. 'You are way too harsh on yourself, Ellie,' she sighs. 'You always have been.'

'Not really, Mum. I had every opportunity in life given to me by you two. When you think about what *could* have happened to me, I've got no right to be like this.'

'Nobody else thinks that but you. Absolutely nobody,' Dad says. 'When any child goes through something like you did, it has lasting effects. When people say that to you they're not just saying it to make you feel better. There have been studies on childhood development that prove it.'

'Yes, I know all about those. Colette made sure I did.'

Mum leans back in her chair. 'Why do you think it went so wrong with her, Ellie?'

I've never fully explained to my parents why I stopped seeing Colette so abruptly. They pressed me for an explanation, of course, but when a person who is mid-breakdown decides to dig in their heels, people tend to back off quickly, worried that they'll do something completely unthinkable. I owe it to them to explain though, I know I do.

'She wanted to try something new,' I say.

'What kind of something?' Dad asks.

'She felt that CBT for the agoraphobia could only take us so far. So she suggested something similar to the way PTSD is sometimes treated. It's called exposure therapy.'

Mum leans back in her chair. From her expression, she immediately understands the implication of this. 'That presumably involves delving into your past a lot.'

'Yes.'

I couldn't claim that Colette had sprung it on me. In fact, she'd first raised the idea at the initial session, then repeatedly dropped it into conversation subsequently, suggesting that it was something we might try at an undefined point in the future, when I felt comfortable. 'It's not something we'd rush into,' she said. 'It requires a commitment, and an understanding that it might be difficult at times. I only want you to do it when you feel you trust me.'

'I do,' I said. It was true.

She explained that the therapy works on the basis that PTSD sufferers use avoidance or 'safety-seeking' techniques, in my case refusing to acknowledge or talk about the early years of my childhood. This can prolong or intensify PTSD symptoms because, when a person avoids certain situations, thoughts or emotions, they don't have the opportunity to fully process their experiences. Exposure therapy aims to eliminate avoidance behaviour by confronting the very situations a person fears – by imagining or vividly reliving them – thereby lessening anxiety. That's the theory anyway.

'So you'd want me to talk about things that happened when I was young?'

'Yes.'

I felt the sharp half-moons of my nails digging into my palms. 'I don't even like to *think* about it, Colette, let alone talk about it.'

'That's because, at the moment, doing so involves re-experiencing the more upsetting memories. You're avoiding the trauma reminders, even though those reminders are not inherently dangerous.'

But that wasn't the only reason. Not in my case.

'I just want nothing to do with that place anymore,' I explained. 'I don't feel part of it in any way and I refuse to let it define me. It's not *me* anymore. In fact, I feel as though it never was me, that what happened didn't even happen to me, but someone else.'

She began to jot something down.

'I *like* it this way,' I continued. 'I like being an ordinary English girl, with two nice parents, who grew up in a lovely place where nothing very exciting ever happens beyond

winning best-kept village or the vicar starting to wear a toupee.'

She looked up. 'That's not the whole truth though, is it, Ellie? Recognising your past doesn't have to mean allowing it to define you. But the fact is, it did happen. It *is* part of you, whether you like it or not.'

I don't know what occurred to change my mind, beyond a sharp sense of duty to my family and an intense dislike of letting people down. I felt I had no choice but to give it a go. And the trust issue was significant. That led me to believe that perhaps this could be the key, after all. That if I just took this one painful step, I might be able to lock away all my troubles for good.

It didn't work out like that.

I called time on the first session before our hour was even up and raced out of the place. It was only two years ago, but my main recollection is not what I said, or what Colette said, but how I *felt*, with my nerves rattling at every word, spoken and anticipated. Afterwards, the glorious realisation that *I did not have to do this* – not any of it – hit me like blinding sunlight.

'We suspected it was something like that,' Dad says now. 'It was almost inevitable. You'd been the same since your early teens. You never wanted to talk about it. Mum and I would try to encourage you to open up about what happened beyond what you'd told us in the first couple of years. But there came a point when you just seemed to turn your back on it all and stubbornly refused. After then, we didn't want to force the issue. It felt cruel.'

I top up my wine glass and take a large mouthful.

The heat of the alcohol slips down my throat and I look up, fortified. Perhaps it's that I have reached such an intense

state of self-loathing after what happened with Guy that I don't feel I deserve to avoid this pain any longer. Perhaps it's simply that hitting the age of thirty-four feels like as good a time as any to break the habit of a lifetime. Or perhaps it's more practical, the unavoidable recognition that this is simply not going to get better by itself.

'Tell me about it, will you?' I say to them both.

They exchange glances. 'Where do you want us to start?' Mum asks.

'How about the day you found me.'

Chapter 25

Harriet, 1990

As the humanitarian convoy approached the Romanian border, the atmosphere among the volunteers seemed to shift. The last overnight stop before they reached their final destination was at a soulless, Soviet-style hotel and it was outside that, with church bells tolling somewhere in the distance, that Harriet stood with Colin and the others. Marie, a representative from one of the two charities accompanying them, had asked the group to gather round. She had a south London accent, a light brown complexion and beautiful jet-black braids, which she tucked behind the silver hoops in her ears. Harriet had interviewed her after they'd first set off from the UK and was struck by her knowledge and passion. But as she addressed the others now, there was the faintest touch of apprehension in her voice that had been entirely absent before.

'I need to mention a few practical matters before we get to the orphanage,' she told them. 'The first thing I ought to prepare you for is the smell. It's pretty awful. There are no toilets so the six hundred children are using sewers directly

in the floor. Also, ladies, if you've got something to tie your hair back with, now is the time to do it. Most of the little ones have had their heads shaved, but not all. Those with hair are crawling with lice.'

They'd read about Romania's orphanages in the newspapers, of course. Marie's charity, which operated globally, had already been out here several weeks earlier. But although images of starving, naked and sick children found in overcrowded state institutions had shocked the world, what the volunteers were about to walk into took on a new immediacy. A collective paralysis had descended on them as Marie finished her speech. 'If anyone who heard that wants to turn back now,' she said, 'I'm afraid it's too late. So, come on, folks. We're in this together.'

In the months following President Nicolae Ceaușescu's fall in a bloody uprising in December 1989, it was estimated that one hundred thousand children were in state orphanages, though that figure was still growing. The astonishing scale of it had been the result of Ceaușescu's family policies during his twenty-four-year reign, during which he wanted to boost the population and create a 'Citizen's Army'. 'The foetus is the property of the entire society,' Ceaușescu announced. 'Anyone who avoids having children is a deserter who abandons the laws of national continuity.'

Motherhood was now a state duty to be rigorously enforced by the secret police. Abortion became illegal for women under forty with fewer than four offspring. Contraception was banned. The result was babies and more babies, a far greater number of unwanted children than desperately impoverished parents could afford to feed. So they were encouraged to hand over children into state care, where they ended up in one of

around seven hundred institutions, the true horrors of which were only beginning to be uncovered.

The orphanage was a colossus of a building, three storeys high and pockmarked with brittle exterior paint, its arched windows criss-crossed with bars. As Harriet clicked open the passenger door of the van, her eyes were drawn heavenward. At a window on the second floor, she saw the outline of two children, one gazing silently at them, his eyes muted and dull, the other rocking back and forth.

Marie was met at the door by the orphanage director and Harriet followed them inside. The stench of urine and faeces hit her like a blast of hot wind. Her eyes skittered around in the dim light, to the rot on the walls, the dirty, cold floors, the squalor in every corner. Before she could fully take it in, three boys appeared from nowhere, followed by a surge of other children. When they realised there were strangers in the building, they emerged from every direction, frantic-ally pushing each other out of the way, amidst a melee of noisy squabbling and excitement. Their heads were shaved and dotted with scabs, their limbs thin and clothes imbued with dirt. Harriet couldn't place an age on any of them, something she attributed at the time to the chaos of the moment. On later reflection, she would realise that, mal-nourished and underdeveloped, they simply looked younger than they were.

'Hello ... hello there,' she said, through a smile, as she made her way through the crowd. Colin by now had an arm round one boy, then another. 'Why don't you be my helper, come and show us round?' The others jostled for Harriet's attention, demanding hugs, reaching for her hand. She tried to clutch them all, one after another.

Shortly afterwards, they were given a tour of the building. A set of stone steps led to the basement, where in one room the stench was so powerful that one of the volunteers had to run for the door to be physically sick. The washing machines were all broken and soiled nappies were laundered by hand in sinks with an intermittent water supply. Across the room, stinking pieces of cloth hung from strings. These were the 'clean' nappies. Every corner Harriet turned brought new horrors. Rusting pipes, black mould, a repugnant residue on the floors that she couldn't identify.

It was when they turned into one large room that Harriet felt her knees slacken. There were sixty or so babies, lying in rusting cots, several piled into each one. Some were covered in their own excrement and urine. They were empty-eyed and malnourished. Some were naked, all were filthy.

But the most disturbing thing of all was not the smell, nor the squalor, but the silence. Child after child sat or lay in rows, but none of them cried, nor played, nor made any noise at all. The first lesson they'd learnt in their short lives was that it was pointless to cry out, so they were either entirely still, or rocked back and forth soundlessly.

Her eyes lowered to the cot next to her, where a little boy sat. He looked about eighteen months old but was almost certainly older, his pale blue eyes fixed on the wall. He wore a knitted bonnet tied underneath the soft skin of his chin and was so still that if it hadn't been for the faint rise and fall of his little chest Harriet wouldn't have believed he was a living, breathing person.

She stooped down, and reached through the rusty bars for his hand. His tiny fingers were icy cold. 'Hello, sweetheart,' she said softly, stroking them. 'Hello, darling boy. I wonder

what your name is?' It was as if she wasn't there. He made no noise; his eyes didn't even flicker.

'They're never picked up or played with.'

Harriet gently released the little boy's hand and stood up to face a young man in his early twenties, wearing jeans and a smart jacket. He was tall, at least six foot three, with sensitive brown eyes and what her mother would approvingly have called 'a good head of hair'.

He introduced himself as Andrei Rucarenu and, though he spoke with a Romanian accent, his English was impeccable. He had been working as an interpreter for Unicef for the last few weeks. He had the look of a man who was deeply, irreversibly affected by what he'd encountered.

'It doesn't help that they're hopelessly understaffed,' he explained. 'There are forty children to every one of the women who are supposed to be looking after them.'

Andrei told Harriet that the little girls and boys were not just physically deprived but emotionally too. This dark, disgusting, cold room was where they ate, slept, existed. 'To call it living would be entirely the wrong word,' he added.

The next few days involved a lot of hard work. The volunteers and charity representatives knew they were barely scratching the surface of the multitude of problems, but dwelling on that would've been no good to anyone. All their band of electricians, plumbers, nurses and paediatricians could do was knuckle down to the task in hand. They managed to get the lighting up and running and made a start on fixing the roof. They scrubbed algae from surfaces and blasted the shower room with an acid descaler to remove the limescale, behind which a layer of excrement had been trapped. There

was corrosion in every pipe. Dirty rags in every room. One by one, the children were examined by medical staff, given vitamins, food and clean clothes.

'It feels like all too little in some ways,' Harriet told Andrei as they sat on the steps at the front of the building, bright sunshine overhead.

'It is, but it's at least a start,' he said.

Harriet had met many exceptional people in her time as a news reporter and she now classed this urbane, intelligent Romanian man among them. Not just because of the quiet efficiency with which he worked, nor even the spontaneous singing sessions he instigated with the children, filling the orphanage with the sound of their voices. It was his determination to make a real difference. Being an interpreter was simply not enough for him.

'I've wanted to be a police officer since I was five years old,' he told Harriet. 'It was all I ever wanted to do. I found out yesterday that I have been successful in my application to join the local force.'

'Oh Andrei, that's amazing,' she gasped. 'Congratulations.'

He nodded and looked at the floor. 'I don't think I'm going to take it.'

'Why not?'

'Because I want to do something about this.' He nodded towards the door. 'I've never felt a stronger calling in my life.'

What happened over those early days came to transcend the tools, equipment and elbow grease. The volunteers played games and involved the older children by getting them to stir pots of paint and pass them tools.

Harriet was due to fly back to London on the evening

of the third day, while most of the others remained. This included Colin, who wouldn't be home for another three weeks. He'd already asked if he could take her out when he returned, and she'd accepted.

That morning, she ought to have been gathering last snippets of colour for her piece, but she found herself seeking him out. She located him on the second floor, where he'd been painting since daybreak – covering the grimy, crumbling walls with a white emulsion that looked like cream cheese when it was smoothed on. It was a vast dormitory and she watched him from the door as he'd stopped to chat with two little girls. He was making them smile by drawing pictures for them on an unpainted section of wall with his brush. Neither of the girls spoke English, of course, and Colin only knew a few words of Romanian, but they were managing to communicate somehow.

Harriet had encountered the two girls a couple of times since their arrival. They'd stood out because they were inseparable, so much so that at first she'd assumed they were sisters. The taller girl was clearly the more streetwise and the self-appointed protector of the other child, whose eyes were full of trepidation whenever she couldn't immediately see her friend standing next to her, ready to square up to anyone who meant trouble.

Harriet watched as Colin drew a flower on the wall before handing the smaller girl his paintbrush, inviting her to make her own picture. She hesitated, looked confused. It struck Harriet that no British child of her age – seven or eight, she'd guess – would be short of ideas about something to draw. A heart, an animal, perhaps a little house. But she didn't seem to have ever held a paintbrush. If she'd been in the orphanage

since she was a baby, as so many of them had, she would almost certainly have never even *seen* a little house. There were no days out or jolly trips from here.

So the little girl didn't draw anything and instead put the paintbrush firmly back in its pot. Harriet wondered if she detected some annoyance or irritation, but then the girl cast her big eyes up at Colin and did the most extraordinary thing. She reached out for his face, pressing her fingers against his cheeks as if she was checking he was real. He blinked, not knowing how to react. Next she wrapped her arms round his waist and squeezed him. He froze, unsure of what to do, and Harriet moved to join them.

'Hello there,' Harriet said gently, as the little girl looked up. 'What are your names?'

Neither understood, so Colin, who'd been introduced to the children by Marie earlier, answered for them. 'Harriet, I'd like you to meet my new friends. This is Tabitha,' he said, gesturing to the taller girl. She stepped forward, accepting Harriet's hand to shake without hesitation.

The other little girl didn't move at first. But eventually she lifted her eyes to Harriet and a smile flickered at her lips. 'And this is Elena,' he said. 'I call her Ellie for short.'

Chapter 26

Harriet, 1991

Harriet couldn't pinpoint the exact moment when she'd realised that she might be in love with Colin. But she knew when the first unsettling rush had come – when she'd watched him put his arms around those little boys. She'd seen kindness amidst the worst atrocities before, of course. Those were the glimmers of light that made her job possible. So why it should have pressed some unseen button inside her this time was never clear, especially as she'd already discovered that he drove like an old woman and was still living with his mother, which ought to have been an automatic turn-off.

The truth was, she couldn't get enough of him and the feeling seemed to be mutual. Plus, once she'd met her, it turned out she liked his mother very much, assuring Colin that he had no need to keep apologising for this *absolutely* temporary arrangement, one that would only be in place until he'd saved the deposit for his own flat. Far from being an omnipresent force at Chalk View, Hazel Heathcote was hardly ever in, preferring the company of her bridge club or

church friends. She went on a 'retreat' every so often, which Harriet initially thought sounded dreadful, but the way she'd describe it made it seem more like a girls' holiday, involving lots of country walks, gossip and Cadbury's Crème Eggs in between the praying.

Colin slept in a room at the top of the house, which felt like an entity of its own. When Harriet wasn't abroad, they were often there. In their first months together, it had been nice to go on dates in town, to catch a show and introduce him to friends, before returning to her tiny flat. But Chalk View – with its garden, expanse of space, fresh air, birdsong and convenient position on the end of the Metropolitan line – had thoroughly won Harriet over. After she'd stepped off a flight feeling grubby and exhausted and in need of a strong cup of tea, it was there that she increasingly wanted to be.

One Sunday morning while Colin's mother was out, she drifted downstairs and found him at the kitchen table, flicking through a newspaper. It wasn't the one she wrote for; Mrs Heathcote had been loyal to her favourite mid-market tabloid for years, leaving Harriet baffled as to how someone could read such bigoted bile and still manage to be as kind as she was.

'I haven't persuaded your mother to jump ship then,' she said, leaning down to kiss him.

'Oh, I wouldn't take it personally,' he chuckled, turning over the page.

The orphanages in Romania were still making front-page news, largely because, despite continued denials of their existence by the authorities, more were being discovered. Hospitals in which babies had been crammed into basements. Institutions for children with disabilities, where young boys,

girls and teenagers were all mixed together with little super-vision, drunk staff and an intermittent water supply.

Harriet had been sent by the news editor to one of these places, a few months after her first trip to Romania. It was described as a 'special hospital', in which 250 children with varying degrees of disability were packed into six decaying rooms. The children had no more than the most basic education, wandered around aimlessly, and signs of abuse were barely concealed. The resident psychiatric doctor, a small white-haired man, had shown her round impassively. When they reached one cot, where a boy of around seven or eight was sitting silently in a grubby pair of pants, the doctor lifted the child's arm then let it flop down. 'Imbecile,' he told Harriet, devoid of compassion. The experience had chilled her to the bone.

Western governments were now sending aid, though packages were often going in the front door and out the back – donated goods were being sold on the local market or kept by employees for themselves. But all anyone could do was keep doing their bit. Colin's fundraising efforts and those of his colleagues had continued apace since his first visit to the orphanage – and he'd used school holidays to visit twice since then. Harriet had stayed in touch with Andrei Rucarenu, who was now working tirelessly for a British charity, having been appointed 'Country Director'.

It was clear from what both told her that the building had improved significantly. The walls were clean and painted with illustrations of cartoon characters. The old, rusting cots had been replaced by new ones, donated by Mothercare. The toilets and showers were working and that dreadful, all-pervasive smell had finally gone. But the number of carers hadn't

changed and neither had something else more fundamental than any piece of equipment or newly painted window.

'Everything all right?' Harriet asked now, pouring herself a coffee as she sat down next to Colin.

'Yes, fine,' he shrugged. 'Just thinking about all this.'

'I'm going to speak to my editor about going back to the orphanage for a follow-up piece,' she said. 'To show him how far it's come along since you first went there.'

He took a sip of his drink and frowned.

'What is it?' Harriet asked.

'I know it's closer to habitable,' he told her. 'I know we've got the toilets working and the kids now have food to eat. But it's clear to me that the problem isn't just with the facilities and infrastructure. It's that these children are stuck in these godawful institutions full stop. What they need goes far beyond a few teddy bears and a clean sheet.'

'What are you saying?' she asked.

'They need a family, Harriet.'

She lowered her eyes to the newspaper. MEET THE BRITISH COUPLES ADOPTING ROMANIAN BABIES, the headline read.

When she looked up, Colin's eyes fixed on hers and she felt an unpleasant skip in her heart. Her first instinct was to reach down and turn over the page, pretend she didn't know exactly what was going through his mind. But for reasons that she would grapple with for a long time afterwards, she didn't.

'You're still upset about that little girl, aren't you?' she said.

'Ellie,' he replied, though Harriet already knew her name. She also knew that the little girl's best friend Tabitha had recently attracted the attention of an Italian couple. They had successfully applied to adopt her, which meant that, within a few short months, while one little girl would be flying off to

start a new life in a comfortable home in a suburb of Bologna, the other would have to stay and face a bleaker future.

'I can't bear the thought of that little mite being left there,' Colin confessed.

There was no point in tripping out a series of glib reassurances and telling him the girl would be all right. Instead, she heard herself saying: 'Neither can I, if it means anything.'

He looked up. 'Okay. Then the question is: what are we going to do about it?'

Chapter 27

Ellie

📷 *Instagram*

EnglishCountryGardenista

670
posts

57.7k
followers

949
following

ELLIE HEATHCOTE

I love this time of year, when the last days of June roll into high summer and all the preparation we did back in early spring really starts to come together. I bought this gorgeous 'Black Dragon' wisteria from @GardensToGo_ and honestly cannot believe how well established it's become in so short a time, with beautiful, long plumes of cascading flowers. The company have an incredible array of plants — I could while away hours scrolling through the ornamental grasses and

herbaceous perennials on their website. You can find out more at www.gardenstogo.co.uk. All gardening equipment gifted by gardenstogo.co.uk – links in my stories. #Ad
#Thisgirlgardens   #Myhappyplace   #digforvictory #beddingplants   #wisteria   #junefloweringclimbers #summercolour   #Englishcountrygardener   #gardener #gardening   #garden   #gardenlife   #flowers   #plants #gardens #nature #gardendesign #gardenersofinstagram #growyourown #gardeninspiration #greenthumb

@rachelgreenfingers:
Wow, they've grown since you first posted the seedling pic. What have you been feeding them – Shredded Wheat?!

@EnglishCountryGardenista:
Nothing but light and water – lots of it!

I make a start on responding to the dozens of others but run out of steam, even though – as this post is an advertisement and therefore I was paid actual, hard cash for it – I really need as many people as possible to engage. The photograph that accompanies the sponsored post is quintessentially Instagram: a painstakingly constructed image of a woman who looks as free as a bird, without a worry on her mind. It bears little relation to the reality.

Two days after my birthday, I have hardly heard from Guy beyond a response to a text I sent asking if he was coming over on Tuesday.

Really busy this week, Ellie – sorry. We'll sort something soon though. Looking forward to it 🙏 x

> Great, me too. When are you thinking? x

To which he didn't reply at all.

I snuggle into Gertie, as rain runs in rivulets down the windows, and decide to message Lucy to ask for advice.

> Should I press him about what 'soon' means?
> Should I even contact him at all?

> **Oh, definitely. I would always text a man in this situation.**

Another arrived a second later.

> *** Full disclosure: My response rate isn't great. In fact, it's possible I'm literally the worst person on earth to ask.**

I shift Gertie over a little and click on Guy's account. This morning he re-posted an Instagram Story he was tagged in by @KellieYogini, who works in his studio. He's lying, bare-chested, flat on his back in a trendy, stripped-brick room, his legs pointing to the ceiling. Above him, the dip of her hips balanced on the soles of his feet, is @KellieYogini, whose taut, tanned body stretches out horizontally like Captain Marvel in Lululemon.

He's added the caption:

> By nourishing someone we are advancing their vitality and nurturing their health. We are helping them on their journey, physically, emotionally and spiritually. Who will you

nourish today? #yogaman #nourish #positivity #spirituality #mindbodyandspirit

I resist the urge to swear and click off my iPad.

'Come on, Gertie.' She follows me, wagging her tail as I grab my waterproof coat and wellies. I open the door to find the rain torrential. The dog whimpers and backs away, leaping on the sofa and cementing herself between two cushions. 'Oh, I see. I'm on my own then.'

For the next two hours, I tend my garden as if it is a glorious sunny day, ignoring the fact that I am quickly drenched from top to toe. I also mulch the grass, stake out the plants by the back wall, prune a rampant forsythia. By the time I return indoors and have showered, I'm clear-headed enough to compose an email.

Dear Guy,

I'm very sorry for what happened on my birthday. It was true that I felt sick and also that my mum had prepared a dinner. However, there's something else I haven't been completely open about and I'd love it if you'd let me explain.

Ellie x

It sounds coy and mysterious in all the wrong ways, but in the absence of an alternative, I press send and head to my bedroom to dry off my hair. It only takes a minute before I am hit by a wave of self-doubt, obliterating every positive feeling I had when I stepped in from the garden. One thought in particular kicks me in the gut: Why am I so bad at keeping hold of the people who mean anything to me? Anyone, that

is, except my family: my lovely mum and dad and, in Lucy, someone who doesn't merely feel like a sister, but a better version of me.

I stayed up with my parents until 2am on my birthday. There were times, amidst the blur of wine and the come-down from my adrenalin, when it almost felt cathartic. It was only as I began asking questions about Romania that I realised how many you accumulate when you refuse to talk about a subject for years and years. I concentrated mainly on the parts I knew I'd like hearing about, such as that hug with Dad. It was the first time I'd embraced a grown-up in my life. They weren't my parents then, of course, just Harriet and Colin, two strangers with pale skin and kind eyes, speaking softly in a language I didn't understand.

My parents did most of the talking, Mum in particular. Her recent trip to Bucharest for the *Observer* – to write about Romania thirty years after the orphanages hit the head-lines – had brought back memories for her too. She travelled, initially to Iași in the east of the country, then to Bucharest, with a British charity who are doing incredible work with an all-Romanian team of social workers to ensure as many vul-nerable children as possible end up in loving families, rather than institutions. 'Perhaps you could read the piece when it's printed?' she suggested, though I didn't reply to that.

Mainly, though, we didn't talk about what Romania was like today, we talked about what happened all those years ago, as questions began to bubble up in my head faster than they could keep up with. What did I look like? How did we communicate? And finally: why me? Why, of the six hundred children in that orphanage, did you choose me?

It didn't surprise me that, in the rush of American and

Western European couples to adopt in the years after the orphanages were uncovered, babies would be top of the list, not children who were eight years old like me and who already bore so many emotional scars. I can't imagine there was anything unusual about me, anything that made me stand out beyond the fact that my friend Tabitha had found a home and I hadn't. I suppose that made them take pity on me, rather than on anyone else in the place. But that didn't make me special, only lucky.

I could just as easily have been left behind. Plenty of children were, including one whose unknown fate has caused me to feel more anguish in my life than I've ever been able to come to terms with. I lie back into the soft folds of my bed and, for the first time in a long while, when my thoughts drift to Tabitha, I don't fight them. I don't push them away. Instead, I let them billow up and settle in my mind: memories of my first friend, someone I loved in a world in which love simply didn't exist.

Chapter 28

I don't recall a particular moment when I first noticed Tabitha in the orphanage. Like me, she had simply always been there, as much a part of it as the rotting mattresses we slept on and the mould that clung to the walls. I knew we'd both started off in the basement though. That was where you came from when you'd never had a mother, or at least not one you'd ever known. It was there that the babies lived, often in darkness, nearly always in silence. I don't know why they didn't cry, but I must have been the same. There was no point, I suppose.

I have almost no memory of being down there, beyond knowing I was terrified about the move upstairs to be with the bigger children. Even when I got there, things remain hazy. There are swathes of time that I've either lost because I was too young, or actively blocked out. Despite this, I still remember not merely the general nature of life there but also – though more rarely – odd details or conversations that have survived like single scenes in a damaged reel of film.

I could tell you what happened my first night on the second floor, for example, because I woke up warm and soaked with urine, before the soles of my feet were thrashed

as a punishment for wetting the bed. I didn't do it again for weeks, then one night it just happened. I couldn't help it. That time, one of the educators, Felicia, stepped in and saved me from a beating. She was soft-natured, a sweet woman who was treated with suspicion by the other staff. I'd seen her successfully intervening before, on that occasion to protect a boy. 'He's got a heart condition, you're going to kill him!' she'd gasped, though I'm fairly sure that particular child died a couple of months later anyway. Quite a lot did. We were constantly sick.

There were certain things I accepted simply as part of life that now, from the comfortable position of hindsight, I see rather differently.

The smell, for example. This was one of the things that Dad told me later had hit him like a ton of bricks the first time they entered the orphanage, yet oddly, I don't ever remember being bothered by it. I know there was excrement on the walls and in the latrine of course; I recall the urine-soaked sheets and the fact that 'washing' meant simply dunking them into the same freezing bath water as the children. It *must* have smelled horrific, but that's not something that stands out in my memory.

Hunger is another thing it's hard to fully reimagine, at least the intensity of it. But then it is, by definition, a transient force. I do know that our bellies were never fully satisfied though and that eating the sour boiled cabbage we were given was simply a question of alleviating the pains in your stomach.

The point I'm making is that the worst thing about the place really wasn't the squalor or cold, nor the sickness and hunger. It was the casual, day-to-day violence. The older kids fought constantly. They'd beat each other up or brawl

over pieces of cheese or bread, but smaller children were their favourite target. When they were caught at it by staff, the punishment was further assault: kids were ordered to hit each other. Failure to do so resulted in the hardest whack of all, from the educators themselves. Looking back, everyone seemed to be hurting each other and some hurt themselves. One girl when I moved upstairs would bang her head against the wall every night.

I didn't have it worse than anyone else, I do remember that. We were all beaten, it was just the way things were. And when another child hit you, you hit them back because you had to – even me, a natural born weakling. These small atrocities were part of our lives and we were collateral in an atmosphere of humiliation and cruelty. I hated it, I feared it, but I also assumed this was how everyone lived.

This is all hard to make sense of now I'm an adult, in particular the behaviour of the staff. My impression from memory is that, while I think there were one or two genuine sadists, most of those who looked after us were simply crushed by a pitiless, inhumane system. Some, such as Felicia, did have empathy but any expression of this would result in their own punishment by the crueller, more 'experienced' workers.

Whatever the case, I was not a fighter by nature. I kept my head down. I tried to be noticed as little as possible. In this sense, finding Tabitha in the next bed to me was a disaster.

She had always drawn the wrong kind of attention and was constantly being smacked across the head or face for giving cheek, for being late, for fighting or taking too much food. But she managed to give the impression that it was all water off a duck's back. The first night she ended up in the bed next to mine is one I remember with startling clarity.

Perhaps my imagination has filled in the gaps. Either way, I recall trying to avoid making eye contact with her. She was having none of that.

'Hey!' she said, as I pretended to sleep, my back turned to her. 'What's your name?'

I froze, refusing to acknowledge her.

'Hey you!' she repeated, prodding my shoulder. She tutted when I didn't respond. 'You mustn't want one of these then?'

I heard a crunch and rolled over, screwing up my eyes to see her in the half-light. She was eating.

'Shh. Don't tell anyone,' she said. 'You can keep a secret, can't you?'

'What ... is that?' I whispered. She reached under her pillow and pulled out a rag, glancing at the door before she unwrapped it. With a grin, she displayed three biscuits, stacked on top of one another.

'Where did you get those?' I said, in disbelief.

'Who cares? Want one?'

I stared at the biscuits. I could smell them and I felt saliva gathering at the sides of my mouth. I shook my head.

'Suit yourself, but after dinner today you're going to die of starvation. Your arms are like sticks.'

I looked at them and frowned. As far as I was aware, my arms were no thinner than anyone else's and what happened at dinner hadn't been unusual. The cleaner on duty had got around the fact that pieces of cheese were numbered for each child by splitting them in two. She took the larger chunk for herself, leaving us with half-portions of an already meagre offering.

Tabitha wouldn't drop the subject. She yammered on about the scumbag cleaner, about the rest of the staff and about my

arms, until in the end I accepted half a biscuit. The sweet, grainy crumbs dissolved in my mouth and I was torn between wanting to savour it and needing to chomp it down before we were discovered. Then she moved on to the gossip from the boys' dorm where, she told me, the supervisor had last night broken up a fight and as a punishment ordered those involved to hit each other. And although part of me wanted her to go to sleep, certain she was going to land us with a beating of our own, another part of me was mesmerised.

'How do you know all this?' I asked.

'Friends in high places,' she grinned.

After that first night, we went from being virtual strangers to barely out of each other's presence. She had a tough, animal quality that made me feel braver, just for being around her. She was my superpower: when she was around, I could get through anything. Also, I recall – rightly or wrongly – that she made me laugh. I don't ever remember either laughing or even *hearing* laughter until that point, yet afterwards I have memories, as clear as day, of the two of us suppressing giggles after dark.

One night as the moon shone outside and the echoes through the dorm room had died down, she handed me one of her biscuits just as another girl appeared from nowhere. She tried to snatch it out of my grasp, but Tabitha leapt up as quick as a panther, grabbed the biscuit and shoved the girl so hard that she fell backwards onto the floor.

'Do that again and I'll strangle you,' Tabitha snarled.

The girl snorted. 'Who'd want to be Visinel's pet anyway?'

Things started to slot into place after that comment. Visinel, the caretaker, *did* treat Tabitha like his pet, as if she was somehow under his protection. She had hardly taken a

beating for months and he, I was now sure, was the source of the biscuits. I was also aware that some of the other kids were jealous, though she was far from the only one to be singled out. A couple of the older girls had attracted his attention too. And, although this was all vaguely unusual, I hadn't thought much of it until he started taking Tabitha and those older girls into a room and locking the door. There were a couple of times when the night supervisors banged on the door and told him to open up, but it never stopped him. I don't know whether I knew then exactly what was happening behind there, or whether I've just worked it out since. But it wasn't long before neither Tabitha nor I liked the taste of the biscuits, no matter how hungry we were.

Chapter 29

The Italian couple who applied to adopt Tabitha looked and sounded like nobody I'd ever come across before. They were tall and sleek and beautiful. The woman's lips and fingernails were painted rose pink and her long hair swept into a smooth, dense knot at the nape of her neck. Her husband's eyes were the colour of the sky on a hot day. They paid three or four visits to prepare for Tabitha's departure to Italy and each time they brought toys – dolls and teddies that she refused to share with anyone but me – and sugared almonds with smooth, coloured shells. Tabitha called the woman Mamma Giulia. The man was simply Papà.

She could not believe her luck. Neither could anyone else. Although a stream of prospective parents had started coming to the orphanage within weeks of the television cameras arriving, all anyone seemed to want was the babies. 'They think you're a character. Don't knock it,' Felicia had said to her, as she brushed Tabitha's hair before one visit. She had been told to put on a pale dress, pink cardigan and a pretty pair of unscuffed shoes – clothes that only ever appeared on such occasions.

'I've asked them if they'll adopt you too,' Tabitha told me. 'They say they can't because there isn't room for two children, but if you're adopted too we can visit each other and write letters. Mamma Giulia says they teach you how to do that at school.'

Some of the girls in our dorm told Tabitha that in Italy they cut open children's heads and fed their brains to monkeys. Tabitha told them to shut up, but I could see that the thought worried her. 'They're being stupid,' I reassured her. 'They're jealous, that's all.'

'Are *you* jealous?' she asked me. I shook my head, because even then I knew that that was what she needed to hear.

'Well, you don't need to be,' she replied. 'I just know you're going to get a mother and father too.'

What I hadn't realised at that point was that my world had already started spinning on a different axis the day two strangers called Harriet and Colin had walked through the doors of that orphanage. I only found out months later that they wanted to adopt me. My reaction was one of wild disbelief – and hope. If I had reservations about going to live somewhere different from Tabitha they were minor, because the truth was we had no idea how far England was from Italy. We imagined visiting each other at weekends, writing to each other every day. The days of sleeping in beds next to one another would be over, but we would still be in constant contact and any temporary periods of separation would all be worth it.

I don't know how long it was before Tabitha was due to leave that she was told about Mamma Giulia's illness. Her departure had certainly felt imminent. Her new mother, we were informed, was now in hospital and may not ever leave.

179

She was too poorly to make the journey back to the orphanage and in no fit state to look after a little girl. Just like that, there was no new mother and the adoption was off. Tabitha was distraught.

'If I could just *get* to them,' she whispered to me desperately one night. 'I could tell them that I wouldn't be any trouble. I could be a help to Papà while she's in hospital. I could look after him, then when Mamma Giulia is well enough to come home I can nurse her too.'

But weeks went by and, while my own adoption was progressing, the decision about Tabitha seemed to be final. I would go. She would stay.

She started fighting again, getting herself in more trouble than ever before. Without the scrutiny of her prospective parents, Visinel began to summon her to his room again. Most of the time she went without arguing and would emerge flat-eyed and sullen. But once, when she refused, he took a stick to her backside, leaving angry welts rising from her skin that she showed me later that night.

I wished above anything else that Colin would just come for another visit. Everything could be solved then. He'd been a few times with the other teachers from his school in England and when he next did I planned to tell him that I simply couldn't leave without Tabitha. He would have to adopt her too. He and Harriet were so nice that I was certain he'd agree. But he never came and I started to worry that perhaps Harriet was sick too and my own adoption was off, which would've torn me in two but at least meant I didn't have to leave Tabitha here by herself.

'You don't need to worry. They're coming for you,' she told me. 'I know it. You're going to be fine.'

The night Tabitha escaped through the window of the dorm, part of me had been expecting it. Kids were always running away. They ended up on the streets, stealing, begging – surviving in whatever way they could, something I knew from the tales we heard when the police brought the odd one back. What was a surprise was how she did it. Our dorm was on the first floor, too high to jump from. Nobody had ever even tried it.

Much of my time at the orphanage remains hazy, my memories like looking back through the murk of an aquarium. I genuinely have no idea if some of them are real or imagined. But I recall the night Tabitha ran away with crystal clarity. It happened exactly as it did in every dream I had about it in the subsequent years, right down to the way her small face appeared at the side of my bed, her dark eyes coated in a film of frightened tears. I could feel her breath on my skin, but when I opened my mouth to ask her what was going on, she just raised a finger to her lips and shook her head. She hesitated long enough for me to see the pain in her expression, before she stood up and walked away, tiptoeing past the end of each bed as she crossed the long room.

By the time she pushed open the window, I had already guessed what she planned to do. I wanted to scream, so loudly that it might tear my lungs, but I couldn't in case I alerted one of the educators. Instead, I was forced to watch, deafened by the boom of my own heart, as she climbed onto the sill.

It took only a few short moments after she leapt for chaos to ensue. For girls to scramble out of their beds, staff appear from nowhere and for me to run to look too, certain that she would be dead. But as I pushed my way to the window,

I caught sight of a small shadow stumbling across the street, making her escape.

In the weeks afterwards when the cops hadn't brought her back, I felt lost. The ache in my gut was bigger than loneliness or fear; it was closer to a bereavement. The days stretched ahead of me. Night involved fractured sleep. I couldn't quite believe or accept that she was gone. And although my heart told me she'd done the right thing – the idea of her staying in the orphanage while I left for England was unthinkable – I couldn't reconcile that with just how much I missed her.

Oddly though, of the plethora of emotions I felt at that time, it didn't occur to me to be afraid for her. She'd been tough. She could handle anything.

It took years for that perspective to change and when it eventually did, recognition of the reality of her circumstances was like a punch in the gut. As an adult I came to recognise that she was no fighter at all. She was a helpless little girl, lost in a country in the midst of a turmoil all its own.

Chapter 30

The first Tuesday night I've spent alone since Guy first started coming over here passes without a response to my email. By Thursday, hitherto one of 'our' days, there's still nothing. Meanwhile, his Instagram Stories are dominated by the exhibition in London and include a video of a demonstration he took part in, which involved lying on the floor as a woman did a handstand on his thighs, each leg spread horizontally like an iron girder.

While my mood refuses to lift, outside my plants are drunk on sunshine. Vibrant blooms jostle and spill onto the lawn; nasturtiums snuggle next to cornflowers and zinnia, while the spikes of hollyhocks nudge four feet of crimson splendour. Clumps of catmint bubble along the side of the path and each tiny jasmine flower has opened up, producing a dense, creamy mass on the pergola. I'm in the process of deadheading some phlox, when Jamie's van pulls up outside.

'Hey there,' he says, opening the gate. 'Only a small delivery today.'

'Oh yes, I was desperate for some garden ties.' I paid £2.99 for them just so I could have someone to chat to, despite the four hundred I already have in my shed.

Catherine Isaac

'Where's my girl?' He grins and for half a moment I think he's referring to me. He drops to his knees as Gertie hurtles towards him.

'Time for a cuppa?' I offer, as he ruffles her fur.

'It's a bit tricky today, Ellie,' he says, standing up. 'I'm going to the hospice Mum was in. I offered to help with their new garden. So – any tips would be gratefully received . . .'

'Hmm. Don't take too many tea breaks?'

'Noted.' He hesitates. 'Maybe they won't mind if I'm a few minutes late.'

I make two mugs and we sit side by side under the shade of the cherry tree. He tells me that he's only recently started to volunteer, but is already struggling to find as much time as he'd like; he plays in a local rugby team, which tends to eat up his every spare minute. That and seeing family and friends – of which there seem to be dozens. Mike is the one he talks about most. He is getting married next year and Jamie is to be best man, something he's excited about and dreading in equal measure. He assures me he's no public speaker. There is also a Greg, a Diane and Rachel, the last of whom was in the year below us at primary school. I remember her as a sweet, funny girl with an extraordinary voice that won her the role of Nancy in the school performance of *Oliver!*. Something in the way he talks about her makes me wonder if there's more to their relationship than just friends.

'How are things with you and your man?' he asks.

'Not great,' I confess. 'I can't stop thinking about it.' I tell him about the tickets Guy bought, the sweat I leaked into the upholstery of his car and how I ended up spending my birthday having a heart to heart with my parents instead.

'And he hasn't phoned?'

'No, he just texted to say that he isn't coming over.'

'Maybe he's just a dick then,' he shrugs.

I snort. 'I'm fairly sure that isn't the issue. This is not the nuanced and insightful opinion I was hoping for from you.'

'Yeah, whatever,' he grins. 'He clearly doesn't know a good thing when he sees one. That's all I'm saying.'

I take a sip of my drink. 'Have you ever been in love?'

'Me? No.'

'Not the romantic kind?' I ask.

'Oh, I wouldn't say that. I think I'm just holding out for the right girl.'

It strikes me that Jamie could be attractive, in a certain light. There's something solid and straightforward about him, and a confidence that has grown with age. There are still glimmers of that shy kid, of course, but he holds himself in an entirely different way, one that suggests, rightly or wrongly, that he could more than look after himself.

Somehow, I can imagine exactly the type of girlfriend he'd end up with. She'd be pretty but wouldn't realise it, even when he'd joke that he was fighting above his weight and absolutely mean it. She'd be a primary school teacher or specialist cancer nurse, universally popular and loved for her sunny disposition. She'd have no hang-ups beyond a dislike of some minor cellulite and every year they'd go on holiday with friends, to Cyprus or Turkey, or another warm destination where they'd enjoy all-inclusive drinks and—

'Ellie?'

'Sorry. Miles away. You must be ready to get back into the dating game again soon?' I ask. 'Surely you've got a couple of groupies in Sweden by now.'

'That's a long way to go for a date,' he laughs.

'Oh, that reminds me,' I say, leaping up. 'I bought your book! You're going to have to sign it for me.'

I head into the house and return with the book and a pen, before handing them to him. The look of astonishment on his face makes me laugh.

'Where on earth did you get this? I *know* you didn't pop over to Sweden for it.'

'Didn't I say you could get anything on the internet these days?'

'I think this could be my first ever UK sale,' he says, shaking his head.

'The first of many, I'm sure.' He opens the book to the title page and pauses as he contemplates what to write. 'Oh God, the pressure. This is like trying to think of something really good to write on someone's leaving card.'

'You'll have to get used to it,' I reply. 'Hey, I bet your mum would've been really proud of this.'

'Oh God, she'd have been unbearable. Neighbours wouldn't have heard the end of it. The thing about being raised by a single mum is that nobody else can take credit for their child's accomplishments.'

He lowers his pen. 'I meant to ask: what do your mum and dad think about what happened with your man? You said you had a heart to heart with them.'

'They think I should go to see my therapist again. They're probably right.'

'So why don't you?'

'I'm scared.'

'Is she that bad?'

'Colette? God no, she's lovely.'

Then a text arrives on my phone. I balance my empty mug on the grass and open it up. It's from Guy.

**Hello Ellie. So sorry I haven't been in touch. Things
have been crazy. I'll explain when I see you but I'm
free on Tuesday if that works? X**

I feel my heart swell and look up at Jamie. 'It's from him. All
isn't lost after all.'

'Well. There you go then. You'll definitely have to go and
see your therapist now, won't you?'

'Yes. I agree.' I inhale deeply. 'The problem is, she won't
want to come to the house. I'd have to go to her. Plus, one of
the reasons I stopped going was that she wanted to "explore"
my childhood. My ... *early* childhood, that is. I don't like
doing that, to put it mildly.'

'You mean, the place you lived before you came
to England?'

I nod. He places his cup on the grass by his feet and
straightens up again, crossing his arms over his chest. 'It
must've been tough coming here the way you did, at that
age. Hardly knowing any English. None of us knew a word
of *your* language – apart from "Salut", which Mrs Hennessy
got us to all learn for your first day.'

'Sweet gesture, but I didn't enjoy that. I'd have preferred
to slip in to the back, unnoticed.'

'But you settled in so quickly,' he says. 'You made friends
straight away. It wasn't long before you were just like any
other kid. It was as if you'd been there for ever.'

'My eight-year-old self would have been very happy to
hear that. Hey, you still haven't signed my book.'

'Sorry, I'm an amateur. I keep getting distracted.' He picks
up the pen and starts to write.

Chapter 31

I don't remember anything about my journey from Romania to the UK. Mum and Dad say I slept most of the way, waking only when my in-flight meal arrived. They discovered later that I'd hidden the bread roll and pack of biscuits in my pockets for some future, unspecified emergency. I wore a pink T-shirt with Minnie Mouse on the front and a new pair of trainers with soles that lit up when I walked, items brought by my parents. There is a picture of me wearing them, taken in Heathrow, smiling as I held Dad's hand on British soil for the first time. But as I was swept along to my new, better life, there was also an urgent topic on my mind.

I'd babbled on and on in Romanian, from the moment I got into the car at the airport. My new parents barely understood a word – it was beyond anything they had picked up from the Romanian audio course they'd been cramming for the last couple of months. But there was one thing I kept repeating. A name. Tabitha.

My first year in the UK is a blur, but I have a few stand-out memories. I remember worrying about where my next glass of water was coming from. Biting into the cling film

wrapped around a sandwich, having never seen such a thing before. I was constantly hoarding food and Mum would often find bars of chocolate or fruit and cheese under my pillow. I was obsessed with where Tabitha was for a long time after I arrived in England. I asked about her constantly, begged Mum and Dad to speak to the orphanage to see if she'd been found, because I couldn't live with the idea that she'd ever returned there. I had only a few photographs of her that had been taken by Dad and my favourite showed the two of us, standing in front of our adjacent beds, holding hands. I used to sleep with that picture, kiss it at night, before tucking it under my pillow to keep it close to me.

But however much I missed her, no part of me wanted to go back to Romania and the orphanage. I made that very clear to the stream of translators and social workers, counsellors and officials, who'd arrive at the house and fill me with anxiety by their mere presence. I wanted to stay in this warm, safe place that was full of food and music and where we did jigsaws and made cakes. Instead, I set about trying to persuade my new parents to find out what had happened to Tabitha, so that they could bring her to England too. Once my language skills had evolved enough to communicate this, they didn't say an outright no like the Italian couple had when Tabitha wanted them to adopt me. But of course they didn't say yes either. All of which was immaterial because absolutely nobody knew where she was.

Mum had promised to keep checking to see if my friend had ever returned. I've since learnt that Mum was in touch with a man who'd by then become a close friend of hers – Andrei Rucarenu, the Romanian director of a British-based charity. I don't know him as well as she does, but he's always

been a compassionate, urbane and infinitely likeable man, with a fierce determination to do the right thing by the children of his country.

He promised that, if Tabitha ever returned to the institution – or indeed any of those his organisation worked with – he would be in touch immediately. A few weeks later, Mum sat at the end of my bed and stroked my hair as I asked about my friend for the umpteenth time. 'I'm sorry, darling. Nobody can find her. But if anyone does, they will let us know straight away.'

As crushing as it was to have no idea of her fate, I was also relieved she had never gone back to the orphanage. Wherever she was, it would surely be better than there.

I concluded that perhaps she had found some parents like mine. Because, although I knew that people in Romania were generally not as wealthy as in the UK, I also knew – because Mum kept telling me – that the rest of the country was nothing like the orphanage. Not by any means. In fact, she'd said, it was a beautiful place, full of warm, welcoming people, plenty of whom were part of a loving, happy family. I thought about Felicia, one of the kinder educators at the orphanage, and remembered the affection with which she'd talked about her own three daughters. Perhaps she wasn't the exception, after all.

Right from the start of my time in the UK, the focus of all my efforts was on trying to fit in. That, I was convinced, was the key to ensuring I'd never be sent back. My first major introduction to British children was at Sarah Hardy's birthday party, a week before I officially started school. Sarah and I were to be in the same class. Her mother – a former colleague of Dad's – had given the impression that the party would be low key; 'just a handful of friends'.

Mum took me shopping a couple of days before, telling me through a combination of sign language and a Romanian dictionary, that I could choose whatever I wanted. I picked out a pale yellow dress with little painted tulips, netting under the skirt and a ribbon tied at the back.

My hair smelled of shampoo and was so clean that it squeaked. My nails were neatly clipped, without the half-circle of dirt I'd always thought was permanent. I had colour in my cheeks and the hollow pains in my stomach had gone. In a matter of only weeks, I already looked and felt a world away from the girl who'd stepped onto a plane a thousand miles away. 'So pretty.' Mum had smiled at me. Being pretty wasn't something I'd given a second thought to until then.

Logic tells me that I must have been apprehensive, but the overwhelming feeling I recall on entering that party was wonder. At the attractive house with its huge front door and white, arched windows. The balloons that floated up in the hallway as I stepped in, clutching my new father's hand, curling shyly into his side. My senses were over-loaded with squeals of laughter, twirling dresses, music and wrapping paper. I could tell Dad was worried about there being so many kids, but Sarah's mum just knelt down and said some kind words. Their translation was beyond me but their meaning wasn't: we are going to make sure you're all right here.

She took me by the hand, as Dad hovered. He wanted to stay, but after a few minutes I insisted he left like everybody else's parents had. When he arrived to pick me up, twenty minutes early, I was playing musical bumps. My cheeks glowed and my belly ached from sponge cake. He didn't need

me to say what was already clear to everyone: I'd had the most wonderful time.

Over the next decade, I became as much of an English little girl as anyone who had happened to be born here. I joined the Brownies, ran for the county, stood for school council, made more friends, passed exams. I achieved a Gold in the Duke of Edinburgh Award scheme and went to a garden party at Buckingham Palace – home of the Queen of England herself – to collect it. I spoke with an English accent, I had a British passport and two English parents. As far as I was concerned I was now English.

For Mum, though, it was not as straightforward as that. She wanted to make sure that I didn't turn my back on my Romanian roots and tried to angle my education and upbringing to reflect them. She cooked Romanian dishes and urged me to maintain the language. She continued to teach herself Romanian and stayed in touch not just with Andrei, but with several other Romanians she'd met and befriended during the adoption process.

She kept assuring me that, despite what I'd been through, Romania was a place of medieval castles and gothic churches, with charming towns and wonderful, warm people. She even got in touch with a local au pair from Suceava and invited her over for chats in my mother tongue. I went along with it for a while, then simply refused.

I couldn't tell you the exact point the switch was flicked. One year after I arrived in the UK, perhaps two? All I know is that it was decisive. I didn't want to know about anything to do with my old life. I didn't want to talk about it, I didn't want to think about it.

Perhaps this is why I've never felt any inclination to go looking for my birth mother. I don't hold the slightest resentment against her for giving me away. I know enough about Romania's history, about the poverty, the politics and the fact that she was one of hundreds of thousands of women left with no choice but to do what she did. But while I don't think about her, or my birth father, or any theoretical brothers or sisters, there is one person I've continued to think about endlessly, whose fate consumed me for years after I stopped talking about everything else to do with my past.

So when Mum comes to knock on the door of my annexe one afternoon, telling me she wants to talk about Tabitha, there is a moment when I struggle to comprehend the statement. In the immediately preceding moment, I'm preoccupied with thinking about Guy and what I'm going to say to him the following day. To hear Tabitha's name makes my heart jump and my first assumption is that Mum wants another conversation like the one we had on my birthday. That she wants to discuss my feelings, explore memories. The last thing I'm expecting is the conversation that actually follows.

'Do you remember walking in on your dad and me a couple of weeks ago? We were having a ... difference of opinion.' She perches on the arm of my sofa and only then do I notice that she has a foolscap folder in her hand.

'In the kitchen, you mean?' I ask, pulling on my wellies and glancing at the weather outside.

'Yes. It was because I'd found something when I was writing the piece for the *Observer*. I didn't mention it the night of your birthday because there was so much going on already.'

I straighten up and look at her. 'What was it you found?'

She opens the folder. 'It was just after I'd returned from Romania. I was doing some online research and stumbled across the archive in a French magazine.' She removes a printout, walks towards me and hands it over. 'It's a piece of photojournalism, won a couple of awards apparently. The picture that caught my eye was taken in 1991. When I read this girl's story and saw the name and dates ...'

My eyes scan a double spread dominated by a single, land-scape photo and a headline that reads ENFANTS SOUTERRAINS.

'It means "Underground children",' Mum says, but it's the image that interests me more than the words. It's of a girl with a sweet face, almond-shaped eyes of a dark brown hue and high cheekbones.

My hand shoots to my mouth.

'It says her name is Tabitha in the caption,' Mum says. 'Do you think that might be her?'

My head swims. It's been so long since I saw her in person. We were both so young when we were together that if I'd been relying on memory alone I don't think I'd ever recog-nise her, no matter how important she was in my life back then. But I'd kept the picture of the two of us on my bedside for a long time after I moved to the UK and Dad gave it to me; it came to university with me, then back here when I moved into the annexe and has been in that plastic crate in my wardrobe ever since.

'I think it could be,' I tell her. 'Just wait here a minute.'

I pull off my wellies and go into my bedroom, stand-ing on the dressing-table stool to pull down the box. It takes me a couple of minutes to find the picture and when I do, my heart clenches. There are no smiles. We simply

194

look small and skinny and lost, which I suppose is exactly what we were.

I take it back to Mum and we put the two images next to one another. There's no question: it's her.

'What's this piece about anyway?' I ask. 'Have you translated it from the French?'

She hesitates. 'It's about the homeless living in tunnels under Bucharest's main railway station. A lot of them had had an institutional upbringing. They'd previously lived in the orphanages.'

The images depict a nightmarish existence, cramped, overcrowded and dirty.

'As you know, I contacted the Romanian authorities about Tabitha years ago and she'd disappeared off their radar. I really didn't know whether to show you this.'

She looks up at me, sees my expression and takes the article from me, placing it back in the folder. 'I was genuinely torn about it, especially after what your dad said. But you made me promise when you were a girl that if I *ever* discovered anything about Tabitha I'd tell you. So I have.'

I nod. 'Thank you. I . . . it's good to know that at least she was still alive.' But my voice wavers. Tabitha might have been alive when that photo was taken. She might have been free. But that was years ago. Contemplating her chances of survival in those conditions makes me feel sick with despair.

Chapter 32

The following morning, I'm editing a post when someone bangs on my door. *'Ellie!'*

I open up to find Oscar on the doorstep in red wellies that appear to be three sizes too big for his feet.

'Have they grown yet?' he asks, stepping inside.

'Have what grown?'

'My tomatoes. I'm having them for lunch. I don't normally like tomatoes but I'm making a deception.'

'I think you mean an *exception*?' I suggest, looking up to see Mandy attempting to tiptoe her way through a puddle in cork wedges, rain battering her hair.

'Oi! Mister! Don't go running ahead like that!' She reaches my door and steps inside. 'Honestly, these flippin' tomatoes. They're all I've heard about today.'

'I'm afraid they won't be ready for a while yet,' I tell Oscar. 'It will probably take until September.'

He holds out the fingers of one hand and starts counting down on them. *'January, Decembuary, June, Octember . . .'* He pauses and looks up. 'That's ages away.'

'Yeah. Sorry. But the plants *have* grown!' I say brightly,

turning to his mum. 'Leave Oscar here and we'll potter in the greenhouse, if you like.'

Mandy doesn't get the chance to contemplate the offer before Oscar runs towards the greenhouse, bursts through the door and rushes to his tomato plant, which I have been nurturing with the care you'd devote to a rare, prize-winning orchid. He peers at it and frowns.

'Where are the tomatoes?'

'You'll have to give them a chance to grow, but they will. Look, they're starting to flower – can you see? That's what they do first.'

'I didn't want flowers,' he adds, sullenly.

'Well, I'm afraid you're stuck with them if you want them to become tomatoes. Wait here, I think the rain's stopping.'

I go into the shed and return with the children's gardening set I ordered online last week. It wasn't expensive, just a little canvas carry bag, with a hand trowel and fork, gloves and a matching bucket. He accepts it with such effusive thanks that I'm almost embarrassed and dives outside to test it out.

He's a bit disappointed that I refuse to allow him to do his favourite job – turning on the sprinkler – given that the grass is already like a swamp. Nor will I let him loose with the hosepipe – the last time it was he and I who were left hydrated, rather than the plants. Instead, I suggest we do a little weeding, which I discover after popping to the loo for a couple of minutes was a reckless idea, judging by the number of bedding plants he's uprooted.

'Look how many I've got, Ellie!' he says, pointing to a heap of lobelia. 'Did I do well?'

I turn to Google for suggestions and come up with a worm hunt. Obviously, there is no horticultural merit in this, but

he's certainly entertained and soon we are on our hands and knees, arm-deep in soil.

'I'm going to keep this one as my pet,' he says, holding it in his palm. 'I'm going to look after him for ever.'

'For ever is quite a long time in worm years,' I point out.

'He needs a name.'

'How about Wriggles?' He scrunches up his nose, unimpressed. 'Wormy?' I suggest.

'Those names don't suit him.' Then he peers at the creature, searching for inspiration from his appearance. 'I'll call him Ellie.'

Mandy appears on the patio, clearly not going to risk the path this time. 'All done. Have you been good for Ellie?'

'Yes and I've got a pet.' He runs at her, brandishing the worm somewhere in the area of her nose. Mandy shrieks and suggests that he should *get that bloody thing away*. I step in and tell Oscar that Ellie – Ellie the Worm that is – needs to live here but he's welcome to visit again. Mandy pulls a face that indicates doubts about my sanity, but decides not to argue if it means she doesn't have to take it home.

Oscar lifts up the palm of his hand to address it directly. 'Make sure you are good for Ellie,' he says earnestly, handing him to me.

'I'm sure he will. But I'm just going to put him back down in the soil for a little while. Worms like their freedom.' I lower it to the ground so it can wriggle away.

'Thanks for my bucket and tools,' Oscar says.

'Thanks for helping in the garden,' I reply.

Then he reaches out and throws his arms around my waist, squeezing me as tight as he can manage. A surge of warmth rushes through me, despite my knowledge that his filthy,

wormy fingers are pressing into my back. 'What's ... what's this for?' I ask.

He pulls away and looks at me. 'Because I love you.'

Then he marches towards the gate, swinging his new gardening kit by his side.

Chapter 33

Guy arrives at eight and my heart swoops at the sight of him on my doorstep. He plants a slow kiss on my cheek and I invite him inside as Gertie hurtles out of the bedroom. He automatically reels back, but I scoop her up by the flanks before she can reach him, tickling her under her ears until she settles and trots off. I fix us some drinks while he sinks onto the sofa; my chest is knotting in anticipation of the conversation I've been steeling myself for ever since sending my email. I still haven't resolved how much I'll tell him and now find myself deferring the entire thing in favour of small talk.

'Have you seen Elijah lately?' I ask.

'I'm having him this weekend. She's off to a festival.' I've noticed that his ex – Stella – is never referred to by name. It's almost as if to say it out loud would be to acknowledge not merely that they had a past, but the dreadful reality that, as Elijah's mother, she will inhabit a small corner of his life for ever more.

'Are you doing anything special with him?'

'You know, he's happy just watching *Kung Fu Panda*. He must have seen it a hundred times but it never seems to get old.'

I hand him a glass of Sauvignon Blanc. 'I'm told it's very good.'

'Not *that* good,' he grins. He takes a sip, then puts the glass down on the table. 'Sorry I've been elusive lately. It wasn't intentional – things are just crazy right now.'

I wait for him to expand on this, but he doesn't, instead stretching his arm across the sofa as he looks at me, taking me in. 'You look utterly gorgeous.'

He reaches around to the back of my neck and gently caresses my skin with his fingers, before pulling me towards him for the sheerest kiss. My heart surges at the touch of his lips, but I remind myself that I must not get into anything physical with him until I've broached the issue I've promised I would. But as I open my mouth to speak, he does too and we end up in a verbal cha-cha-cha of 'you first's and 'after you's. It's he who eventually concedes.

'Did you see what happened to my account this week? My followers jumped by over a thousand.'

'Oh, I did notice actually. That's great! What do you think prompted it?'

'Popsugar ran an article called "Shirtless Men Meditating",' he replies. 'I was number twelve.'

A laugh bursts out of me, which I quickly suppress. 'That's brilliant. Gosh, what a coup.'

'I know!'

He looks so happy that I feel happy for him, recalling that same feeling I had when *my* account started to take on a life of its own.

'Overnight, I'm almost at four thousand followers. If I carry on like this I could be at the ten K mark by autumn, which means I'm *this* close to getting my posts sponsored.' He begins

to remove his sweater and as he pulls it over his head a scent rises, half warm skin, half essential oils. Something stirs inside me. 'I was wondering if I could come and take some photos in your garden?'

'Oh sure,' I reply, flattered and a little surprised. 'Whenever you want. It's looking really photogenic out there at the moment.'

'It would also mean you could maybe re-post the pictures to your account,' he tells me. 'You wouldn't mind, would you?'

'No, not at all.'

'Hey – why don't we do a series?' he suggests. 'We could do some stories together, then you could do a video about me, introducing me to your followers.'

I shift in my seat awkwardly, trying to work out if there would be any way to do this that didn't jar. But I can't help coming to the conclusion that, from the perspective of my own followers, it would look a bit odd.

'Yeah, I'm sure we could come up with some ideas,' I say, diplomatically. 'I'll get my thinking cap on. I just . . . I need to bear in mind that my own followers are only really there for plants.'

'Right, right,' he nods, then turns a frown on me. 'What do you mean?'

'Well, if I suddenly switch focus and start writing about wellbeing and yoga, I'll start losing people. They'll wonder what's going on.'

When it becomes clear that the knot on Guy's forehead is not going to fully unfurl, I curse myself for being so selfish. 'Forget I said that,' I reply, waving my hand dismissively at my own stupidity. 'I'd love to help. In any way I can.'

His gaze makes a sultry drift across my face before settling

on my mouth. 'Thank you, Ellie. I'm really just starting this journey. It means the world that you'll be there with me for it.'

He picks up a strand of my hair and lets it slide through his fingers. He's about to move in to kiss me again, when I feel an urge to address the issue I've been avoiding. 'Guy, I promised I'd explain about what happened on my birthday.'

He pulls back. 'Oh yes.'

All the words I've been thinking about for most of the afternoon start jostling in my head and I suddenly don't know where to begin. 'I need to give you some context first.'

'Sure,' he says gently.

'When I was younger, before I came to live with my mum and dad, I . . . was initially brought up somewhere else.'

He ponders this for a moment. 'They're not your real parents?'

'Not biologically, no.'

'You're adopted?'

'Yes.'

'Cool,' he says, reaching out to pick up his glass. 'So what's that got to do with what happened on your birthday?'

'Well, I thought maybe I ought to start from the beginning.'

He takes a sip of his drink. 'Okay.' He smiles.

'So the thing is . . .' I continue, but then I notice his eyes slide to the right and realise that he's subtly checking the kitchen clock. 'Though . . . No, I'll get straight to the point, shall I?'

'Whatever you think is best.'

I decide I must have imagined it.

I inhale deeply and look at him. 'Sometimes I feel weird when I go out. You know. Panicky.'

He looks concerned. 'Oh, is this an anxiety thing? I can show you some exercises for that if you like. So, what . . . it's when you're in a car?'

'Well. Yes.' For some reason, implying that my issues are confined to when I'm in a vehicle, as opposed to just *everywhere*, feels slightly easier.

He leans forward and puts down the glass, then returns to pick up my hand. 'Ellie, I *understand*.'

'Do you?'

'Absolutely.' He starts to stroke my knuckles. 'My mum was involved in a car accident a couple of years ago.'

'Oh . . . God, really?'

'It wasn't anything serious, fortunately, but she hurt her pelvis and, even when she recovered, for years she hated getting in the passenger seat of a car. She took the train everywhere. It's all good now though. It passed. I'm sure it will for you too.'

His fingers have now made their way gently up my arm and are tracing my collarbone. 'You know, you'd have loved the Mind and Body show.'

'I saw the videos. It looked wonderful.' He begins circling the nape of my neck. 'I'm really sorry, Guy. I'll give you the money for my ticket. I really do feel awful about it. Here, let me get my purse—'

But he grabs me by the arm and gently pulls me onto his knee. He turns my head towards him and softly, oh so softly, sinks his mouth into mine. My entire body goes fuzzy, my limbs weak with longing.

'Ellie, stop worrying,' he says, between kisses. 'There's no way I'm going to let you pay. It's all fine. I promise.'

'You're sure?' I whisper.

'Absolutely.' Then he kisses me again and soon we are on our feet and he's leading me to the bedroom, where I usher Gertie out and close the door.

Afterwards, Guy sleeps. He always does, as if whatever cocktail of chemicals he's just released has a narcoleptic effect on every limb and organ in his body. It never lasts for more than ten minutes, which I usually spend on my phone until he rouses. But this time, I close my eyes and sink into sleep too.

I dream about the orphanage. About its mould and rust, layers of dirt and stench of fear. This time, it isn't about the day Tabitha jumped out of the window, but the time Visinel beat her, after she'd refused to go with him into his room.

They're in our dorm, his eyes fixed on her fragile frame as he moves towards her. But now, I am not eight years old. I am caught in a slipstream of time, watching the scene unfold not as a child, but the adult version of me. Who knows more, has seen more, who understands what's happening and has the ability to stop it.

He yells and grabs at Tabitha's clothes. I run towards them. The air around me is cinematic, rushing past at high speed. But, no matter how fast my legs move, I'm not getting anywhere. The realisation that I can't reach her, I can't save her, hits me like a tsunami and I stumble to a halt. 'Get away from her,' I scream. Tabitha's thin arms are trembling. 'Get your hands off her.'

Visinel raises the stick, bringing it down so hard that the air whistles. '*NO!*'

'Ellie!'

I wake up with sweat soaked into the hair above my neck. I register Guy's expression and the acid burn in my chest.

205

'Sorry,' I mutter.

He runs his hand through his hair, blowing out his cheeks. 'Christ. You'd have thought the house was on fire.'

'I had a bad dream,' I mumble.

He looks genuinely worried. 'Ellie, you were . . . hysterical.'

'Sorry,' I say again, pushing myself up as I feel the blood return to my cheeks.

He inhales, pecks me on the cheek, then turns away to grab his pants from the floor. 'What time is it?' I ask, as he stands and pulls them up over his buttocks.

He picks up his phone. 'Eleven. I need to go.'

'You could stay over,' I suggest hopefully.

'Not tonight, I'm afraid. I've got too much on tomorrow.' He bends to kiss me again, this time on the lips. He pulls away and holds my gaze, tucking my hair behind my ear. 'Still beautiful.'

'I'll come and see you out,' I say, starting to move.

'No, you stay there. And don't let any more of those nightmares disturb your beauty sleep, will you?'

Then he opens the door and heads outside as Gertie jumps on the bed and I snuggle into her neck instead.

Chapter 34

Harriet, 1992

Until the moment Harriet had entered the UK with an eight-year-old Romanian child, she had never considered herself to be one of life's risk takers. Ironic for a war reporter, perhaps, but she prided herself on it. It was what had kept her alive all these years.

Yet, even before they'd started the adoption, it felt as though something fundamental had changed in her, that some mysterious internal procedure was recalibrating her system. The feeling was most acute when she arrived at Heathrow, clutching Ellie's hand while Colin guided them towards Customs. There, they calmly announced that yes they did have something to declare and presented officials with a mountain of accumulated paperwork. Everything suddenly felt very risky indeed.

To reach this stage had taken six months and scores of meetings with child protection services in both the UK and Romania. Between the translators and the home visits, the bureaucracy sometimes felt overwhelming and the pace

glacial, leaving the 'honeymoon' phase of Harriet and Colin's marriage scarred by a simmering anxiety that their plans might crumble at any moment.

By now, stories were filtering out of Romania about cash being offered for children by overseas couples desperate to adopt. One German family had been on the brink of securing their legal adoption of a little boy from the same orphanage as Ellie, when someone else swept in with the money and the child disappeared overnight. The authorities were under pressure to curb such abuses and while every process Harriet and Colin had followed was above board, they started to fear that it wouldn't be completed before international adoption from Romania was outlawed completely. But that fear was confounded, and, within a day of the final stamp appearing on a piece of British paperwork, they had leapt on a flight to Bucharest and brought Ellie to her new home.

After months of delays, Ellie's first three weeks in Britain passed quickly. Harriet had taken time off work, as much as she was allowed, and had secured the written agreement of her editor that she would cover predominantly domestic stories at least for the next year. Everyone who knew about Harriet's situation had been compassionate, her employers included. They'd all seen the news reports, after all. Colin meanwhile had handed in his notice, but planned to contribute all he could to the family income by tutoring maths in the evenings. These were sacrifices, of course, but under the circumstances, hardly felt worthy of the term.

Given the environment in which Ellie had so far grown up, both Harriet and Colin had prepared themselves for the worst kind of difficulties. But her transition was nothing like they'd imagined. There would be plenty of times in the coming

year when they would marvel at the apparent ease with which she'd settled, at how eager she was to fit in. Despite the barriers of language and culture she was, fundamentally, the sweetest girl, a delight to everyone who encountered her.

It was a time of endless discovery for Ellie. Harriet would watch and remember every revelation: the look on her face the first time she tasted jelly and ice cream, closing her eyes as if to intensify the pleasure. The way she would sink into bed and stroke the duvet against her cheek, having never felt anything so warm and soft. She discovered music in the form of Colin's CD collection, which she'd spend hours rifling through like a puppy eager to play with everything in its path. Motown became her music of choice and anyone entering the house for weeks over that first autumn would be bombarded by a series of toe-tappers from the Temptations or Stevie Wonder.

Contrary to all the warnings about low IQ and developmental delays, the pace at which Ellie learnt English vindicated Colin's view that their daughter was a very bright girl indeed. He read to her every night, starting with picture books for younger children, such as *The Tale of Peter Rabbit*, before progressing to *Alice's Adventures in Wonderland* and *The Worst Witch*. *A Bear Called Paddington* was her favourite and she'd home in on the part where Mrs Brown said: 'In London, everyone is different, and that means anyone can fit in.'

She made friends quickly and parties followed, then sleepovers, from which Harriet would collect her the next morning and be told by parents how good she was, how polite, how *lovely*. The thing everyone loved most was hearing Ellie laugh. She seemed to need only to look at Colin for him to set her off by pulling a funny face; these tickled her

so much that she would release loud, hysterical peals, which rendered anyone nearby helpless to resist joining in.

'It's as if the poor love had never laughed before in her life,' Colin's mother had said.

Harriet would cling to these memories, but could never claim that every minute was like that.

The first time she tried to persuade Ellie into the bath, the little girl refused, backing away until her spine pressed against the wall and shaking her head violently, convinced that *this was it*: the thing that finally proved this new place was too good to be true. Having spent her entire life being washed with freezing water in the orphanage, it took months before she was fully confident that the shower at Chalk View would be warm, that it wasn't some trick that would leave her bones rattling from cold for hours afterwards. The hoarding went on for months too. Biscuits and other food items were constantly going missing from the cupboards and later found under pillows or in wardrobes.

Then there was the issue of Tabitha. On the plane from Bucharest, neither Harriet nor Colin had any idea of the drama that had happened only a few weeks earlier with Ellie's friend. They assumed that she was exactly where they'd been told she'd be: with a family in Bologna.

But even before Ellie could speak English, they'd realised that something hadn't worked out – and for many months afterwards, *Tabitha* would crop up in every other conversation. It would be the name she'd whisper before bedtime and cry out in her dreams. Ellie was obsessed and Colin worried that she'd never settle until they could reassure her in some way.

Yet when Harriet's friend Andrei made enquiries with the

orphanage the message was far from reassuring. The police had not picked her up. She had not returned. As far as they knew, none of the authorities had any idea where she was. None of this was unusual, nor especially surprising. It was just another child who had slipped off the radar in a time of chaos and change. She had to be *somewhere*, naturally – but she might as well have disappeared off the face of the earth.

Then there was the day Andrei and his wife Gabriella came to dinner. Harriet and Colin had enjoyed the couple's hospitality on two occasions during visits to Romania while the adoption was going through. Wanting to return the favour when the Rucarenus were next in London, she invited them over to sample her Beef Wellington.

They'd had a genial evening full of shared jokes and the odd political discussion, until the conversation turned to the recent ban on overseas adoptions from Romania, which had been driven by irregularities and corruption.

'Yours has been a success story,' Andrei had told Harriet and Colin. 'Nobody could ever suggest otherwise. But the same cannot be said for everyone. The focus now has to be trying to support vulnerable families so that children from orphanages can be reunited with their loved ones – as well as reducing the number of youngsters entering the system in the first place. In cases where they can't return home, the aim is to build new families by fostering in-country adoption. You do understand, don't you?'

'Of course,' she said quietly. And she absolutely did, as strange and unsettling as it was to recognise that.

In the run-up to the adoption, neither she nor Colin had doubted that bringing Ellie to the UK was the right thing to do. How could it not be when they'd been driven by pure

love and a desire to help a child who otherwise would have faced a bleak future?

And yet, during the course of the conversation with Andrei that night, a view formed that existed in parallel to her own actions: that the future of Romania's children couldn't be in overseas adoption. It had to lie within the country itself.

'Does it make me a hypocrite to say I agree with you?' she asked Andrei. 'Yet, at the same time I wouldn't change a thing.'

'Of course not,' he replied. 'You two did something magnificent for Ellie. Nothing is ever going to change that. But the solution we need to work on cannot involve simply removing children from the country. The real victory would be to keep our children safe and happy within Romania.'

By now, Ellie was used to Harriet and Colin's dinner parties. She enjoyed creeping downstairs in her pyjamas, persuading the grown-ups to watch a dance routine, or let her throw the dice in Trivial Pursuit. Now, she appeared at the door, smiling hopefully as Colin beckoned her in.

'Hello, trouble,' he grinned, as Harriet enveloped her in a hug. 'You should be fast asleep by now, but come and say hello. Andrei, you remember Ellie. Gabriella, this is our daughter.'

'Hello again, Ellie! How wonderful to see you!' Andrei exclaimed. He hadn't seen her since she'd moved to the UK. He turned to his wife and, in the light of her minimal English, translated Colin's words. He spoke a language that Ellie hadn't heard spoken in a mother tongue for quite some time.

Her reaction was as quick and devastating as cardiac shock. Her cheeks blanched and her frame seemed to freeze. And at some point in the conversation that followed between the

Romanian couple, everyone in the room became aware that something was wrong.

'Is everything all right, darling?' Harriet asked.

Panic showed in the whites of Ellie's eyes. Colin took her hand and Andrei realised that the source of the problem was *him*.

'I ... I was just introducing Ellie to Gabriella,' he explained, before turning to the little girl and adding hopefully: 'I'm sorry if I gave you a fright. My wife doesn't speak English yet, not like you. I hear you're a star student.'

Ellie wouldn't speak and in the absence of an explanation, Gabriella turned to her husband to seek one.

'Ce se întâmplă?' she asked, perplexed. *What's going on?*

Ellie fled from the room and raced up the stairs, until she was hammering on the door of Mrs Heathcote's bedroom, demanding to be let in. Harriet went after her, but Colin's mother insisted she'd handle it and gently shooed her away, telling her she should go and enjoy the rest of her evening. But nobody could by then. They passed two hours of polite chat and disappointing cheesecake, before the Rucarenus left amidst a blizzard of apologies and promises to keep in touch.

'What did she say?' Colin whispered to his mother afterwards, as Harriet hovered at the door. Mrs Heathcote was lying propped up by pillows on her candlewick bedspread, the television on low, with Ellie curled into the dip of her arm, fast asleep.

'It was when she heard the language,' she whispered back. 'She thought they were here to take her back.'

Chapter 35

Ellie

Colette opens the door to her office with the air of a latter-day Mary Poppins. Straight-backed and with an efficient smile that gives the impression that she's here to sort out all this fuss.

'Good afternoon, Ellie. How are you?' she asks, as if I last saw her yesterday, not over two years ago.

'Fine,' I say automatically, as she closes the door. 'Apart from being a gibbering wreck, obviously.'

I spent time choosing the right outfit before I left, aiming to look fashionable, but with optimum levels of comfort. Now I'm here, damp rings are visible under each arm of my softspun top and there is blood on my trousers from the hangnail I tore off on the journey. It was every bit as bad as I knew it would be, despite Dad's efforts to distract me by chatting. When he ran out of steam, he switched on the midday radio show just as the presenter announced, 'Today we'll be discussing the House of Lords, pancreatitis and sex shops on the A1.' He turned it off again.

Colette invites me to sit, which I do, in a chair that is new

and more comfortable than the last. She sits opposite me and crosses her legs. She's wearing glossy brogues, wide-leg trousers and a pale blouse buttoned up to the spot where her clavicles meet. The ensemble has a slightly masculine edge that counterbalances the soft features of her face and the swish of her honey-coloured bob.

'You certainly don't look like a gibbering wreck,' she says. 'That's a lovely outfit.'

I lift both arms in the air. 'The sweat rings set it off a treat, don't they? They're a special, exclusive embellishment available to agoraphobics, nervous wrecks and general wet lettuces.'

'That's a lot of self-deprecation in one sentence, Ellie.'

'It feels rather justified at the moment,' I say.

She opens my file. 'So . . .'

'Did you finish *The West Wing*?' I ask.

She looks up. 'What?'

'Last time I was here you were making your way through the box set.'

'Oh. Yes, actually.' She looks down again.

'What did you think of the ending?'

She tilts her chin as she looks at me. 'Ellie, shall we get started?'

'Okay. Though, I ought to say . . . about the last time I saw you. Sorry for leaving so abruptly.'

'It's quite all right. I went shopping instead.'

My mouth parts.

'Just kidding.' She smiles. 'And *I* ought to say: well done for coming here. I know how difficult it is. Now why don't you tell me what's been happening?'

It's Guy I tell her about first. How we met. How I have

growing feelings for him. And that, while I know how attracted he is to me – he doesn't even attempt to hide it – I am painfully aware that the thing that is stopping this from evolving into a proper relationship is my agoraphobia.

I feel self-conscious, like a teenager writing to a problem page. So I also tell her about the growth of my Instagram business, the one area of my life that is going well. I don't want her to think I'm a complete loser. She asks about how my anxiety is currently manifesting and I tell her about the day Gertie ran outside, then Guy attempting to take me to London. And the nightmares.

'Are they about the orphanage?'

I nod.

'Can you tell me what happens in them?'

I feel my teeth grind as I regret even mentioning them.

'Ellie?'

'They're predominantly about Tabitha.'

She doesn't need to look at her notes. 'Your friend.'

'Yes. I hadn't realised I'd told you about her.'

'Only briefly, same as everything to do with your past. It was very obvious how important she was to you.' There's a pause, a held breath as I sense Colette is working out which way to take this conversation. 'Why don't you just tell me a little bit about her, Ellie? What was she like?'

There are dozens of things I could say about Tabitha. That she was tough and generous and loyal. That her presence was the only bearable thing about the place. But that ultimately she ran away to live a life I can't even bear to imagine. The heat of tears begins to press behind my eyes.

'Ellie, I want you to know that nobody is going to try and make you talk about something you don't want to,' she says

urgently. 'Last time we saw each other, I felt it would help to explore these aspects of your life. But I don't *ever* want us to reach the stage we did last time. If you feel as though it might cause you so much distress that it becomes impossible to carry on, then we just won't do it. It's as simple as that. We won't even go there.'

I become aware that my hangnail is bleeding again. 'Do you think there are ways of helping me without raking over my past? Without me talking about the orphanage or Tabitha or anything at all to do with that?'

'Absolutely,' she says, with an enthusiasm that doesn't match her expression. 'CBT is very effective and we can focus on that to get you out of the house. The last thing I'd want to do is scare you off. Then, *if* in the future you feel you can revisit some exposure therapy, we'll do so. But slowly. Or possibly even never. The point is, I will be guided entirely by you. There is no pressure.'

I don't say it out loud, but there absolutely is. I know it. If I don't get myself sorted out quickly, this thing with Guy won't last. It already feels fragile enough for me to fear losing him, just like so many others I've ever cared about.

Chapter 36

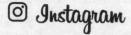 **Instagram**

EnglishCountryGardenista

690
posts

58.8k
followers

939
following

ELLIE HEATHCOTE

I devoted some time to organising the potting shed today and think Marie Kondo is on to something when she says that tidying up can change your life. I'm the worst person for seeing something online and feeling I just have to buy it, hence all the unnecessary clutter that had been stuffed in my little space. So I threw out the bits that didn't bring me joy (three broken hosepipe adaptors, some rusty pruners and an old propagator). The result is a lovely area in which to sit, have a brew and contemplate my next gardening job. Do any of you have a potting shed? I'd love to know what you get up to in it. Clean answers only please 😊 #pottingshed #thisgirldigs

#gardensofinstagram   #EnglishCountryGardenista
#englishcountrygardens   #shedsofinstagram   #gardener
#gardening #garden #gardenlife #flowers #plants #gardens
#nature #gardendesign #growyourown #gardeninspiration
#instagarden #gardenlove #growyourownfood

My sister's face appears at the door. 'What the … Why are you sitting in the shed?'

'I'm relaxing. It's really nice,' I reply.

'Jesus, Ellie. Try a spa break, it'd blow your mind. Why would you sit here when your house is four metres away and has a sofa and well-stocked fridge?'

'I'm going to get back to work now anyway,' I say, standing up. 'You can join in if you like?'

'You're okay – I've just had a manicure.'

'When?'

'2017. Oh, come inside for a cup of tea. I don't want to hang about out here unless the sun comes out again.'

I follow her inside with Gertie trotting behind, and flick on the kettle.

'How did the first session with your shrink go?' she asks.

'Good,' I say, though my heart starts flapping like a rolodex every time I think about it. 'How's Jakob?'

She sighs dreamily. 'Absolutely lovely, so something's bound to go wrong soon.'

Lucy's new love interest is a documentary film maker from Norway and, at thirty, is older than her. They met in the fancy bread shop she goes to on Saturday mornings, to buy the cinnamon swirls she then spends the afternoon attempting to run off. He seems very keen even though the first text she sent him was an accident and included a link to Ted Bundy's

Wikipedia entry after she'd Googled it while watching the Netflix documentary.

'How long has he lived in the UK?' I ask.

'Eleven years. He moved here for the climate.'

'Is he a masochist?' I ask, glancing outside at the clouds.

'No, an asthmatic. He's from Tromsø, which is beautiful but way inside the Arctic Circle and the cold was causing flare-ups. His doctor actually advised him to move to Spain.'

'Lucky for you that he didn't. So he's definitely not married?'

'Nope.'

'Nor a drunk, a drug addict, a psychopath, or—' The hum of an engine cuts off my sentence. I glance at my sister in panic as an irrational thought swoops through me. This could be Guy again. Lucy's sixth sense kicks in.

'Ooh. Is this Mister Loverman?' She stands and looks out of the window. 'Well, there's a man walking up the path and he's rather lovely ... No, hang on. No. This isn't the bloke I've seen on Instagram.'

I work out that it's Jamie before I even open the door, at which point Gertie bounds over and starts jumping up and down like she's on a piece of string. 'Down!' I command. She ignores me completely.

'Oh, she's fine,' he laughs, picking up the dog as her tail thrashes and she whimpers with pleasure. 'Were you expecting someone else?'

'No, come in, I've just put the kettle on.'

Jamie looks different today. I can't put my finger on why because when I deconstruct his features they're the same as always. The broad shoulders and thick waistline that suggests a hearty appetite and no interest in getting up before sunrise to do burpees. The dusty hair that is vaguely unruly, though

I hesitate to use that word as it implies he even attempts to keep it in check. He has definitely caught the sun over the summer though; Grandma would've described him as *brown as a berry* and I make a mental note to remind him about the importance of SPF at some point.

I can see Lucy checking him out as they exchange introductions, before he lowers his thick lashes and says, 'You know, if you're busy I won't stop. I haven't even got a delivery – I was just passing and wanted to mention something to you.'

'Oh, what is it?'

'Well, you said the other day that you felt bad relying on your parents to walk Gertie. And I was thinking: I wouldn't mind doing it. She's a fantastic little dog. I'd love it.'

'That is *so* nice of you,' gushes Lucy, sliding a meaningful look in my direction.

'It is,' I agree. 'But Dad walked her earlier. I don't think her short legs would withstand another bout of exercise in one day.'

'Ah, right. I'll leave you to it then.'

'Oh, don't do that.' Lucy leaps up. 'Stay and have a drink with us. Ellie?'

'Like I say, the kettle's boiled,' I tell him.

'Oh, please. The sun *is* over the yardarm,' Lucy says. It is five past five.

'Sorry but I haven't got any wine. The supermarket shop isn't due until tomorrow.'

'G&T then,' Lucy grins.

'All Jamie wanted was—'

'I can mix a couple of cocktails if you like,' he offers. I turn to look at him, surprised. 'I told you I was a bartender once. It was my first job. Awful place with a manager who could've been running North Korea, but it did teach me a few things.'

'Are you basically telling me you could rival Tom Cruise in *Cocktail*?' I ask.

'That might be a stretch but I can whip something up if you've got a couple of spirits and some odds and ends in the fridge?'

He asks for cranberry juice, ginger ale and angostura bitters, none of which I have. But I manage half a bottle of gin, sugar to make syrup and a lime that, he assures us, 'can make anything taste good'. Lucy pops to Mum and Dad's house and returns with a cocktail shaker and crystal glasses, setting them down in front of Jamie.

'I can't wait for this. Are you going to fling that thing over your shoulder?'

'I'm not that good. In fact, you might want to take cover,' he suggests.

He picks up a bottle, balances it on the back of his knuckles and flips it, catching it with the same hand in time to pour the liquid into the cocktail shaker.

'Oh *come on*, you clearly are that good,' my sister exclaims gleefully.

Except, he isn't. Not really. But that's what's so funny about the whole thing. There is something faintly impressive but predominantly hilarious about the flair moves Jamie goes on to *almost* achieve. He rolls, he throws, he flings – and pulls it off not because his moves are smooth, but because they're the opposite. Our favourite tricks are not the perfect ones, but those that leave him scrambling after the dropped cocktail shaker or chasing the dog when she trots away with a quarter of lime he inadvertently catapulted across the counter. At the end of these theatricals, Lucy is wiping tears of laughter away, as Jamie declares the result to be a 'gimlet', which he garnishes with evening primrose petals from the garden. However he made it, it is delicious – silky and sharp all at once.

'Bloody good work,' Lucy says approvingly. 'It's not a *quick* process though, is it? You must've ended up with one enormous queue of girls waiting to be served when you were a bartender. Or was that the idea?'

'I was way too shy to chat up girls, hence resorting to acrobatics. Though, given the quality of them, you might wonder how I ever lost my virginity . . .'

'How long have you worked for this garden centre then?' Lucy asks.

'Three months. It's only really to fill in the gaps in freelance work.'

'Jamie is a children's book illustrator,' I explain. 'He's like J. K. Rowling in Sweden.'

He snorts and shakes his head. 'Hardly. Though I do have a bit of news on the books front.'

It turns out that the agent representing the author – Ulrika Sjöblad – has sold the book to publishers in six countries, including the UK. It will hit British shelves in time for Christmas and there is talk of a book tour in Germany. He's been told it might involve a speech or two.

'In *German*?' I ask.

'I do hope not. It's stressful enough in a language I actually know. Public speaking isn't really my thing.'

'Everyone feels like that in the beginning,' Lucy tells him. 'I used to hate giving lectures.'

'Come off it, Lucy. You've always been a big show-off,' I say sceptically.

'That's where you're wrong. I was worried sick every time I had to do it at first, but it gets easier – just like everything if you do it often enough. And before that, you just feel the fear and go for it anyway. Otherwise none of us would ever do anything worth doing.'

The way she glances at me makes this feel like a lecture, especially as I know Colette's homework tasks are sitting on a sheet next to my bed, entirely uncompleted.

'Excuse me a minute,' I say, heading to the bathroom. When I return I find Jamie alone in the kitchen, dropping the strawberries I picked from the garden earlier into the blender.

'Your sister has adjourned to the patio now the sun has come out,' he says, screwing on the lid before setting the machine going.

'What have we got here?' I ask, raising my voice above the hum.

'Strawberry Daiquiri.' He opens it up. 'I've gone easy on the booze though. It's lethal if you don't – so sweet you hardly notice the alcohol.'

'This is turning into quite the party,' I say, pushing my glass towards him.

'Oh no, it has to be a clean one,' he insists. I watch as he runs my glass under the tap, before drying it with a tea towel and pouring in the contents of the blender.

'No decor on this one?' I ask.

'Not even a paper umbrella.'

I take a sip and lower my glass, realising his eyes have softened on my face. Warmth spreads from my neck to my cheeks and I wonder if it's the alcohol or some vague nostalgia from our school days. He continues to hold my gaze beyond the point at which I can pretend it isn't happening.

'Pip,' he says, out of nowhere.

'Wh . . . what?'

He reaches out and his fingertip hovers an inch from my cheek before he presses it gently against my skin. My eyes half-close sleepily and, when he withdraws, my heart seems to expand into the space between us.

'You had a strawberry pip on your cheek,' he says, holding up his finger to show me the evidence.

I blink. 'Right.'

Lucy appears at the door. 'Just wondered . . . oh, sorry. I'll leave you to it.'

'We're coming now,' I say, straightening up and following her out.

But this, it turns out, is only the start.

Jamie decides to leave the car and, as the sun sets behind the cherry tree, the rest of the evening unrolls into itself. We order pizza and make more cocktails. We play Primal Scream, Simon & Garfunkel and a dozen other forgotten albums. Jamie attempts to teach Gertie to 'sit' and fails miserably. We start an impromptu pop quiz – Guess the Intro – and I sweep to a decisive victory that's no less satisfying for knowing that Lucy is only twenty-four and therefore files Girls Aloud under 'classical'. We talk about politics and books and apart from when the subject of Grandma comes up, which makes me feel a bit wistful, it is predominantly an evening of rolling, helpless laughter.

When it finally ends in the early hours – with Lucy disappearing to her room across the garden and Jamie's taxi arriving too quickly for goodbyes – I close the door and start to clear away the mess. As I pick up the chopping board and tip the remainders of strawberry stalks into the compost bin, it occurs to me with a surge of happiness that Jamie has become something that I haven't had in a very long time: A friend.

Chapter 37

Having a sex life again has been a revelation, hedonistic in ways that I'd entirely forgotten were possible. I love how alive my body feels when I'm in bed with Guy, as well as the physical yearning I feel in anticipation of it. That said, things have changed since I was last doing it regularly – even if I have only endured years, not decades, of chastity. I'd watched *Fleabag* and worked out that sex these days is altogether more edgy than it used to be.

Despite this, when Guy slaps me playfully on the bottom midway through what began as a tender love-making session, my body tenses. At first I wonder if it's an accident, then he does it again: a sharp little wallop with the flat of his palm that makes my flesh wobble. For the rest of the time he's inside me, my brain works overtime, questioning if there's something wrong with me for not finding this a turn-on. After all, it's what people do in a post-*Fifty Shades* world.

'That was amazing, wasn't it?' Guy says afterwards, as he curls me into his arm.

'It was!' I say, politely.

I get up to go to the bathroom and splash water in my

eyes, feeling oddly empty. I decide to jump in the shower and when I emerge a few minutes later I find him propped up in bed, the swell of his muscular forearm behind his head. He lifts up the quilt and invites me to snuggle in. When he kisses me on the temple, it releases a swarm of relief in me that I wish would go on and on. But a thought pierces through me and I realise what the issue is. It's not the bum-smacking. It's something far bigger than that – and for as long as I fail to address it, things are never going to progress as they should between Guy and me.

'I need to tell you something,' I say.

'Sure,' he replies. He looks at my expression and something in it makes him anxious. He pushes himself up and swallows. 'What is it, Ellie?'

I look him directly in the eyes. 'I'm seeing a therapist. I've got agoraphobia. That's why you and I never go out anywhere and only ever meet here.'

He blows a long trail of air out of his mouth, inflating his cheeks. 'Oh, thank God,' he chuckles. 'Sorry, I was convinced you were going to tell me you had an STD then. Go on, please. Tell me all about your therapist.'

'Uh . . . okay. Well, it's going well,' I continue. 'She thinks it won't be long before I'm back to my usual self.'

He nods. 'That's good. Really good to hear.'

I don't know what to say then. His reaction feels subdued, but then that's probably the best I could've hoped for when I've worried for weeks that this revelation would cause him to leap up and run out of the house.

'So we should arrange to go out at some point, don't you think? Maybe I could come to your place or meet your friends, or colleagues from the studio?'

'Yeah, we'll do that. Why not?' he says, leaning in to kiss me. Before his lips make contact, I pull back.

'Is there a reason why we only ever get together on Tuesdays and Thursdays?'

He shrugs. 'Of course not. It's just work and other commitments. It means I know not to arrange anything else on those days. It's not a problem is it?'

'No. Not at all,' I say, because, for now at least, I'm in no position to suggest an alternative.

I dread the second session with Colette for reasons that go beyond my having to get there. But what's bothering me more than anything – the fact that I haven't done my homework – is not the first subject she homes in on.

'You've been having nightmares again,' she says, reading my sheet.

'They're not unusual when I'm feeling stressed.'

'About Tabitha?' I nod silently. 'Would you like to try talking about her again?'

I bite the inside of my mouth. 'Okay.'

I take this as her cue to fire questions at me, to thrash out what I remember from when I was a little girl and shove it down my throat until it comes out of my ears in a sane-shaped bubble. But she doesn't say anything. For a while we just sit until I can't bear it and start talking just to fill the silence.

'She was the only thing that kept me going at the orphanage. She was my friend, though at the time I don't think any of us really knew what the word meant. I worked out that she was being abused by a caretaker at the orphanage, or perhaps I've only worked that out since, I'm not entirely sure. She was supposed to be adopted, by an Italian couple, but it fell through. Then just before I came to the UK, she ran away.'

'Do you know what happened to her?'

I shake my head. 'She was never found by the authorities. But Mum found a picture recently. It was published in a French magazine about a year after I last saw her. She was homeless, living in the tunnels under Bucharest train station. Nobody knows what happened to her after that.'

Colette takes this in and seems to think carefully about her next sentence. 'You were coming to see me for a long time before you mentioned Tabitha.'

'Yes.'

'Why do you think that was?'

'Because she's part of my past and I can't talk about my past. I stopped a long time ago.'

'But you were still wondering what happened to her? She's been on your mind all this time?'

'Yes,' I confess. 'I was obsessed with her when I first came to England. At first, I imagined her finding some happy family like the one I had. But as I got older, I worked out how unlikely that was. Now I'm an adult, it's worse. I know what happens to little kids who run away and have to survive on the streets. They don't end up like Hansel and Gretel with a happy ending. She'd be lucky to survive at all.'

'But you don't know that, Ellie. This awful, parallel life exists solely in your imagination.'

I look up at her, with a stab of annoyance. 'Colette, I don't know how much you know about Romania in the 1990s, but I'm not being overly pessimistic. Do you want to know what I really feel about whatever happened to her? *Guilt*. For getting what I got, when she got nothing. That's what makes all this,' I tap the side of my head, 'so frustrating. I have no right to be messed up. There's nothing you can say to me that will persuade me otherwise: I have no right at all.'

She takes off her glasses and leans on her elbows. 'That's not how it works, Ellie. You already know that. Everyone carries different-shaped scars. These are yours. And whether you realise it or not, you're making progress.'

'Well, I haven't done my homework,' I say, feeling suddenly contrary.

'Which part?'

'The part that said I had to leave the garden for a short, accompanied walk.'

'Did you attempt it?' I don't answer, which is an answer in itself. 'But you managed to come here.'

'Only because I had to. My dad virtually bundled me in the car and put his foot down before I had a chance to tell him I'd changed my mind.'

'I know it's hard, Ellie. But don't forget you can take someone with you on the first walk.'

I don't think she realises how little that would help. The mere mention of a family member coming along would have them falling over themselves to be *the one*, then they'd make an enormous fuss throughout. Faced with the glare of their loving but suffocating gaze, I am convinced I'd prefer the unthinkable: to do this on my own. The question is, am I even capable?

Chapter 38

Something about the second session with Colette leaves my skin crawling. I can't decide if it was talking about Tabitha or the idea of embarking on regular walks that keeps pounding me with waves of anxiety. Either way, I am on the verge of adding a pack of Marlboro Lights to my trolley during the online supermarket shop, when Mum appears at my door, carrying a bag from her favourite deli.

'Why don't you come over and eat with us tonight?' she suggests. 'I picked up a few treats.'

'But you and Dad normally go for a drink with the Miltons on a Thursday. I hope this isn't on my account?' She doesn't respond immediately. 'Mum, I'm *fine*.'

'I'm sure you are. Just ... is everything going all right with Colette? You seem a little ... I don't know.'

'I'm not a little anything,' I insist.

'All right then,' she replies, lifting her hand in surrender. 'You know where I am if you need me.'

The beauty of client confidentiality is that I don't have to tell my parents about the homework. I could easily inform them that Colette set me the task of bingeing on Danish porn and Special Brew and they'd never be able to confirm anything to the contrary.

I can't stop thinking about it though. The homework stays at the front of my mind for the next few days, including when I'm in bed with Guy, which doesn't make ideal conditions for intimacy. Still, normal service has been resumed on that front: the moment I suspected he was contemplating slapping me again I performed a kind of stunt roll across the bed. He didn't try it again.

I've also been trying out Mindfulness techniques, inspired by Colette's enthusiasm for the practice and a post in which Guy was posing in front of a sunset in a small pair of yellow shorts, with the caption: 'Yesterday is history, tomorrow is a mystery, but today is a gift. That is why it is called present.' It's unquestionably one of his most eloquent, so I casually forwarded it to Lucy to make sure she'd seen it, then sent her a text pretending it was an accident.

As ever, the only thing that seems to stop my brain skipping from one useless, non-specific worry to another is being in the garden. My dahlias have frothed into a vivid pink display, while the delphiniums are in high bloom, their tall spikes of pink and blue rising above the flower beds. But the unquestionable star of the show is the sunflower Oscar and I planted in April. I've been meticulously fertilizing and protecting it from pests and now it rises over the other flowers in the garden, its imperial yellow petals fluttering like the mane of a lion. When he turns up this week he rushes straight over, his eyes wide as he gasps: 'Is that *mine*?'

We spend some time taking photos of him with it, while he entertains me with his repertoire of jokes.

'What do you call a man with a banana on his head?' he asks.

'I don't know, what *do* you call a man with a banana on his head?'

'Poo head.' He bursts into peals of hysterical laughter. This is typical of Oscar's material, which always involves a punchline that includes 'fart' and/or 'poo', and ideally makes no sense whatsoever.

'Brilliant,' I say. 'Your delivery is certainly spot on.'

By the time Mandy has finished cleaning and he trots off with a bag of tomatoes, my mood has lifted a little. It's a feeling directly attuned to the sunshine on my skin, soil under my nails and also, I must admit, the image of Oscar's face as he gawped at his sunflower. But as I head inside and I catch a glimpse of Colette's homework sheet, I feel an intense stab of resentment.

It feels like an imposter in my bedroom, in my world. Why would I put myself through this, when I've already got everything I need right here? For the first time since I returned to Colette it occurs to me in a fully realised form that *I don't need to*. I'm a grown woman. I can do what I want. As soon as I have recognised that the best course of action is simply to tell Colette that I'm just not going to do it, I feel empowered to the point of elation.

I take a deep breath and pick up my phone, to discover a new text from Guy.

Just been invited to a family wedding next month. Fancy being my plus one? X

I lower myself onto the bed and read it again. When I'd said I wanted to go out with him, I'd expected a couple of hours in the pub. Not a *wedding*. The thought that he wants to introduce me to his friends and family fills me with an equal measure of happiness and horror. I throw down the phone and pick up my iPad, perching on the edge of the sofa as I Google two words – 'occasion wear' – and watch as the results filter onto my screen.

Oh, my heart ...

The designer gowns are divine, but even those within a high-street budget are glorious: silk halter-necks, asymmetric maxi dresses, elegant jumpsuits in every colour and fabric. I click on a long green dress with a wrap waist and a fluid pleated skirt. I imagine myself stepping into it and zipping up the back, twirling in front of the mirror before Guy arrives to pick me up. The thought evokes a scene from every American teen movie: Girl in a prom dress. Boy in a tux. Standing in a hallway anticipating not just one night, but a moment in time, after which everything would change. I snort at the silly comparison, then realise that my heart feels so full it might shatter.

Chapter 39

The star jasmine plant I ordered yesterday is standing at my doorstep in a plastic pot, supported by a five-foot trellis.

'How gorgeous,' I exclaim.

'Must be my new aftershave.' Jamie pokes his head out from behind the plant to hand me the signature machine.

'Very funny,' I say, signing my name. 'God, it's huge. I wasn't expecting it to be so mature.'

'Do you want to send it back?'

'No, I love it. I just need to work out where I'm going to put it.'

He hesitates then says: 'How are things with your therapist?'

'Oh, fine,' I reply breezily. 'Yeah, pretty good. Pretty ... fine.'

He nods. 'Pretty fine is better than pretty awful.'

'Yeah.' I force a smile, then immediately cave in. 'Urgh, all right, I'm having a nightmare. Why don't you come in and I'll tell you all about it?'

We sit at the kitchen table while he throws a ball for Gertie and I fill him in on the first two sessions and my wedding invitation.

'Sounds like it's pretty serious between you and this guy these days then?'

'Well, I want it to be,' I say. 'I guess it's hard to believe that someone like him would be interested in me some-times though.'

'Don't be daft. *Someone like you*,' he mimics, shaking his head. 'Anyway, if he's invited you to a wedding he's obviously more than interested.'

'Yes, I hope so,' I say, feeling my spirits lift. 'So, any solutions?'

'I hate to say it, but you're probably just going to have to . . .' His voice trails off as if his mind is elsewhere.

'Jamie?'

'Sorry.'

'I just need to get on with it, don't I?'

'I was trying to think of a way to sound more sympathetic.'

'I don't want sympathy,' I tell him.

'Then yes. Get on with the walk.'

I twist my bracelet around my wrist and look up. 'Will you come with me?'

Only as he considers this do I realise how much I want him to be the one. He lowers his eyes and I am transfixed by his lashes, how long they are, the way they frame his face.

'Okay,' he says.

I inhale sharply and smile. 'Great. Maybe tomorrow?'

But he fixes the amber flecks of his eyes on me. 'I'm not available tomorrow.'

'Oh. All right.'

'Let's do it now. Come on.'

He reaches out and touches my fingers. His feel warm and strong and slightly rough. I squeeze them without even thinking about it and he responds with a softening of his features, before standing up.

He leads me by the hand to the door. I think about breathing exercises. I think about anti-anxiety techniques. I think about a sentence that plays on repeat in my brain: *This is no big deal, really.*

'How far are we going to go?' I ask, when we're outside and in front of the gate.

'Let's just see how the mood takes us,' he shrugs. 'I reckon the best approach is to not think about where you're going or how long we'll be. Just put one foot in front of the other. Hey, I've got an idea. Have you got any headphones?'

I run back for the ones I keep in my sideboard, return and hand them to him. He plugs them into his phone, passes me one bud and tucks the other into his own ear. Then he scrolls through his music as we walk down the path again, to the gate. He presses play.

Nina Simone. 'Feeling Good'.

We'd listened to it on the night of the cocktails and pop quiz, to its deep, bluesy vocals that soar like a magnificent, pitch-perfect cry. He takes my hand again. My palm is slick with sweat and I'm self-conscious about that but not enough to let go. I look up at him and am struck quite suddenly by how physically big he is. The simple registering of this fact, of his broad shoulders and thick forearms, is the most reassuring sensation. But I still can't move when he takes his first step through the gateway. Our arms stretch out comically in the gap between us and my earphone pops out until he moves back, allowing me to quickly replace it.

'You'll be okay,' he says. I nod. All I can do is go with him.

We are soon on the path outside Chalk View. Then we are

walking across the meadow, our ankles swishing through the long grass with a quivering sun overhead. Our pace is neither slow nor fast, but it is decisive enough to maintain a steady momentum. We don't stop to look back. Heat collects in the creases behind my knees and there are moments when I'm so aware of my thrashing heart that it feels like it could break my eardrums. But as the space grows between us and home, I try not to think about my physical self beyond the press of Jamie's hand in mine: the warmth of his skin, the strength of his grasp, his fingertips against my knuckles.

At times I feel as though I'm the protagonist in a movie, in which the fields and the sky and swaying wildflowers are all just scenery, a background. This thought doesn't distress me though. To my surprise, none of it does. And by the time we have walked to the kissing gate at the edge of the woods, and taken the bridleway that leads up the steep escarpment, I realise I am okay. I really am okay.

We keep walking.

We talk about Billie Holiday and the ginger ale his mum used to make. I tell him about the time I came up here with Lucy and she climbed a tree then couldn't get down until I ran all the way home and got Dad. We discuss our school days and how once, when he was fifteen, he bumped into an old teacher while she was buying a bra in Debenhams and didn't know where to put himself. We talk so much and walk so much that before I have even registered it, we have completed a loop of the woods and have re-emerged in the field in front of Chalk View, with the red bricks of the house in sight and Gertie yapping at the gate.

'Hello, my girl!' I laugh and my steps quicken until I'm there, I'm home, being jumped on and snuggled by my dog, who appears to think she hasn't seen me for a week. I stand up and find myself looking at Jamie's chest.

'What just happened?' I ask. 'And why doesn't it always feel that easy?'

'It will,' he smiles. 'It *is* easy.'

'Well, you made it feel that way.' A bolt of heat surges to my cheeks.

'I can't take credit for that. That was all you, Ellie. You did that.' I blink, taking in that fact.

'Same time tomorrow?' he asks.

'Great,' I say, as he heads towards his van, and it occurs to me that he clearly was never busy tomorrow after all.

Chapter 40

The following day it rains in the way that it only can in summer if you live in the UK. Slanting, horizontal drizzle that seeps into every pore of your skin and gives the impression that it's simply never going to stop. I foolishly assume that this means the walk with Jamie is off, and my relief is followed by disappointment in myself, a feeling that if I don't commit to stepping outside today, then what happened yesterday will never be repeated.

I need not have worried. He turns up at 4pm as promised, with a large bag, from which he pulls out two pairs of waterproof trousers.

'Where did you get these?'

'My cousin John is a Scout leader. I knew he'd have masses of this stuff and I didn't want you coming up with any excuses. Here you go.'

He throws me a pair, which I wrestle over my jeans, while Gertie barks in alarm, convinced a Gore-tex monster is attacking my legs.

'They are a bit over the top, aren't they?' Jamie laughs as we head to the door. 'We look like we're preparing for a trip to the moon.'

'I might as well be going to the moon the way I feel,' I say.

'Ah, you'll be okay. Shall we take the dog with us?'

I look down. 'Should we go for a walk, Gertie?' Her ears prick up and she yaps. 'This is a big moment.'

'Come on then.' He grins decisively. 'Grab your poo bags and let's do this.'

I dress Gertie in her own waterproof coat, step outside holding her lead, and she tugs me along to the gate. 'What are we listening to today, DJ?'

He takes out some ear phones. 'I put together a mixtape.'

I bat my eyelids jokingly at the romantic implications. 'A *mixtape*?'

'I mean, no. A playlist,' he squirms. 'Just a few songs to ease the pain.'

'Of course. I didn't . . . you know, *mean* anything. Obviously.'

'No. Of course not.'

I reach for his hand and we step out of the gate. In the immediate seconds after this, the sky seems to swell and wane. Then he presses play and Gertie pulls at the lead as we start to walk.

We make our way up the hill, as Jamie's *not-a-mixtape* unrolls into 'She's A Star' by James and 'Here Comes The Sun' by the Beatles. It follows with Queen, Laura Marling, Aretha Franklin, Amy Winehouse and Echo and the Bunnymen. There's eighties disco, nineties indie, jazz and Americana. I judge the distance not by how far we go, but how many songs we listen to and today it's fourteen in all.

Sometimes I simply let this soundtrack drift over me; at other points he lowers the volume and we chat. The whole way, he's there next to me, and I focus on the clasp of his fingers and the feel of his palm against mine.

*

The next time I open the door to Colette's office I'm feeling rather good about myself. Possibly smug. 'You look like you've had a good couple of weeks,' she comments.

I hand over my homework sheet. 'Yes, I think you could say that.'

After each walk I had to rate my anxiety levels from 1 to 10 and write a sentence or two in the box about what I was feeling. All the way down the page the rating decreases and by the final entry this morning the box includes words like 'surprising' and 'in parts enjoyable'.

'This is wonderful, Ellie,' she says, scanning the sheet. 'A great start. So where did you go?'

'Just for a walk in the fields around the house. Not once but four times. I took Gertie twice. And I went out by myself. Well, just me and the dog. It was only for a few minutes but I did it.'

She looks up. 'Must be nice to know you're able to take your dog for a walk.'

'I wouldn't describe the experience itself as entirely nice. It wasn't quite *relaxing*.'

'I don't suppose you expected it to be.'

'No, but it wasn't as bad as I'd thought it would be. Even getting here today felt kind of undramatic.'

'Why do you think it was better than you'd anticipated?' she asks.

'Because my expectations were so low,' I shrug.

She smiles. 'Anything else?'

'Well, I created a safe environment around me. I listened to some songs – the kind of music that makes you calm but also sort of brave. I went with someone I trust but who isn't as invested in this as my family are. He held my hand, which really worked. It made me feel like I wasn't alone. But I don't feel any pressure with him. He is a very calm person to be around but still persistent, somehow.'

'In what way?'

'It was raining on one of the days and I thought: "Right, this is my excuse not to go", but then he turned up with some waterproofs and he'd made a mixtape for me – although it wasn't really a mixtape. It was just a bunch of songs he knew I'd like.'

'Guy sounds like a real keeper.'

I snap up my head. 'Oh no – it wasn't Guy. This was the delivery man.'

Her pen stops and she looks up at me.

'He's called Jamie. He delivers my plants. He's a friend now too. But no, I'd never do something like this with Guy.'

'Oh. Why not?'

I'm tempted to ask if she's ever dated before. Ever been at that stage of a relationship in which you present the best version of yourself and nothing less. The bit where your legs are permanently waxed, underwear always matches, tempers never flare, smiles don't falter.

Guy has already seen enough of my faults and he's still around, so I'm not going to continue to thrust them in his face, any more than I'm going to start farting in bed with him. That might be human reality, but it's the fastest way to demolish a honeymoon phase.

'It would put him off,' I say simply. 'It's hardly a turn-on all this, is it? Anyway, he's very busy. He's a yoga teacher and has got a big private client list.'

'I think you mentioned that,' she says.

'Plus, he's grown his Instagram account enormously

recently and has a really active social life. It's one of the things I love about him.'

'That social life is something you want to be a part of?'

'Absolutely. As soon as possible. He's invited me to a wedding. I'm determined to be there.'

'Aha. So that's the prize.'

'Absolutely. I keep imagining myself in a beautiful dress, on the dance floor with him and . . . I'm aware this sounds like I want to be Cinderella. Sorry.'

'What are you sorry for?'

'Ah, you know. It's frivolous. Pretty shoes and romance.'

'Pretty shoes and romance sound like something a lot closer to *living*. It really doesn't matter what your motivation is, Ellie, as long as it helps you.' She pauses and takes a sip of her coffee. 'And the idea of going to this wedding doesn't make you feel too anxious?'

'Of course it does. If you asked me to fill in one of your "fear ladders" it'd be through the roof. The thought of walking into a big hotel room with loads of other people and a man I am in—'

'A man you are in love with?'

'A man I am in a relationship with. The point is, the stakes are high. As they always are with something you want. Those are the things I want to do with Guy and be able to do them without worrying that I'm going to lose it. Believe me, Guy could have any woman he wants. So I suppose there is an element of . . . I want to be worthy of him. To be the person he thought he was getting before he knew about my issues.'

'But that's not who you are, Ellie.'

'Not yet,' I correct her.

She thinks about this and nods. 'You're right. Not yet.'

Chapter 41

I'd forgotten how fast Mum travels by foot. She bounds rather than walks, with the kind of energy that I'm sure can't be the norm for her age. Gertie scuttles at her ankles as if I'm not even here, though given that Mum and Dad have been her regular walkers for the last two years, I can hardly accuse her of disloyalty. Our country walk is a spontaneous venture, prompted by the convergence of a sunny day, a visit by Lucy and the fact that I can now attempt this without a drama being inevitable. Leaving home wasn't completely without incident, of course. Even pulling a cardigan over my shoulders as I stepped out of the gate unleashed the dreads, but I reminded myself that the feeling would pass and, sure enough, as we leave the Coach and Horses car park behind us and head across the fields, it has.

'You're not on the run from snipers now, you know,' Lucy calls out as we trudge uphill in Mum's wake.

'Sorry, am I going too fast?' She turns briefly, her boots slowing on the path, before continuing, clearly not that sorry.

'When I was five, I assumed I'd be able to catch her up at some point,' Lucy mutters between breaths. '*You* never had any trouble though.'

'I was fitter in the days when I was running every weekend.'

'You should start again,' she says. 'Not competitively, of course, but it'd be a great hobby for you. You really enjoyed it once.'

'Maybe. I'm not really thinking that far ahead though, yet. I'm supposed to be taking baby steps.'

'Oh, fuck that,' she exclaims, pausing for breath, her hand pinned to her hips. 'I mean, Ellie, you're out. If I were you I'd be running around this field singing "The Hills Are Alive"!'

What I don't explain is that, despite me putting on a good display of being relaxed and happy, my agoraphobia will always be a ghost waiting in the wings, biding its time before its presence is again felt. Colette says I shouldn't fight this feeling, just observe it, watch it, keep doing what I'm doing. Which I am, dutifully, but it does stop me short of skipping around like Maria Von Trapp.

We cross the field and reach the edge of the woods, as Mum turns to us. 'What was that song you girls used to sing, the one you learnt at Brownies? It reminds me of walking up here.'

'"Do your balls hang low?"' Lucy says.

'It was "Do your *ears* hang low?",' I correct her.

'It might have been that in *your* Brownie pack.'

We find a spot to eat our picnic and lay out a blanket, stretching our legs in front of us as we unwrap Mum's homemade sausage rolls, Kettle chips and chilled watermelon slices.

'If you're not up for running, what about giving some of your old mates a ring?' Lucy asks, continuing a conversation that I'd thought had ended. 'You could go out for a few drinks.'

'I'm not at the *going out for a few drinks* stage just yet,' I say.

'And when I am it'll be *you* who will be roped to the pub first, I'm afraid.'

'Absolutely fine by me,' she says, catching a flake of pastry on her fingertip. 'So, these sessions with your shrink . . . what happens exactly? Whatever she's doing seems to be working a treat.'

'It's cognitive behavioural therapy. I like it because it homes in on a specific, current problem – my agoraphobia – rather than banging on about anything that's screwed you up in your past.'

'Hmm,' she says. 'So you don't even talk about Romania?'

'Nope.'

'Huh.'

'The CBT is going really well,' I say, stressing the point.

'Yeah, I can tell,' she concedes, propping her elbow on her knee. 'I don't know, I just . . . I get why you wouldn't want to talk about the past all the time. Who would? But doesn't part of you want to know about where you came from? To try to make sense of what happened to you?'

Mum flashes her a look that says, *please shut up, darling*, the kind that never, ever works on Lucy.

'I'm talking about all the things that made you the person you are . . . the political and economic context, or what happened to the other kids you were with – the ones that left *and* the ones that stayed. Have you read the *Observer* piece that Mum wrote? They published it last weekend.'

'No,' I reply.

'You should. It's really good. It feels incredible that this happened in your lifetime, let alone to *you*. I just know that if it was me—'

'But it wasn't,' I interrupt.

She closes her mouth. 'Sorry. I didn't mean ... '

But she doesn't finish her explanation. 'No, it's fine,' I say, patting her hand. 'Don't be silly. Shall we get going again?'

We pack away what's left of the food and follow the steep path downhill. We're only a few minutes in, when the heel of my boot slips on a stone and my ankle gives way. I stumble backwards, instinctively reaching out and falling onto my hand. I inhale sharply as the skin tears on a rock and look down to see a glossy line of blood dripping from the ball of my thumb to my wrist. My head begins to swim.

I become aware that Lucy is fussing and Gertie is barking, both sensing my panic, as sweat pricks on the back of my neck. It feels like the start of an attack until I sense the hot, firm grip of Mum's hand on my arm.

'All right?' she asks calmly, handing me a napkin from her rucksack.

I nod and press it against the cut, before wiping the blood away. Then I stand up and I do what I've been doing all my life. I start again.

Chapter 42

Mum's car pulls up outside the house as the tail lights of Jamie's van are disappearing in the other direction.

'Give him a beep!' Lucy exclaims and, with lightning reflexes, thumps the centre of the steering wheel. Mum tuts at her impertinence as Jamie comes to an abrupt halt and begins to reverse. As he draws up alongside our car, he catches sight of me in the back and smiles, raising his hand to wave. Lucy sighs and turns around.

'Can't you fall in love with *him*?' she hisses. 'He's bloody lovely.'

Now *I* tut and open the car door, picking up Gertie.

'Hello there,' he says cheerfully, stepping forward to greet the dog, who is wriggling in my arms to reach him. 'The bulbs you ordered are outside your front door.'

'Ah. I sometimes forget you're here for business and not just . . . pleasure.' My ears warm and I wish I'd chosen a different word.

'What are you serving up today, bartender?' Lucy asks, closing the car door. I lower Gertie to the ground, where she starts attempting to lick Jamie's ankles.

'Much as I would love to spend another night losing to you both at Guess the Intro, I can't today.'

'Have you got many more deliveries?' I ask.

'It's not that. I'm being taken for dinner by my publisher so I need to dart home and spruce myself up.'

'That's so exciting, Jamie.' As he holds my gaze, his mouth softens, prompting a burst of something sweet at the pit of my belly.

'So how's your love life?' Lucy asks, a subject she quizzed him about extensively a few weeks ago.

'Oh, not much to report,' he laughs.

'I've found myself a Norwegian,' she announces.

'Have you? Well done.'

'He's a significant upgrade on what I'm used to, I assure you,' she continues, then glances at me. 'Well, I'll leave you both to it, shall I?'

As Lucy and Mum disappear into the house, I look up at Jamie. He looks down at me. It is an oddly awkward moment. 'I'm glad I bumped into you. I've actually got something for you. Apart from the bulbs, I mean.'

'Oh, the organic seaweed extract? I've been waiting for that ever since they sent me some copper slug repellents by mistake.'

'No, it's . . . wait here.' He returns to the van as the sun filters through the branches of the trees and Gertie disappears under the patio table for shade, lowering her head onto her paws for a snooze. He returns with a small, leather-bound book, which he clutches to his chest as if he's never going to let it go.

'I painted a couple of pictures of your garden,' he says.

'Oh!' I say, surprised. 'Are they . . . in there?' I gesture to the book.

'Yeah,' he says, but refuses to unclasp it. 'It's not a big deal – I do this kind of thing all the time when something takes my interest. It's a good excuse to experiment with different techniques. The first one wasn't great. Like I say, I was experimenting. So I did another and . . .'

'How many pictures did you do?' I ask.

'A couple.' He shifts to the other foot. 'A few.'

'Can I see them?'

'Oh. Yes, of course.' He unfolds his arms and hands me the book.

I open it to find a sketch depicting my annexe from the opposite side of the patio. It's in early summer, when the flowers had almost but not quite reached peak cottage garden whimsy. He has captured every exquisite detail: the peachy glow of light as the sun sets, the patterns in the lichen on the stone walls, the way the daisies grow in the gaps of the path. He perfectly depicts the strength and beauty of the weeping willow, its curtain of elegant, fluttering leaves.

'That one isn't the best,' he mutters, turning over the page before I've properly had a chance to look. 'This one's better but . . . to be honest, that's not the greatest either.'

'Did you paint them from memory?' I ask.

'Partly,' he says. 'Partly from your Instagram page too.' He peers in and frowns, dissatisfied at something else. 'I kept going and I did more pictures. I'm not one hundred per cent sold on any of them. In fact, I'm not sure why I even gave you this. Actually . . . I don't know what I was thinking.'

'They're stunning, Jamie,' I tell him, refusing to hand it back as I start flicking through. Each one is created with a combination of paint and pencil and captures every subtle detail perfectly, from the dewy grass to the glittering sunshine on the roses. This is more than a gesture. It represents hours upon hours of his time and talent.

'It's . . . just the best thing, Jamie. I'll treasure it.'

He gives a brief nod, satisfied. My phone beeps.

'Sorry,' I say, withdrawing it from my back pocket. It's a text from Guy.

> **Hey. I'm going to be passing in about thirty mins and thought I'd pop in. I've been thinking about you a lot. Certain parts of you in particular . . . xxx**

My heart soars. 'It *is* Wednesday, isn't it?' I ask.

'Last time I checked. Why?' Jamie glances down long enough to see Guy's name on the phone. He looks up and I register the slow movement of his Adam's apple as he backs away.

'Sorry. I'll . . . leave you to it,' he says.

I want to say more, to tell him how overwhelmed I am, how grateful. But none of the right words come to me and I'm conscious that I urgently need to shower before Guy arrives.

'Thanks, Jamie. The pictures. They're . . . lovely. Stupid word, but . . . really. Listen, I hope your meeting goes well, okay?'

'Yeah. Thanks,' he says, and off he goes.

As his van disappears down the hill, Lucy appears at my side. 'Aw, has he gone already? What's that?'

I show her the book. 'Jamie painted these for me.'

She starts flicking through. 'Oh my God. He did this? For you?'

'Yes,' I say.

'Shit.'

'Look, I've got to go, Guy's on his way over.'

She closes the book and looks at her watch. 'Is he going to be long? I'd love to meet him but I've got a work event tonight and I need to get back.'

'Today isn't a good day anyway,' I say, deciding not to explain that I'm responding to a booty call. I walk her towards the gate. 'You know, I really enjoyed today, Lucy. It was good, wasn't it?'

'It really was,' she grins, putting her arm round my waist. 'And the next step, by the way, is *you* coming to my flat to meet Jakob.'

'I'd love that.'

She is about to leave, but as she reaches the gate she pauses. 'What's up?' I ask.

'I know I was joking before about Jamie,' she replies. 'But you do realise he is absolutely crazy about you, don't you?'

Chapter 43

Harriet, 1993

Even before Harriet had taken a pregnancy test and discovered it was positive, she'd felt wrung out by Sarajevo. The city had been under siege for nearly eighteen months and Kosevo Hospital had particularly suffered its toll. She'd visited on a clear, starry night, arriving as another bullet-riddled ambulance trundled past the freshly dug graves in the cemetery and pulled in to the emergency entrance. Mountains of blood-stained sheets were piled up outside the garage, waiting for a lorry with fuel to take them to an incinerator. There was no point in going to a laundry with only occasional water and often none at all.

Inside she had been shown round by Dr Farouk Kafedzic amidst an atmosphere of total chaos. Amputees' beds were being wheeled to parts of the building that didn't leave them exposed to the sniper positions on the hills. The only sources of light were the nurses' stations and the glow of the moon through the windows. Dark, over-crowded wards were packed full of patients whose chances of recovery after their fragile bodies had succumbed to mortar shells or bullets were variable to say the least.

Dr Kafedzic, meanwhile, was a man on the verge of a breakdown. 'A mortar shell landed among children playing in the old city yesterday,' he told Harriet wearily. 'Three were killed instantly, another ten ended up in here. We managed to save all of them, except a little girl. She was seven.' His eyelids closed, but momentarily, as if he couldn't bear the images in the darkness behind them. 'This is not what I became a doctor for. I have seen things that no human being should see.'

Harriet kept thinking of those words, long after she'd landed on UK soil, stood in a toilet cubicle at Heathrow and watched a blue cross develop on a white stick, before grabbing a cab to take her home to her family. Her eagerly awaited return to war-reporting following the twelve-month break to settle in Ellie had been very different from what she'd envisaged.

She'd enjoyed her stint in the newsroom and was pleasantly surprised by the challenges it threw at her. Now, back on the front line, she found she simply couldn't stand being away from Ellie. She'd always missed people back home on her trips away, but what she felt for her daughter just didn't compare. For the first time in years, when she envisaged herself back in Fleet Street full time, the thought did not repel her. In many ways she wished she felt differently. Because the world still burned and it needed journalists to uncover the worst and best of human acts with courage and sensitivity.

But she'd never flattered herself into thinking she was unique. There would be other reporters – and more women, at least she hoped so. Because the world might have needed her, but now a new baby did and so did Ellie. No, that wasn't quite right. It was Harriet who needed them, more than she'd ever imagined she would.

Colin was overjoyed about the pregnancy, cheerfully dismissing friends who told him that with a newborn around he should never plan to sleep again. He didn't mention the sleepless nights they'd been having with Ellie since the day she arrived or that, though he had no experience of babies, he hoped he was already a father in all the ways that mattered. Still, he was anxious about how Ellie might react to the idea of making room for an interloper.

'Did she have nightmares while I was away?' Harriet asked. They had flared up again in the aftermath of the dinner with the Rucarenus and although they had begun to peter out a couple of months later, Harriet knew they hadn't seen the back of them altogether. In fact, she'd slipped into Ellie's room a couple of nights before she left for Sarajevo and found her twisting under her duvet, as if sleep was a source of agitation, not release.

They'd discussed accessing the child counselling services that had been offered after the adoption, but quickly discovered that Ellie had an aversion to clinics and local authority waiting rooms, and any suggestion that a stranger would want to talk about her life in the orphanage caused her such distress that it seemed counterproductive.

'It's been fine,' Colin told her. 'She's been to Brownies and had Helen and Jo over to play. We did some jewellery making.'

'*You* did some jewellery making?'

'Well, I *supervised*. I'd tried to teach them the rules of cricket but they were having none of it.'

Colin was right to worry about how Ellie would react to a new baby, but not for the reasons he imagined. They tried to involve her in the pregnancy, taking her to antenatal appointments and to pick out clothes, lemon-coloured sleep suits suitable for whichever sex the baby turned out to be. They suggested naming the baby after characters in Ellie's favourite books (Charlie from *Charlie and the Chocolate Factory*, or Lucy from the *Chronicles of Narnia*). But she monitored Harriet's growing bump with suspicion, if not outright hostility. Harriet only worked out what the problem was on the day she felt the first twinges of labour.

She'd been driving Ellie and Jo home from school one Tuesday afternoon, two weeks before her due date. The plan had been for Ellie's friend to come for dinner but Harriet dropped her home early, explaining to her mother that *something* might be happening.

'Is the baby coming?' Ellie had asked, as Harriet put on her seatbelt.

'It might be,' she smiled, glancing in the mirror. 'Honestly, though, I've no idea. I've never done this before.'

Ellie looked out of the window. She seemed upset. 'You'll never be able to adopt Tabitha now, will you?' she asked quietly.

'Oh Ellie,' Harriet sighed. There was no point in repeating the fact that nobody knew where Tabitha was.

In the event, three more days came and went before Lucy was born, during which Harriet was astonished to discover that absolutely nobody had been exaggerating about the pain involved. Soon afterwards, Colin brought Ellie into the hospital room to meet her new sister, her eyes cast downwards as she refused to lift her chin.

'Hello, gorgeous girl,' Harriet said wearily, beckoning Ellie into her arms. As Ellie snuggled into her mum's hospital gown, tiny snuffling noises drifted from the cot, and she froze. 'Would you like to come and meet the new member of the family?' Colin asked. He lifted the baby out of the cot and brought her over to his daughter. She straightened up and examined Lucy's curled fingers, her soft, pink skin. 'Do you want to hold her?'

It took a little coaxing, but eventually Ellie did as Colin suggested and took the seat next to Harriet's bed, where the baby was placed in the crook of her arm. Her mouth trembled, then she looked up. The smile that followed seemed to begin in her heart and radiate through her whole being.

Several months afterwards, it occurred to Harriet that Ellie hadn't mentioned Tabitha for a long time. Colin surmised that Lucy had plugged the gap in her life that had been left when Tabitha jumped out of the orphanage window. It was feasible, of course, but Harriet felt certain there was something else going on besides that.

Ellie, she realised, had become a master of self-preservation. Harriet had seen with her own eyes how close she had been to her friend in the orphanage, then afterwards how the mystery of her whereabouts had tormented her.

She'd long ago started to package memories of her past life into a box and bury them in a corner of her mind, never to be opened again. Now, she'd clearly felt her only option was to do the same with Tabitha. In some ways it made sense. It was certainly a relief to see her happy. But, as Harriet would later observe, the problem with some boxes is that they never stay shut, no matter how hard you try to nail them down.

Chapter 44

Ellie

I was only looking for something to help me cool down. It's the hottest of August days, the kind too rare in the UK for anyone to ever bother installing air con, a decision I curse nonetheless, along with the stickiness that has been clinging to the small of my back all morning. I'd gone up to Mum's office knowing that everyone was out and she wouldn't mind me borrowing her fan.

As I reach the top of the stairs, the *Observer* magazine catches my eye, sitting on her desk on a blue folder. I suspect instantly that it's the edition that ran her article about Romania and when I see a Post-It highlighting a particular page, I walk over and touch the glossy cover, recalling Lucy's words during our walk.

If it was me, I'd have to know . . .

I lower myself onto the chair as my heart starts to beat in a queasy rhythm. Counter-intuitively, I open up the magazine and begin to read.

It is nearly three decades since the fall of Ceauşescu
exposed the horrors of Romania's orphanages.
Harriet Barr was among the first journalists to
visit the institutions in 1990, discovering infants
hidden away in filthy conditions, lying silently in cots.
Today, she returns to the country to learn what has
happened since.

It's the pictures from the early nineties that leave me momentarily unable to draw breath. The shaved heads. The rusting
beds. The tiny, cold-looking bodies. The photographs are
crystal clear and the colour vivid, with several pages of
images, including one of Mum in the orphanage where I
lived. She looks young and serious-minded, her red hair held
back with an Alice band as she reaches out to a little boy
who sits on a mattress, a knitted bonnet tied under his chin.
Once I begin to read, I can't stop, taking in the description
of what Mum and the others found: the squalor, the smell. I
have an odd sense of detachment as I read, as if the words are
somehow separate from my own experiences.

Back in 2000, over 100,000 children were still living in
orphanages in Romania. Today, there are 6,000, living
in 181 institutions, a fall of nearly 95 per cent. Even
this number is considered to be too high for charities
operating in the region, which want all orphanages
in the country to be closed down within the next five
years. They attribute some of the enormous strides
to Romanian teams on the ground, which showed
compassion, courage and a commitment to totally
transform the childcare system. 'Romania now leads

the world in demonstrating how it is possible to change systems by freeing children from institutions and getting them back to the love of families,' says Andrei Rucarenu, the country director of one British-based charity. 'But the job isn't done.'

I read on, about a large orphanage my mother visited during her trip to Iaşi for this feature. It housed two hundred children at one point and only closed for good this year, after a lengthy programme to find a safe, loving home for each child. In many cases, this meant being reunited with their birth families – because most 'orphans', both in Romania and elsewhere in the world, still have a living parent or other relative, but are taken into state care for reasons that include dire poverty, disability and discrimination, all of which may make it impossible for families to care for them without support.

'These days, the remaining institutions are a long way from the horrors that were revealed in the early 1990s,' Rucarenu continues. 'The buildings are in a better state now, but they are still bleak and soulless, with nothing warm or cosy about them. They remind me of a big, scary school in which the home-time bell never goes off. Imagine how that feels for a young child. They are regimented. There's no privacy. The children have no personal possessions. The ratio of qualified carers to residents is also still very low. Youngsters remain at risk of abuse and neglect, both from staff and older children. All of this means that this really is no way to live. What they need is the same thing as any of us: the love of a family.'

When it is not possible to place children with either
their birth family or a foster family, they may move to
a 'small group home', a bright and welcoming building
which, while not the same as a family environment, is
the next best thing. It's little wonder why the charity
now places so much emphasis on working with local
professionals to prevent the separation of children
from their families in the first place.

The article goes on to talk about partnerships and child protection volunteers, about the vast improvement in knowledge
and skills – and how funding, which initially came from
abroad, is increasingly from companies that operate in the
Romanian market or private donations made by big-hearted
Romanians. There is an understanding, it says, that what
makes a nation civilised is not merely its infrastructure – but
how it pools resources to help its most vulnerable members.

It is, I can't deny, a generally hopeful piece. I can see why
Mum and Lucy thought I should read it. But as I turn the
page, there is a separate section that is rather less heartening.
It's clear that while the institutions of the 1980s are a thing of
the past, their legacy lives on for those who experienced them.

Even after leaving the orphanages in the early 2000s,
the children continued to exhibit physical, emotional,
social and cognitive developmental delays. Young
people with an institutional upbringing are easy
targets for exploitation and trafficking. Statistically,
about 40 per cent of children who stayed until they
were 18 ended up begging or turning to prostitution.

The piece interviews several former orphans, institution-alised at the same time as me. One 32-year-old man spent his childhood in state care from the age of two months, but ran away at twelve and was eventually rescued by his older brother, who was twenty. He now lives in a small apartment outside Bucharest, running an NGO that helps children who have had a similar upbringing. Another woman is living in a hostel, but remains upbeat about her future; her boyfriend works in McDonald's and has won a scholarship to study at university. They plan to move in together and get married.

The least hopeful ending comes in the form of a haunting image of a woman who spent nearly a decade in exactly the same orphanage as me, though of course I don't recognise her. Her name is Violetta. She's five years older than me and ran away at thirteen. She's still homeless, addicted to Ketamine and 'Legale', a legal high that is no longer in fact legal. She looks shrunken, ravaged.

'My closest friends are dead,' she says—

It's at that point that I can't read on. I feel a surge of anger that makes me want to rip the magazine in two. Instead I go to stuff it in the folder. As I open the flap, only then remem-bering that I'd actually found it out on the desk, I catch sight of a copy of the photograph of Tabitha and me, the original of which is in my own wardrobe. I place it on the desk and pick up the document beneath – a copy of a Romanian birth certificate. The name on it is written in typed, faded letters: *Tabitha Florescu.*

I don't understand the Romanian words beyond the most basic of them, so put it to one side and remove all the rest of the papers. There is a small stack of official documents, inter-leaved with written notes in Mum's light, Teeline shorthand. Her hieroglyphics make them indecipherable to me, but there is the odd longhand sentence – *Phone call with Philippe Broudeur (photographer) 06.06.18* – that makes it absolutely clear what has been happening over the last couple of months.

'Ellie?' I spin round on the desk chair to find my mum at the top of the stairs. Her eyes dart from the folder, to the picture, then to me. Her chest rises.

'You've been looking for Tabitha,' I say.

She sighs. 'Yes.'

'Have you found her?' I ask urgently. My heart thrums as she walks to the chair opposite her desk.

'No,' she says, sitting down dejectedly. 'I'm afraid I haven't. I'm so sorry, Ellie. But I honestly don't think she'll ever be traced.'

Only as I exhale do I realise exactly how much hope had been concentrated in that single held breath.

'Why didn't you tell me you were even looking?' I ask.

'Because I feared exactly this. That I wouldn't be able to find anything out, or at least nothing that would reassure you. I must admit I thought I'd get further than I did. I'd assumed that, with all the systems in place these days, I'd at least have a chance of tracing her. Andrei and I tried everything but in the end it came to frustratingly little.'

I glance down at the picture of the woman, Violetta, her thin arms mottled with the scars of addiction. I feel my throat thicken.

'Could she still be at the station, like this woman?' I ask.

'I don't believe so,' Mum says. 'It seems that Tabitha left not long after the picture of her was taken as a little girl. I spoke to the photographer, much to your father's chagrin. It was years ago that he'd encountered Tabitha, but those images won him an award and he hadn't forgotten her. She was one of a little group that stuck together, apparently. They begged from commuters and helped a couple of shopkeepers stock shelves for payment.'

'How does he know she left?'

'Because he went back a year later to document changes to their situation. He discovered that the police had dispersed many of the children – most had gone back to homes, a couple of others had made their way to the abandoned construction sites around the city.'

She rubs her temple and glances at the notes. 'I decided to do some further digging. Andrei helped – again. As far as he can tell, Tabitha was never returned to an orphanage. *Any* orphanage. He looked at all the relevant records and then, when that amounted to nothing, he even went to the train station with that picture, on the off chance that anyone remembered her. He found one woman who said vaguely that she thought she did, but had no idea where she'd disappeared to.'

Mum moves the first couple of pages to one side and picks up the birth certificate.

'Meanwhile, I managed to trace her birth mother,' she continues. 'I thought it might be a possibility that Tabitha had tracked her down at some point in her life. But when Andrei went to the address on the orphanage's records, he learnt she had been living with a new husband and two children. She died of cancer in 2015. Her husband hadn't even been aware of Tabitha's existence. All of this brought us to another dead end – and the inevitable conclusion that wherever your friend was now, nobody was going to be able to find her.'

I knew this of course. It's why I've tried my best not to

Catherine Isaac

think about Tabitha's fate for years. But the knowledge that this is really it – that I'll truly never find out what happened to the only friend I had in that place – seems to smother me.

As pressure starts to build behind my eyes, Mum rises from her chair and leans down to me, wrapping her arms round my shoulders. 'Oh, Ellie, I'm so sorry. I really wish I could have given you some answers.'

I shake my head, sniffing myself together. 'It's okay. You tried. Thank you. God – and you must thank Andrei too.'

'He feels as frustrated as I do.'

She pulls away and sits opposite me. 'Do you think she's dead?' I hear myself saying.

And there it is. My worst fear, out in the open.

Mum's shoulders slump. 'I've seen enough of the world to know that people *can* defy odds, even when they're stacked against them.'

'But, realistically, if Tabitha had done that and now had a nice job and home somewhere she'd show up on some employment records, wouldn't she?'

Her brow tightens. She thinks carefully about her response and the weighty responsibility it holds. 'I don't know, Ellie,' she says quietly.

But I think she does.

Chapter 45

EnglishCountryGardenista

730
posts

58.9k
followers

954
following

ELLIE HEATHCOTE

The tree I love more than any other in my garden is the weeping willow. This gentle giant, with its feather leaves, was planted by my late grandma and grew at a rate of knots, so that within a few short years it had risen over everything else in the garden. Its branches are flexible but strong; they can bend without breaking. It can weather storms and, above all, has a remarkable ability to regenerate. Willows are easy to grow from a cutting because their tissues contain a natural, root-promoting hormone. They can be started at any time of year in pots, or outside in late winter or early spring, and grow up to 50 feet within 15 years. This ability to grow so quickly is why, in many parts of the world, the weeping willow is held up, above all, as a symbol of renewal, strength and hope.

#thisgirldigs #gardensofinstagram #EnglishCountryGardenista #englishcountrygardens #weepingwillow #gardener #gardening #garden #gardenlife #flowers #plants #gardens #nature #gardendesign #growyourown #gardeninspiration #instagarden #gardenlove #growyourownfood

@Misusmiggins
Where did you get that nail polish Ellie? And how on earth does a gardener keep their hands looking so nice?

@Pastelgardener
@misusmiggins I'm usually terrible for forgetting to wear my gloves and the result has been scraggy nails for years. But I'm off to a wedding soon so thought I'd make an effort.

The wedding is in two weeks and it is clear that it is not on Guy's mind to the same extent as mine. I am consumed by the impending event, probably more so than the bride herself. Guy, on the other hand, has hardly mentioned it since he first invited me, something that feeds my growing paranoia about his feelings towards me – and convinces me in my more neurotic moments that he regrets asking me altogether. It is during one of these that I decide to compose a casual-sounding text asking about the plan on the night – whether we're getting a taxi and, if so, at what time. I press send just as Dad arrives to take me to my session with Colette.

'All set?' he asks, as if we're off for a trip to the seaside.

'Nearly. Give me a minute.'

I know my anxiety will bubble under the surface during the eighteen-minute journey — twenty-three if there's traffic — but that it will be better as soon as I arrive. I also know that I will later reflect on the experience and conclude that this time wasn't as bad as the time before, just as that time wasn't as bad as the time before that.

As summer draws to a close, there has been a sense of change and renewal in my life. I've been going out more. Not just on walks in the countryside that surrounds Chalk View, but also as far as the village. I've strolled past my old primary school and seen the children in little uniforms through the railings, playing hopscotch like I used to with Jo and the others. I've been to the Post Office and stood in the queue, chuckling when the lady behind the counter enquired about the contents of a parcel and its sender replied, 'My teeth'. (He went on to explain that it was destined for a denture repair company.)

I've taken cream tea with Mum in the café Grandma used to love, going through the ritual as she taught me — jam first, clotted cream second. I've promised Oscar I'll go to one of his assemblies. I've browsed round the little bookshop in Chorleywood with Dad and on the same day we stumbled across the sign for Green Fingers garden centre. I knew I couldn't let the moment pass.

As we pulled up to the gates, I felt my heart rise, but it was an entirely pleasant sensation that continued as I browsed through rows of evergreen and deciduous shrubs, hedging and climbers, grasses and alpines. They had a superb range of fruit trees — damson, mulberry, pears and gages — and I watched as a group of women took part in a hanging basket workshop.

I'd texted Jamie, to ask if he was at work, the moment we'd stepped through the sliding doors and, having not heard back, approached a member of staff to see if they knew where he was, imagining him in the back somewhere, hair awry as he heaved boxes into the van. But he was on a day off, at a meeting in London.

I came away feeling deflated because it's been a while since I've seen him. He only rarely stops for a tea after he's delivered something these days and somehow I'm starting to get the feeling he's humouring me. He doesn't seem to go out of his way to see me any more.

Now I'm concerned that my only friend is no longer interested in spending time with me, or at least not as much. It's hardly surprising in some ways, given that he's been organising Mike's stag party and his book publication is imminent. He has so many other people to go out with. But I instinctively feel that something else might be at play: that he may have become involved with someone romantically.

If that is the case, Jamie is not the kind of man to offer this information freely, even in response to my sister's direct questions about his love life. He's too discreet to say if he was going on a first date and would only announce that he had a significant other at the point when she became just that – significant. He might not ever feel the need to announce it. Why would he? Who am I, after all, but an old acquaintance, rekindled? This time six months ago we barely even remembered each other's names.

Thoughts such as these are often in my mind lately, especially when I'm flicking through his paintings. Every time I look at his book, I see some new detail, a ruffle of peonies or the silky ivory petals of the lilies that stood in pots by my front door back in June. On Friday night as I was doing just that, I felt compelled to order a raft of gardening equipment that I really don't need, paying extra for Saturday delivery. Then Green Fingers had the audacity to send a replacement delivery driver because Jamie hadn't been on the rota for that day.

We arrive at Colette's office, where Dad takes a seat in the waiting room with the *Guardian* crossword, as she invites me in. 'How was your journey?' she asks, closing the door.

This is before she's taken out her folder, so I know it is polite conversation, not a subject she wants to explore as part of the session.

'Well, I didn't throw up, so definitely a success.'

'You're looking a lot more relaxed than the first time you came to see me.'

'I am. Some days still feel easier than others though.'

'That's normal, Ellie.' I catch a glimpse of a spider plant on her window sill that looks yellowing and limp.

'You're overwatering that,' I say.

'What?'

'That plant. It doesn't need much liquid and would be better in a slightly less bright position.'

'Thank you,' she replies. 'How is your medication working for you at the moment?'

I'm back on a low dose of antidepressants, prescribed at my first GP visit in years, during which Dr Zacharia also took the opportunity to check my blood pressure, quiz me on my weekly alcohol intake and book me in for an overdue smear test.

'It's fine. I'm not convinced it's this that's worked miracles, but then I'm here so I can't really argue with it. I still think the CBT is the most effective thing. And the walks. I've been taking the dog out every day.'

'With your delivery man?'

'It tends to be Mum these days. Jamie's book looks like it's about to really take off, so he's busy. I still listen to his playlists though. They're kind of . . . comforting.'

'You imagine him being there with you?'

'No, nothing like that.' I force out a laugh, though the truth is that I have started a little ritual every time I go out and it hasn't failed yet. I close my eyes and try to conjure up the precise feeling of my hand in his the first time we stood at the gate. The pressure of his fingers, the warmth of his skin. It leaves me fortified, with a sense of self-belief and calm. Then I press play and step outside.

'And how are you feeling about your past at the moment? You told me last time that you'd read the piece your mother had written about Romania and said we'd come back to it. Do you feel ready to talk yet?'

She clearly thinks it's significant, a step forward, that I am confronting my past rather than running away from it. She was so impressed by the whole thing that by the end of that session I wished I'd never mentioned it at all.

'I really don't think it's necessary,' I say. 'The CBT is working well, isn't it?'

A long pause follows. I'm determined not to fill it. This time, I decide to let it run and run until it's *her* who has to break it. It goes on so long I become convinced that I could sing all three verses of the national anthem and she still wouldn't have cracked.

'I don't regret reading the article,' I hear myself saying. 'But I do really wish my mum had found out something about Tabitha. The fact that she went to all that effort and came up with nothing makes it almost worse. I'm not saying I thought . . . there's just no closure, you know?'

'Of course,' she says carefully.

'Not knowing is the worst thing. Your head fills the vacuum with theories, good and bad. And I know the fact that I'm in the dark doesn't *necessarily* mean the worst. But her chances were awful.' I lift up my chin and look at her. 'It must be your turn to speak now?'

'Closure is a difficult thing when you have so many unanswered questions. By the sound of it the only option might be to try to gain some acceptance that you may never know what happened to her. As hard as that is. Ellie, I think you need to find a way of saying goodbye to Tabitha – somehow.'

I find myself examining the spider plant again, my gaze drifting over the long tendrils that curl down from the window sill.

'Do you think you'd ever consider going back to Romania?' she asks and my head snaps back to her.

'No. Never. If that's what you mean by saying goodbye, then no. That's not a good idea.'

'Why is that, Ellie?'

I shift position in my seat. 'Well, it's obvious.'

'Because you are afraid?' she asks gently.

'Of course.'

'But nobody is going to take you to an orphanage and lock you away there now,' she says. 'Perhaps that could be a way not merely to say goodbye to Tabitha, but to your past as a whole.'

'No.' I shake my head. 'I don't think so. I'm not going to do that.' I decide to change the subject. 'Have I told you I'm going to a wedding?'

She smiles. 'You have. How are you feeling about that?'

'Excited. I'm still worried about having a panic attack, of course. Which is annoying because I'll only have one if I'm worrying about it and ... well, I'm worrying about it.'

'Actually, I had a thought about that,' she continues. 'All your tasks have been in daytime hours so far, haven't they? You haven't been out in the evening.'

'Not yet.'

'Then I think that should be this week's homework. Before you go to this wedding, make some kind of social engagement one night. It doesn't need to be fancy – just a drink in a pub with your boyfriend.'

'You mean Guy?' I say stupidly, because of course she does.

'It can be anyone you like, as long as it's a practice run and you take someone with you. Someone who makes you feel safe.'

Chapter 46

Sharply crisp autumn sunlight greets me the following morning, shining on the berried trees and illuminating the shrubbery. I wake up and start work early, clearing the leaves gathered in the corners of the garden and filling a Tupperware box with conkers that have dropped under the horse chestnut branch drooping over my hedge. I work all the way through lunch, forgetting to eat, and by mid-afternoon the light is so perfect that although I hadn't planned a photo shoot, I can't let the opportunity pass.

I set up my tripod in front of the Michaelmas daisies and the katsura trees, wishing their burnt-sugar aroma was somehow broadcastable through social media. I know before I've even downloaded them onto my computer that the photos are some of my best this year, a splash of reds, yellows and oranges that will need minimal alteration on Photoshop. I'm heading inside, when I hear the thrum of Jamie's van.

'Hello!' I say, as he opens the gate. 'Gosh, it's good to see you. We've been like ships in the night lately. I hope you've got time for a cuppa?'

He hesitates and pushes his hair back.

'Oh go on,' I urge him. 'Or I could make it a cocktail?'

He laughs and the dimples in his cheeks suddenly appear. 'It's a bit tricky at the moment, Ellie. I've just had another commission for a children's book.'

'Oh wow! Jamie, that's brilliant.'

'Same publisher, but the deadline is tight so I'm working flat out. Probably why you haven't seen much of me lately.'

'I did wonder,' I reply, feeling relieved that there is a plausible explanation. 'Then you surely need a break?'

'Wish I could,' he replies. Only now, as he hands over the signature machine, there's something about his demeanour that makes me not believe him.

'How about coming for a drink with me tonight then?' I blurt it out, entirely unplanned. And yet, I realise straight afterwards how much I want him to say yes. 'Oh, come on. It's been a long time since I've been to the pub with anyone. I'm buying!'

He breathes in. Smiles. 'Okay, why not. I'll pick you up at seven-thirty.'

I'm tonging my hair later that afternoon, when I have the most infuriating conversation with my sister during a video call. 'I'm not convinced you should have asked him out,' she says. 'Not if you're seeing Guy.'

'I haven't *asked him out*. Jamie is my friend.'

'He's not your friend. He's a very decent human being who has feelings for you that clearly diverge wildly from your own about him. You're stringing him along.'

'I am not! I never would!' I realise I am squeaking now. 'Lucy, you're wrong about his feelings. He's never shown the slightest interest in me beyond anything platonic. And if he did . . .'

'Then what?'

'Well, he'd have no *right* to. I've made it clear that I'm already seeing someone.'

She rolls her eyes, as if she's dealing with an incompetent customer services assistant. 'I know you're out of practice, but falling for someone doesn't work like that, Ellie.'

'Oh, I give up,' I say.

'Maybe you should be straight with him then. It'd be the nice thing to do. Leave him to get on with his life.'

'What, and not see him *at all*?' I'm squeaking again. I can't help it. I'm horrified by the thought. 'I didn't say I had *no* feelings for him. I have lots of feelings for him. I just don't want to have sex with him.'

The sentence rolls off my tongue like a steam train and, as soon as I've said it, I am not merely questioning the assertion, but – worse – thinking about having sex with him. I feel a bolt of hot adrenalin, first between my legs then right up to my cheeks.

'Oh fine,' she says. 'You've convinced me. Go on your date. See if I care. Just do me a favour and let me know if you end up shagging him, won't you?'

I decide to end the call.

He arrives at 7.32pm in jeans and a pressed cotton shirt that leaves wisps of hair just visible above the top button, kissing a tiny, raised mole that I've never noticed before. He is standing straighter than usual, his shoulders pulled back in a vaguely unnatural posture.

'You look lovely.' There is a shy note in his voice, as though he has something hot in the back of his throat.

'Thanks,' I reply with a *this-old-thing* shrug. I'm wearing my favourite boots with jeans and a cashmere jumper that I bought in the Hush sale a year ago and which has languished in my wardrobe since. It feels like a solid combination: the familiarity of my footwear and the almost-newness of the sweater, finally freed from its prison.

After dropping Gertie with my parents in the main house, we walk to the village. It takes ten minutes, at a brisk, down-hill pace, and when we reach the car park, my steps slow. It's been nearly three years since I walked into this pub. Or indeed any pub. A place that, on a Friday night, will be full of people, possibly two-deep at the bar. If I let myself dwell on this fact it has the potential to end badly, so instead I turn to Jamie, taking a moment to drink in the sheer height and breadth of him, the strength of him.

'Well, here goes,' I say.

He responds with a look that says *you'll be fine* and opens the door. 'After you.'

I step in, half-expecting everyone to turn and look, like that scene in *An American Werewolf in London*. But nobody even registers us. Conversations continue. Card games are played. Pints are pulled. Not a single gaze is cast in our direction. We find a spot by the fire and Jamie offers me the seat facing out.

It is a proper country bolthole of a pub, with a rabbit warren of bar rooms, low, beamed ceilings and eccentric flourishes such as a huge jar full of cricket balls on the bar and a mural of ordnance survey maps papering one wall. There is also a laissez-faire approach to taxidermy, with various stiff, ancient-looking creatures peering out from shelves, and soft woollen blankets scattered on leather seats.

I wrestle off my coat as Jamie goes to the bar and scans a

chalkboard menu of ales with names like Crop Circle and Grumpy Bastard. A staff member comes over to feed a log into the fire, which crackles and roars.

An old man sitting alone strikes up conversation with Jamie. He looks as much a part of the furniture as the creaky bar stools and woven rugs, and once he's started talking it's clear he's not keen to stop any time soon. But if Jamie minds, he doesn't act like it. He listens and nods, and occasionally laughs, even beyond the point when the barman has completed the order and he's paid for the drinks. As the man slaps Jamie on the shoulder, it occurs to me what it is that everyone likes about him. If he comes across an old man who's slightly the worse for wear, he doesn't try to avoid him. He takes the time to chat, to treat him with consideration and kindness, even if he'd rather be somewhere else.

And I know he'd rather be here with me. I do know that. He finally gives the man a gentle buddy slap on the back and returns, setting down a glass of wine and a pint on the table.

'Sorry about the delay,' he says.

'Do you know him?' I ask.

'The old guy? No, he just wanted someone to talk to. He was telling me about his daughter. She lives in Chicago and has just had a baby. She's offered to pay for the flight and he's desperate to go, but is terrified of flying. He's seventy-seven and has only been on a plane once, more than thirty years ago.'

'Oh, so you had his life story?' I smile.

'Most of it, yes,' he laughs.

'What did you advise?'

'I didn't.' He shrugs. 'Sometimes it's better just to listen.'

'Your listening certainly helped me,' I say.

'Good.' He smiles and raises his glass. 'Cheers to that. And to you.'

I lift my glass and gently chink it against his, before taking a sip. 'You know ... I've never really said thank you, Jamie.'

'For what?'

'You know *for what*. I honestly think that if you hadn't taken my hand on that first day, I'd still be sat at home in a cloud of Marlboro Lights.'

'No, you'd have got there in the end,' he says confidently. 'Well done for quitting those things though.'

'Yeah. They're shit, aren't they?' I look up at him. 'I think what I'm really thanking you for is ... not writing me off as a complete fuck-up.'

He chuckles into his beer and shakes his head. 'Sorry. Ellie, you do make me laugh sometimes though.'

'And not in a good way ...' I say, joining in.

'*Always* in a good way.' He places his drink on a beer mat. 'You know, you're just your own worst enemy. You're not a fuck-up. On the contrary. You're amazing.'

He says the words so lightly that you'd think he was stating, not an opinion, but a fact so irrefutable that it was on a par with *you're a human*. Then he smiles and takes another sip of his Crop Circle.

Chapter 47

We talk till closing time, as the fire crackles and my belly warms with just enough but not too much booze. Every so often, I'm struck by how wonderful it is to be cosy in a country pub, in the company of someone I feel completely comfortable with but never bored. Someone with whom I can be entirely myself, my faintly ridiculous and definitely screwed-up self, and know for certain he doesn't look at me in anything other than pools of flattering light.

It's one of those evenings in which three hours disappears in minutes, the kind I haven't had for years. I have that same childlike feeling I got at birthday parties in the first years after arriving in the UK. That aching happiness, the desperation for it not to end.

The conversation rolls into memories from school and I ask him whether he was bullied, saying I remembered seeing him outside the head's office one day with his mum.

'I had a tough time in the last year of primary school, yeah. There were two kids – Graham Parry and James Bent – who'd steal my lunch, call me names. I got a new pair of trainers and they threw one on the flat roof. Nothing major but enough to make a kid miserable,' he confesses. 'My mum found out about the shoes and was straight in, but it didn't really end until I went to seniors.'

'What happened then?'

'I reinvented myself,' he grins. 'Developed a bit of a swagger. It was all a front, obviously – I'm about as much of a hard man as Fozzie Bear. But it's surprisingly easy to look tough when you're thirteen years old and nearly six foot tall. I never attracted that kind of attention again.'

'You were a big softie disguised as a tough guy, then.' I can't help smiling.

'Correct.'

'Well, good for you. I'm sorry you had to go through that though.'

'Ah, it was a long time ago. I bumped into Graham last year, as it happens, working in a mobile phone shop.'

'Did he say anything about what he'd done when he was younger?'

'No, he just tried to flog me an iPhone X. I declined, but filled out a customer service form on the way out, rating him two out of ten and suggesting that the company should do something urgently about his halitosis.'

Later, I discover that he'd kissed my old friend Helen at Jeremy Harding's seventeenth birthday party. He refuses to reveal a single detail on the grounds that 'a gentleman never tells'.

'Oh, come *on*. I need the gory details,' I say. 'I mean ... *did* you?'

'Did I what?'

'Consummate it?'

'Under the stairs of Jeremy Harding's house? What kind of slag do you take me for?'

Soon, last orders have been and gone and the landlady is beginning to clear the tables.

'I think this is a hint,' he says, nodding to her as she liberally applies antibacterial spray on the table next to us.

As we leave the pub and start to head home, my thoughts are misty from wine and the feel of the heat of him against my arm. The moon is a shimmering disc of light, turning the meadows mint green as we begin the trek uphill. We walk slowly, and chat for most of the way, about the similar somethings and nothings that have peppered the whole evening. We are halfway home when I feel Jamie's hand on my elbow.

'Come here,' he says and before I can argue he's climbing over a gate, offering me a hand.

'What are you doing?' I ask, but take it anyway. I climb over to the meadow on the other side, where we are just a few steps from the banks of the River Misbourne.

'Lucy and I used to drink from this water when we were kids,' I say, walking towards it, the grass swishing against my ankles. 'It's filtered through the underlying chalk, according to my dad. That's what makes it so pure and clear.'

I tiptoe over mounds of anthills that sprout tiny yellow rock roses, then pause as I stand next to Jamie on the grassland, to take in the view. We are surrounded by hills to the west, where the valley dips and undulates in a soft, patchwork blanket. The outline of a church spire is just visible among a dark frill of trees and the scent of chimney smoke perfumes the night air. And above the woodland and fields, the ridgeway tracks and the wildflowers, the stars are incandescent, shining pearls in a black, velvet sky.

England, I think, you really are beautiful.

I become aware that Jamie's eyes are on me and turn to

meet his gaze. The way he looks at me recalls the moment back in summer when he reached out to take the strawberry pip from my cheek with his fingertips. Warmed by the memory, I hazily, unthinkingly, reach out to touch his face in the same spot that he touched mine.

My fingertips barely brush the skin beneath his eyes, just above the line of soft bristles. I sweep them gently, less than an inch across, and his eyelids close involuntarily. His mouth parts, releasing the faintest noise from the back of his throat. I lower my hand and take a step closer, until the buttons of my coat catch against his sweater. His eyes open heavily and scan my face. My breathing slows and I feel his left hand slip into mine.

It is in this strange, sultry bubble that my conversation with Lucy returns to me like a crack of lightning. Panic rushes up in me.

What is it that I'm doing here, I think – standing drunk in a field with heat throbbing through me? What about Guy, the closest thing I've had to a boyfriend *in years*? Someone for whom I was driven to confront my demons, to return to Colette, to leave my house time and again, even back in the days when I was convinced it might kill me.

What, exactly, am I doing here?

I take a step back, shaking Jamie's hand away from mine. I cough, bring myself back to my senses.

'Well,' I say cheerfully, 'I can't wait to see Colette after tonight. I should get an A plus for this.'

He blinks, his thoughts a second or two behind mine. 'Sorry . . . what?'

'Tonight was this week's homework.' I grin.

'Oh,' he says, taking this all in. 'You mean like the walks we went on when you first started seeing her?'

'Yes!' The smile lines by his eyes have disappeared in the glow of the moon. 'Obviously, it goes without saying that I wanted to go out with you anyway. But this – yes, it was homework. It's been fun, though, hasn't it? And I'm really grateful – again.'

'Um ... yeah,' he says, but now he sounds vague enough to make me worry that I've offended or hurt him. I try to think of a way to explain.

'Because I'm going to a wedding with Guy in a couple of weeks, it's obviously really important that it goes well,' I begin babbling. 'So Colette suggested I have some kind of trial run, with someone I trust. I can't think of anyone I trust more than you, Jamie. I really mean that.'

But he has the air of the man who has been kicked in the balls, wounded and speechless. It's the last thing I wanted but before I can say anything else, he shakes his head and takes a step away from me. 'I don't think I can do this any-more, Ellie.'

'What do you mean?'

'I mean ... you've got a boyfriend.'

'Yes, I know, but you're just my *friend*, so what's wrong with that? There's nothing more to it between you and me – and he certainly hasn't got a problem with it.'

His jaw moves imperceptibly.

'What is it?' I press on. 'Seriously?'

'Nothing.'

'Oh, for God's sake! Am I supposed to *guess*?'

I can tell from the way he's breathing that he's angry or upset, or some other emotion I don't recognise in him. 'Look, I'm not one for big speeches, Ellie. But I ...'

His voice trails off but he doesn't need to finish his

sentence. As we stand in the moonlit countryside I realise I already know. I've been denying it because I couldn't stand the thought of not seeing him anymore, which is what I'd have to do in the light of Guy. But I've known for a long time. Lucy was right. And it's going to ruin everything.

'You're not ... *allowed* to fancy me, Jamie,' I say, illogical in my frustration.

He laughs, incredulous. 'What?'

'I just mean: I've got a *boyfriend*. I've got Guy.'

His chest rises. 'Yes, I know. And that's fine,' he says, though it sounds anything but. 'I do realise, Ellie, that you don't feel the same way about me as I do about you. I can live with that. Almost. But I tell you what, that ... prick just doesn't deserve you.'

I gasp. '*What* did you call him?'

'I'm sorry, but he doesn't.' He is defiant, entirely unapologetic.

'Have you been speaking to my sister?' I demand.

'What? No. My friend Gail does yoga at his studio. He's constantly flirting with other women there, Ellie. He sounds like a real lech if you ask me and—'

'A ... lech? Are you serious? Fucking brilliant. You're basing your judgement of a man you've never even met on some bullshit *your friend Gail* has told you?'

Because it absolutely is bullshit. I don't need to go to the studio and watch Guy teach his students with my own eyes to know that there isn't a grain of truth in this. He has a naturally warm, flirtatious manner, a playful nature and a personality that is *magnetic*. People, men and women, want to be around him, including me. Unapologetically me. That, whatever Jamie has convinced himself, does not make him a lech. As I fizz with indignation, a trace of regret appears in Jamie's expression.

'Look, Ellie,' he sighs. 'I'm not going to stand here like an idiot and list all the reasons I think you are ... say the things I want to say to you. You already know what I think of you. It's already obvious. And yes, it is a punch in the gut when I see you to know that it is entirely unrequited. But do me a favour and at least find someone better than that guy.'

I am gripped by an incendiary rage now. How *dare* he.

'Don't you tell me what to do,' I say, my jaw set. 'You have absolutely no right, Jamie. No right at all. Besides, what is it you've got against him? Aside from envy? Are you *jealous* because he's got loads of followers on Instagram and a six-pack?'

He lets out a bitter laugh. 'I do not give a shit about his followers on Instagram and I do not—' He glances down briefly. 'Okay, I *do* hate him for his six-pack. But that's not the main reason. The reason I resent him is because you think the world of him and he is completely undeserving of that opinion. He swans in and out of your life, turning up twice a week like it's some kind of one-stop shop, and worst of all, he doesn't make you happy. He just makes you insecure.'

'One-stop ... how dare you! He absolutely *does* make me happy. All of that makes *you* the prick here, Jamie. Not him. You.'

My head throbs with regret now that I ever shared my thoughts and fears about my relationship with Guy. Angry tears swell in my eyes and he's about to fire something back, but stops and raises his hands in surrender. 'Okay. You're right.'

Now I'm crying. I'm nearly gasping for breath, trying to

push great big sobs of despair down my throat, but it's not working. I'm furious with him. This could have been a perfect evening yet he's ruined it with all this crap.

He lowers his head. 'I'm sorry.'

I don't say anything. I can't bring myself to. Instead, we walk in silence back to Chalk View and mumble our goodbyes by the gate, before he makes to leave.

'Will I see you tomorrow?' I sniff, business-like.

He just stops still, his big frame silhouetted against the moon. When he finally answers, I can no longer see the shadows on his face.

'It's like I said. I can't do this anymore, Ellie. I'm sorry. I just can't.'

Then he turns and crunches his way back down the hill.

Chapter 48

Oscar has finally got to pick his tomatoes. He is beside himself over his little crop, and tells me proudly that they'll help him hit his five fruit and veg a day.

'I also had a Jaffa cake this morning,' he adds, which is the first thing all day that has made me smile.

Two weeks after the row with Jamie, I'm still not feeling right and this can't only be attributed to nervousness about the wedding party tonight. I'm continuing to go out for my walks. I'm persevering with the CBT exercises. I've been to Colette once, had Guy over three times and even went to the little arthouse cinema in Chesham with Lucy, to see a movie and pick at some popcorn. None of these things have prompted a tidal wave of anxiety, at least nothing I can't cope with.

Anxiety isn't the right word to describe how I feel about what happened. I don't think there's even a name for it, not a single word anyway. It is a kaleidoscope of emotions: indignation, fury and, above all, sadness. I am bereft without him, heartsick at the idea that I'll never see him again, but simultaneously so angry and raw that it feels as though there's no going back. How could I pick up the phone now to place an order for a heavy-duty garden arch, just so he has to deliver it?

As the wedding has crept closer, there was a point when I'd have done anything to talk to him about it. But what he said hasn't just stopped me from baring my soul to him, now or in the future. It put a different perspective on all those moments we'd had in the past.

'Are you still going to come to one of my assemblies?' Oscar asks. 'There's one after half term.'

'Okay then. I'll be there.'

'Definitely?'

'Yes.'

He grins. 'I think you'll like it. There will be lots of singing,' he says, launching into a rendition of 'Baby Shark', thus guaranteeing that its chorus will be jangling around my head for at least a week. Oscar has been here most of the morning. It's an inset day at school, which Mandy hadn't realised when she booked a doctor's appointment straight after cleaning. I said I'd keep an eye on him for half an hour, but then he begged to stay, so she took the opportunity to get her eyebrows threaded too.

'These carrots are coming along nicely,' he says, parroting me as he examines the vegetable patch.

'We'll dig them up in a few weeks and cook something with them,' I tell him. 'A vegetable curry maybe. Speaking of which, you must be hungry?'

'Starving,' he says.

'Come on then. Take your wellies off at the front door and I'll whip us something up while you wash your hands.'

I chop up some carrots, celery and pitta strips to dip into little pots of hummus and peanut butter. I've been snacking on this a lot lately in a bid to take my mind off not smoking. But after the Jamie debacle the chickpeas just aren't cutting it and I came very close last night to digging out one of three emergency cigarettes I have stashed in the shed.

My phone pings and I open up a text from Guy.

I'll collect you at 6.45 for the wedding tonight, that okay?

Jamie's accusations have left me sensitive to every nuance of Guy's texts, and I feel a stab of concern about the lack of seductive undercurrent – or kiss. Should I be worried about the fact that he used to text me at all times of day or night to tell me how he couldn't get me out of his mind? It would leave me thinking about him for hours afterwards, picturing the sinews in his arms, the tight knit of his body, those endless eyes. Although there is absolutely nothing wrong with this text, Jamie – *bloody Jamie* – has left me paranoid about everything.

Great. See you tonight. Looking forward to it xx

I also can't stop thinking about the other accusation. Much as I'm convinced it's rubbish – gossip from *his friend Gail* would hardly stand up in court – the idea that I'm being played for a fool is horrible. After the seed was planted, it has somehow taken root and started to make me question my own feelings about Guy. I occasionally feel as if I'm looking at a beautiful, critically acclaimed painting that, for all its dazzling qualities, no longer touches my soul. And I question whether he makes me feel all the things you're meant to when you meet someone: in love with the world, with life, with yourself.

I shake the thought from my head as I bring the plate of crudités to the table. As Oscar makes fast work of them, I whiz up some raspberry lemonade from the glut of soft fruits I froze after picking them a couple of months ago.

'Gosh, you really were starving, weren't you?' I say, filling a glass and putting it in front of him. He's finished the entire peanut butter pot, so I take it to the kitchen to replenish. When I bring it back, he dips his celery in and scoops it up into his mouth. 'I love hummus,' he says, gurning as it sticks to the roof of his mouth.

'That one isn't hummus, but feel free to keep eating as it'll stop me from stuffing my face with it.'

'Why do you want to stop eating it?' he asks.

'It's pretty high in fat, that's all, so I shouldn't eat too much when I've got a dress to fit into tonight. You don't need to worry about that though. Help yourself.'

'What is it if it's not hummus?' he asks.

'Peanut butter,' I reply.

He stops chewing and lowers his celery stick. 'Are there any nuts in that?'

'Yes, of course. Why?'

He swallows, a long and hard movement that gives the impression that something remains lodged in his throat. 'I'm allergic to nuts,' he says.

I feel a sudden and heightened sense of the blood running through my body, rushing into my ears.

'What do you mean?' I ask.

'I'm allergic,' he repeats. 'To nuts.'

'But . . . you've just eaten a whole bowl of peanut butter. Two, in fact.'

'I thought it was hummus.' As the sunlight shines through the window, I register two pink patches on either side of his neck. My mind races. Nut allergies don't have to be serious. I know that. I *think* I know that. Do I?

'Are you sure about this?' I ask. 'Wouldn't your mum have said something?'

But she hadn't known he was staying for lunch. He's never eaten here before and had no plans to do so. Why *would* she have mentioned it?

There was a piece in the local newspaper recently about someone who'd nearly died because they were simply on the same flight as someone who'd opened a bag of nuts. All it took was for them to breathe in an infinitesimal fragment and it left them in a critical condition. I look at Oscar and try to remain calm, or at least give the appearance of it.

'So this allergy. What *happens* when you eat nuts?'

He sees the panic in my eyes.

'I don't know,' he replies, looking worried.

'How do you know you're allergic then?'

'I don't know,' he repeats, his voice getting higher.

'You *must* know!'

He sits up, shocked. Frightened.

'Sorry. Sorry,' I mutter reassuringly, rubbing his back. 'I'm sure it's absolutely fine. But look, do you get poorly or something? Has your mum or a doctor told you not to eat them?'

'You should phone her,' he suggests.

'Good idea.' I pick up my phone, fumbling as I scroll to Mandy's number.

'Are you feeling all right?'

He shakes his head. 'No. I feel really weird.' His face is definitely redder. The blotches underneath his ears are getting bigger.

'In what way?' I ask, pacing. 'Can you breathe all right?'

He starts panting.

'I feel dizzy.'

'Okay.' I press dial.

'And I've got a headache.'

'Oh God,' I mutter.

'I think I need to lie down,' he adds.

'No don't do that,' I say, as the phone goes to voicemail. 'Or maybe ... do. Oh, hi Mandy. I wondered if you could give me a ring back urgently please. Nothing at all to worry about ... though I need to speak to you immediately if possible. Thanks.'

I put the phone down and he is now lying on the sofa groaning. 'What's happening?' I ask.

'My toe hurts,' he says. 'But also my tummy too. I feel really hot. Urgh!'

I pick up the phone again and leave another message for Mandy. Then I try Mum and Dad, even though there's little they can do from their walking holiday in the Cotswolds. I consider Jamie for a moment, but instead decide to Google *nut allergies*, briefly alighting on an NHS article that says it's not necessarily serious, which then diverts to several more alarming news stories. 'Maybe I should phone an ambulance,' I mumble, which he hears and begins moaning about his toe again.

It's this that convinces me that it can't be serious. I'm going to look like an idiot if I phone an ambulance. But what if I'm *that* person, left in charge of a small human being for the first time and who's screwed it up so badly that it has critical consequences? What if I'm sitting here contemplating all this while he's dying on my sofa?

'Okay, Oscar, let's go.' He groans and looks up.

'Let's go where?'

'I'm going to drive you to hospital.'

Chapter 49

I find Mum's car keys on the table in her hall and pull the door closed. I still have no idea whether Oscar is sick or not. One minute he's groaning, the next it's as if he's forgotten the whole drama and starts weeding the path.

'You're definitely feeling ill, aren't you?' I ask, as I lead him to the car.

'I feel *very* funny,' he says gravely, and although I'm still full of doubts it's enough for me to open the door, put him in the back and jump in the front.

It's been more than three years since I've driven a car. My panic is now so sharp I can taste it. I put the keys in the ignition and the urgent whisper of my inner voice makes me freeze. *Get back in the house. You can't do this. You cannot drive a car. Not after three years. Not without another adult present. Get back in the house* right now *or something very bad is going to happen.*

I turn back, feeling a bead of sweat trickle in a straight line from my armpit all the way down to my waistband.

'Strap your seatbelt on, Oscar.' Then I check the mirror and put the car into reverse.

He leans forward. 'I don't know how. And where's the car seat?'

Another bolt of panic. I consider phoning a taxi, then realise they probably wouldn't have a car seat either – and that's before we get onto the thought of Oscar having a meltdown in the back of a stranger's car. 'I think if it's an emergency, you're okay not to have one. Wait there, I'll get a cushion.'

I yank on the handbrake, open the door and run into the annexe, where I grab a couple of cushions. Once Oscar's seated on them, with the seatbelt fastened around him, I get back in, put the car in reverse again and press my foot gently on the accelerator. When it doesn't move, I press harder, misjudging the bite point as the car judders back. Even though I quickly snap away my foot, the bumper clips against the stone wall. Oscar shrieks. My blood pools.

'Don't worry!' I say, but I'm now actually panting. I close my eyes and take a moment to compose myself. I count steadily from one to five on the out breath, repeating it as I breathe in. I don't look for distractions. I tell myself I'm going to ride this out.

'Why aren't we moving?' Oscar pipes up.

I put the car in gear and begin to drive.

The journey feels surreal, like watching a speeded-up black and white movie. Every function of my body is misfiring. My knuckles are drained of blood, my muscles are trembling, my arms are cold and rigid. Cars seem to come at me like ghosts in the night, each one making my heart skip and thump and miss the odd beat entirely. Everything I've learnt from the past few weeks with Colette, the theory and the logic, now only exists in a compartment of my brain that I can't access.

It rubs off on Oscar. He senses my fear, mirrors my anxiety. By the time I am at the car park of the hospital, he has started to sob.

'Please don't worry, sweetheart,' I say gently as I open the door.

I get him out and am halfway across the car park, when I spot a sign saying this is a pay and display. After fumbling in my pockets, I realise I don't have a penny on me. Why the hell would they make parents bringing their sick children to A&E pay for parking? What sort of money-grabbing—

I stop and look at Oscar, who begins to cry again. 'Please don't worry. Come on, darling. Put your arm around me,' I say, bending down to hook his hands around my neck as I lift him up. I run across the tarmac, deciding I'll respond to any parking tickets with a sternly worded letter at a later date.

We burst into the reception of A&E and discover a queue at the counter, of six adults and what appears to be five patients. I stand at the back and after a minute register how slowly it's moving. A noise is released from Oscar's mouth. I can't tell if it's a yawn or if he's gasping for breath. I tap the shoulder of the man in front.

'I'm sorry . . . I think this child could be seriously ill,' I tell him. 'Would you mind?'

People are kind. I'd forgotten how kind they could be. Each person and their child allows us to move to the front of the queue and I gabble something to the lady at reception, who tells us to take a seat. A nurse calls our name soon afterwards and I carry Oscar into a sparsely decorated triage room. It's white and clinical, except for an alarming attempt at a Buzz Lightyear mural, in which his slightly wonky face reminds me of some of Salvador Dalí's early work.

Oscar sits on my knee and looks at the nurse with wide, frightened eyes.

'Who have we got here?' she asks cheerily. 'Hello, Oscar, nice to meet you.'

She turns to me. 'Are you Mum?'

'No, I was babysitting,' I say, dispensing with the introductions to get straight to the point. 'I gave him some nuts without knowing he had an allergy and I can't get in touch with his mother to ask how serious it is. He's had some strange symptoms – he looks red and blotchy and he's breathing oddly. Also, he feels ill and he's been dizzy.'

He nods, verifying my account. 'And my toe hurts.'

'Is that right?' she smiles, typing something into the computer. 'All right, young man, let's take a look at you.'

I carry him to the bed, lie him down and take off his shoes. I am wrestling with a Velcro strap when my phone rings. 'This might be his mum,' I say, looking at the nurse.

'Take it,' she says, ignoring all the signs to the contrary.

I press answer. 'Mandy. Oh, thank God. I'm in casualty with Oscar. He told me he has a nut allergy and, well, I hadn't known anything about that so I gave him this entire bowl of peanut butter. Two, in fact. I obviously don't have an epi-pen and I couldn't get hold of you—'

'He told you he's got a nut allergy?'

I swallow. 'Yes.'

She begins to weep. At least, that's what it sounds like for the first few seconds, until I realise that she can in fact hardly speak for laughing. 'Oh my God, Ellie. He does *not* have a nut allergy. Oh, what *is* he like . . . you poor thing. Ha!'

I glance at the nurse, who is taking Oscar's blood pressure as he lies groaning on the hospital bed. I think of all the children waiting outside, the sympathetic parents who've just let us barge past in the name of a medical emergency. I cup my hand over the phone.

'Then *why would he say that*?' I hiss.

'Sorry,' she says, composing herself. 'He doesn't understand the difference between having an allergy to something and just not *liking* it. This started when his friend Zachary at nursery — who *has* got an egg allergy — told Oscar that it meant he didn't like eggs. Since then Oscar's gone around telling everyone he has a pear allergy. Or a broccoli allergy. All it means is he doesn't *like* it.'

'But he ate an entire bowl of peanut butter,' I say. 'He definitely liked that.'

'He's obviously over that particular phase then. Oh God, I can't believe you've taken him to hospital. Oh Ellie, isn't he a little bugger?'

I put the phone down and am forced to explain all this to the nurse, who is remarkably understanding and assures me I did the right thing under the circumstances.

'Why did you tell me you felt funny?' I ask him, as I'm putting his shoes back on.

'I did,' he shrugs.

'I think sometimes if grown-ups worry, it rubs off a little,' says the nurse.

'And I've definitely got a sore toe,' he adds.

Chapter 50

Harriet

Shortly after Ellie's sixteenth birthday, Harriet was back at work full time and at her desk in Fleet Street. She was about to head to Brixton for the second day running, where riots had broken out following the fatal shooting by armed police of Derek Bennett, a 29-year-old black man. As she stood up and grabbed her jacket, the editor's secretary Pam appeared at her side.

'Have you got a minute, Harriet? Jerry wants a word.'

Harriet got on well with her boss. He wouldn't ever become one of the legendary editors – he was no Harold Evans or Robin Esser. But his editorial judgement was good, and he fought his journalists' corner with the zeal of a lion, albeit one who'd avoided dirtying his hands as a reporter and climbed the corporate ladder via the subs' desk. Still, he'd successfully seen off budget cuts, political interference, awkward advertisers and dealt with some of EC1's finest drunks – again, usually from the subs' desk – with a cool head.

'I wondered if you'd consider writing a first-person piece

for us,' he said, as she entered the room and closed the door behind her. 'I thought it would be interesting to read about your experiences with your daughter. Eleanor, isn't it?'

Harriet felt her spine tighten. 'Elena. *Ellie*,' she corrected him.

'I got the idea after reading this,' he said, tapping on a news article in the *Guardian*, sitting on his desk. Its title was CEAUȘESCU'S CHILDREN – *what happened next to the Romanian orphans adopted by British couples.*

It detailed an extensive study by Professor Julian Steadman and his team at the British Psychiatric Institute that had been conducted on fifty-five of the several hundred children adopted from Romania and brought to Britain to live. They'd studied the children, not merely in the aftermath of their arrival in the UK, but also their progress in the eight years afterwards.

> The children arrived in the UK with unique problems.
> The younger ones showed a limited capacity to
> move and speak and many had difficulty giving and
> receiving affection. They rocked back and forth and
> many displayed 'quasi-autistic' symptoms. At first,
> none of the youngsters knew how to play. Going outside
> was a terrifying experience for many because they were
> so unused to it.

The article added that the length of time spent in an institution was the most significant factor in developmental delays and psychiatric problems. Around forty per cent still had contact with mental health services. Professor Steadman was quoted:

Catherine Isaac

'Many of the children have made remarkable progress
since being removed from the orphanages, but it is
worth noting that sometimes problems can take years
to be fully realised. You can't simply take a child whose
entire life has been lived in a tiny cot and suddenly say:
"There you go. You have the world at your feet." The
human brain does not work like that.'

'I'm not for a minute suggesting your experience has been
like this, obviously,' said Jerry. 'From what I hear, Ellie is a
terrific girl. Really, I thought it would be good to show the
other side of the coin. An unqualified success.'

Harriet shifted onto her other foot. 'Would you mind if I
said no, Jerry? The thing is, Ellie's sixteen now. It's a tricky
age. I don't think she's one for the limelight.'

He smiled. 'Rather like you then?'

'You know me, Jerry. Never become the story.'

'Bit late for that, isn't it?' he chuckled. 'Okay, don't worry
about it. Thought it worth asking. I'm just glad it's all worked
out for you and the girl. Let me know if you change your
mind though, won't you?'

She never did. But she would remember that newspaper
article often in the coming years. It would spring to mind
when Ellie said or did something to remind them that, despite
appearances, she wasn't unaffected. How could she be? But
although there had been nightmares and odd but rare incidents in which they would find her quivering, suddenly and
for no apparent reason, until the day Harriet received a call
from Ellie's roommate Carolina at university she hadn't fully
appreciated what had been lurking in the shadows of her
daughter's mind.

Arriving at Ellie's hall of residence, she and Colin found her pale and trembling in her bed. Harriet packed her bag as Colin led Ellie to the car, like a knight in shining armour, with the eyes of a broken man.

As Ellie curled in the back, wrapped in a blanket with her temple pressed against the cold window, there were too many questions to say out loud, their worries too big to express. So they drove in silence through the black night as the blur of street lights led them to Chalk View.

Ellie seemed to recover quickly at home and, though Harriet knew that appearances could be deceptive, she was an optimist. After a few weeks of home-made food, movies on the sofa and time in the garden, Ellie was soothed back to her old self.

Even though she would never return to university – to Harriet's quiet dismay – she would ultimately make her way to London and again Harriet would hear herself saying the same words as when she was a child. Ellie was thriving. In fact, she thrived for more than a decade until things started to go wrong again. When Harriet opened the door to Ellie after she'd fled London, her high-flying job and fully functioning life, she knew instantly why she'd returned.

But it wasn't until months later, when the glow had returned to her daughter's cheeks, that Harriet realised Chalk View hadn't merely become her refuge. It had become her prison. The question she kept asking herself now was: what would it take for Ellie to finally escape for good?

Chapter 51

Ellie

The wedding is at Bosworth House, a glamorous sprawl of a hotel that commands its forest landscape like a Jacobethan dominatrix. We arrive via a long avenue lined with lime trees and classical statues, floodlights guiding us to a large turning circle. Sweeping stone steps lead up to a neatly cropped, lawned terrace. The place is colossal, the ultimate display of Victorian ego, a stately beauty surrounded by lush countryside.

'Wow,' I say, stepping out of the taxi.

'Like I say, Mimi's parents are loaded,' Guy replies, rolling his eyes. But then he spots someone on the stairs and waves. 'Jimbob!'

He marches off towards a tuxedoed man lounging on the stone banister, gazing at his phone. There is something Gatsby-esque about the pair, as they chat under the glow of an overhead lamp. Guy's dinner suit is more formal than anything I've seen him in before, yet he owns the look completely – every angle is sharp and tailored, his white shirt crisp against the faded tan of his neck.

However, as I stand watching him, traces of the orange and neroli oil from his bristles lingering on my cheek where he kissed me briefly in the taxi, I feel uneasy. Not about him, or at least, not just about him. *Everything* has felt wrong since this afternoon.

My mind has been in a discombobulated, paranoid state since I returned from the hospital. I spent hours in the bathroom as my stomach churned, convinced I'd never leave. My hand trembled as I tried to put my make-up on and I had to restart the process several times. Even now, the skin under my eyes feels pink and sore.

As the taxi pulls away, I am left at the side of the circle, acutely aware of my aloneness beneath the swollen sky. I look up and feel the gallop of my heart beneath my ribs. I am suddenly pummelled by the thought that Jamie might be looking at this pink sky too, right at this moment.

I wonder if he has been thinking about our argument as much as I have. I wonder if he regrets it. A shock of tears springs in my eyes and I blink them away, forcing indignation to billow up again. I glance over to the staircase as Guy slaps a chummy hand into the other man's, then swings his left palm into a slap between his shoulder blades. Smiles glint. Laughter is released into the air.

I tell myself that it's not a bad thing that I'm standing by myself. It's better like this. I don't want Guy to go on about *how I'm feeling, how I'm doing*, like Jamie would. If he was here showing all kinds of concern, it might draw attention to my anxiety. It might indulge it and feed it, like stacking peat on a fire. That's what I tell myself, at least.

My heels sink into the gravel as I focus on slowing my lungs, but a shot of sweat pricks under my arms. I tug away the pits of my dress. I'd tried it on dozens of times before tonight and, in the soft light of my bedroom, had been pleased with the way it cinched my waist and how the fabric drifted down my back. Now, it feels scratchy and exposes too much skin.

'Ellie. Over here,' Guy shouts, beckoning me. I snap out of my thoughts, paste on a smile and tramp towards him, clutching the skirt of my dress.

'Hello!' I say to his companion. I'm too bright, too loud, too conspicuous.

'Hello there,' he grins.

'Come on, let's go and grab a drink,' Guy says and the two men head up the steps as I trail behind.

A red carpet leads to the entrance, flanked by flamelights that shimmer orange and yellow. I find myself floating towards the door, adrift amidst a sea of silk dresses and a fug of perfume. There is a shriek of laughter and music from inside. The evening already has a bacchanalian feel. As we stand in line to be greeted by the bride and groom, I silently, internally chant my own mantra. *You will enjoy this. This is wonderful. Exactly what you wanted.*

By the time I've smiled and moved down the line saying, *lovely to meet you!* and *have you had a wonderful day?* I find I've arrived inside without fully knowing how I got here. Now there are more people, friends or family of Guy's, and he's talking to them and introducing me to one or two. I think I'm making the right noises, but words and phrases tumble into the room like bubbles, before drifting away, unconnected to one another.

'Darling! Guy! Over here!' I turn around and see a woman who looks to be in her sixties. She has a wispy, light blonde bob and is deeply tanned, with a line of vivid orange lipstick smeared on her mouth, a fraction outside her lip line. She's wearing a heavy-set gold necklace that sits amidst a slightly puckered décolletage and, despite being no more than five foot two in block heels, she stomps towards us like she's preparing to batter down a door with her forehead.

When Guy says this is his mother I try not to look surprised, even though it is impossible to identify a single physical feature they have in common. He introduces me by name, though gives no explanation that we're here together, and she responds with a cursory hello, before hooking her arm through her son's.

'I need to talk to you,' she announces, prising him away. Their discussion takes place a few feet from where I'm standing and ends when she plants a kiss on his cheek like a full stop, before wiping off a smear of lipstick with the heel of her hand.

'Your mum's nice,' I say pleasantly, as he returns to me and she marches away. 'Can I meet your brothers?'

'That's an idea. Come on, let's go and look for the gang,' he replies, taking me by the hand. He leads me through the crowd, though at one point turns so quickly that I push into a woman and slosh her drink down her dress.

'Oh God, I'm so sorry. I—' But Guy still has hold of me and hasn't noticed me stumble.

'*Guy! Stop!*' He turns sharply and looks alarmed. 'Could I . . . just have a minute?'

'What's the matter?' he asks, frowning.

Someone pushes past, elbowing me in the small of my back. 'Nothing . . . I . . . does this dress look okay?'

He looks at it, a touch bewildered, and says, 'It's absolutely fine. You look lovely. Now stop worrying.' I restack my spine.

'Was everything all right with your mum?'

'Oh, you mean the private conversation? She just wanted to . . . honestly, it's not even a big deal.'

'What isn't?'

'The fact that Stella's here.'

I'm so unused to hearing this name that it takes me a moment to place it. 'Your ex?'

He nods. 'She's friends with Mimi. I didn't know for certain but I assumed she would be coming. I'm not going to let that bother me though, I assure you.'

I blink, wondering how I'm not going to let it bother *me*.

Chapter 52

The champagne helps. At least, the first one does. The next one just leaves me queasy and ill-equipped to keep up with the names of those to whom I'm introduced. There's a Phineas and an Uncle Angus, two Hughs and a Fortescue. It starts to become like that memory game when you're supposed to recall every item hidden under your bed. I hover on the edge of a group of three women. One does PR for Gucci. Another is a fine art dealer. A third – Arabella Something-Double-Barrelled – is following her father into politics.

I've never been intimidated by the idea of privilege or money. Everyone I know started life with more than me and it never stopped me getting along with people, whoever they were. At eight years old, thrown into an unknown world, I did not sink – far from it. I swam. I tell myself I can swim again.

But perhaps I was just braver then. Perhaps there is something inherent in adulthood that has weakened and chipped away at me. I tell myself to get a grip. They're only people. It's only a party. There's nothing frightening about this. Yet the more I linger on the edges of the group, the less part of it

I feel. I am a little girl standing on her tiptoes, trying to peek through a window at the grown-ups.

'Is it the bride or groom who you know?' I say randomly, but the woman I addressed is talking to someone else before I've finished the question, having apparently not heard me.

'Sorry, did you want something?' She turns and a wrinkle appears above her pale, freckled nose. Her companion, a tall man with skeletal cheekbones, glares at me from underneath an unruly fringe.

'No, nothing,' I mumble and slink into the background. Guy is on the other side of the group, deep in conversation.

'Lovely venue, isn't it?' I try again, the moment one of the men on the edge of his group disengages from them.

'Oh, it is. Some of the frescoes are a bit flashy though. The ceiling looks like the inside of a big Christmas cake.'

I laugh. 'It's Hugo, isn't it?' I ask.

'Hugh,' he corrects me.

'Pleased to meet you.'

He takes my hand and squeezes it. There's something a touch sleazy about it, but at this stage I don't care. 'You must be Stella.'

'Oh. No, actually ... I'm Ellie,' I say awkwardly.

He looks over at Guy and raises an eyebrow.

'*Hugh! Come and get your photo taken for Insta!*'

Arabella ushers the group into formation: some kneeling, some standing at the back. It is a riotous arrangement, with jazz hands at the back, the odd rude gesture and one girl at the front who gives a peace sign. I hover again, until Guy calls out.

'Ellie? Come on, get in!'

I shake my head. 'Oh ... it's okay, I don't mind sitting it out.'

'Ellie's got fifty thousand followers on Instagram,' he says. Arabella lowers her phone.

I don't bother correcting him that it's closer to sixty.

'Well, you'd definitely better get in then!'

As the evening progresses, I feel stone cold sober. Adrenalin isn't merely the antidote to the small amount of alcohol that I've had, it also entirely removes my desire to drink any more.

'You actually make a living out of social media?' Arabella asks later. 'Aren't you clever? I'm so impressed!'

Arabella is quite sweet, even if we established immediately that we know none of the same people, go to none of the same parties, listen to none of the same music and, after she learnt that my Instagram account has a gardening theme, could only offer the information that she bought her grandmother some potting gloves from Liberty for Christmas.

'I am totally addicted to Instagram, for fashion mainly. I do follow Guy though. I love the way he's all about emotional empowerment and rebalancing of the mind.'

The thought of what Lucy would make of that sentence makes smile into my drink, though who am I to scoff? If I had more emotional empowerment and rebalancing of the mind I'd probably cope with this evening better. Still, I remind myself that I *am* getting through this. At no point is it actually enjoyable but there is a sense of accomplishment in knowing that I'm hanging in here, however woolly and disconnected I feel.

I briefly meet Guy's eldest brother – William, the cardiac surgeon. He's a nice man who is ten years older than Guy and we bond briefly over his passion for gardening, which he tells me is unfulfilled on account of his busy work and family life and the rather diminutive plot in his Putney townhouse.

For much of the night though, Guy is elusive, drifting in and out of group conversations, occasionally stopping by to ask if I need a drink, before being swept away. He has a lot of people to catch up with. I see enough of him to know that he's getting spectacularly plastered and, while I'm the last person to judge, at some point in the evening, his mood switches. He goes from being a happy drunk – the kind who laughs at anything and is loud, tactile and funny – to something more melancholy.

It's about an hour after the first dance, on a rare moment when I'm alone with him and the subject of his work comes up. It turns into an anecdote, bordering on a rant, about a disagreement he's had with the owner of his yoga studio.

'Do you know what he said? That I was "arrogant". Fucking arsehole.'

I purse my lips together sympathetically.

'Do *you* think I'm arrogant?'

'No, not at all.'

'If I leave, he wouldn't be able to replace me.'

I look up. 'What do you mean? Are you *planning* to leave?'

'I'd love to. It's been such a disappointing summer,' he sighs. My chest contracts at this assessment of the time we've spent together, yet it's clear that he isn't saying this to be hurtful. 'I just feel totally miserable that I didn't get to travel. I can't bear being cooped up for much longer. I need to get out of the country again. Staying here is stifling me.'

Quite suddenly, he stands up, swaying as he almost spills his drink. I grab it and put it on the table for him. 'Going for a slash,' he says and walks away, weaving through the tables.

As inebriated as he is, the moment Guy leaves, I feel as though I've lost my anchor. Arabella and Hugh are now engaged in a conversation with another couple, hooting with laughter. I pick up my drink and pretend to sip, feeling my spine slacken into an arc. I put my glass down and instead take out my phone, my crutch. I click on Instagram, where I've received dozens of responses to today's post. As the disco lights flash above and the DJ plays something I vaguely recognise by Rihanna, I reply to a comment about gerberas.

That's a lovely idea **@gardendaydreamer**. Nothing brightens up a winter display like

Then I stop. I force myself to click off the sentence and instead text Lucy.

At the wedding. Very sober. Dress looks crap.
But in the words of Elton John, I'm still standing.

She replies immediately.

I've been *dying* for an update but didn't want to text in case I was interrupting. First of all, send me a pic of the dress, because I don't believe you. I know you look gorgeous. Also – and mainly – WELL DONE. I'm so proud of you, Ellie. Seriously.

Three dots begin to undulate, indicating that she's writing something else. They go on and on, before eventually disappearing altogether.

Were you about to say something? You were writing something for ages then?

Catherine Isaac

Are you around tomorrow?

Yes why? Is something wrong?

I just need a chat, that's all.

Have you split up from Jakob?

The three dots appear again, then disappear. I persist.

Seriously – what is it? You're worrying me.

Just, I love you okay? We'll talk tomorrow. For now, get a drink down you and don't fret about the dress.

Lucy, I want to know what's going on.

What's going on is you need to go and have fun. Over and out.

Chapter 53

I look up across the dance floor and see Guy in the midst of a heated conversation with a woman. I don't need to be told that it's Stella, I already know. She's the most striking woman in here, though hers is a different kind of beauty from the immaculate grooming around us. Her thick, dark blonde hair tumbles around her neck. One spaghetti strap of her lipstick-red dress has fallen off a shoulder. She is barefoot, having abandoned her shoes at some earlier point. They are in semi-darkness, illuminated intermittently by the lurid flash of disco lights.

I am mesmerised. By the way she tosses her head furiously and his eyes burn when he looks at her. This does not have the mundane air of a squabble about next month's diary commitments. They are like two dancers clinched in an Argentine tango. Sweat beads at the bottom of my spine and I take a mouthful of wine that does nothing to help.

When he grabs her arm and she shakes him off, I lower my head, taking out my phone, seeking another distraction, hoping that Lucy has texted again. But she hasn't. I click it off and look up, but Guy and Stella have disappeared.

'Coming for a boogie?' Arabella is tugging me by the

arm and before I can argue I'm on the edge of the dance floor trying to remember how to move my feet in time to the music. It doesn't help that it's the worst song ever – after 'Baby Shark' of course. But even with the delirious squawk of 'Cotton Eye Joe' pounding through the speakers, people are bouncing about enthusiastically. I pretend to enjoy myself, hoping to fake it till I make it. 'Love this one!' Arabella giggles, as the bars of another song open.

'You Are The Best Thing' by Ray LaMontagne. Track number 6 on Jamie's not-a-mixtape. A song full of rousing trumpets and soulful lyrics and a drum beat that makes you remember why you're alive. I'm hit by a shot of pure, white-hot regret. By the thought that if I was here with Jamie everything would be all right. More than all right. It would be luminous and easy and filled with laughter.

Instead I'm here with Guy and it's none of those things. I take a lungful of dry ice and excuse myself from Arabella, before heading away with the song strumming my breastbone. I need air. I need a cigarette.

But the exit isn't where I thought it was and after several turns through corridors lined with princely portraits of men in wigs and racehorses in ornate gilt frames, I find myself in a drawing room. Its dark olive wallpaper is dotted with tropical birds and flowers. There is a flamboyant antique rug, a stuccoed ceiling and an abundance of ornaments, lamps and piles of books that sit upon heavily curlicued sideboards. I register a lingering scent of burning cedarwood when a footman appears at the door with a silver tray. 'Are you lost, madam?' he asks pleasantly.

'I . . . yes, I think I might be. Sorry. I wanted some air.'

'Of course. Let me show you the way.'

He leads me through a series of rooms with sprigged

wallpapers, chintz, checks and panels. Everything, everywhere is grand and old – ugly in parts and beautifully, scrumptiously English. A door finally opens onto a stone terrace at the side of the building and, after asking if there's anything else I need, the footman leaves me to lean on a lichen-patterned balustrade and breathe in the night.

'Oh. Sorry. Do you mind?' A woman appears behind me, holding up a cigarette.

'Not at all,' I say and she lights up.

'I'm giving up tomorrow.'

'Hard, isn't it?' I say, gazing longingly at the glow on the end of her Marlboro Light.

'Oh . . . do you want one?' she asks, after a languorous drag.

I plan to say: 'No thanks, I really shouldn't', but the words that actually come out are: 'Oh go on, you're a life saver.'

She passes me the packet and offers a light. I lean in and suck it up.

I've thought about this moment endlessly since my last cigarette, as if it was some tantalising, glorious, unobtainable thing. Something far bigger and better than the reality, as it turns out. I only have to take the first puff to recognise it for what it is. A monumental let-down.

My thoughts turn to Guy again. These days, it's as if he's a different man from the one who came to visit me at the start of the summer. The way he'd look at me then, with desire in his eyes, is not something I've seen recently. In bed, he's never anything less than technically proficient, but there have been times when I've felt more like an *outlet*, than the subject of any true passion.

I feel an urge to stub out the cigarette but don't want its original owner to know I've wasted it. So I merely stand with it redundantly burning down between my fingers.

'Are you all right?' she asks. I realise my hands are trembling.

I nod. 'Yes. Thanks.'

'You're sure? I need to get back but if you want me to get someone for you . . .'

'No. I'm fine. Thanks for this.'

'No problem. That dress is fab, by the way.'

I feel my heart lift. 'Really?'

'Oh yeah. Amazing colour on you.' She smiles.

As she disappears, her words bolster me. I'm grateful for the solidarity, repeating her sentence silently as I walk to the steps at the end of the terrace and drift downwards, without knowing exactly where I'm going.

I reach the bottom and turn to look at the manicured gardens. I feel chilly. I need to get back. I'm about to retreat when I hear something a little further along the wall, coming from behind one of the turrets. I realise how much I don't want to be here. I turn around and take the first three steps up towards the terrace, when I hear it again. A groan, a sound like someone is hurt or in pain. I instinctively think of Tabitha and my stomach twists.

But I close my eyes and ground myself firmly in the present day, balling up my fists as I gallop back down the steps and around the corner.

There, I find Guy and Stella.

Her back is pressed against the wall, her hand on the space between his shoulder blades as he buries his head in her neck. Their kisses are breathless and primitive; they are devouring each other. Her chiffon dress is split to the thigh and his arm has disappeared under its ruffles all the way to the inside of his elbow. I back away silently and I run.

Chapter 54

Dawn breaks like a knife blade in my head. I've had less than an hour's sleep, instead spending most of the night reliving the events of the party.

I sit up and push away the covers as I spot my dress, my beautiful dress, puddling on the carpet. There is a streak of filth on the hem and my shoes lie next to it, scuffed with a dirty tide mark. I stand up and realise with a wobble that I feel hungover, though that's hardly possible. I pick up my phone to see if Guy has texted. There's just one message, from Lucy, telling me she'll be over at eleven.

I'm hit by a tidal wave of contradictory emotions.

I never want to see him again. I want him right here, right now.

I need an explanation. I know there isn't one.

I hate him for what he did, for his casual cruelty. But most of all, I hate myself.

I can feel myself slipping down a spiral of self-loathing. Why wasn't I good enough? Or irresistible enough? Or just *enough*?

The thought that Jamie might ever find out about what

happened last night is even worse. He'd be within his rights to gloat, and if he didn't – if he was sympathetic – that would be worse still. Gertie jumps on the bed and I bury my face in her fur as another thought occurs to me: Guy never even liked my dog. He thought she was a pain in the neck, which she *is*, but she's my pain in the neck and I love her. I give her a protective squeeze and head to the shower.

The water is too hot but I stand until it stings my skin then emerge into my bedroom to find my phone ringing. It's Guy. I consider ignoring it, but swipe the screen and answer before I can stop myself.

'Hello,' I say, coldly, clutching my towel around me as I sit on the edge of the bed, my thighs damp and pimpled.

'Morning,' he replies.

It's only one word but I can already tell he's not sorry. Mildly sheepish. Hungover. But sorry? No. At least not enough.

'So . . . last night was a bit weird.' I say nothing. 'I had way too much to drink and . . . oh, Ellie. I know I was bad. Was that you at the back of the hotel?'

'Yes.'

'So you saw . . .' He's clearly not going to finish his sentence.

'You and Stella? Yes.'

'Ugh. That sucks. I'm cringing,' he sighs.

It becomes apparent that this is all he has to say on the matter. I'm aware *I've* had moments throughout my life when I've felt out of my mind. But I've always known the difference between right and wrong, understood the concept of common decency. It feels appropriate to point this out.

'How could you do that, Guy, when we were on a date together?'

'I know, Ellie. I know. Urgh! I was so drunk. It was a big mistake.'

'I don't ... I honestly don't know what it is you're phoning for.'

He seems to take umbrage at this. 'I phoned to see how you are,' he says. 'I *thought* I was doing the right thing. Clearly not.'

'I caught you *in flagrante* with the mother of your child last night, Guy. I don't know what it is you expect me to say. "Oh, never mind – what time are you coming over on Tuesday?"'

'I've already explained I was drunk,' he says, as if patiently addressing a slow-witted child. 'It was a one-off. I can hardly believe it myself – the woman is an absolute dick. *And* I've said sorry. What more am I supposed to do?'

'You were not supposed to do what you did in the first place.'

'Hang on a minute. You don't *own* me, Ellie,' he says.

'I never said I did!' I protest.

'But, Ellie,' he says, gently again, 'that's exactly how you're acting.'

'No, I'm not,' I reply indignantly. 'I've never complained that you only come over here twice a week, as if you're booked in for a chiropody appointment. I haven't raised the fact that we've been seeing each other for months but you act like I'm just there for your convenience. But you can't possibly believe it's okay to do what you did last night. Surely?'

'Can we just take One. Step. Back,' he continues acidly. 'Last night was a mistake. But could you just rewind and point to the bit at which we agreed we were exclusive?'

A knot forms in my chest. 'I ... but I assumed—'

'You assumed what? That I'm your *boyfriend*? That we're

going to start having Sunday lunch with my parents and cosying up on the sofa in our slippers on a Saturday night? I never signed up for that. So you assumed wrong.'

The worst thing is that, on one level, he's right. He never gave any indication that he was interested in me in any meaningful way whatsoever. But there is a hollow feeling in my stomach as I think about the implications of his words. 'Does this mean you've been seeing other people at the same time as you've been seeing me?'

He sighs. 'Look, Ellie. I didn't phone up to have this conversation this morning but it's probably good we did. I think it would be better for both of us if I didn't come and see you anymore. It's not your fault, but you've been expecting too much from this. I like you, Ellie. I want you to know that. You have a good soul. But I can't be in your life in the way you want me to.'

I am momentarily stunned by the raging injustice of this – that *he* gets to dump *me* after last night. 'But . . . I—'

'You don't need to say anything,' he says, soothingly. 'I want you to know that you are a beautiful person and your scars will heal. Sometimes we need to break before we shine. At times of trouble—'

'Hang on. Is this a motivational quote?'

'I'm simply saying, Ellie,' he continues smoothly, 'trust that an ending is followed by a beginning. Try to see the light beyond the storm. Feel your heart and—'

'Oh, do shut up,' I say and end the call.

When Lucy arrives, I fill her in on the whole night. She makes me an omelette. We drink tea. I do some crying.

'You can tell me you told me so.'

She tuts. 'As if. I wish this hadn't happened to you, Ellie, but at least you've seen him for what he is. I never met the guy but he comes across as a self-absorbed prick.'

The word flashes in my head, a reminder of the row with Jamie.

'The important thing is this: I know you're upset but you mustn't let this set you back on all the progress you've made with Colette. Please. I know *this* – he – was your motivation. But you've got a whole world to get out and discover with or without him.'

I sniff and nod. 'So . . . what is it you were talking about in your text last night? I've been so wound up I'd forgotten all about it.'

Her demeanour changes. She puts her mug down on the table and clearly has something big to tell me.

'Is this something to do with your lovely Norwegian?' I ask. 'I hope so. I need some news to cheer me up . . .'

'It doesn't matter,' she says.

'What doesn't?' I frown.

'We can talk about it another time.'

'Talk about what? Lucy, what are you hiding?'

She lowers her eyes and almost winces as the next words come out of her mouth. 'I've been offered a job.'

'Oh. How fab! I didn't know you were looking. What is it?'

'It's . . . at the National University of Singapore.'

I feel my wrist go limp and realise a moment later that tea is dripping on the floor.

'It's a really good opportunity.'

'Oh. I see.'

'And . . .' She takes a deep breath. 'Ellie, I've said yes. I've taken it.'

I try to keep my voice steady. 'Right. Wow. Gosh, con-gratulations! What about Jakob?'

'He's ... coming with me.' Every word sounds like an apology.

I let her announcement sink in, allowing it to filter through my brain long enough to plaster on a smile. 'Lucy, that is just *brilliant*.'

'I'm really sorry, Ellie.'

'You daft thing. Don't be,' I laugh. 'You'll be amazing! Come here, give me a hug.'

As we stand in an embrace, I squeeze my eyes tight. When I open them and pull away, I have to quickly turn to the kitchen to hide the tear spilled on my cheek.

'I thought about not going, just so you know. This hasn't been an easy thing to decide.'

'Not because of me, I hope?' I manage to grin again. 'Lucy. This is the chance of a lifetime. Think of the sun! And sky-scrapers and cocktails!'

She smiles uncertainly. 'They're putting me up in a swanky apartment for the first few months. It's got a pool.'

'And presumably you'll be back every so often?'

'Twice a year, maybe more. Perhaps you'll feel able to come and visit one day.'

'Well, there you go then! I'm unbelievably proud of you.'

I repeat those words constantly over the course of the next hour. I reassure her, I congratulate her, I tell her she is doing the right thing.

I save my crying for the moment I close the door behind her, when I leak tears and feel paralysed with despair. Eventually, I pad to the kitchen and remove a bin bag from the cupboard, before returning to my bedroom, where I stuff my dress and shoes inside the black plastic like I'm a forensics officer collecting evidence from a crime scene. I take the bundle to the front door, intending to put it in the outdoor bin. But as I click open the lock, and go to step out, I am engulfed by a feeling as hot and powerful as the backdraught from a burning building.

I stand at the threshold, looking into the garden. The leaves of the snowy mespilus have turned scarlet and crimson. The asters have brought vibrant, light purple colour to the border. The forest pansy has turned yellow and the late summer crocuses have appeared in large, leafless blooms from the bare earth, their waterlily petals a striking pinkish purple.

The thought of going out there makes my limbs begin to judder and shake, and sweat bead at my neckline. I place my foot on the patio outside and feel the air change. Then I step back, close the door and bolt the lock.

Chapter 55

 *Instagram*

EnglishCountryGardenista

769
posts

59.3k
followers

954
following

ELLIE HEATHCOTE

The temperature has dropped and the days of sitting outside in a T-shirt to watch the sun set with a G&T are pretty much gone. There's no denying it, summer is well and truly over for one year * **SOBS** *. But it isn't all bad! Today, I layered up, took myself outside and enjoyed the chill on my cheeks and the benefit of a warm drink after my hard toil. Despite the challenging conditions, the chrysanthemums are still blooming, the geraniums are in full flower and the begonias are working hard too. They don't have much longer left, so I'm enjoying them while I can and filling my notebook with ideas for my autumn and winter garden.

All, of course, with a fabulous, upbeat soundtrack (though 'Walking On Sunshine' was pushing it a little under today's cloud cover). What jobs have you been doing since the weather turned? #EnglishCountryGardenista #thisgirldigs #englishcountrygardens #Octobergardens #gardener #gardening #garden #gardenlife #flowers #plants #gardens #nature #gardendesign #growyourown #gardeninspiration #instagarden #gardenlove #growyourownfood

The relief of sleep is immense. So dense and warm that I don't even dream. Dropping off last night felt like slipping into a silky bath, deep and comforting and safe. These days, I stay in bed not merely all night, but for hours beyond the point at which hazy light begins to blur into the gap in the curtains. When I wake it is reluctantly, peeling open an eyelid to register the glow of digits on my bedside cabinet. 12.43pm. I sink further under my quilt.

What rouses me eventually is a craving, a visceral need to reach under my bed for the cigarettes and ashtray. A dusty, decaying aroma rises as I lift them onto my bedside cabinet, but I fall short of finding it offensive. Others might, though nobody has been inside my annexe for weeks except Gertie, to whom I cling like she's a lifebuoy, and Mum and Dad, who I don't allow near my bedroom. I keep the door firmly shut, awaiting their departure, so I can return to bed. I sometimes have a long wait.

They come over as often as their ability to create flimsy excuses allows. Mum hovers in the living room, saying everything too casually: *Could I tempt you for a walk today, Ellie? How about you pop over for dinner tonight?* or – more directly – *If you need to talk, we're here. Not that I'm pressurising you.*

All of which translates as: *What the fuck is happening here? AGAIN?*

She brings home-baked bread and fancy deli items, hearty soups and sweet things, food designed to fortify, nourish and encourage a failing appetite. Most end up being chucked out, though she must never know that. Dad also arrives to walk Gertie every day and of the two of them, it's his expression that's hardest to handle.

I sit up, plump my pillows and light a cigarette, inhaling as deeply as my lungs allow before they begin to object, brushing a greasy strand of hair out of my face. There's something deeply luxurious about smoking in bed, I think. Prunella Scales used to do it in *Fawlty Towers*, with a box of Milk Tray in the other hand. If that's not living I don't know what is. I place the filter in my mouth and pull out my iPad to check how last night's Instagram post is performing.

The answer is, beautifully. Which is gratifying given that my process has altered slightly of late. This image of the *Cotinus coggygria* was not taken yesterday morning as it says in the caption. It was rooted out from the archives of my computer and selected from the images I took this time last year. I always end up with hundreds more photos than I can use and it fills me with a certain satisfaction to know that I'm now putting them to good purpose. It seems thrifty and rather practical, like Kirstie Allsopp making a nifty pomander from dried lavender and an old pair of tights.

I sink into my bed again and reply to some comments.

@ontariogardener
Have you had any snow there Ellie?

@EnglishCountryGardenista

Not yet! Plenty of rain though. No chance of a drought in my garden right now.

@Lauramanners

I love your shrubs. Are there any I could plant at this time of year?

@EnglishCountryGardenista

Absolutely! Lots of shrubs need to be left until spring (ornamental grasses or borderline hardy plants such as cistus or salvias, for example). But go with something like witch hazel or hydrangeas and make sure you dig over the whole border at least a spade's depth, then work in lots of well-rotted compost and you're ready to go!

It's nice to stay in touch. It reminds me that I'm human. That I might be sitting here surrounded by fags and Diet Coke cans, having not faced anyone from the outside world for ... I hardly remember now. But, on Instagram, everything remains the same. On Instagram, I am still @EnglishCountryGardenista. I still advise you how to handle tender perennials and prune a pear tree. I can still tell you how to deal with acid soil and the best position to plant nasturtiums. I can still dig and mow and cultivate and grow and do it all with a pin-sharp eyeliner flick and bubblegum-pink Hunter wellies. Or at least do all this in the pictures.

Maintaining my social media presence without moving from my bed might seem cynical, but I have a living to make and the money I got from selling my 1900 edition of *The Gardens of Gertrude Jekyll* will only last so long. I have not taken up any offers of new work, but most of the sponsor-ship campaigns that I was contracted for have gone ahead as scheduled, using pictures I'd already taken. I've had to make my excuses on at least two that were due to run next month because I simply haven't done the photo shoot. But this is the best I can do right now. Given I'm in the throes of what I'm fully aware is an episode (nothing as dramatic as a *breakdown*, whatever Lucy calls it), it is surely to be commended that I'm still vaguely functioning enough to continue with self-employment for now.

I click through my computer and find another contender for tomorrow's photo. I'm in this one. My hair is wanded into lustrous waves, I have a face full of make-up and look every bit Instagram Me. A woman with no flashbacks or nightmares or the insidious sense of threat that lives constantly between the thudding in her ears.

After I've replied to everyone, I answer the call of my bladder and empty my ashtray, watching as the swirl of toilet water struggles to flush the mountain of butts and leaves a residue of nicotine tide marks. My loo really has earned its keep lately. I've thrown all sorts down there in a bid to avoid putting the bins out. I could ask Mum or Dad, but so far I've tried to maintain the impression that I'm still going into the garden and they're pretending not to notice evidence to the contrary. I realise I'm going to have to either broach that sub-ject soon or actually open the door and put the bin out, but for the moment, the thought makes me feel ill. I head back into the kitchen to make coffee. As I fill up the machine with water, I lift my eyes to the window and look outside.

So this is what happens when you don't weed the beds or deadhead your roses.

There's a strange and wild beauty in what I see – Miss Havisham's house in horticultural form. The unseasonably warm weather has led a mass of new shoots to pop up from the cracks in the flags. The borders are a tangle of browning, overgrown stems and anything that was blooming in late summer – the phlox and foxgloves – lies dead and decaying. Sludgy water spills from stacks of pots and overflows from the wheelbarrow. Of the flowers, only a few cling on, roses with wilted heads and pansies battered by rain that lie like muddy handkerchiefs. And at the far end of the garden is Oscar's sunflower, withered and brown, but still standing.

I realise I'm scratching my forearms and decide it's time to drag myself into the shower. As I head to the bathroom, I hear the thrum of an engine and thoughts of Jamie hit me like a flash flood.

I am gripped by the thought that this could be him, even though I have nothing on order. It's feasible, though I haven't heard a word from him since our argument. I'm continually torn about whether I want to see him or not. For the most part, I simply cannot face him – yet I've still managed to place four orders with Green Fingers in the past weeks for items I don't even vaguely need. They sent a replacement delivery man every time, which makes me suspect Jamie has actively requested to be put on another route. *That's* how much he doesn't want to see me.

Obviously, there hasn't been the slightest clue on social media as to what he's up to. He's still not on Instagram or Twitter, and only has his half-hearted Facebook account for which he still hasn't even uploaded a profile picture. In this vacuum, my imagination has run wild. I've considered the possibility that he's had a shotgun wedding with the nice cancer nurse-cum-primary school teacher I'd partnered him off with and is now toasting their nuptials on a balcony in Alicante. Or, and I suspect this really is the case, he's just quietly getting on with his life, exactly as before, and wants nothing more to do with me ever again. For different reasons than Guy.

I've seen plenty of *him* on social media. He's been pictured repeatedly with @KellieYogini in a variety of local beauty spots, often with his ankles twisted round her neck, and always accompanied by some quote about *making a connection* or *being someone's earth*. The frequency and nature of these pictures is starting to give the impression that they are designed to make someone jealous. Someone other than me, of course. I do wonder sometimes what Stella must make of it all.

I creep to the window and peer out. When I see it's a Green Fingers van, my brain puddles with the possibility that this – finally – could be him. The van door opens. Two boots crunch on the ground under the door. I look down at my crumpled, fetid PJs and dash to the bedroom to pull on some clean jeans. When I return to find a brush, it occurs to me that Mum and Dad might have ordered something. But they're out, so he'll either just drop off the delivery and leave *or* come over here.

I'm dousing myself in dry shampoo and deodorant when there's a knock. I walk to the door before I can change my mind and turn the lock. Opening it feels like a rush of cold air sweeping through my body, chilling my bones.

But it is not Jamie. The man at the door must be in his mid-seventies, with a thin face framed by steel-rimmed glasses that make him look like Postman Pat. He smiles cheerfully. 'Hello! Can you take a parcel for the main house?'

I taste bile in my mouth. 'Yes. Of course.'

A gust of wind from behind him reminds me that I am facing the outside world and the moment I have the parcel in my hand, I want to shut the door. It's addressed to Dad.

'You need to sign for it,' he says, handing me the signature machine. I scrawl my name, and thrust it back at him. I'm about to close the door, but hesitate.

'How's Jamie?' I ask.

He frowns, trying to place the name.

'He used to be my delivery man,' I explain. 'Hasn't been for a while but I assume he's still working at the company?'

'Oh ... Jamie. Big bloke?'

'Yes.'

'Tall?'

I nod. 'Yes.'

'Friendly chap?'

'Yes, that's him,' I say.

'He's on a couple of weeks' leave, I think.'

Relief sweeps over me. I decide there and then I'm going to order some plants, timed precisely for his return to work. Before then I can get outside and tidy up the beds. I could say I've been sick, ideally with something people are actually sympathetic about, like laryngitis or shingles – something solidly unpleasant and worthy of compassion.

'When is he back? Next week? The week after?'

'Oh! No, hang on. I think he might not be coming back.'

'What?'

'Yes ... did he say something about going to live in Sweden ... ?'

'He's moving to *Sweden*?'

'That can't be right, can it? I don't know. Maybe it is. Do you want me to phone the office to find out?'

333

A sickly feeling rises up my chest. 'Yes, please.'

I stand back from the door, trying not to shiver as he telephones the office and ends up in conversation with a receptionist called Shirley about her dog's rheumatoid arthritis. When he gets onto the subject of Jamie, he explains that a customer is asking after him and wondered if she could confirm what he'd thought was the case about Sweden. Her response goes on for ever, a drone of chatter and half-heard explanation that only finally ends when he says, 'Rightio. I'll let her know.'

'What did she say?' I ask.

'She's just been on a data protection course,' he says.

'What?'

'Apparently I'm not allowed to say where he's gone,' he replies.

'But . . . we were friends,' I argue. 'We *are* friends. I just . . . has he really gone to Sweden, do you at least know that?'

'Sorry, I don't.' He lowers his voice conspiratorially. 'He *has* left though – that I can say for definite.'

Chapter 56

Lucy is leaving for Singapore in six weeks. She's been very busy. There's a lot to organise when you're moving to another continent. I knew she was coming over today because she texted me, but when she knocks on the door, I still jump like a child spooked by noises in the night. I let her in and she surveys the living room, her lip tightly curled.

'What's that smell?'

'I don't know.' I sniff my left armpit. I do know.

'Ellie, you need to empty your bin. It stinks of fags in here. You do realise Mum and Dad *know* you smoke, don't you?'

'Have they said that?' I ask, alarmed.

'Believe it or not, that's the least of their worries. For God's sake, at least open a window.'

She marches to the kitchen and reaches for the latch.

'*Don't!*' She turns. 'Please. I prefer it like this.'

She sighs. 'Ellie, I'm sorry, but you're just going to *have* to let some air in here.'

She pushes the window open and a cold breeze rushes in. Goosebumps prickle along my arms, which I fold tightly across my chest.

'Come and sit down,' she says, gesturing to the sofa. I do as I'm told. 'What's going on?' she asks. This gentle voice is infinitely harder to take than the one when she's being a pain in the neck.

'What do you mean?' I ask.

She swirls her hand around and I realise she's referring to my appearance.

I tug the belt to my dressing gown tighter. 'I'm allowed a lie-in, aren't I?'

'This is more than a lie-in. You look like you've been crying for a week. You're refusing to go to see Colette. You're not looking after yourself.'

'Well, I'm sorry if I don't look like Grace Kelly. I'm tired, that's all.' I stand up and walk away, marching to my bedroom, where I scratch under the bed for my cigarettes. I find one and light up, then return to the living room with it flagrantly clamped between two fingers of my right hand.

'What happened to your inside smoking ban?' she asks. 'Couldn't you at least *vape*?'

I let out a long plume of smoke. 'Have you come here to lecture me, Lucy? Because, as they say in all the best movies, *I'm not in the mood.*'

I wait for her to fire back a response. But she suddenly looks so unbearably sad that I can't bring myself to meet her eyes.

'I didn't come to lecture you.' Her larynx sounds thick and woolly. 'I came here to try and help. Because, I'll be honest, Ellie, I don't think Mum and Dad know how any more. But now I see that *I* don't either.'

'I don't want help,' I shrug.

'Yes, I know. That's what I'm worried about.'

Then she doesn't say a thing. For the first time in all the years I've known her, I appear to have silenced my sister.

'Is this about Guy? Or Tabitha? Or *me* – the fact that I'm going to Singapore?' The question bursts out of her as if it's all she's thought about.

But it's impossible to answer, at least in the way she wants me to. I don't have the ability to deconstruct which setback engulfed me, tipped me over the edge. What I'm feeling seems completely disconnected from any of those events. I'm barely even thinking about them any more. So I give her the closest answer to the truth.

'This is about none of those things, Lucy.'

It's only about me.

There's no real way of explaining. How do you explain to someone your absolute and certain knowledge that if you leave the confines of your house something terrible will happen? And how the fact that you do not know what the *terrible thing* is only adds to its immensity. How do you explain the overwhelming threat posed by what is beyond your door, the threat only you recognise and register, through something that can't be rationally outlined, but is closer to a kind of sixth sense? The answer is, you can't, because you'd sound like a lunatic. Even I know that and I'm the one thinking all these things.

Either way, she isn't listening. She sits forward on the sofa, her eyes glazed. 'I won't go if you don't want me to,' she says. 'I could never forgive myself if I was the cause of . . . if you did something and I was to blame and . . .'

I sit down next to her on the sofa. 'What are you saying? You're worried I'm going to kill myself?'

'Yes. We all are.'

'Lucy, listen to me. I'm not going to do that. Okay? I promise you. I absolutely promise.'

'Have you ever thought about it?' she asks, lowering her chin. 'Tell me. I need to know.'

'No. Never.' I'm not sure this is one hundred per cent true. There have been bleak moments, but they have been fleeting. I don't want to admit they're real by saying it out loud. 'Plus, even if I had – which I haven't – I'd never have the guts to go through with it. The thing is, Lucy, *nothing* would depress me more than the idea that I'd held you back from your dream job and your dream man. So you're just going to have to go to Singapore and that's that.'

She lowers her eyes. 'Wherever I am, I want you to know that I will be there for you on the phone or Facetime at any time of the day or night. You mustn't ever, ever think you're alone.'

'I know that,' I say shakily.

She sniffs. 'I'd love you to meet Jakob, you know.'

She's imagining dinner à trois at one of her favourite London restaurants. She's thinking about clinking glasses and laughter, sharing anecdotes about our childhood and squeezing his hand secretly under the table. Absolutely none of which is going to happen.

'He sounds lovely,' I say.

'Well, I've *earned* him. You've got to meet a lot of dickheads before someone like him comes along, just remember that. You, Ellie, only met *one* dickhead. Count yourself lucky. Though I'll give you this, he really was a supreme dickhead. Did you notice what happened on his Instagram feed yesterday?'

I look up. 'No. Why were you looking at his Instagram?'

'Working out a way to use my voodoo doll. Someone had called him out about that post you sent me a while ago. What did it say: "Yesterday is history, tomorrow is a mystery, but today is a gift. That is why it is called present." Rather good, wasn't it? It was a quote from *Kung Fu Panda*.'

'You're joking?'

'Someone threatened to report him, a heated exchange followed, and now he's deleted his account. Tea?' she asks, and heads to the kitchen.

'Um . . . okay.'

'So what about Jamie? Have you seen anything of him?'

'He's not working for Green Fingers these days.'

'Oh. Really?'

I swallow. 'I didn't mention this but we had a falling out.'

'What about?'

I consider telling her the whole saga but feel urgently in need of retiring to bed. 'It doesn't even matter now.'

'Ellie, I'll phone him. Can you give me his number?'

'No!' I say, alarmed. 'Absolutely not. Promise me you won't try to find him.'

She frowns.

'Seriously, Lucy. Don't.'

'Okay. I won't do anything you don't want me to. But . . . can I ask you one thing?'

'Of course.'

'Please just give Colette a ring. For me.'

But I can't answer her. Because just the thought of it is completely exhausting.

Chapter 57

The days begin to blend into one. There are no mornings, afternoons, evenings or night-times. I am simply either awake or asleep, and I know which I prefer. When I'm not in bed, I do one of three things. Watch Netflix. Post on Instagram. Or look online at what some of the people who once had a place in my life are doing.

Guy is now in Indonesia. He reactivated his account and posted a photo on Instagram today, or maybe it was yesterday, in front of the Uluwatu temple with the balls of his feet tickling his eyebrows. He was deluged with admiring comments about his 'one-legged king pigeon', which is apparently a yoga pose and not an alternative to turkey on Christmas Day. I don't feel numb to him exactly, but neither do I feel any of my previous longing, or even, surprisingly, anger. I don't actually feel anything, other than a complete disconnection from any of my old feelings about him.

I also find myself drifting onto social media platforms I don't usually visit and typing in the name Tabitha Florescu. Predictably, I find nothing. So instead I end up searching for old school friends. I don't know why. But I discover that Isabel

340

works in the human resources department of a hospital in the West Midlands. She has a long-term girlfriend called Ashanti and a puppy called Villanelle. Helen has a high-flying finance job and lives in Hong Kong, where her hobbies include feng-shui, networking over cocktails and dating pneumatic Australians called Jack, Jake, Nick or Luke.

And Jo, it seems, is doing exactly as Jamie said: living two miles away with her parents and two children and working as an environmental lawyer in east London. She's going through a divorce. Of all of them, she's the only one I've considered contacting. I even got as far as composing a message on Facebook. I know I should, that she might be lonely or in need of a friend at a time like this.

But what do I have to offer? How could I possibly help? Plus, knowing Jo, she'd want to meet for drinks or go looking for a new boyfriend. She might already have booked a singles holiday and try to persuade me to go with her. I can't do any of those things. So instead, my long message sits as a draft in the depths of my little-used Facebook account.

Then there is Jamie, the only man on earth, it seems, not on social media. Except, when I search on Instagram under the hashtag *#DannyOchIsbjörnarna*, it unleashes a stream of images from book events in Stockholm. Jamie isn't tagged in any of them as he doesn't have an account, but he is pictured in at least a dozen different stores, surrounded by children and parents. Then, one evening, as dusk becomes twilight, an event appears on Facebook, advertising a short UK book tour to celebrate publication of 'the most magical children's book you'll read this Christmas'.

Danny and the Polar Bear
Listen to author Ulrika Sjöblad read from this future clas-
sic, while budding young artists can join illustrator Jamie
Dawson for a drawing workshop. 3pm to 4pm, Saturday
December 1st, Hatchards, Piccadilly.

I click on the link.
'Going?' it asks.
For a fleeting moment I almost consider checking my diary.

My sleep is disturbed that night. I can't remember the last
time I had insomnia – for weeks I have crashed into a near
unconscious state at any hour of the day when I've felt inclined
to climb into bed. Tonight, although I drift off repeatedly, it's
never for long and my dreams are odd not merely because of
their fragmented nature. In them, Jamie and I are standing
at the gate outside Chalk View, like we did the first time we
walked together. The field is dredged with wildflowers and
the sky a yawning, cobalt blue. Skylarks circle above, butter-
flies swoop and dive.

I should be sick with fear but I'm not. Now, everything is
the same but slightly different, as if I've stepped through an
alternative set of sliding doors. In this version of my world
there is no Guy. There is no cancer nurse–cum–school teacher.
There is only me and Jamie. But we're not just friends.

The reason I know this is that, instead of clasping my
fingers before we walk across the field, he turns to me and
lifts my hand to his lips. He tenderly kisses my knuckles, his
melting brown eyes on mine. Something surges through
me: a rush of euphoria, an explosion of lust, an indefinable,
dynamic thing that's as pure and clear as a mountain stream.

Suddenly, that something is unmistakable. This is love. This brief kiss is one of an infinite series, the first chapter in a book that does not end here, but only starts. Then I feel the tug of my sheets and open my eyes to find Gertie attempting to lick my feet and everything exactly the same as it was before.

Chapter 58

For the rest of the night, I lie in bed with my laptop, Gertie by my side as I interact with a few followers and drift onto my favourite accounts to comment on their posts.

@Bobturpin
You're planting under some pretty mature trees there. I always find it impossible to get anything to thrive in those conditions. Do you have any tips?

@TheMontyDon
I love those pruning shears. Which brand are they?

I do this for much of the night and, unsurprisingly given the hour, receive a limited response, at least from anyone living on my side of the planet. But as people wake up, so does my Instagram feed. One of the first notifications comes from a well-established influencer called @GardeningBetty, who comments on the picture I posted yesterday.

Gorgeous. Ellie, you are the best advert there is for getting outdoors, despite the weather. An inspiration!

My fingers hover over the keyboard. I begin to type.

Actually **@GardeningBetty**, I'm not an inspiration. I'm a fraud.

I sit and look at the words, feeling an almost preternatural urge to hit Enter. To blow the whole gaff. To tell the world that no, on the contrary, I can't even walk out of my own front door and have been bypassing this bothersome issue by using old photos that I pretend were taken this week. Would that be the right thing to do? It would certainly be the honest thing to do. Gertie appears at the side of the bed. I lift her up but she wriggles away and hops down again, circling the room before she disappears and returns with a ball. She drops it on the floor and yaps. I throw it across the room.

We repeat the exercise approximately thirty times, until I'm irritated and weary, but most of all conscious that I have no right to be. She needs exercise. And though I feel lousy texting Mum to ask if she's free to walk her, I have no alternative. She responds to say she'll be over in an hour. I use the time to drag myself into the shower, wash my hair and pull on some clean clothes. I even put on some mascara. It's all a disguise, of course, though not a good one.

Mum appears at the door in a Barbour jacket and bobble hat, her phone loaded with Radio 4 podcasts. She walks in and coughs, her throat catching on the half can of Febreze I've unloaded into the atmosphere. Gertie jumps up and down, lavishing Mum with affection.

'You're her favourite human these days,' I say.

'She's just excited about her walk,' Mum replies. 'Why don't you come with me? Even just for five minutes. This place is so stuffy, I know you'd feel better if you got some fresh air.'

'I'm tired, Mum. I didn't sleep very well last night.'

'Well, I was thinking of making the Christmas cake later today. Will you come over? You and Lucy used to love joining in.'

I feel a pang of nostalgia at the thought of my sister and me excitedly stirring the mixture, before helping Mum to tip in the dried fruit, which there was so much of that she'd had to soak it in brandy in a washing-up bowl. The memory is completely at odds with the way I feel now, but I can see how much Mum wants me there. 'Yes, all right,' I say, though I already know I won't go.

She brightens. 'Oh, good.'

When she's gone, I return to my computer and read my un-posted words. I gently rub my finger on the return button, but delete them and shut down my laptop.

Instead, I pick up my phone and scroll to Colette's office number. It goes straight to voicemail, but I don't leave a message and decide to try her mobile.

'Hello, Ellie. Nice to hear from you.' It sounds like she's been expecting this call for some time.

'Sorry to phone on your mobile. I hope I'm not disturbing you?'

'Not at all. What can I do for you?'

'Well, first of all, I need to let you know that I haven't done my homework. I'm really sorry. I don't know why. It's been impossible.'

'I didn't imagine you would have, Ellie,' she replies. 'When your mum phoned to cancel the last appointment, she said you'd been finding things hard.'

'Did she tell you I can't leave the house? I mean, *at all*?'

'She did.'

'I have tried but I really can't do it and now I'm at rock bottom. Did she tell you that?'

'Something along those lines. Have you spoken to your GP about adjusting your medication?'

I might have known this would come up. 'The medication wasn't working.'

'You stopped it?'

'Look, I know you're going to say I'm not meant to change anything without consulting the GP but I was feeling rotten well before I stopped. The tablets were making me feel worse. I'm convinced they were contributing to how bad I felt.'

I can sense her disapproval. 'All right. But you need to speak to your doctor about an alternative. In the meantime, if you want to see me, I will squeeze you in tomorrow.'

I feel a wave of sudden optimism.

'Colette, that would be great. I honestly think that if anyone can help me it's you. Thank you.'

'Two-thirty?'

'Yes. Absolutely.'

'Just so we're clear, Ellie. The appointment is here, at my office.'

I suspected she might say that but I still feel as though I've been winded. 'But I . . . my mum told you. I told you. I *cannot* leave the house. I'm just not able, Colette. I understand that you had that policy when I was *slightly* bad. You made that clear and I respect that. But this is far worse.'

Catherine Isaac

She pauses long enough for my hopes to rise. 'Ellie, you know you can get yourself here because you did it for weeks.'

'Everything was different then,' I say, my voice cracking. 'Look, I understand it's a pain for you.'

'That's not the reason.' There is empathy in the way she speaks, and hesitation. She's thinking about this, I can hear it.

'If you were just willing to make an exception, just once, I *swear* it would be worth it. One session. That's all I'm asking. I will cover your petrol . . . in fact, I'll pay double time.'

There's a pause. 'Ellie, I'm sorry, but I'm not coming to you,' she says finally. 'The appointment is in the diary. I'll see you tomorrow.'

No, you fucking won't, I think, as she ends the call and I throw the phone at the wall, watching as it bounces off my Farrow and Ball French Grey and leaves a pebble-shaped chip in the plaster.

I sit on the edge of my bed, fury racing though me. Then I stand, pick up my phone and walk to the living-room window, clicking on the camera. I don't open it. I don't need to. Even through the glass you can see the mess, the debris, the decay. I remove the lens cover, point and shoot. I capture everything: the saturated leaves that have piled into the corner. The soggy stems that have wilted into the ground. I capture the mud and the mess, the chaos, the dead and the dying.

Then I sit on the sofa, with Gertie curled up on my feet, and compose an Instagram Story, uploading picture after picture and adding a paragraph to each one.

If you've been following me for a while and stumbled across

348

the pictures in this Story, you'd be forgiven for wondering what's going on.

Where are all the winter flowering shrubs and vibrant berries, the neatly arranged pots and the hanging baskets filled with winter foliage? The answer, I'm afraid, is that they don't exist. Not this year.

These pictures, I'm sorry to say it, were taken today. All of them.

As you can see, there are no winter cherries, no evergreen viburnums. Nothing but a mess. I haven't touched the garden for weeks. And the reason for that is that I haven't been able to step outside my front door.

As most of you are here for the gardening pictures and advice I won't bore you with the detail, except to say that, mentally, I have not been in a good place. I have suffered with agoraphobia for all of my adult life and, while there are long periods when it's under control, at other times it's so severe I can't even leave my bedroom. That's where I spent most of the last few weeks.

During that time, I did something I'm not proud of. I continued posting pictures about sunshine and flowers, pretending everything was tickety boo. I reasoned that if I could keep one part of my life in order – this, which means so much to me – the rest would follow.

It amounted to a big fat lie. It disrespected anyone who has taken the time to follow me.

To me, Instagram has never been about filters and Photoshop, but community. So there's no defence for what I've done.

All I can say is, I'm sorry. I really am.

I publish picture after picture, caption after caption. It occurs to me only briefly to question why I'm doing this. Perhaps I want to do something brave and real, something true to myself. Perhaps I am feeling so self-destructive that this is the fastest way to undo everything I've achieved in the last couple of years.

An icon appears below the story to show that someone has read it. Then another. As the number of views rises, it strikes me that if this really is my aim – to show people the real me – then I've only half-done it. What, after all, is the point in having lots of followers if the person they think they're following doesn't actually exist?

I go to my bedroom and open the wardrobe, standing on my stool to take down the photo of Tabitha and me. I take a copy on my phone, then head back to the sofa.

Instagram

EnglishCountryGardenista

791 posts **62.6k** followers **987** following

ELLIE HEATHCOTE

I want to tell you a little bit about me. Not gardening me, or Instagram me, but the real me. The name I was given when I was born was Elena Balan. I spent the first years of my life in Bucharest, Romania, and this picture, taken in 1990, is one of the few that exist of me there. I'm on the left, next to a little girl called Tabitha. Those rusting beds are where we slept in the orphanage and like tens of thousands of children, we'd been there since we were babies. Tabitha ran away shortly after this, while I was adopted by a British couple.

For those of you old enough to remember the news stories about Romania's orphanages, you probably don't need me to describe what they were like. For anyone else, you might consider Googling the subject. I will simply say that they were the last places on earth where any child should be raised.

I have spent much of my time since I moved to the UK not merely trying to forget this phase of my life, but to deny its existence. I refused to accept that it would ever be allowed to influence the person I went on to become. That turned out to be a fruitless task. Human beings are shaped by our past whether we like it or not.

Acknowledging this is one of the reasons why this feels like a good time for me to bow out of here. It might be just a break, it might be for good. Either way, I want to end on two important notes. First, thank you for your friendship, your loyalty, your chats about peat and fertiliser, worms and wisteria. People who don't like social media will never understand this side of it. But for those who know, you have helped me enormously and brought a lot of support and friendship into the life of someone who otherwise would have had none. Most of all though, I'm sorry. I'm sorry for all kinds of things but mainly this: that I am not the person I let you believe I was.

#thisgirlgardens   #autumngardens   #gardenistas #orphanagenumber3   #bucharest   #romanianorphanage #mentalhealthmatters   #romania #LaCentruldePlasamentTrandafirGalben

I publish the post and for a moment afterwards, I watch. The first response arrives within a minute. It's from someone called @RamseyLad, who says:

Priceless. You filthy Polish fake.

I can feel every tiny blood vessel in my body constrict. Part of me wants to wait for my followers to respond, to leap to my defence. But no matter how hard I stare at the screen, nothing comes.

I click on @RamseyLad's profile and see that he's a follower of mine though I don't remember him ever commenting before. He has a biblical quote in his biog and a Britain First hashtag. Another comment appears from him.

You're not fit to clean my fucking shoes

My heart begins to flap. I scroll up to the settings and, before I can change my mind, I log out of my account on my iPad and uninstall the app. For good.

Chapter 59

It takes until the first week of November for something to change, on a morning that begins with glimmers of pale sun filtering though the gap in my curtains. Gertie sees me rouse and jumps on the bed. I snuggle into her fur and consider closing my eyes again, when I hear something outside. Banging. Voices. I pull the quilt up to my face and listen.

Someone is in my shed. I sit up sharply. Who the *hell* is in my shed?

I leap out and wrestle on my dressing gown, before opening the bedroom door. Gertie scuttles behind to the window, where I am confronted with a sight that makes me think I'm hallucinating at first.

My sister has a spade in her hand. Dad is holding a rake.

Instinctively, I bang on the window. They both look up, register me and reply with two pleasant waves, as if we're in a parallel universe in which this kind of thing ever happens. Then Lucy bends to a flower bed and jams the spade in the ground, while Dad tugs the rake over the grass. I run to the front door and unbolt the lock, inhaling deeply before I open it. The cold air hits me like a firecracker. Everything is too bright, too sharp, too *outside*.

'Morning,' they chime.

'What are you doing?' I demand.

'Have you got any gardening gloves?' Lucy asks, apparently not hearing me.

'We've decided to give you a hand, just sort out the worst of the mess,' Dad explains.

'It's not a . . .' But I don't finish my sentence, because it is. For a moment I don't entirely know what to do, other than retreat into the house and sit at the window, watching.

It would be funny if it wasn't so painful.

Lucy handles the leaf blower like it's a weapon in an armed shoot-out, her brow squished in furious concentration. Despite this, she's useless with it, repeatedly clogging up the netting with leaves, at which point she unplugs it before manually attempting to unblock it. I tap on the window on her fourth attempt and she turns to me, testily.

'*There's a knack*,' I shout through the glass.

The brow furrows again. '*What?*'

'There's a knack to it,' I repeat. '*A. Knack.*'

She drops it to the ground and walks to my door. She knocks. I brace myself and go to open it.

'Are you trying to tell me something?'

'I'm just saying that there's a knack to it. You don't have to do it too hard, you just have to hold it in the correct position. Treat it with respect.'

'Why would I do that? It's an absolute bastard.'

'Oh, it's not bad,' I say defensively. 'I got it free for a sponsored post. It does work as long as you know how to do it.'

'Well, perhaps you could come and show me.'

I cross my arms and step back. 'I did not ask you to do this, Lucy,' I say. I can see irritation billow up behind her eyes. 'But . . . for the record, I appreciate it.'

This is a lie. I know it *should* be true. But as I watch them hack away at shrubs, yank at perennials and, in the process of *clearing*, make far more of a mess than nature alone would, it feels like a violation. Like someone giving a bed bath without prior warning, let alone requesting consent – convincing themselves they're doing you a favour when they shove a wet sponge in your most intimate parts.

They continue for another hour, my sister muttering angrily under her breath, Dad coming over to inspect, Mum appearing at the door carrying three steaming mugs. They all stop for a jolly tea break before she joins in too. I watch with a knot in my chest as she begins lobbing the heads off my Honeybun roses, presumably in the belief that this constitutes deadheading. When Lucy emerges from the shed brandishing a hedge trimmer, I can take no more. '*Stop!*'

She looks up and gives it a little rev. 'Everything all right?' she asks, proving once and for all that she is a psychopath. I step away from the window and grab my boots.

The first time I go outside I can only stand it for a few minutes before I excuse myself to go back inside to the toilet. I am mainly dying for them all to just leave so I can smoke a cigarette in peace and return to bed. I don't know how it is that I end up drifting outside again. It almost comes as a shock to realise that I am on my knees, with cool winter sunshine on my back, my hands deep in the cold soil.

After that, time passes without me fully registering it. When I eventually do look at my watch, it tells me that I've been outside for nearly two hours, though that hardly seems possible. I accumulate three garden bags of waste, as the soundtrack of blackbirds and song thrushes competes with my family's chatter.

It happens in a blur, momentum building as my lungs burn with clear air. As the sun goes down, my fingers are numb, my thighs are beginning to ache, my feet throb. All four of us pack away the tools and head into my parents' house and although I feel tired, it's in a different way from the last few weeks. There is a hot glow on my cheeks. And although I'm still dying for a cigarette, the thing I want most is to sit by the stove in my parents' kitchen and eat a bowl of thick, home-made soup.

Chapter 60

I spend the next few days in the garden, heading out each morning for reasons I can't fully explain beyond some kind of muscle memory. It doesn't feel good to be outside, but staying in feels worse.

It seems fairly sudden – a recognition one day when I walk out of my front door that there is an energy in my limbs that definitely wasn't there a few weeks ago. My thinking feels sharper, my heart lighter.

'Thought you might like some tea,' Dad says, placing two cups on the bench. 'Wow, this really has had an overhaul. Should I take some pictures for you?'

This is how we did it when I first started my Instagram account. Before I'd bought a tripod or a proper camera, I'd rope Dad in to help out, insisting that he didn't need to know anything about light or composition, just to press the button.

We take lots. Some are pretty good. My favourite is one that he captures when I'm off guard, of me kneeling beside the vegetable patch, soil smeared on my forehead.

'Do you remember joining the synchronised swimming team?' Dad asks, randomly.

'Vaguely,' I say, because it can't have been for more than a couple of weeks.

'You'd been in England for eighteen months and, although we'd taken you to a pool, you'd never been taught to swim formally – weekends were usually packed with English lessons and other activities. You could manage a doggy paddle, but that was it. Synchronised swimming was all the rage at the time and your pals at school were trying out for a squad. You were determined to join in.'

'Oh dear. Oh God yes ...'

'You went to the first sessions and the idea was that after a month they'd pick the best. There were fifteen girls and fourteen places.'

I smile. 'And I was *The Chosen One*. I must've been terrible.'

'I was furious that they hadn't let you in.'

'To be fair, you probably *do* need to be able to swim to be in a synchronised swimming team, Dad,' I say.

He pulls a 'meh' face, refusing to concede the point. 'I thought you'd be upset, but you just shrugged it off and asked Harriet to start taking you to the pool at weekends, so you could try again at the end of the year.'

'So the moral of this story is that I should take up synchronised swimming?' I put my camera back in its case.

'I think you know the moral of the story. You were never the kind to just give up. So how about going back to Colette?'

'Very subtle. I think I've probably been blacklisted by Colette after all the missed appointments.'

'I doubt it, Ellie. Have a think about it anyway.' He mooches into the house and about a minute later I hear the gate open.

'Can we go on a worm hunt?' Oscar yells, sprinting towards me, stumbling in his wellies.

'Oscar! Don't go off ahead! And don't run in the house!' Mandy appears at the gate, sweating in exasperation. 'Thank God. I had visions of him redecorating your carpets with all that mud.'

'He's fine, honestly,' I say, ruffling his hair.

'Do you want me to keep this one in the house with me?' she asks, lowering her voice conspiratorially. 'Your mum told me you haven't been . . . feeling well lately.' She accompanies the last three words with a slightly embarrassed expression.

'Er, there's no need. He's fine to hang out here.'

'Can we grow another sunflower?' he asks.

'It's four degrees and forecast to snow tomorrow, so probably not. But we'll find you something to do.'

'Well, as long as you're sure,' Mandy says, already heading into the house.

'Is it really going to snow tomorrow?' he asks, following me to the shed.

'So I believe.'

'I hope some polar bears come and visit. But Mum says the only pet we're allowed is a guinea pig.'

'Oh, you like polar bears, do you? Wait until I show you a book I've got.'

I pop into the house and take my copy of *Danny och isbjörnarna* from out of the drawer. As I'm heading back outside I flick it open and see the message Jamie wrote, back in the summer after our conversation about my first day at school.

For Ellie. Bravest girl I ever met. Jamie Dawson. Oh, the irony.

I hand it over to Oscar. 'Someone I know drew those.'

'Is that the man who can moonwalk?' he asks.

'Yes, how did you know?'

'He told me he drew books,' he says. 'I don't understand any of this.'

'It's all in Swedish, but you can look at the pictures. Plus it will be available in English soon. Jamie's having a book launch in London – you should ask your mum if you could go. He'll be doing drawing workshops. I'm sure he'd love to see you.'

'You could take me to his book lunch.'

'It's not a lunch, it's a *launch*. There's no food.'

'We could order pizza,' he suggests.

'It's not that kind of thing. Anyway I can't go, I'm afraid.'

His expression darkens. 'You mean like you didn't go to my assembly?'

I was supposed to attend Oscar's school for his event one morning in early November, but in fact was lying in bed surrounded by fags as I binge watched the third season of *Nailed It* on Netflix.

'I'm sorry about that,' I say, sheepishly.

'Did you have a dentist's appointment?'

'No.'

'Was it a funeral?' he asks.

I frown. 'No.'

'Did you have a car crash?'

'No, I was just busy.'

He suddenly looks angry. 'No, you weren't! Don't lie!'

'What do you mean?' I ask, taken aback. It's clear we've stumbled onto a subject about which his feelings are more raw than I'd thought.

'I'd saved a seat for you specially and told my teacher you were coming,' he says, blowing out his cheeks.

'Did you?' I say weakly, feeling a swell of shame.

'There was a surprise for you. I'd drawn a picture of *our* sunflower. It got put up on Mrs Gilmour's big screen. I stood up and told everyone that I'd planted it in your garden, then

I was *meant* to point at you. But you weren't even there so I looked stupid.'

His bottom lip is wobbling.

'Oh Oscar, I'm so sorry. I really am,' I say, with a rush of regret.

'You were just here doing your gardening. That's all you *ever* do.'

I feel my chest brace. 'Look, I'm really sorry but . . . please don't talk to me like that. I know Mum wouldn't be happy about it.'

'She wouldn't care. She said you're weird,' he fires back. 'She said all you ever do is stay in the house and if she was single she'd be out on the town, not at home like a mad old woman.'

'She . . . called me a mad old woman?'

'Why didn't you come to my assembly, Ellie?' he asks, tearfully. 'If you'd really wanted to come you would. And if you really wanted to go to the book lunch you would do that too.'

He turns and starts running to Mum's house.

'Don't go in with your wellies on!' I call out after him. He comes to an abrupt halt and sinks onto the patio. Then he wrestles off his footwear, stands up and marches through several puddles in his socks, before stepping into the house.

My eyes drift to the gate. It's open and I hadn't even realised. I wander over to it and click it closed as an unsettling vision appears in my head. Of me, at eighty years old, doddering about this garden like the *mad old woman* Mandy clearly believes me to be. But it isn't the thought of gnarled fingers or curved spine that chills me. It's the thought that the house next door is empty. Gertie, my only friend, is gone. My parents are long dead. And I'm completely alone.

Chapter 61

Returning to Colette involves more than simply picking up the phone and booking myself in. After all the false starts, she'd be within her rights not to have me back, even if logic tells me she can't have signed up for a job like hers without expecting a few hiccups. Despite this, I have a certain amount of commitment to prove. I don't want to return empty-handed – and I'm not talking about buying her flowers.

I dig out my homework sheets from the folder I'd buried in a kitchen drawer and review my weekly targets. I run through the Beck Depression Inventory, a self-scoring system designed to monitor the scale of relapses. This, officially, is big. But I already knew that. I re-read the weekly target sheet she showed me when I first returned to her. To the average, non-affected person, they sound laughable. *Go to the local supermarket (accompanied). Walk to the village (alone).* No matter how insurmountable they feel to me, I do as I have before and start with baby steps, namely, *Walk for five minutes outside your home (accompanied).* It's with Dad the first time, Mum the second. The third I'm on my own. And so it all begins.

I throw away half a box of Marlboro Lights and buy some

patches. Lucy was right about Mum having known about my habit for some time. She tries to persuade me not to tackle this now, worried I'm doing too much at once. But oddly, having a nicotine craving on which to focus is a distraction from the other stuff I'm grappling with.

I also meet Jakob. Lucy brings him along to her final dinner at home before she leaves for Singapore – and I immediately recognise him as the antithesis of some of the egomaniacs my sister has dated in the past. He's all big beard and dimpled smile, with an accent that sounds more English than half the English people I know. He is wearing a spectacular patterned jumper, which he tells us casually was knitted by his mother, a biochemistry professor. He is somehow immensely clever and sophisticated, but without any airs or graces whatsoever. Part of this is down to his huge, roaring laugh, which makes you feel witty even when you've said something so lame you ought to be cringing into the carpet. It is the most wonderful night, full of silly jokes and memories and delicious food. By the time they're getting their coats on to leave, Lucy is flushed with happiness and wine, judging by the faint red stains at the edges of her mouth.

'You definitely think he likes me then?' she whispers drunkenly, as Mum is busy pressing a Tupperware box full of leftover torte into his hands in the kitchen.

'He adores you,' I say, under my breath. 'More importantly, he respects you.'

'I know. It's *so* hot,' she grins.

But then it's time for her to leave for Singapore and that's when things get tough again. There are a few days when my fragile sense of stability nose-dives. Yet, my anxiety never feels insurmountable, my self-doubt doesn't achieve the vice-like grip of previously. We Facetime on her second day there, which proves to be the start of a regular three-times-a-week video call. The intervening days are punctuated by constant WhatsApp messages, her favourite being photos of amusingly translated menu items, such as 'Soup for sluts' or 'Deep Fried Farmer'.

I begin keeping a diary. Without my daily Instagram captions to produce, it seems to be an outlet for *something* and, though I start off writing solely about my agoraphobia, my entries begin to drift elsewhere. I predominantly write about Tabitha. Not for me, but her. I feel as though I owe her that much. She may have been lost to a cruel chapter of history, but she can continue to exist in every word I write down, every memory, good and bad, that I consign to paper.

When I'm not writing, I spend much of the day outside. I photograph everything but instead of posting my efforts online, I print out my favourites and keep them in my journal. This usually amounts to three pictures per day, to document my evolving garden. Because it *is* evolving, albeit slowly. I have to remind myself of that sometimes, on the freezing days when the ground is too hard to concede an inch to my spade. I also remind myself that the lack of light and vivid colour is *not* a bad thing. Because as sure as the sun rises every day, it will not last. The bare soil and cold frost is simply nature's way of proving that everything changes. Sometimes you've got to shed all your leaves to be able to grow.

By the time I go back to Colette, I've already made progress. I still feel sheepish when I return, but I get no sense of resentment from her. On the contrary, she welcomes me back with open, patient arms. It's during my first session that the issue of the orphanage comes up. This time, it isn't her who raises it, but me. I tell her that I'm writing down my memories of Tabitha and that contrary to what I might have imagined, I am finding comfort from it.

She wonders if I feel ready to talk to her about the subject, or to my parents again.

That night, before I have time to change my mind, I ask Mum if she'll watch a documentary with me called *From Romania with Love*. I've been aware of its existence for some time and know she watched it when it was first screened on ITV a few years ago. I couldn't even contemplate the idea at the time.

The programme follows the real–life stories of three people who were adopted from Romanian orphanages by British couples back in the early 1990s. By the time it was screened, they were in their twenties. In all cases, they've been raised by loving families. They're young, bright and *sound* very British, just like I do. Two came to the UK when they were toddlers and can't remember anything of their orphanage. One was there until she was older than me, aged ten.

There is an uplifting conclusion to the programme; the journeys it features are enlightening, the reunions touching.

But there is no escaping from the fact that the footage and photographs from the orphanages in the early 1990s are har-rowing. To me, these are not merely images of thin, starving babies, they are long-suppressed memories brought back to life. I knew these films existed of course and have simultan-eously managed to avoid them. Now, as I watch them silently on the sofa next to Mum, cocooned in a soft blanket, it's hard to put into words how I feel. Angry? God, yes. My anger is electric. But more than that I'm sad and bewildered, not just about what happened to me, but about the world we live in. Most of all, I'm flooded by some other emotion that seems to stem from the pit of my belly, hollow and raw. By the end, I am wrung out; my cheeks sting with the salt of my tears.

'Are you okay?' Mum asks softly. She reaches out for my hand and when I let her find it, she clutches it so tightly that my knuckles jam together.

I sit up and wipe my face with the ball of my other hand. 'Yep.'

There seems so much to say yet I'm unable to say anything at all. Because what is overwhelming me is not the reminder of the squalor, nor the cold, dirty conditions and the violence we accepted as completely normal. It's not even its juxtaposition with this house, its warmth, its comfort and the pretty bedroom that my parents gave me. Materially, these differences are vast, yet the value of what Mum and Dad gave me amounted to infinitely more.

Oddly, although I imagined what I'd just watched would encourage the worst kind of memories, the one that pushes right to the front of my mind is of a day when Mum took me to buy a party dress, only a few weeks after I'd arrived in the UK. It was not the dress I was dazzled by. She strapped me into the car seat and handed me the pretty bag containing my new clothes, before planting her lips on my forehead, as softly as you'd kiss a newborn baby.

'Come here,' she says now, opening her arms. As she folds me into her embrace I realise we haven't hugged like this since I was a girl. Far from feeling silly and childish, right now this is the only place I want to be.

'Thank you,' I say into the wool of her cardigan.

She pulls away slightly, frowning. 'What for?'

I brush away the damp stinging my cheek and look into her eyes. 'For being my mum.'

Chapter 62

Harriet, the present day

Harriet gets nervous before making speeches, though people never believe this. They think that a background in war-reporting gives you immunity from the irrational but very real terror of saying something idiotic in front of several hundred people. But the spasms in her gut before she steps on a podium refuse to settle until the moment she begins speaking. Then, as a curious silence descends on her audience, the possibility that she's managing to entertain them makes her jitters begin to subside.

'There are two questions I'm always asked when people discover I was a war correspondent,' she says, addressing a gathering of audiologists in a plush Oxfordshire hotel. 'The first is: Weren't you scared? The second is: Where exactly did you go to the loo?'

You might wonder what particular interest a group of audiologists have in newsgathering during the late eighties and early nineties and the answer to that is none. There rarely is a connection. But, without planning to, Harriet has somehow accrued a neat sideline in speaking to all manner of groups – architects, neurologists, rheumatologists; the medical profession in particular seems to like her and several such groups invited her back to their next conferences immediately. This recently happened with the National Association of Chiropodists, which was especially handy as it came hot on the heels of a gig with the Independent Footwear Guild and meant she could recycle an excellent gag about ingrowing toenails.

She only throws in the odd joke, though – that's not what audiences want from her. They book her because of a fascination with what she'd experienced, the people and places she'd encountered. They wanted to know if she'd ever knowingly put herself in danger, how close she'd ever come to losing her life, of how affected she was by some of the things she'd seen.

'A foreign correspondent gets to do their job, then leave. They can be parachuted out of a place and into the next. In that sense, you are by definition detached. But did that mean I didn't care about what I saw, or was unaffected by the plight of those I met and interviewed? Absolutely not. I don't know how anyone could fail to be moved by much of it.'

She takes a sip of water.

'It was an immensely satisfying and enjoyable career though – as well as an occasionally near-lethal one. I was never bored. And I liked to think that what we were doing was important. I never had ambitions to have one of those jobs that *mattered*, but that's what I ended up doing in my own small way. I was glad of that. Glad that what my colleagues and I wrote had the capacity to change public opinion, or open the eyes of those back home who otherwise wouldn't have known anything about what was going on in some parts of the world.'

She takes questions from the audience, the first from a

gentleman a few tables away. 'Do you think there's too much ego in news reporting these days?'

She considers the question and smiles to herself. 'Well, my number one rule when I started out was to keep myself out of the story. To never become personally involved in the subject matter. It was a rule I felt strongly about, but which I did break, on just one occasion.'

'What happened?'

'It turned out to be the best thing I ever did.'

She stays for a drink afterwards, chatting to the host on her table, a woman about her age who tells her that she's stubbornly refusing to retire, and the chairman of a hearing aid company sponsoring the event. They're a fun group, interesting and full of good humour, but she makes her excuses when she can and heads to her hotel room, hoping Colin is still awake.

It's a very nice suite. They were generously upgraded and it has a charming view over the croquet lawn and a selection of swanky toiletries that Harriet intends to take home for the downstairs loo. Colin is propped up on top of the duvet, in a fluffy robe, his glasses perched on his nose as a television programme she's certain he didn't choose drones on in front of him. He's nodded off. She smiles and slips off her shoes, crawling onto the bed next to him. She curls her arm across his body and he responds by gasping like he's just been given the kiss of life.

'You frightened the life out of me,' he says.

'How romantic,' she replies.

He chuckles and sits up to remove his glasses and rub his eyes.

'Fancy a nightcap if I order room service?' she suggests.

'Oh, go on. You're a terrible influence.' Then he swings his legs out of bed and adds: 'Before I forget, your phone rang tonight. It was Andrei. I think he's left you a message.'

'I wonder what that's about,' she said, surprised. 'It's ages since we last chatted.'

It was too late to return the call now of course, but she listened to the message while Colin scanned the room-service menu.

'Harriet, I hope you and the family are very well. I wondered if you could give me a call when you've a moment? Nothing to worry about. I'll explain all when I hear from you. And I'll look forward to talking – it's been too long!'

She phones back after breakfast the following day. Andrei is his usual jovial self and she is making a mental note to take him to lunch next time he is in London, when he starts talking about the orphanage where Ellie spent the first years of her life. It had been closed in the 2000s as part of the major deinstitutionalisation project that would ultimately be replicated across Romania. Some of the children there had been placed in a new, purpose-built 'small group home', jointly run by a British charity and the local authority.

'A man called Cristian Lungu turned up there this week,' he says.

'Should I have heard of him?' Harriet asks, idly piling clothes into her overnight bag.

'No, not at all. But a friend of his had read something on the internet. He sent me a link. I don't know if you're aware that Ellie posted something online about spending the first part of her life at the orphanage?'

Harriet closes the case and zips it up. 'She mentioned something. She's not on any social media any more though. She didn't get a very positive reaction so decided to come off it. I think it's for the best, at least that she has a break.'

'Mr Lungu repeatedly tried to send her a message apparently, but had no response. He wanted to talk to her. It's very awkward as I didn't know whether it was a question simply of Ellie not wanting to talk.'

Harriet stands up, letting this sink in. 'Was he at the orphanage himself?' she asks.

'No,' Andrei replies. 'Not him, but his wife. Tabitha.'

Chapter 63

Ellie

With the day of Jamie's book event looming, my thoughts about what to do have veered from one standpoint to another like a drunk driver. I tell myself he will want to see a friendly face. If so, I want it to be mine, even if I'm blotchy and red with blind panic.

Once I've accepted this, a host of technicolour scenarios play out in my head, including one in which I arrive at the bookshop like it's the final scene of a Hugh Grant film and we kiss under the paranormal teen fiction section before riding into the sunset. Of all the problems with this fantasy the main one is that *going for a walk (alone)* or *driving to the local supermarket (accompanied)*, is very different from getting the Tube and travelling all the way to London on the first Saturday of December, even with my mum and dad in tow, which they'd simply *have* to be.

I decide to just see how I feel on the day. That's all. Only when it arrives, I spend the morning pruning the wisteria and Japanese maples, avoiding any decision until the actual deadline, which, by my calculations, is about 12.30pm.

When 12.30 comes, I make the decision to go – and it's firm enough for me to put away my tools and make myself presentable. As I'm rummaging through my wardrobe, I am hit by a wave of regret that I spent so much money on a dress for Guy's second cousin's stupid wedding and not this. When I think of all the gorgeous outfits I could be wearing, the shoes I could have paired them with, I'm furious with myself. Still, I do dig out a nice knitted dress I used to wear in winter for special occasions and team it with ankle boots and tights. I tong my hair, I flick on some eyeliner, I look in the mirror and ask myself, again, if I really want to do this. This time the answer is a sure-as-dammit yes.

I walk over to the house to see which of my parents are free and even before I've opened the door it occurs to me that I should've checked first. I find it empty. I phone Mum as I lock up and step back into the garden. 'I thought you'd be back from Oxfordshire by now.'

'We had a late breakfast and decided to stop off and see Jill and Tony in Abingdon while we were in this neck of the woods. What's the matter? Are you all right?'

I study the gate queasily.

'Ellie, have you looked at Instagram?'

'No. It's not that – I was just thinking about going out, that's all . . . but it doesn't matter.'

'Okay.' She hesitates. 'Don't forget Mandy is here this afternoon. She couldn't do yesterday because of some emergency with her mother.'

'That's fine. I need to go. See you later.' I end the call as Mandy is walking up the path, with Oscar behind her.

He isn't skipping like usual and instead skulks behind his mum.

'We won't trouble you today,' Mandy tells me curtly. 'Oscar's going to sit inside. He's got his iPad. He's going to watch his YouTubers.'

I lean my head to the side to see if I can catch his eye. He refuses to come out from behind Mandy's legs.

'Okay. I was thinking, though, Oscar: I really want to make it up to you for missing your assembly. I'm sorry I let you down.'

He peers out. 'I'm sorry I was mean. Can we plant some tomatoes again?'

'It's not the right time of year. But' – I glance at Mandy, addressing the next sentence to her rather than him – 'my friend Jamie has an event today in London, Piccadilly. It's for his children's book and there will be lots of activities. It should be nice. I'd be very happy to take Oscar if he wants?'

Oscar looks up at her. '*Please*, Mum.'

She studies me, unsure, her usual desire for peace tempered presumably by concern about leaving her son with someone she considers 'a mad old woman'.

'I don't know . . .'

'Oh *please*, Mum!'

She looks at me. 'Are you sure you'll be all right with him?'

'Absolutely certain,' I reply, not even remotely certain.

'I'm really not sure.'

'I understand if you don't feel comfortable with it. Sorry I mentioned it.'

'Mum!' Oscar pleads.

She looks at him and sighs. 'It would give me a chance to do a bit of my own Christmas shopping, I suppose. Oh, go on then.'

Oscar runs towards me and grabs me by the hand. 'Okay

then,' I say, taking a deep breath. 'Shall we go and have some fun in London?'

This time, we borrow Oscar's car seat from Mandy's Fiat and pop it into Mum's Volvo. The drive to the station is still hairy, but I manage to get there without anything approximating a melt-down, nor any alarming physical symptoms other than a slightly raised heart-rate and knuckles the colour of egg white. The radio helps, as does Oscar sitting in the back crooning along with Elvis to 'Blue Christmas'. We get stuck behind the Rotary club float, but it at least distracts my passenger, who takes the opportunity to wind down the window and yell his entire Christmas list at Santa, who merely waves back, in between fortifying himself with mulled wine. The wait on the station platform is also fine, even when I'm clutching Oscar's hand, cold biting my cheeks as I watch leaves dance on the tracks and feel the first inklings of disconnection. A thudding in my ears. A swirl of nausea. Then the train arrives amidst a screech of hot metal and we hop on.

Agoraphobia and public transport are notoriously poor bedfellows. But, today, I'm going to be okay, I already know that. After all, I've done this before. I lived in London once. I saw it all. The nosepickers, the man-spreaders, the sneezers, the people who think it's a good idea to eat a McDonald's Filet-O-Fish in a confined space with little circulating air. I've experienced the intense claustrophobia of rush hour, the hot, angry press of bodies. This train isn't anything like that, at least not this far outside central London. At least not yet. For now, there are enough seats to find two together and as we sit, I clutch my bag to my chest.

Oscar chats relentlessly as we hurtle towards our

destination, mainly about the fact that he's going to be in a nativity play. 'It's a big part,' he says. 'I just can't remember what it is.' When we've ruled out the roles of Joseph, a shepherd, a wise man, a sheep, a donkey and a lobster (which he assures me is an important one), he finally exclaims: 'I've remembered: I'm a Gabriel!'

Passengers shuffle in and out at the first stop like the pieces on a chessboard. The closer in we get, the more of them there are, all sharing the same air. But I can do it. I *am* doing it. My head is clear and focused and I'd already mentally mapped out a plan to change at Baker Street, take the Bakerloo line to Piccadilly Circus, before walking to the bookshop. We pass through Chorleywood without incident. Rickmansworth too. With each stop, more people embark, but I cope, I absolutely cope. But when we're almost at the mid-point of the journey, the train doesn't pull away after a handful of passengers have stepped off. Instead, the entire carriage is emptying, until Oscar and I are the only ones left. I glance around, holding my breath. Either something amazing is going down in Harrow on the Hill, or we've come to an unexpected stop and are not going anywhere.

Chapter 64

I beckon Oscar to stay by my side as I peer out of the door to see the crowd following instructions to exit the platform. I take his hand, step down, and we are swept along in a wave of stress and shopping bags, squawking pigeons and crying children. I start considering plausible possibilities. A terrorist incident? A suicide on the line? Something *bad*. Yet for all my catastrophising, the thing that's uppermost in my mind is not the infinite number of potential disasters, but a single small and very personal calamity: namely, that unless there's another train right behind this one there's no way we will make it to the book launch in time.

'Are you all right there, miss?' A man wearing a TFL uniform approaches me.

'I'm just ... what's happening?'

'The line is closed for planned works, sweetheart. Didn't you see the signs at the station when you got on?'

'I might have been distracted,' I mumble.

'There's a bus replacement service if you head outside.'

'I love buses,' Oscar says.

'Will it get us to Piccadilly Circus in thirty minutes?'

He sucks his teeth. 'I think you'd be lucky.'

Outside, there is a twenty-strong queue for the bus, but an electronic sign tells me that one is due any minute. As we stand in line, I feel hot and cold all at once. But one minute passes and instead of a bus pulling up, inexplicably, the expected time of arrival on the board jumps forward by 15 minutes.

I dig my nails into the palms of my hands. But this isn't anything like the sweeping physical sensations of a panic attack. My reaction is entirely logical and completely justi-fied – *because we are about to miss Jamie's book launch.*

A text beeps on my phone. It's from Lucy.

Are you around for Facetime in five mins? xx

I text back.

No. I'm at Harrow on the Hill station. No wifi.

How come?!!! Are you with Mum?

But I haven't got time to respond. Instead, my head is whiz-zing with possible solutions to our problem when another text arrives.

What's going on? Are you all right?

I'm with Oscar, trying to get to Jamie's book launch.

HURRAH! GO GET HIM!

I tut.

> We're not here to GO GET HIM. We're not
> even going to make it. Metropolitan line
> closed, bus hasn't turned up, no taxis.

Her response arrives with lightning speed.

> UBER! I'll send you the link.

So I stand in a windy London street, fumbling with the app, before managing to install it, add my details and, I think, order a car. It arrives in four minutes, we pile in and I tell the driver where we're going, only to learn that he already knows this.

Of course, driving anywhere in central London is a mug's game. The roads are congested and unforgiving; traffic doesn't flow, it splutters. However long you think the journey will take, double it, then add a bit extra. I know all this. Yet the moment I realise that, short of being airlifted, there is no way I'm going to make it to the bookshop for even the last five minutes, it's like a kick in the stomach.

Still, I mutter a few prayers. I stick on another nicotine patch for good measure. As we're travelling down Park Lane, approaching the dazzling entrance of the Dorchester with its terrace of lit Christmas trees, I check the time and feel awash with despair.

'Are we going to make it?' Oscar asks.

'I don't know. Oh, Oscar ... we might not. I'm so sorry. With all this traffic and the train and ... I feel terrible. I've let you down again.'

'It's okay, Ellie,' he reassures me with a smile. 'Can we still go to London though, just you and me?'

I decide not to tell him that we're already here. 'Yes. We can still go to London, just you and me.'

I look out of the window, feeling regret creep up on me. I know Jamie wasn't even expecting me, but I wish I'd got my act together earlier so I could have been there for him. I take out my phone and compose a text.

> I hope it all went well for you today. I bet you were amazing. Believe it or not, I tried to come and almost made it but the Metropolitan line was closed! Argh. Really sorry I missed it.

I press send and lower my phone. Then I re-read it, twice. It suddenly doesn't feel enough. I type another message.

> I'm really sorry full stop xxx

'Here you are.' The driver pulls up outside the bookshop and I try to pay him, only to be informed that this isn't necessary either. I step out and Oscar follows me. The street is bustling with shoppers and bright with the glare of Christmas lights. I pause to take it all in.

Here I am, in one of London's busiest streets three weeks before Christmas, surrounded by people and noise. Yet the air is flowing freely through my lungs and none of it feels threatening. Not the beeping horns, nor the delighted laughter of excited children. Not the shoppers emerging from Fortnum and Mason, carrying hampers and bags of posh chutneys and Christmas puddings. Not the high-pitched beep of a flashing green man, nor the clash of carols emerging from adjacent shops.

Oscar and I approach the window of Hatchards and my breath catches. There is a huge, beautiful display devoted to *Danny and the Polar Bear*, with row upon row of gorgeous, glossy copies, standing proud around a sign that reads: A FUTURE CLASSIC: MEET THE AUTHOR AND ILLUSTRATOR TODAY AT 3PM.

The sight of Jamie's face makes my limbs soften. There is no filter on that photograph, but his handsomeness shines through. I'm again struck by something beyond curiosity, a fizzing disbelief that I couldn't recognise this when I first met him.

'Is that Jamie's book?' Oscar asks.

'Yes. Shall we go and buy a copy?'

The shop has stood in this spot since the 1700s, four elegant floors of sweeping bookshelves and antique tables, arranged with suggested reads. I head towards the enormous swirl of a staircase in the centre of the room and, as Oscar races ahead, I climb up behind him to the first floor. I can see where Jamie's event has taken place as soon as I reach the top: on the opposite end of the long room, beneath a Georgian window, decorated with swags of pine and baubles. There are a series of small tables and beanbags, arranged around a larger one stacked with books. The shop is still busy but this particular party is over, the main players have gone home. The children who came to listen and draw, their parents, the author – and the illustrator.

'Looks like we missed the drawing workshop?' I say to one of the two young women dismantling the event.

'Oh, I'm afraid so,' she replies, gathering up an armful of

paper and pencils. 'There are some signed copies of the book left though. They'll make a lovely Christmas present. We've sold a load of them today.'

Oscar is already at the table, flicking through a copy of *Danny and the Polar Bear*. I pick one up too and run my fingers over the image on the front. I open the cover and find two signatures: short, choppy letters that read *Ulrika Sjöblad*, then underneath: *Jamie Dawson*, written in his elegant, assured swirl.

Oscar sits on a beanbag reading as I take two copies – one for me, one for him – then, as I turn to the till, change my mind and decide to make it three. I go to stand in line at the cash desk, close enough that Oscar is still in my sight, when I hear a voice from behind.

'There's a discount for that many copies.'

I spin round to see Jamie, in the flesh, for the first time in what suddenly feels far too long.

Chapter 65

I feel a surge of elation at the sight of his face, the big, broad frame that somehow seems vaguely out of place amidst the dainty refinement of this bookshop.

'I can't believe I missed your event.'

He shakes his head. 'I can't believe you came.'

'Well, I *tried* to come. I was scuppered at every turn. How did it go?'

Before he can answer I'm at the front of the queue, while Oscar rushes towards him and starts yapping about moon-walking and what happens in a drawing workshop. As I pay for the copies, I glance over to see Jamie taking him to a table and picking up a Sharpie. He begins drawing, as Oscar looks on.

I make my way over after paying for the books, arriving in time to see him putting the finishing touches on Oscar's own polar bear picture, which Jamie suggests he should now colour in.

'You really didn't need to buy those, Ellie,' he says, standing up. 'I've got copies at home I could give you.'

'I don't know much about the book trade but surely the first rule of becoming a bestseller is to not give them away for free. They're beautiful, by the way. So did lots of people turn up?'

The hint of a smile appears at his lips. 'More than I was expecting, though admittedly that didn't amount to much. A lot were mates though. They're in the pub if you want to join us? Might be a bit packed in there, that's the only thing.'

The thought of standing in a busy pub makes my neck prickle, but I'd gladly put up with it if I could. 'I've got Oscar with me, so I'd better give it a miss. I'm really glad it went well though. Just think, you could've been an internationally bestselling illustrator all this time, instead of delivering compost.'

His eyes burn into mine. 'Delivering compost had a lot going for it. I miss it.'

Heat builds around my neck and I try to swallow but everything happens slower than usual. 'Have you actually moved to Sweden, Jamie?' I ask.

He releases a spurt of laughter. 'No. What made you think that?'

'Your replacement at the garden centre thought you had.'

'I spent a week on tour, then stayed a bit longer for a holiday. Did a bit of moose-tracking. Saw the northern lights. It was nice to have a break, you know.'

I nod, as the bag I'm holding slips from my fingers to the floor. Jamie picks it up and passes it to me, causing a tiny electric current as our hands brush.

'What do you think?' Oscar runs over to show Jamie his picture.

'Wow. I wish I'd thought to make the polar bear in the book red and green.'

'Can we go to London now?' Oscar asks me.

I grin. 'Yes, why not.' Then I look back at Jamie.

'Maybe we can catch up another time,' he says. 'A drink perhaps. Though, I promise it won't be anything like last time. None of that nonsense.' He takes a deep breath. '*I'm really sorry too, by the way.*'

'You've got nothing to be sorry about. You were right about Guy.'

'I shouldn't have said those things. I'm totally embarrassed. Mortified, actually. Especially about all the other stuff I said.'

'Why?' I ask gently. 'Is that why you haven't been in touch?'

'I made a complete fool of myself.'

I shake my head. 'Jamie, you didn't.'

'Well, that's kind of you to say, but it's fine anyway. All in the past. *All* of it. And if it's all right by you, I think we should pretend none of it ever happened and go back to how we were. Friends.'

'Friends,' I repeat. And just like that, my Hugh Grant moment drifts away like a plume of smoke.

Chapter 66

Oscar and I go shopping. We start next door in Fortnum and Mason, soaking up the atmosphere, which is busy, but lovely too. I load up a basket of goodies from the food hall, protesting with an 'oi!' when he pops in a candy cane, before promptly buying it anyway. I also get a small hamper, filled with things Mum will go mad for – caviar, chocolates, rose-petal jelly. Every so often I am struck again by the idea that *I am in London*, buying presents for the people I love.

After a phone call with Mandy to let her know all is well, we stroll to Hamleys and spend an hour amidst the chaos of a toy shop I loved as a little girl. I buy Oscar a present – a little remote-control car, my pre-Christmas treat – before we stop off for a pizza.

'I'm glad we did this,' I say, as we head to the Tube to start our return journey. 'I can't think of anyone I'd have liked to come to London with more.'

'Shall we come again tomorrow?' he asks.

I glance down at him. 'Probably not.'

On the Tube home, I let Oscar take the last remaining seat and find myself pressed up against a throng of people with only a hamper basket between us. But once we're on the final stretch of the Metropolitan line, the crowd thins and three seats next to Oscar are clear, so I take one.

'Ellie?'

The woman opposite me has a face that is instantly familiar, yet it takes a beat of recognition for me to catch up.

'It's Jo,' she says. 'Do you remember me? My God ... it must've been what – thirteen, fourteen years?'

The girl who used to share lifts with me to cross country as a child is fleshier around the face. Her hair has been highlighted and now, instead of the long mousy curtain that would hang around her ears at university, she is full-on blonde, with a choppy, stylish bob. Despite the years – and I think it's actually fifteen – there are certain features which are instantly and uniquely her: the sweet asymmetry of her mouth, the quirk of her eyebrows.

'My God, Jo. I can't believe it!' I laugh because any ability to be articulate has left me.

'Is this little chap yours?' she asks, smiling widely at Oscar.

'Oh! No. This is Oscar.'

'I'm just here because of the assembly,' he tells her.

'Right,' she grins, deciding not to worry about what this means.

'You look amazing, Jo.' It's obligatory but true.

'That's the heartbreak diet for you,' she shrugs.

'I did hear you'd got divorced. I hope you're okay?'

'Oh, I'm all right. As all right as you can be. Never thought I'd end up back here with two kids, but when something like this happens you need to be close to your parents. Sounds pathetic from a grown woman, doesn't it?'

'Er ... no, actually.'

Catherine Isaac

'You know . . . I thought I'd have bumped into you before now. I'm amazed I haven't when we live so close.'

'Yeah,' I shrug apologetically. 'I don't get out much.'

I can tell from the wavering of her smile that she realises that there could be more to this than a glib expression. 'Well, listen, I've joined the running club that meets in the village – you should come along. We start in the car park of the GP practice every Monday and Wednesday, then on Saturday mornings there's a long run. It's great. Lovely bunch of women. Very supportive.'

I lower my eyes and pick at the edge of my nail. 'I'm sorry we lost touch, Jo. That was my fault.'

'No, not at all,' she insists. 'All those things I said . . . I was too immature to understand what you were going through. I did try to ring you afterwards though. Just so you know.'

I nod. 'I know. It's hard to explain why—'

'You don't need to explain,' she smiles. 'It's just great to see you.' She turns to Oscar. 'Have you been Christmas shopping?'

'Yes, I got a remote-control car.'

'Gosh, aren't you lucky? My kids have been told they're getting nothing before Christmas Day. They did start writing their lists in July, mind you.'

'Well, I owed this little guy one for coming with me today,' I smile. 'He helped me out a lot. He was my plus one at a book launch. Remember Jamie Dawson from primary school?'

She frowns, trying to place the name. 'Yeah, I think I do. He was a nice kid. What – he's *written a book*?'

'Illustrated one. He's very big in Sweden,' I tell her.

Her expression seems to shift. 'Are you and he . . . an item?'

'Oh no.' I shake my head decisively. 'He's just a friend.'

I think about saying something more because this feels like too flippant a description, but we're suddenly at our stop. We gather our bags and head outside, tramping up the steps until we're in the car park.

'Well, lovely to meet you, Oscar.' She looks up at me and smiles tentatively. 'It's been *so* great to see you, Ellie.'

'And you.'

Just as I'm feeling slightly light-headed at the idea of fifteen more years passing, she pulls a business card from her purse. 'Don't be a stranger though, will you? I'd love it if we could go for a coffee some time.'

Chapter 67

Six months later . . .

'Oh, Gertie. You'll be all right on your own for a bit. I'll be back soon, I promise.'

The dog looks perplexed as I tug on my running shoes. She's not entirely pleased about recent developments, in particular the idea of being left alone for the odd hour instead of having my round-the-clock attention. Still, when Jo picks me up at 6.45pm, my friend greets Gertie with all the right cooing noises and leaves her sufficiently satisfied to eventually slink away to her basket.

'They gave us *four days*' notice for parents' evening, can you believe that?' Jo is telling me, as we drive to the clinic car park where the running group meets. 'It takes place at three o'clock in the afternoon, slap bang in the working day.'

'Surely you haven't got anything better to do . . . like a job?' She laughs.

'I don't think our school approves of parents having jobs. They get in the way of all the sports days and cake bakes.'

In the fifteen years that have passed since Jo and I last

spent time together, our lives have diverged so completely that on the surface you'd think we would have little in common. She's been married and is a mother. I've never come close to either. Yet nothing that's happened to us in the intervening period has fundamentally changed the people we were. From the first coffee we had together, everything slotted back in to place. We talked in the shorthand of shared memories and it felt like we'd been apart for weeks, not more than a decade.

'How did you feel after the big run on Saturday?' she asks.

'I needed a very long soak in the bath.'

'Ha! The next day is always the worst. I had a gait like John Wayne on Sunday.'

When I first joined the running club, I was the slowest in the group. But it didn't matter because the fastest members simply looped around us during breaks and if I *was* annoying everyone they were too generous to say. Tonight, as we set off with the others in the all-female group, it is clear yet again that this endeavour is not about the speed we reach or the miles we clock up, at least not *only* that.

We set off towards the Fox and Hounds pub, passing a Labrador lolloping out of the vets with its owner before we reach the end of the path that runs along the river. It's a bright, sunny evening, with a honeyed light that shimmers on the water, but there is enough of a chill in the air to be perfect for running. Soon, my body is warm and my pumping blood has reached the tips of my fingers and toes.

As we run, we talk. Occasionally it's about big things such as climate change or cancer scares, but mainly it's about a broad range of smaller topics that keep us ticking along and laughing most of the way. Philip Pullman's best novel. Carol

Vorderman's teeth. Teenagers' bedrooms. The hunky Pest Control man from the council.

'I joined this group four months into my maternity leave,' says Dianne, a fellow runner, as we stop for breath. 'There was one point in my life when these women were the only adult company I'd had all week. I'd have gone mad without it. Sometimes, all you need is a good natter to lift your spirits, isn't it?'

Yes, I think. Sometimes, that is all you need.

I sit in Colette's office the following afternoon and can't take my eyes off her spider plant. She has it on a bookshelf now, and it's so big that its slender leaves tumble down onto the wall below, cascading in little offshoots.

'You were right about the water and sunlight,' she says. I nod obligingly. 'So in the last session we started talking about your Instagram message, the one you posted before Christmas.'

'Feels like a long time ago now.'

'I think it was very brave to write what you did. With the benefit of hindsight, do you think you did the right thing?'

'Yes,' I reply. 'Did you read it?'

'I did, as a matter of fact. How did it feel to be so open with everyone?'

This isn't an easy question to answer. 'On the one hand it felt good to say: here I am, Unfiltered Me, take it or leave it.'

'And on the other hand?'

'Well, there were trolls. There always would be for something like that. But that's okay because I dealt with it. I deleted the app.'

'You didn't remove the post?'

'No.'

'Why not?'

'Because I'd said all that stuff for a reason. I wanted it to stay, even if I myself was leaving. I must admit though ... I miss being on it. Instagram I mean.'

'Having lots of followers made you feel good about yourself,' she says.

'I suppose so. I don't think my motives were purely that shallow though. I liked being creative. I liked the people I met on there, most of them anyway. Plus, it was my *career*. I only had a few sponsors, and they were all understanding when I wrote to them to explain I was having a break, but it effectively cut off a significant source of income, until I can pin down a full-time job.'

'How is the job hunting going?' Colette asks.

'To be honest, I've enjoyed working for Green Fingers so much that I've not devoted as much time as I ought to it.'

The garden centre firm took me on in February to cover maternity leave for the marketing manager for their nine branches. It's fantastic in many ways – based in the office of their largest site, which is less than five miles from home. But it's only two days a week and will come to an abrupt end at the start of next year.

'You wouldn't consider starting up your Instagram account again?'

I take a long breath. 'I don't know.'

I'm aware that in the context of mental health, no one has a good word about social media. It's not just the tinpot psychologists on daytime television who cite it as damaging to self-esteem – there have been plenty of studies from more illustrious sources that show a correlation between usage and levels of anxiety and depression.

393

Colette writes something down in her notepad, then looks up abruptly. 'You know what? I think you should consider it.'

'Really?'

'Yes. You had an overwhelmingly good experience when you were on it. It's been an outlet for your creativity and you said yourself it was your saviour at one point.'

'But what about my last post? I'm sure there will be more abuse.'

'Perhaps. So why do you *think* I would suggest it?'

I consider the question. 'Oh. Okay. You think that *not* going on there is an "avoidance technique". That I'm running away from the problem rather than confronting it.'

'Maybe you should become a therapist.'

'I can't think of anything worse,' I say and she snorts.

'All those keyboard warriors, Ellie, all the nasty things they write ... they're just *words*. You can survive *words*. You've already survived far worse and all when you were just a little girl. And yes, you bear your scars but you must realise that you've turned out well, all things considered. Your family and friends certainly think so.'

I lower my eyes.

'That silly man giving you trouble on the internet can't hurt you. He can only insult you and all that does is make him look rather pathetic.'

'I'll think about it,' I reply. 'Maybe we can talk about it next time we get together.'

'That's fine. And it's your decision. Have a think while you're away, perhaps,' she says. 'When do you leave?'

'We fly out on Monday.'

'How are you feeling about it?'

I inhale deeply. 'Conflicted.'

'Well, that's not a surprise. Not only have you overcome a significant relapse in the last year, but you're returning to a place with very difficult memories for you. Not to mention going to Tabitha's home and meeting her family . . .'

I can feel my face start to colour, my jaw loosen. 'I'm sure this was your idea,' I point out. 'Do you remember telling me it would be the best way to say goodbye?'

'I still think it is a good idea. The point I'm making, Ellie, is that if you feel anxious, you must remember that *anyone would* in these circumstances,' she continued. 'Feeling overcome by emotion isn't the same as having a relapse. It's normal. Try not to fight these feelings and don't be afraid of them. Just go along with them and remember everything you've learnt.'

But this pep talk isn't necessary. I am feeling mentally stronger than I have for years. That doesn't mean I am sure that my agoraphobia won't ever come back, or that I'll never experience that terrifying rush of cortisol at the peak of a panic attack again. What I *am* now certain of is that I'm better equipped to deal with either scenario should it arise again. I know the drill. I have the capacity to beat it. No matter how bad things are, I know from rock-solid experience they *will* get better.

Of course, there is still a sliver of doubt. My running, my rekindled friendships and my new lease of life is one thing. Getting on a plane and travelling to Romania is quite another. But the fact is I have to. If not for me, then for Tabitha and the memory of everything we went through together.

On the drive home, Dad listens intently to a feature on *Woman's Hour* about activists in Saudi Arabia that has just neatly segued into another about pelvic floor exercises. The discussion with Colette about my Instagram account leaves my phone burning a hole in my pocket.

As we head into the village, I take it out of my bag and flick through the app store, hesitating over the Instagram logo before clicking the button to reinstall it. I hold my breath and type in my login details, then watch as we take the road towards our house and months and months' worth of activity loads onto my screen. It constitutes not so much a series of notifications as an *explosion*. I've never seen anything like it. A lot has happened on here while I've been away, it seems.

The first is that I've lost a huge number of followers, which is only to be expected from an account that's been dormant for so long. I feel less bothered by it than I thought I would. What's really astonishing though is the number of likes on the post I wrote back in October. There are more than *three thousand*. Moreover, as I flick through the comments – from regulars such as @DaisyFallowes and @Rachelgreenfingers, from @hopesandhouseplants as well as dozens I've never seen before – they are overwhelmingly supportive.

@Muddybootsandmarigolds
Ellie, you are incredibly brave posting this. My brother had agoraphobia and he went through hell. You have nothing to apologise for. I hope you keep up the posts as we would all miss you so much on here, but right now, do what you need to do to get better. Love to you and Gertie xxx

@ontariogardener
I'm still haunted by the images of the Romanian orphanages

back in the nineties. I've always wondered what happened to the poor children who suffered through that. I understand what you're going through and why you feel you need to go, but please know that to me you have never been more of an inspiration.

Another leaps out, from an account in Romania.

@Andreea_filipescu
I was also raised in an orphanage – the Hospital for Irrecoverable Children – which I'd been placed in as a baby because I'd had polio. I was two when I was adopted by my parents and came to live in Cluj-Napoca. I don't remember anything about my time there but I have heard such horrors, that can only be a good thing. God bless you, Ellie. Like all the children there, you deserved better than the hand fate dealt you.

There are more. Hundreds more. All well-wishes and messages of support. Some are from those I know, others from strangers, sharing their own experiences and thanking me for my honesty. I keep scrolling and read every one, knowing that it will take me a day to reply to them all, though I definitely will. Among this, I search for the comments from @RamseyLad, the last ones I read before I removed Instagram from all my devices.

I'm sure I remember his username correctly, and certainly I remember how quickly he posted so his comments should be right at the bottom. But when I scroll down, all I can find is a barrage of objections by other users, apparently directed at him. They're telling him to shut up, calling him out for trolling. Several write that they have reported him to Instagram and requested the suspension of his account. I type in his username and keep on scrolling. But my supporters were apparently successful. @RamseyLad is gone.

Chapter 68

EnglishCountryGardenista

792
posts

39.6k
followers

958
following

ELLIE HEATHCOTE

You might find it hard to believe, but this thriving Japanese maple was looking rather pathetic not so long ago. It had come under attack from frost at the end of last year and, though the trauma to its delicate young growth wasn't immediately apparent, scorching and brown patterns soon began to appear under the leaf veins. It was so bad at one point that I nearly gave up on it altogether. Instead, I trimmed away the nasty bits and left as much living stem as possible, before applying a top dressing of fertiliser. I created a shelterbelt of small-leaved lime to protect it from the threat of further harsh conditions. I fed, watered and generally looked after it, and look at the reward: glossy, mustard-yellow leaves that are a picture of good health.

This small horticultural triumph got me thinking. Even the hardiest species can be susceptible to trauma, whether from a cold winter, long drought or an attack of greenfly. Plants suffer, just like people. But if you give a living thing the conditions it needs — in this case, water, light and nutrient-rich soil — it has the best chance not merely to survive, but thrive. With love, attention and perseverance, even a hopeless case can have a bright future ahead. #gardenersofinstagram #Englishcountrygarden #japanesemaple #femalegardener #thisgirldigs #Englishgardenstyle #gardendesign #growyourown #gardeninspiration #instagarden #gardenlove

Morning light casts shadows on the sleepy hills and fields that stretch out before us. The countryside is serene and almost still, with only a whispering breeze rustling in the trees. Jamie lifts Mum's bag into the boot of his car and places it next to mine.

'Is this all you've got, Harriet?' he asks.

'I always travel light,' she tells him, opening the rear door while I climb into the passenger seat. 'It's very good of you to give us a lift, Jamie. Ordinarily Colin would but it's his friend's seventieth and he's on a golfing holiday.'

'Oh, I didn't realise Colin was a golfer,' Jamie says.

'Oh God, he's not. It'll be a miracle if he returns without decapitating someone.'

Jamie laughs. 'Well, it's really no trouble to give you a lift. I wasn't doing anything more interesting, believe me.'

Mum's gaze slides towards him briefly, suggesting that she *doesn't* believe him.

He slots his key into the ignition and turns to me. 'How are you feeling, Ellie?'

'Bit nervous,' I reply. 'It's been a long time since I've been on a plane for one thing.'

'Oh, they haven't changed. Food is still rubbish.'

'I don't think I'll be very hungry anyway,' I say, forcing a smile.

We chat for most of the journey about the last time Mum and I were abroad together, on a family holiday to France when I was sixteen. We recall long, hot days of swimming in the sea off the Île de Ré, eating fresh moules for dinner and Lucy burying me in the sand.

My thoughts drift to the three days ahead of us. The trip isn't a holiday – not by my definition. It's more of a journey of rediscovery – or perhaps closure. It might, of course, be nothing more than an ordeal. But that possibility makes me no less sure that I'm doing the right thing. That this is the final step in my recovery and that I simply have to do it. We find a space in the short-term car park and Jamie insists on coming into the terminal, waiting with me on the concourse while Mum goes to the bathroom.

'Oh, I nearly forgot,' he says. 'I made you a mixtape for the trip. I'll send you a link for your phone.'

'You made me a *mixtape*?' I say automatically, but the laugh we both start fizzles out before it really begins.

He looks suddenly shy, unable to meet my gaze. Strangely, though, I can't take my eyes off him. The way the bristles on his jaw fall in crazy directions. The curve of his shoulders. Those gentle brown eyes.

'Will you share it with me before I fly?' I ask.

He looks up. 'Sure.'

Then I hear myself saying: 'You know, I would really like it if this *was* a mixtape, Jamie.'

A slow smile creeps to his lips. 'Then that's what it is. A mixtape. Just for you.'

I feel something brush against my fingers and realise it's him, reaching for my hand. He clasps it tight. I hold my breath. I'm about to tell him that I have the strangest feeling of déjà vu, when the words dissolve on my tongue. He lifts up my arm to press his lips against my knuckles. Something surges through me and that something is unmistakable. A rush of euphoria, an explosion of lust, an indefinable, dynamic thing that's as pure and clear as—

'All set?'

But now Mum is by our side and our hands are released. I find myself nodding and saying *thank you* and *I'll see you on Monday*, then we've parted and I'm drifting towards Passport Control with an overwhelming and urgent sense of having failed at something. We reach the entrance and, as Mum begins piling toiletries into a square plastic bag, she looks up and lets out a long sigh.

'What's the matter?' I ask.

'Have you really not worked out what you feel about him yet?'

'What do you mean?'

'I'm wrong then? You wouldn't mind if Jamie walked out of here and this weekend met somebody else?'

I feel my expression drop.

'You're probably right,' she continues breezily. 'No point rushing into these things. I mean, I married your dad after knowing him for twelve months and look how that turned out.'

When I don't answer, she fixes her eyes on me, deciding to spell it out. 'Twenty-eight years and counting, Ellie. That's how that turned out. Don't believe anyone who says patience is a virtue. A whole wide world has opened up to you. Good things are waiting, but you've got to go and get them. Nobody is going to do it for you.'

I turn and scan the terminal building but Jamie is no longer there.

'He's by the lift,' Mum says, then looks at her watch. 'You've got four minutes.'

I thrust my own toiletries into her arms and start to run.

I push through a long line of package holiday-makers and dodge several luggage trolleys. I reach the lift moments before Jamie is about to step in and tap him on the shoulder. He turns and blinks in surprise. Before I can change my mind, I decide to say something that now feels as immense and unavoidable as the sea.

'I love you.' I hear the words, but am unsure whether it was me who said them, so I decide to repeat them. 'I love you, Jamie.'

He looks, above all, shocked. The kind of shocked that makes your knees give way, or possibly your hair turn grey. But it's momentary. He smiles and that smile expands into a laugh that is full of disbelief and joy, but stops almost as abruptly as it came on. Then he reaches out to cup my face in his big hands and I stand on the balls of my feet to allow the tingling warmth of his kiss to spread all the way down to my toes.

Chapter 69

From: Tablungu@hotmail.com
To: E.Heathcote@gmail.com

12 December

My Dear Elena,

I can hardly believe I am writing to you. I have thought about you many times over the years, but truly never imagined the day would come when we would be in touch. I pinch myself that you will be reading these words in your home in England.

Now I am sitting down to write, I do not even know where to begin. I should ask straight away that you forgive my mistakes in English. My conversation is better than my writing, at least I like to think so! So what can I tell you? You already know that I am married to Cristian. We have a six-year-old daughter, my beautiful Daniela (I know a mother is not supposed to say this but it is true – she really is so beautiful, on the inside too!). We live on the outskirts of Bucharest and, although the house is rather small,

it is cosy and the village pretty – a nice place to bring
up children.

Cristian I know has told you that I am unwell. I am writing
this letter in hospital and must say that being in touch with
you is one of the few wonderful things to happen at this
difficult time. But I will have the operation on my heart next
month and I am hopeful that I will be like a spring chicken
afterwards!

It was Cristian's sister who first saw the picture of us in
the orphanage on your Instagram. We looked at your new
photographs and although you look so different, I knew it
was really you the moment I saw you.

I have just read back what I have written and fear I have
already jumped ahead. The past is a terrible place for
you and me, dear Elena. I never talk about my childhood
to anyone except my Cristian. I believe that it is better to
concentrate on being positive and the future – my own and
that of Romania. There is a true determination here that what
happened to us could never happen again. But, for you,
dear Elena, I will go back to the start – otherwise you will
wonder what on earth happened in that large gap in time.

I look up from my phone as we sit at the gate in Heathrow, waiting for our plane to start boarding. It's the umpteenth time that
I've read Tabitha's email, sent months ago and in circumstances
that were different from those today. So much has changed since
December. Yet those first words she wrote to me, as she lay in
hospital feeling nervous but very clearly confident about the
operation, still bring a lump to my throat, every time.

When I first read her story, what had happened to her
in the intervening years, I was frantic, racing through her

sentences and each new revelation. Now, although it involves so much horror, it is also the source of comfort. Without even speaking to her, I can hear her voice. Her letter is a hand stretched across continents, holding mine – one that I'll always have, no matter what.

The email describes her life under the Gara de Nord station, in that year after she ran away. It documents the unbearable heat and freezing cold, the tiny space in which she ate and slept and how at the time there were many other adults and children too – all generations, in fact. She had always been a good fighter and said this became essential. She also learnt to beg and steal, quickly discovering that it was the only way to survive.

I don't know why, but of everything she describes, it is her casual reference to how she and the other children would get high on cans of paint that I find most upsetting. Everyone did it, she explained, and she wanted to fit in. A universal human desire and one I know so well.

> I have not asked my doctor if that is what caused me to be so unwell. I cannot dwell on what I inflicted on my poor baby heart back then. There is no point as in so many other ways I am lucky.

She explains that the police started to regularly come along and try to return the children to the orphanages, so she made the decision to leave the tunnels. Now alone, she found shelter in various places that were, in her words, 'very unsuitable'. She eventually ended up under the stairs of an apartment building and it was there that her life finally took a turn for the better.

Ana and Sorin were a young, professional couple, both born and raised in Bucharest and now living together on the sixth floor of the building. They were kind, the first people since the Italians who seemed to consider Tabitha worthy of empathy. Their decision to take her in would change the course of her whole life.

There was no official adoption, but they did everything they could to give her a normal childhood, and Tabitha decided to adopt Sorin's surname – Dascalu. Despite this, she confesses that she didn't make life easy for them; she didn't do well at school at first and was always fighting and in trouble.

It was as if I could not help myself . . .

But Ana and Sorin refused to give up on her and over time she began to knuckle down. She discovered which studies interested her, and above all, developed an appreciation of the opportunity that these wonderful people had handed her.

By the time she was sixteen, Ana would tell anyone who listened that Tabitha had overtaken her peers academically.

There is no point in fake modesty – I was proud of myself!

She describes one of the best moments of her life as winning a scholarship at the University of Bucharest to study computer science. Her first job was as a junior developer at Microsoft, where she met Cristian. They were married in 2009.

Do you have someone, dear Elena? I really hope so. You and I experienced some terrible things and we more than most need somebody to wrap their arms around us and make us feel safe.

She goes on to say Ana and Sorin now live in Timişoara, where the latter has family. She says that it's a truly beautiful city and urges me to visit, adding that she planned to spend a family Christmas at their house, 'assuming I am well enough to travel'. She ends the email by asking one thing of me.

I know it is a long way, but if you would ever come to Romania again, my greatest wish would be for you to meet Daniela and Cristian. Please do write to me again and tell me more about your life. I have looked at you on Instagram and it was wonderful to hear in your letter that the people who adopted you were as good to you as Ana and Sorin were to me. We are lucky, dear Elena. So many of those with us in the orphanage were not. Though we hold dreadful memories, I always tell Daniela: even when the world is against you, there are still good people. You just have to go and find them.

With all my love from Romania.

Tabitha

xxx

I click off the email and onto Instagram, where I quickly locate the account that belongs to Tabitha's husband. Until she became ill, when the family clearly had other things to occupy their time, he was a regular poster of pictures. There's one from five years ago when her daughter Daniela was small enough to be carried in Tabitha's arms. It's summertime and she is holding the giggling little girl just close enough to reach into a fountain and let the water rush over her fingers.

There's another of the three of them on Cristian's birthday, in which his wife holds out an elaborately iced cake as he blows out the candles. There are one or two of Tabitha by herself, in her cap and gown on the day she received her degree from the University of Bucharest. Then there are the three of them, at their home in the pretty village she talked about, only a dozen or so miles from where I will be sleeping tonight. There's just one picture of her while she was in hospital and, every time I look at it, it makes the hairs on the back of my neck stand up. In that image, she looks closer to the girl I knew than in any other. She's pale, thin and clearly in vulnerable health, but with a strength in those dark eyes that is utterly and wholly hers.

We are greeted at the airport by a smiling young driver who proudly declares, 'Welcome to beautiful Bucharest!' He whisks us to our hotel on the edge of the old town, an elegant pile with all the stylish trimmings beloved of the aristocracy in the 1920s, when its location – Mum tells me – was considered the Broadway of its day.

Checking in is just one surreal fragment of the whole bizarre experience. I can't reconcile this hotel, its crisp white linen and Relais & Châteaux affiliation, with the very different associations Romania holds for me. Despite the surroundings and impeccable customer service, there's no denying that I am on edge. This faint state of alert persists while I unpack and is uppermost in my mind until, an hour before dinner, we take a stroll through the streets. It's then, early on a balmy summer evening, that a curiosity begins to awaken in me.

Bucharest, it seems, is a place of layers and contradiction. Parts of the cityscape would win no beauty contest and are blighted by concrete and peeling communist blocks. But in among those and the shiny new hotels, there are also eighteenth-century Orthodox churches, dazzling belle époque villas and art nouveau buildings. If a city's history is reflected in its architecture, then Bucharest has known as much extravagance as it has constraint and despair.

We arrive at the old town to find it buzzing, with locals enjoying the gastropubs and teahouses, al fresco bars and beer gardens. It's full of vitality and laughter. Mum comments on how clean it is, how safe it feels, how, in her many trips abroad, she found most Romanians to be charming, resourceful and streetwise. For all its vigour, though, the pace of life here feels markedly different from London.

'Nobody looks as though they're in a rush, do they?' she asks, trying to elicit a response from me. But I can only nod in vague agreement, still taking it all in.

We dine in a restaurant where Mum ate once before with her friend Andrei. Caru' cu bere is housed in a gothic building with a stained-glass ceiling, ornate arches and a mosaic floor. Despite the grand surroundings, the atmosphere is fun and informal, with musicians pounding out folk tunes while customers dine on spiced meats, salads and beer.

Mum likes this place, it's obvious. She likes Romania. She was always at pains to tell me that the orphanages never said something dreadful about the country as a whole and now, for the first time in my life, I can understand why she wanted me to know that.

When our pretty waitress arrives to take our order, I can't help noticing her dark eyes and hair, that her skin has the exact same hint of olive as mine. Nor indeed that this is no rarity around here. The thought prompts a memory to bubble up from nowhere.

'Do you know what I thought the moment I first saw you?' I ask Mum.

She pauses mid sip, and lowers her glass of red. 'No. What?'

'I couldn't believe how pale your skin was. I was bewildered by it.'

'*Really?*' she smiles. 'I thought you couldn't remember much at all about that first meeting.'

'I couldn't until now. But, yes, I was fascinated by it – and worried. I thought you might have been ill.'

She laughs into her wine. It occurs to me that this country has never represented more than a series of fragmented, nightmarish memories to me. I've spent almost every day since I left trying to forget it even exists. To wipe clean the slate and restore my factory settings. But as I soak up the energy in this room, I can feel something shifting in me.

I will always feel British. I have a British passport. I sound British. I even act British, as my passionate love of tea and default conversational topic of the weather proves. But within a few short hours of being here, I register something I never thought possible: the first glimmers of connection with where I came from.

Chapter 70

Harriet

Andrei is at the wheel of his very old car, as it heads through the busy streets towards sector 3. He's making small talk, lightening the mood, though the closer they get to their destination, the more difficult that is. He turns a corner into a wide, tarmacked road and Harriet is hit by a feeling that's similar to déjà vu, but entirely more visceral. Her gut tightens as a series of images flash into her head in the same way they're supposed to when you die. The grip of Colin's young hands on a steering wheel. Two small children at the window, heads shaved, eyes dull. A surge of scrambling boys as the door opened. Dank, concrete stairs leading underground, a lightbulb flickering overhead.

The memory of that basement sits somewhere in Harriet's mind like a sunken stone. The silent babies, their skin and bones, the hollow look in their eyes. That's how a human baby looks at you when they've been treated like an animal.

She turns to Ellie and is overcome by a feeling she hadn't expected. Being here with her daughter has brought the life she lived – before she *was* her daughter – into pin-sharp focus. Harriet questions whether the passage of time has made her feel like this, if she's become soft in her old age. But this doesn't feel like a softening. It feels like the opposite.

She is suddenly struggling to deal with the idea that her daughter lived in a place in which nobody would protect her. It makes a wave of maternal rage rise up and make her fists close, her face begin to fill up. She pushes it back, wonders what has come over her, swallows whatever is lodged in her throat.

Harriet doesn't look at her daughter for fear of unleashing a torrent of emotion that it is beyond her ability to stem. Instead she slides her hand across the seat and takes her daughter's. She squeezes it once, then again, tighter. Her eyes remain fixed on the back of the driver's head, aware that Ellie is now looking at her. When Harriet finally turns she silently makes the same promise she's repeated many times: *I'm going to keep you safe. No matter what.*

They turn the corner and there it is.

The orphanage is now derelict. It closed years ago and stands rotting behind tall iron gates, bound together with thick, rusting chains and several large padlocks. As Andrei clicks off the engine, Harriet feels the tension in Ellie's body radiating through her fingers. She wonders if this was as bad an idea as it suddenly feels. It certainly hadn't been on the original itinerary. To Harriet, it had felt like a step too far.

But they'd taken breakfast that morning with Andrei, in a café in one of the grand old buildings that had been con-fiscated by the communist government in the mid-twentieth century, abandoned, then repurposed. They sat among a vivacious crowd, surrounded by the aroma of roasting coffee and sweet cakes, as Ellie had asked: 'How far away is it?'

'The orphanage?' Andrei said, to which she nodded. 'It's a little way away, in Sector Three. About twenty minutes.'

'That close?' she murmured, lowering her coffee. 'Do you think ... maybe we could go there?'

Now, Ellie clicks open the door of the car. She steps out onto the pavement into bright, sharp sunshine. Then she pauses, slides her hands into the pockets of her dress and slowly approaches the railing. Numerous windows are smashed in. The odd item of furniture is abandoned outside. Birds circle above in eerie silence. They and the overgrown thickets in front of the steps are the only signs of life in a place that is, essentially, dead. Ellie watches, her features still and unreadable. She is irradiated with emotion, her lips swollen. She swallows hard.

But they don't stay for long. There isn't really much to see, though Harriet wonders what's behind those splintered doors now. If the cots are still there, decaying like the rest of the place.

'Hey,' Andrei says eventually. 'I've got an idea, Ellie. I think you should come and meet someone.'

It takes about fifteen minutes to reach the one-storey, brick-built house he wanted them to see. It's on the edge of a village, surrounded by farmland. When Andrei knocks on the door, it's opened by a young woman with a baby about a year old perched on her hip. She's strikingly beautiful, in a plum-coloured T-shirt, hair swept into a loose bun. She greets Andrei like he's a long-lost uncle, with cries of delighted surprise.

They talk in Romanian, faster than Harriet can keep up with, before Andrei turns to Ellie and says, 'Mihai, the boy I was telling you about, is out playing football. We can go and say hello in a minute, but Ana-Maria would love to offer you some tea and cherry cake first. She made it this morning.'

It's a clean, pretty house, with bright and modern décor that has the odd traditional flourish – lace curtains on the windows, woven throws on the sofa.

'Come, sit,' she says, as they are invited to gather around a table. They are presented with slices of cake and drink tea, making conversation as Andrei translates. Ana-Maria is a foster mother. She and her husband Florin have taken on three children so far, the most recent being Mihai.

She tells them, via Andrei, that he'd been born into extreme poverty and had been living in an institution since he was two, when his mother died. His father handed him over to the state so he could go and work abroad. Efforts to place him with other members of his extended family proved fruitless and, until four months ago, he had been living in a large state-run orphanage. While this was an immense improvement on the old institutions, it was still big, impersonal and he'd been brutally bullied by the older boys.

As Ana-Maria talks, Andrei explains to Ellie that his transition to family life hasn't been without its problems – 'he is just not used to living like this,' Andrei says. 'But she says he has settled in well under the circumstances. I think he's going to have a bright future here.'

They go outside after the refreshments and Ana-Maria calls out to the end of the street, where three boys are playing football. 'Mihai!'

Prising him away from his game is not easy, but eventually he bounds over, arriving in front of them out of breath and with his forehead glistening with sweat. Ana-Maria ruffles his hair and says something that makes laughter burst out of him and rise like a balloon in the wind.

He and Andrei begin to chat. Harriet can't follow as much as she'd like, but eventually, Andrei turns to Ellie and says: 'I'm explaining to him that you were eight years old – just like him – when you left an orphanage. I told him that you were very glad indeed to be able to find a family. He says he feels the same.'

'I suddenly wish I'd relearnt more Romanian,' Ellie smiles awkwardly.

'What do you want to ask him?' Andrei shrugs. 'I can translate.'

She turns to the little boy. 'I can tell that you enjoy being here. But what is it you like best?'

Andrei asks him the question, then chuckles heartily when he gives his answer.

'The first thing he said was "the food",' he grins. 'But he also says he likes the friends he has made. Most of all though, he likes his new parents. He says that when his mother put her arms around him, he knew he had found the happiest place on earth.'

Chapter 71

Ellie

We head to the Cişmigiu Gardens after lunch, which is where we've arranged to meet. This was the purpose of the whole trip. It's what finally persuaded me that I really had to come to Romania. I knew, after all that had happened, that to stay away was no longer an option – and this certainty only grew in intensity the more times I read Tabitha's letter.

I've been thinking of this afternoon for weeks, playing out every detail of it in my head, in my dreams, imagining exactly what I'll say. But now I'm here, words have emptied from my head and all I can do is drift along with Mum by my side, looking out for the bridge where we've agreed to wait.

The air is warm around my shoulders and the gardens are an oasis, with statues of distinguished Romanian writers standing amidst carpets of colourful flowers and the kidney-shaped boating lake. It's a romantic landscape, with gently rolling grass, picturesque architecture and all the trimmings of an English-style garden.

We've arrived early. This wasn't on purpose, but even when I tried to slow myself down I couldn't. Now we're here, the minutes pass slowly. I can only find distraction in the plants, of which there are plenty to document and photograph amidst the hidden paths that lead to the ruins of an old monastery. Mum and I chat as we walk and my nerves reveal themselves in my babbling.

'I read about this park before we came,' I tell her. 'Apparently when it opened in the nineteenth century, exotic plants were brought from botanical gardens in Vienna and thirty thousand trees were imported from the mountains.'

'That's a heck of a lot of trees,' she says.

'Well, you can never have too many of those.'

The bridge is made of stone and dappled with lichen, spanning the entire stretch of the lake. We stumble upon it almost by accident. But by now it's nearly 3pm and I'd rather be early than late. I let my eyes drift over the linden and chestnut trees that rise above the shallows and a spray of glittering sunlight from the fountain.

Our steps slow automatically as we walk to the mid-point of the bridge and lean on it to look into the water, at our reflections and the stretching, blue sky behind. There are a few seconds of stillness, before a gust of warm wind raises the hair around my shoulders and I lift my head in time to see a little girl skipping onto the end of the bridge.

She looks directly at me and I feel something crack open in my chest. A tiny gasp escapes from my lips. Every feature of her face is a mirror image of Tabitha's at that same age, refracted in several small ways. She has the same long legs. That sloping forehead. She isn't thin like Tabitha though. She's strong and robust, her cheeks slightly rounded and full of colour.

Mum's hand touches my elbow and a prickle behind my eyes runs all the way down my back and across my arms.

I nod. I'm all right. I think I'm all right. Am I? I swallow back the lump in my throat, force emotion down into my chest.

Then someone is calling out a name: Daniela.

The little girl is starting to skip away in the direction from which she came and my eyes follow like I'm watching a will-o'-the-wisp.

It's then that I see her.

A woman with open arms. With dark hair framed by soft copper highlights and a patterned scarf at her neck. With fierce eyes and a defiant curl of her lips. My hand is automatically at my mouth because I never planned to cry and I don't want to and yet now what else is there to do? Because Tabitha is right here, in front of me.

Even from a distance, she looks better than I was expecting. Although the surgery was nearly six months ago, the prognosis remained unclear for weeks afterwards and I was convinced from everything her husband told me that she wouldn't survive.

Although you could not describe her as a vision of health, she insisted in her last email that she was past the worst of it. 'There's always reason for optimism, dear Elena. You and I must grasp hold of that above everything else.'

The little girl trips and I feel my chest brace. She stumbles forward and tries to catch herself but is soon on her hands and knees, howling. Tabitha rushes to her and stoops to assess the damage, kissing away tears. Eventually, the girl nods and her mother wraps an arm around her waist to lift her back onto two feet. Then Tabitha looks up.

When she sees me, every feature of her face blossoms into a smile. She slips her hand into her little girl's and takes two breaths before beginning to walk towards us. Mum and I start to approach too. But after my first steps, even a few extra seconds apart feel too long. I break into a run and so does she.

In the first moments of our uninhibited embrace, the oddest thoughts ricochet in my mind. Of how soft her hair is and how I think we might now be the exact same height, how she smells of apples and toothpaste – such a sweet, clean smell that comparing it with all I'd imagined makes a sob escape from my mouth. She pulls back and looks at me. 'Don't cry, dear Elena. This is the happiest of days.'

I nod and say, 'It is,' but now her own eyes are filling and she reaches out to touch my cheek. My breath catches, I just can't help it. 'It's really you,' she laughs, shaking her head.

'Yes,' is all I can say, 'it really is.'

I'm faintly aware that we still haven't done our introductions, nor even said hello. But, for now, all that matters is she and I, friends and survivors, laughing and crying under the whispering leaves of a weeping willow.

Author's note and acknowledgements

As the section at the front of the book rightly says, this is a work of fiction. The character of Ellie, her story, personality and history are products of my imagination. Nevertheless, writing this book required a significant amount of contextual research about the Romania of thirty years ago, as well as today. For that, I had a lot of help along the way.

I'd first and foremost like to extend my enormous gratitude to the team at Hope and Homes for Children. Particular thanks go to those members of the organisation, both in the UK and in Romania, who were interviewed and read through the book before publication. The charity was started in 1994 at a kitchen table in Wiltshire belonging to two extraordinary people – Mark and Caroline Cook – who believed that every child had the right to grow up in a loving family.

It was a conversation I had with Mark that sparked the idea for Ellie's backstory – even though at the time I was researching something completely different (which didn't make the cut). For that, and for introducing me to the team at Hope and Homes for Children, I am truly grateful. Today, the charity operates in countries all over the world, working

Catherine Isaac

with governments to close down institutions and support the right of all children to grow up where they belong, with a family to love them. To help or find out more about their work, please visit www.hopeandhomes.org.

Much of my research into what it was like to be a child at one of the orphanages was compiled via a combination of news articles, historic footage and old television documentaries. But the most valuable of all forms of research always tends to come from talking to people. I'd like to extend my thanks to Alexandra Smart for sharing her thoughts and experiences with me, as well as her memories about being adopted and growing up in the UK.

For anyone interested in this subject, the documentary *From Romania with Love* is a powerful piece of film-making from 2013 and well worth a watch.

I read a lot about the life of a foreign correspondent before tackling Harriet's story, but if this is an area that interests you, I'd recommend any of Kate Adie's books. She writes so compellingly, with compassion, insight and terrific wit. Harriet is a very different character of course (and I'm certain Ms Adie would never approve of some of her actions), but if there is one area in which she definitely provided inspiration then it was in how much she clearly adored her fascinating job.

For help and advice on the treatment of agoraphobia and PTSD, thank you to Adele Murphy. For her advice on social media, thank you to Kelly Terranova (who you'll find on Instagram as @kellyterranova_).

Thanks also to Emma Wraithmell's dad for bidding in the annual CLIC Sargent charity auction so she could appear as a character in this book. I hope Emma didn't mind becoming

Lucy's best friend and being whisked away with her family on holiday with her!

I'm continually grateful for the opportunity to grow and develop my skills as an author under the guidance of my agent Sheila Crowley. I am indebted to her for the opportunities she has steered my way and for her continued support, which is immense.

Thank you to the publishing team at Simon & Schuster for their commitment to me as an author, which began with my very first book (written as Jane Costello) and continues to this day. Special thanks go to my brilliant editor Clare Hey, Sara-Jade Virtue, Suzanne Baboneau, Polly Osborn, Genevieve Barrett and Alice Rodgers. Thanks also to my copyeditor, Elizabeth Dobson, who did a sterling job in helping me unpick and make sense of a particularly complex timeline.

Thank you to all the authors who have been such a source of support and friendship. There are too many of you to list, but I must give a special mention to Debbie Johnson, who always knows the right thing to say and still makes me laugh as much as she did when we were newspaper reporters in our early twenties.

Finally, as ever, a big thank you to the lovely lot that is my family: Mark, Otis, Lucas, Isaac and my mum and dad, Jean and Phil Wolstenholme.

Discover more novels from Catherine Isaac ...

Messy, Wonderful Us

'What a stunning novel ... I loved it'
Beth O'Leary

In late 1983, a letter arrives from Italy, containing secrets
so unthinkable that it is hidden away, apparently forever.
More than three decades later, it is found ... by the last
person who was ever supposed to see it.

When Allie opens an envelope in her grandmother's house,
it changes everything she knows about her family – and
herself. With the truth liable to hurt those she loves most,
she hires a private detective to find out what happened to
her late mother in the summer before Allie was born.

**But the secrets that emerge go far beyond
anything she was expecting. Now, Allie must find
the courage to confront her family's tangled
past and reshape her own future.**

AVAILABLE NOW IN PAPERBACK, EBOOK AND EAUDIO

**SIMON &
SCHUSTER**

You Me Everything

'Wow. Just wow. If you liked *Me Before You*,
you'll love *You Me Everything*'
Clare Mackintosh

Jess and her ten-year-old son William set off to spend the
summer deep in the rich, sunlit hills of the Dordogne.
There, Jess's ex-boyfriend and William's father Adam
runs a beautiful hotel in a restored castle.

But Jess is in France for a more than a holiday: she
wants Adam to connect with his son. Over one heady,
sun-drenched summer, bridges are built and secrets
uncovered, but there is one truth that nobody – especially
William – must discover.

**By turns life-affirming, heart-wrenching and joyful,
You Me Everything is a tender novel about finding joy
and love even in the most unexpected places.**

AVAILABLE NOW IN PAPERBACK, EBOOK AND EAUDIO

**SIMON &
SCHUSTER**